Until the Sun Falls
from the Sky

Until the Sun Falls from the Sky

from the Sky

Kristen Ashley

Discover other titles by Kristen Ashley at:
www.kristenashley.net

Commune with Kristen at:
www.facebook.com/kristenashleybooks
Twitter: @KristenAshley68
Instagram: KristenAshleyBooks
Pinterest: kashley0155

Dedication

This book is dedicated to Stephanie Redman Smith,
my bestie since forever.
Mainly because she likes her vampires,
her scary movies and her hot guys.
And I like her.

I

The Selection

My dress was blood red.

This, I thought, was farcical. I mean *blood red*? Were they serious?

"Smile. Be nice. Respectful. Always respectful. Remember, you're representing the Buchanans," my mother at my side whispered urgently to me. Her eyes did not leave the length of the hall and her bearing was stiff as we walked side by side.

She was nervous and excited. Unbearably so.

It was driving me nuts.

I didn't need her to say this to me. Since I'd received my invitation to The Selection she'd been coaxing me, coaching me and constantly reminding me that I was a Buchanan and what that meant.

Like I'd ever forget.

In fact, since I was told when I was thirteen what being a female Buchanan meant, I'd never forgotten. Not one word. They were burned on my brain.

I didn't answer her, just stared down the long hall.

It was, as it would be, lush but spooky. A dark gray carpet runner flanked by polished dark wood floors. Matching gray walls with pristine white cornices and ceilings. Every six or seven feet a small, exquisite sconce dripping crystals was affixed to the wall, enough of them to light the way but not enough of them to take away the shadows. Much farther apart along the walls there were doors, all of them closed. At one end was the elevator we rode down however many stories and at the other end was the door to where we were heading.

And in between it was a long walk.

Way too long in blood-red satin shoes with a pencil-thin heel and an ankle strap that was so dainty it threatened to break with every step I took.

"I think these shoes were a bad idea," I grumbled under my breath to my mother.

"Leah..." she started in the warning mother tone I'd heard her use with me many a time over the years.

"No seriously, I fear a massive shoe incident. The Buchanans can't have a massive shoe incident, not at something as important as a Selection. What would that do to our reputation?"

"Don't worry about your shoes. Your shoes will be fine."

"No, I don't think they will. I think we should leave, find me another pair of shoes and come back," I suggested.

"You don't have another pair of shoes that would be appropriate."

She was right about that. Who owned two pairs of sexy, seven hundred dollar, blood-red evening shoes?

"Well then, maybe we'll talk to the powers that be and say I couldn't make it due to possible shoe failure and could I have another go at the next Selection?"

At my words, her head whipped to face me and she looked panicked. This freaked me out more than I was already freaked out at the very prospect of the evening's festivities.

"You *have* to attend *this* Selection. For you, there *is* no other Selection," she hissed, not angry. She was frantic.

So frantic that out of habit, even though I didn't understand her anxiety, I found myself soothing her. "Okay, Mom. I'll work these shoes. It'll be all right."

She took in a deep breath and turned again to face the hall. So did I.

That proved it. She'd been beside herself with glee, and strangely, nerves when I got my invitation. Not because everyone in my entire family thought I'd never get an invitation to a Selection (and I'd been hoping, since I found out who my family was and what they did, that they'd be right) but because I'd received one to *this* Selection.

Though she'd never explained.

"Mom, is there something...?"

I didn't finish. We were five feet away from the door at the end of the hall. It opened. A man in evening dress stepped out and closed it behind him.

I stared at him in shock.

He had to be seven feet tall, very thin, his head shiny and bald. He had a heavy, protruding forehead, no eyebrows, big, dark eyes and long, long limbs that matched his height. His hands were incredibly long and thin, longer than even his body demanded, with slender fingers and knobby knuckles.

Although he was an unusual looking man, he was somehow alluring, even handsome.

His eyes went directly to my mother and he smiled with genuine warmth. He had beautiful, white, strong, even teeth.

Oh my God. Was this what vampires looked like?

At the sight of him, my step had stuttered. My mother put her hand on my elbow to propel us forward the last few feet to stop in front of him.

"Avery," she greeted and smiled up at him.

"Lydia." He took her hand, bent low and brushed it against his lips. "It's always a pleasure," he went on after dropping her hand. "I hear our Lana is faring well."

He knew my sister, Lana. And he knew she was faring well.

This was true. Lana had been to her Selection three years ago. She'd been selected, according to my mother, within minutes of arrival. She'd done very well for the Buchanans; a vampire of some status had chosen her. She was still in her Arrangement with the vampire who selected her without any hint she'd be released.

This was unusual. I'd been told after I received my invitation which heralded the time new secrets could be shared that Arrangements lasted on average two to three years before the vampire released his or her concubine and moved on. Any Arrangement that lasted longer than that was known to be particularly successful.

The Buchanan women for five hundred years had made a habit of such accomplishments. My mother's Arrangement had lasted seven years. She was practically a legend. At least that was what my Aunt Millicent told me with some envy. Her Arrangement had lasted four and three quarter years. The "and three quarters" was a very important addition to Aunt Millicent.

I'd never met Lana's vampire. As an Uninitiated, I wasn't allowed. I didn't even know his name. I had seen Lana countless times since her Selection. She was ecstatically happy though she couldn't tell me why. It was still plain to see she was.

"And this is Leah," Avery said, his words low, giving me the strange impression there was some meaning to them outside of the fact that I was, indeed, Leah.

He'd taken me out of my thoughts and my eyes focused on him to see he was studying me and had his large hand extended toward me, palm up.

My mother nudged me.

I put my hand in his and he brought it up, brushed his lips against it, and then his grip tightened. He didn't let go as he looked in my eyes.

"I've been looking forward to meeting *you*."

Again, there was more meaning to this. More than me being a Buchanan, the first concubine family that put their name to the Immortal and Mortal Agreement five hundred years ago. More than me being the Legendary Lydia's daughter. More than just common courtesy.

"Thank you," I whispered, my voice soft and not my own mainly because he was freaking me out even more.

He smiled at me, dropped my hand and looked at my mother. "Lucien will be very pleased."

My mother dipped her head down and looked at Avery under her lashes before she murmured, "I hope so."

What was this? Who was Lucien and why would he be pleased?

"Who's...?" I started but Avery's long arm swept out, cutting off my question.

He caught both me and my mother in its length and turned. He opened the wide heavy door with no apparent effort and gently led us through.

I blinked at the sudden light.

"Lydia Buchanan, Distinguished!" Avery bellowed from behind us. "And Leah Buchanan, Uninitiated!"

The soft murmur of party conversation suddenly silenced at his words. Everyone turned to stare.

I stared back.

There was a lot to stare at. Too much. I couldn't take it all in.

The room was oval. It was opulent. I'd never seen anything like its simple finery.

Rich blood-red walls, again with the white cornices and ceilings, no windows as we were well below the earth's surface. No paintings, no mirrors, just lots and lots of deep blood red. An enormous oval chandelier illuminated the room, its millions of crystals dancing prisms of light everywhere. There was a plush, blood-red, oval carpet on the floor that didn't reach the edges of the room and you could see the dark, gleaming wood at the sides.

There were people there, maybe a hundred, maybe more. Even with that many people the room was far from filled it was so large. Everyone was wearing black, like my mother. The men in black evening dress with sparkling white shirts. The distinguished ex-concubines (or mothers, aunts or grandmothers of the Uninitiated) in glamorous black gowns. The female vampires, appearing much younger than the males but no less elegant, also in black gowns.

There were maybe only a dozen women wearing blood-red gowns amongst the group and I noticed that my gown was different.

This, I realized instantly, was a tactical error on my part. Even though I was one in only a few who wore red, I was going to stand out.

I didn't want to stand out. I didn't want to be selected.

Damn it all to hell.

I'd put my foot down about the gown. Not that my mother wanted me to wear what some of the other Uninitiated were wearing. However she'd wanted a little more dazzle, which I thought would bring unwanted attention to myself, not to mention, I wasn't a dazzle type of person.

The others had gone full-on dazzle. Unbelievable amounts of jewels at their necks, wrists, ears, elaborate up-dos with sparkling gems affixed in their hair. Eye-catching dresses from wide-skirted, Southern-Belle-on-a-rampage to daringly displayed skin (mostly cleavage and lots of it) to sequined affairs that probably weighed half a ton.

Every single dress, every single jewel, every twisted curl pinned high up on someone's head screamed *pick me*!

My dress was satin, snug-fitting at the bodice, waist and hips. It had a long skirt that was cut on the bias and hung beautifully when I was still and swirled softly around my legs with any movement. The dress bared my shoulders, had an empire waist, subtle cleavage where the material covered my breasts under which it was stitched in gathers to the waistline. The same at the back under my shoulder blades, exposing skin at my back, around my shoulders, at my cleavage, but nothing too bold.

I wore only the Buchanan family's ancient, hand-me-down earrings that had an oval ruby surrounded by diamonds set at the base, a larger teardrop ruby dropped from it. I also wore a much larger oval ruby surrounded by diamonds on my right ring finger.

I'd swept my blonde hair back from my face and fixed it in a twisted chignon at the nape of my neck. I'd done it myself and I didn't think I did half bad.

I looked like I was headed into a Hollywood awards ceremony (at least this was what I told myself).

The rest of the Uninitiated looked like they were no-date girls at a high school prom desperate to be asked to dance.

"Crap," I muttered so low even my mother didn't hear me and she would have at least given me a killing look if she did.

Even so, I saw a few men, their eyes still pinned to me (in fact, everyone's eyes were still pinned to me) smile at my word.

As my mother propelled me down the steps with her hand again at my elbow I reminded myself that I was now amongst vampires. Their senses were heightened to extremes. They could hear better, see better, their senses of smell, taste and touch were vastly more acute, and they moved faster.

Or so I'd been told.

And, it was important to note, they didn't look like Avery. Not one of them did.

They also didn't look like vampires. At least not what popular culture led us to believe was the look of vampires.

They were not thin and pale and wearing red ribbons around their throats to which a cross was affixed. They also didn't have mullets and wear rock 'n' roll clothes.

They were all varying heights but none of them were less than what you'd describe as tall. They had varying body sizes but none of them were slight or slender, nor were they heavy or obese—they were all muscular and powerful. They had all different eye and hair colors.

The vampire women were the same except the muscular part, but not the powerful part, even if this was a perceived power rather than the physical the men displayed.

Their skin was normal-toned, denoting warmth, humanity.

And, lastly, they were all beautiful.

As we hit the bottom step, I controlled my urge to mutter a different, stronger profanity.

The conversation started buzzing again, which was a relief because it meant I'd stopped being the center of attention. This relief was short-lived.

"Lydia." A man, dark blond, green-eyed, tall, gorgeous, was all of a sudden close.

Wow. My first close encounter with a vampire.

"Cosmo," my mother whispered, her head tipped back, that strange, slightly sad but very familiar look she usually had in her eyes had melted away. Instead, her eyes were alight and there was a sweet but sultry smile I'd never seen her wear on her lips.

He bent low and kissed the hinge of her jaw. Something about this gesture was so intimate, I turned my eyes away.

Cosmo. I knew that name. My mother had told me the name only days before.

My mother's vampire.

Oh my God.

"Cosmo, I want you to meet Leah." I heard my mother say and I turned back.

My mother was in her sixties. She didn't look it, nowhere near it. But she still looked older than Cosmo who appeared to be no more than thirty-five. She'd been in her twenties when she'd serviced him.

He moved to me and bent in. I froze as his lips touched the hair at my temple then his head dipped farther, and mouth at my ear, he murmured, "Leah."

A trill raced up my spine.

It wasn't exactly fear. It wasn't exactly *not* fear.

Nor was it unpleasant. Not in the slightest.

How weird.

Please, my mind begged, *don't let my mother's vampire choose me. Please, please, please. That would be both weird and gross. Too gross. Ick!*

His head moved away but his body didn't.

I found my voice and did my utmost to turn it cold and added (for good measure) an icy look on my face when I returned, "Cosmo."

In the presence of my frost, he grinned. His grin made his beauty shoot off the charts. Therefore, I lost the frost and stared.

He turned to my mother and stated, "The rumors are true."

My mother shook her head, giving me a reproving look, but she spoke to Cosmo. "I'm afraid so."

"I like this," he muttered and turned to inspect my face. His green eyes moved the length of my body then back to my face before he continued, "Lucien will like it better."

I felt my body still at another reference to the unknown Lucien. Before I could open my mouth though, my mother spoke.

"Do you think so?" she asked hopefully.

"Oh yes," Cosmo answered, not taking his eyes from mine.

"Who's...?" I began but a female vampire joined our group.

She was tall, thin but curvy, dark curling hair, beautiful blue eyes, and she was wearing a strapless dress with a slit up her right leg that ended high on her hip at a graceful drape of material.

"Finally. Leah," she announced upon arriving at our small group. Before anyone could say anything, she lifted a hand and snapped her fingers.

A waiter bearing a tray of champagne flutes appeared at our sides. Cosmo took a glass and handed it to my mother then another, which he handed to me.

As he did this the female, her gaze on me, begged Cosmo, "Please tell me this will be interesting."

Cosmo, also watching me, affirmed, "This will be interesting."

I was losing patience.

On any day, even a good day, I didn't tend to have a lot of patience. But in these extraordinary circumstances I had almost none. Therefore this wasn't a surprise.

This meant I was also losing my temper, something which also happened easily and, unfortunately, frequently.

"Can someone please tell me what everyone is talking about? Who's Lucien?" My voice was still cold and now also sharp.

At my words, I felt my mother turn to stone in horror at my side. Cosmo grinned. The female examined me for a moment then she threw back her head and laughed.

"What's funny?" I snapped.

She stopped laughing, but even so, it still danced in her eyes as she replied, "I'm Stephanie."

"That's lovely, you being Stephanie and all, but that isn't an answer to my question," I told her.

"Leah," my mother said softly in her mother tone, this one also sounding slightly alarmed.

"Leave her be, Lydia," Cosmo ordered gently. "No harm will come to her."

I felt my eyes grow wide. No harm would come to me?

What did *that* mean?

I thought this whole farce was about urbanity and civility. How could harm come to me? Other than the harm that *would* come to me if I was selected, of course.

"She *is* a Buchanan, after all," Stephanie added before I could form a question.

"Yes. There is that and, of course, Lucien," Cosmo put in and Stephanie turned to him.

"Where *is* Lucien? I thought he'd never miss her arrival," Stephanie asked Cosmo.

"He's going to be late. He's having some difficulty with Katrina. She's..." Cosmo paused and glanced at me before looking back to Stephanie, "not happy about him attending this particular Selection."

I watched, with no small amount of unease, as Stephanie's face grew hard. "What would she have him to do? Starve?"

"I think in this instance," I watched Cosmo's eyes shift to me again before returning to Stephanie, "she would."

"Whore," Stephanie spat with such fierce, terrifying emotion, I couldn't help myself. I stepped back.

"Calm, Teffie, you're frightening Leah," Cosmo warned.

I felt it important to save face. I mean, I *was* frightened. Stephanie was scaring the shit out of me, but I didn't want *them* to know that.

"I'm not frightened, I'm annoyed," I announced. "No one has answered my questions."

Cosmo's eyes came back to me. "You'll get your answers soon enough, love."

That didn't sound too good.

Cosmo moved to my mother and took her elbow. "Let's get you something to eat, my love. I distinctly remember you like to eat."

As Mom moved away with Cosmo I heard her reply in a voice filled with fond laughter, "I remember you like the same."

Cosmo laughed.

I couldn't help it, I grimaced. I mean, even if it was my mom, it was still gross.

"You'll like it too," Stephanie said and my eyes shot to her.

"Sorry?"

"You'll like it too," she repeated.

"What?" I asked, even though I knew.

"The feeding," she replied.

I didn't *think* so.

"I doubt it," I shared icily.

She smiled. All anger out of her expression, she was back to beautiful again. She was also, I noted, not affected in the slightest by my icy demeanor.

Her hand darted out and her fingers closed around my upper arm with a strength that shouldn't have been surprising, but it was.

She led me farther into the room. I saw and felt eyes on us as we moved. She stopped us close to an outer wall in a pocket where no one was near. She dropped my arm and took a sip of her champagne which I found shocking. Firstly, I hadn't even noticed she was carrying a glass. Secondly, I didn't think vampires drank anything but blood.

I took my first sip as well before asking, "Is no one going to explain about this Lucien guy?"

"I think we should let Lucien do the explaining," she told me, her blue eyes on my face.

"What does he have to do with me?" I persevered.

I was, it's important to note, as well as impatient and short-tempered, also stubborn. I had a lot of bad traits. I knew this and I worked on it with people I cared about. Like my mother, my sister, my aunties—even though all of them drove me to distraction a great deal of the time—and especially my friends.

I also had a lot of good traits which meant my mother, sister and aunties put up with me. It also meant I had a lot of friends.

However, I wasn't going to show my good traits. Not tonight.

"Everything," Stephanie responded to my question and then her head moved around sharply right before her eyes narrowed and the scary, hard look came back to her face. "*Fuck,*" she hissed.

I looked in the direction she was glaring. A man was approaching us. Tall, beautiful, dark hair, swarthy skin, and strangely with his coloring, intense light gray eyes.

He was smiling. *At me.* Wolfishly.

I felt another trill race up my spine. This one was total fear. Complete and total *fear.* I'd never felt anything like it and it scared the hell out of me.

Yes, this was true. The *level* of my fear scared the *hell* out of me. Therefore I was doubly terrified.

Stephanie moved slightly, putting herself closer to me and partially in front of me like a shield.

All of a sudden I decided I liked Stephanie.

The new vampire arrived at our group never taking his gaze from my face until he stopped. Then it moved to my throat and I watched in horror as it turned hungry.

Oh my *God.*

The trill up my spine chased back down. This time it was a chill.

"Nestor," Stephanie growled, her alto voice holding a distinct unfriendly rumble.

Nestor looked to Stephanie. "A guard? At a Selection? Lucien's being a very bad boy."

"Leah and I are talking," Stephanie replied.

His lip curled as he spoke. "You're implying you're considering declaring your intentions, right?"

"That's right. Back off," Stephanie warned.

"I'm supposed to believe that?" Nestor clipped.

"You're supposed to adhere to tradition," Stephanie returned.

"*I* am? Did you release Reed and I hadn't heard?" Nestor asked.

"Back...*off*," Stephanie snapped, then she tensed. I heard a feral snarl come from her throat and I looked beyond Nestor.

Two more male vampires were heading our way, both big, both dark, both with dangerous intentions written clearly on their faces.

Something was not right. I had no idea what was going on. I just knew, whatever it was, it didn't bode well for me.

Or Stephanie.

She came closer, crowding me, stepping back, forcing me nearly to the wall.

Terror raced through me and my eyes flew around the room searching for my mother. I wasn't a wimp but these were *vampires*. They had superhuman strength. They had teeth that could tear your flesh. They drank *blood* for God's sake. Human blood! That was what this whole circus was all about!

This Selection, I knew instinctively, had turned from what it was supposed to be—a cultured, controlled ceremony where the Uninitiated were to display themselves in hopes of getting selected to service their master or mistress, as the case may be.

Upon entry it felt safe, regardless of what the process would eventually mean to the selectee.

Now it was anything but safe.

My eyes found my mother and she was staring at me, an hors d'ouevre in her hand frozen halfway to her mouth.

I knew from her pallor that my instincts were right.

Confirming this, I noticed Cosmo had left her. He was moving through the crowd swiftly but surely, his face set and angry, his direction taking him toward Stephanie and me. While he moved, the two new vampires closed in.

Not knowing why, my body prepared to run.

"*Lucien!*" Avery bellowed from the door and everyone, not just Stephanie, Cosmo, Nestor, and the two vampires that had approached, but *everyone in the room* stopped, went silent and turned to the door.

I did as well.

At the top of the steps stood a man.

No, not a man, a vampire.

Man or vampire, he had no equal.

Upon looking at him I felt as if someone had put a hand to my throat at the same time they shoved another in my chest, both at throat and chest I felt a painful squeeze.

Tall, taller than anyone there, at least six foot four, maybe six foot five, he was huge. He didn't have lean, compacted muscle. His muscle was not lean, not compacted. It was massive, powerful—even brutal. His hair was black, so black it shone, and it was thick, even had a little wave. It was too long, not in a way where it looked unkempt, in a way that said he didn't have time to bother with such unimportant things as routine haircuts.

It looked great on him.

Everything looked great on him.

His dark suit, his dark shirt, the fact that he was the only man not wearing a dress shirt and bow tie but that the top buttons of his shirt were open, exposing an attractive column of corded throat.

He wasn't beautiful, he wasn't even handsome, or not your normal everyday type of handsome.

His look was too rough, too rugged, somehow both savage and compelling.

It was crazy to think it but he had the most perfect nose I'd ever seen, straight and long. Ditto with his jaw, square and strong. Ditto with his sharp cheekbones, his full lips, even his chin.

And, fucking hell, his eyes. Black, intense and staring at me.

"Oh my God," I breathed.

Then I watched from across the room in rapt fascination as his eyelids lowered, just partially, hooding those spectacular eyes and his magnificent lips twitched as if he was fighting back a smile.

He'd heard me.

Fuck! I thought.

So much for appearing cold, disgusted and uninterested with this whole mess. I'd practically drooled.

He moved down the stairs, not gracefully but powerfully, his movements somehow seeming to devour the distance.

His eyes left me and he headed toward Cosmo.

"Not so brave now, hmm, Nestor?" Stephanie taunted. I tore my gaze from Lucien to look at Nestor and Stephanie continued, "Leah wouldn't have blooded your contract anyway."

"I didn't expect her to." Nestor was calm, the other two vampires that had started to close in now moving away. "I expected to state my intentions and get her to a contract room. She'd refuse and be forced to leave The Selection. No second chances, alas. Not until another Selection. By that time, Lucien would need to feed, he'll have to select tonight. But Leah wouldn't be a choice."

"Not very bright to expose your plan," Stephanie commented with derision.

Nestor flashed a satisfied smile. "It wasn't mine. It was Katrina's." Stephanie hissed angrily at this news but Nestor ignored her and turned his eyes to me. "Though, seeing you, I would have been tempted, even tempted to coax you to blooding my contract."

He leaned in around Stephanie, ignoring her body tensing again, the growl emitting from her throat.

He got close to me and muttered, "I reckon I'd help you beat your mother's record. Seven years wouldn't be enough of you." He pulled away and said to Stephanie, "Katrina has reason to be angry, just fucking look at her." His head jerked toward me.

"I see her," Stephanie ground out.

"Do you *smell* her?" Nestor whispered almost reverently and I felt that hand at my throat, the other one at my heart, and they were squeezing again. Then Nestor chuckled. "Of course you do, just not your kind of scent is it?"

"Fuck off," Stephanie clipped.

"Will you two quit talking about me as if I'm not here?" I demanded, fed up, freaked out and scared out of my ever-loving mind.

Nestor went still, his brows snapped together, and he gave me a look so ferocious it made me feel as if the moment before I wasn't actually scared out of my mind.

Now I was scared out of my mind.

"What did she just say?" he asked Stephanie on an enraged whisper, but his eyes never left me.

"It looks like Magnus just claimed the Warrington girl," Stephanie told him instead of answering his question. "You don't move fast, Nestor, the only one left will be the Howard."

Nestor's head swung around and we watched a vampire with dark brown hair leading a very beautiful and somewhat less desperately dressed Uninitiated up the stairs.

"Fucking hell," Nestor muttered, shot a glance at Stephanie, swept me from top to toe with his gray eyes, and then he moved away.

"Dickhead," Stephanie muttered.

"Um, do you want to tell me what that was all about?" I asked.

Stephanie took my arm in her hand and moved me into the room all the while talking in a low voice. "The first bit, I'll let Lucien explain to you if he desires. The last bit, you must know. You haven't been to your studies, obviously, but I suspect your mother gave you *some* instruction. I don't know if you're ignoring it or have a death wish."

She stopped and turned to me, we were the same height and her eyes leveled on mine. Hers were serious as she continued speaking.

"Never disrespect a vampire, Leah. Cosmo and I, tonight, will be okay with it. Lucien, never. Don't *ever* disrespect Lucien. After you do your study, Cosmo and I'll not be patient with it either. You need to know this. And tonight any vampire that approaches you, you treat with respect. It's important, to your mother, your family, the legacy of your family past and present, and most of all, it's important to Lucien."

I had to admit I was getting more than a little bit sick of this Lucien business. Mostly not knowing what in the hell everyone was talking about and especially now that I'd laid eyes on him.

However, I wasn't stupid. Stephanie was being serious, she was also being real. She wasn't trying to scare me, she was telling me like it was. She was trying to protect me. Even though she was a vampire, I decided not to throw that back in her face. I might be a lot of things but I wasn't someone who would do *that*.

"Now I'll introduce you to one of my old concubines," she told me, her voice back to friendly and cheerful.

She led me to a man who had to be seventy years old—and, I will add, Stephanie looked about twenty-five—but he was a fit, still handsome seventy-year-old with an even fitter, more handsome thirty-something man with him. The younger was the only man in the room wearing a red bow tie.

A blood-red bow tie. Another Uninitiated. A male one.

Wow.

I tried to be cool even though this was something Mom hadn't shared with me.

It was obvious Stephanie was fond of both the men. They laughed. They chatted. They drew me into their conversation.

After we said farewell, Stephanie led me away and I said, "I didn't know there were male concubines."

"There weren't," Stephanie replied. "But I lobbied The Dominion, which means I bitched and moaned so much that one hundred and fifty years ago they recruited males, thank Christ." She turned to me, plucked my empty champagne glass out of my hand and exchanged it with a full one from the tray of a passing waiter. "No offense." She grinned as she gave me my new glass.

"No offense?" I asked.

She was still grinning when she said, "Girls taste good. Boys taste better."

"Oh," I whispered, looking at the floor and going back to being flipped out by this entire business.

"Not surprisingly a lot of female vamps were pretty pleased at the new recruits. Also not surprisingly so were some males." She chuckled and the sound was nearly as beautiful as she was. So much so, I lifted my eyes to her as she carried on, "Though, some females still prefer their girls. It's the way of the world, no?"

I nodded because it was indeed.

Freakishly, I had to admit, I liked her. Therefore, I got closer to tell her something. Something I hadn't, until that moment, admitted to myself.

"Something's wrong," I whispered and she tensed.

"What?" she asked.

I shook my head and looked around.

Then I caught her eyes. "I don't know. I feel funny." And I did.

After Nestor left...

No, it was before that. After Lucien arrived, it happened. It wasn't the hands at the throat and heart thing. It was something else. Something that tugged at the edges of my consciousness. Something that was making me feel weird, like I was drugged.

I looked at my champagne. "I think I've been drugged," I breathed.

The rigidity left her body, her face grew soft, and she got close. "You haven't been drugged, Leah."

"I haven't?"

"No, you haven't. He's tracking you."

I blinked then *I* went rigid. "What? Who?"

"Lucien," was all she said.

My eyes flew around the room. It wasn't hard to spot him. He was standing with and talking to two men and a woman.

But his black eyes were on me.

"Tracking me?" I whispered, looking directly into those eyes.

Yes, my pet. Tracking you. Marking you. Mine.

I dropped my champagne flute.

In a flash of movement that didn't register on me, Stephanie's hand shot out and caught the glass before it fell to the carpet.

Those words, spoken in a deep, throaty voice, sounded not aloud but *in my head*.

"Oh my God," I was still whispering.

"Yes, honey, tracking you." Stephanie's voice sounded amused and I tore my eyes from Lucien and looked at her. The minute I did she smiled. "Oh, Leah, it's good. When I say that, I mean it's *good*. The Buchanan women have been aiming for Lucien for centuries. *Everyone* aims for him. The only catch that comes close is Cosmo and your mother had him," she paused and grinned a cheeky grin, "and, of course, me." She chuckled then said, "You don't have to look so scared."

"He just...Stephanie, he just..." I stammered then heard more words in my head.

No, Leah. Don't tell her.

My mouth snapped shut. I didn't snap it shut; it just did what it was told.

Oh my God, I repeated in my head, panic overwhelming me.

Relax, my pet. He spoke again, *also in my head.*

Leave me alone! I shouted, yes, yet again, in my head.

I heard his laughter not with my ears. It was even more beautiful than Stephanie's. It was so beautiful, it was enthralling. And it wasn't just amused laughter, it sounded slightly surprised, slightly expectant, even, I could sense, slightly aroused.

What in *the* hell?

"I can hear it," Stephanie said softly, tearing me with a start from my nonverbal conversation. "And see it," she went on and I stared at her. "He's marked your every movement. Even the slightest movement you've made, Leah, he's marked it. His heart is beating in tandem with yours exactly. Everyone knows, every vampire here that is, they can all hear it, see it, sense it." Her voice went softer, turning reverential. "Nobody can do that like Lucien. It's beautiful."

She wasn't talking about him speaking in my head. She was explaining what tracking meant.

Still, I was stuck on another point.

"His heart is beating?" I asked her.

She nodded on another smile. "You've got lots to learn, honey."

I was so shocked at this news I forgot that a vampire across a crowded room was speaking in my head.

"Vampires' hearts don't beat," I told Stephanie stupidly, since she was one, she should know.

"Oh yes they do. You'll see," she sing-songed, grabbing my hand, and she moved me around, heading in the direction of Lucien. "I don't know what he's playing at but enough's enough. I'm hungry."

She was moving us toward Lucien.

No. Really, really, *no*.

I dragged my feet and hissed, "What are you doing?"

She didn't answer my question, instead she said, "I figure he's showing you off. It's his way which is normally quite interesting but right now it's annoying. I'm tired of playing bodyguard. Again, no offense but I want to get to Reed tonight." Her fingers gave my arm an affectionate squeeze and her strength didn't allow me to drag my feet, powering me ever forward.

I tugged at my arm. Her fingers gave me another squeeze, this one different, telling me I would not get away.

I tried something different. "Listen, Stephanie, I don't want to be selected tonight."

"No chance of that," she told me happily as she drew me ever closer.

I stopped talking when I looked at Lucien. His eyes were again locked on me, marking me, as Stephanie said, and finally I got it.

They were possessive, declaring ownership, bottom line, I was his. I could see this even from a distance.

I could even *sense* it.

Others watched, swinging their gazes between him and me.

My heart started beating even faster as the people he was standing with noticed our approach and stepped aside, clearing a path to him.

No! No, no, no, no! my mind shouted, my eyes again locked on his.

Yes, he said in my head.

Seriously, stop doing that! my brain yelled at him.

I heard another chuckle in my head.

I scowled at him.

He burst out laughing, this time not in my head, but out loud.

This was, to all those around him, for no apparent reason and they stared at him, stunned.

But I knew the reason.

My scowl was joined by my nose wrinkling in irritation.

He shook his head, a smile still tugging at his beautiful mouth.

Stephanie brought me to a halt right in front of him.

He was taller than he seemed from a distance, bigger, more powerful, completely overwhelming. He made me feel small.

I wasn't small, not by any stretch of the imagination. I was five foot nine, over six foot in my blood-red shoes. I wore a C-cup bra. My ass was my nemesis, it always had been. It was completely impervious to every diet known to man.

Your normal, average, everyday guy couldn't pick me up, not for more than a couple of seconds anyway.

This man, even if he wasn't a vampire, could have done it. No doubt.

I felt fragile in the face of him. Breakable. Delicate.

All conversation in the room had again died.

The entire room was silent. Everyone was watching.

I opened my mouth to say something, likely something foolish, when Stephanie spoke.

"Lucien—" she began, her voice impatient.

He cut her off. Eyes locked on mine, he didn't lead into it, he didn't even say "hello."

Instead, his deep, strong, throaty voice announced loudly, "I declare my intentions."

Oh shit.

"Thank you, God," my mother breathed happily from behind me.

2
The Contract

"Get out," Lucien growled.

This was not going well and he didn't like it.

Leah glared at him.

Her mother, Lydia, stared in horror—at her daughter's behavior or Lucien's break with tradition he didn't know. He also didn't care.

Cosmo, who had been smiling until the moment Lucien growled, now frowned with concern.

Avery stepped forward. "Lucien, you know the law. You need consent. Your second must be present as must the Uninitiated's Distinguished. Even *you* can't—" Avery started.

Lucien lifted a hand and Avery ceased speaking.

He knew. He'd been fucking well living the nightmare for five hundred years. He bloody well knew.

This was also something about which he didn't care.

"Go," Lucien ground out.

"Lucien, don't do this," Cosmo implored.

Lucien lowered his voice to a dangerous rumble. "Now."

There was a hesitation before Avery, as ever, played diplomat.

Glancing at the occupants of the room, Avery said on a whisper, "There's a way. No one need know, Cosmo. This doesn't leave this room."

"I don't like it," Cosmo replied to Avery.

"Lucien, let me talk to her," Lydia pleaded, her hand coming toward him.

"I will not say it again," Lucien snarled.

With that, they knew they'd tried his patience, they knew what that meant, and without further hesitation, all of them moved to leave.

Including Leah.

"Not you," he demanded and everyone turned.

"What?" Leah asked, her soft, sweet voice grating on his nerves.

"Not you. You stay."

Her eyes darted to her mother, Cosmo, Avery then back to Lucien. "But I thought—"

"Come over here," Lucien ordered, cutting off her words as the others quickly and silently left the room.

She didn't do as he'd commanded. Instead, she looked at the closed door in confusion.

In fact, since she'd stepped foot in the Contract Room she hadn't done a single thing that he'd commanded.

It wasn't just her voice that was grating on his nerves, everything about her was.

He'd expected to enjoy this. He hadn't had a challenge in five hundred years.

He wasn't enjoying this.

"Leah," he called, his voice as strained as his patience.

Her head snapped around. "What?" she asked sharply.

He felt his body go taut fighting back the desire to teach her the respect he was owed.

Instead of acting on this urge, he warned quietly, "Don't *ever* speak to me that way."

She stared at him, confusion warring with fear in her face, another look he hadn't seen in a long time. A look he liked. A look he missed. A look he craved.

This appeased his anger. Not all of it, but enough.

"I don't get it," she said, the same fear and confusion in her voice, and he felt it stir his blood.

Especially the fear.

Every concubine itched to be selected. This served a purpose but it also eradicated the chase, the capture, the taming.

All of which Lucien also liked, missed and most assuredly craved.

Her fear was as delicious as her face, her hair, her eyes, her breasts, that ass, her fucking *scent*, which had practically brought him to his knees the minute he'd entered The Selection and caught it.

As it had done the first time he saw her, smelled her, years ago, after which he'd marked Leah Buchanan as his. Everyone knew it, they had for decades.

Except, of course, Leah.

She kept talking. "I thought if I refused to blood your contract that I was free to go."

Lucien pulled in a calming breath.

It failed to calm him, however, and his voice sounded less impatient when he explained, "If Nestor had declared his intention. Yes. Magnus. Yes. Hamish. The same. Any one of them." He paused, gesturing to the door with his hand to indicate The Selection before he finished, "Me? No."

"Why not you?" she asked.

"Because I want you."

"But I don't want you."

"That doesn't matter. You're mine."

She blinked then rallied, "But, Mom said the rules are absolute. No one breaks them. Ever."

"I'm not no one."

Her head jerked with surprise. "Who are you?"

"I'm your master."

Now she started to look angry. "No one is my master."

"I am."

She stared at him, anger displacing the fear, her hands balled into fists, and she leaned toward him before she declared, "You. Are. *Not*."

He'd had enough.

Come here, Leah.

Instantly she moved to him. Lucien watched as the anger disappeared and the confusion came back.

So did the fear. A great deal of it.

So much the room reeked of it. It mingled with her scent. He had the forbidden desire to snatch her in his arms, rip open her throat at the same time he ripped off her clothes and buried his cock in her so deep, he'd feel his own thrusts as her blood poured into his mouth.

"Stop doing that," she whispered as she halted less than a foot from him.

Silence, he demanded and her mouth clamped shut. *Better*, he told her.

She glared at him, her hands again fists at her sides, but she didn't move away from him. She was straining to do it, but she couldn't. He wasn't allowing it.

It didn't matter, she fought it. He liked that.

Give me your hand.

She lifted her hand to his and watched it move, horror and anger in her eyes.

He turned, his fingers curling around the sharp dagger which was one of four things on the shining oval table next to him.

There was also their contract, as big as a poster board, ivory parchment, tiny calligraphied words from the very top to near the bottom. There was only an inch of space for their signatures. All if it was words declaring her blood his, giving him feeding rights, and in return he'd take care of her. Not through the length of The Arrangement, but until she took her last breath on this earth.

What she did not know, Cosmo did not know, her mother did not know, but Avery *did* know was that Lucien had the five-hundred-year-old agreement altered.

Upon entry to the room, she'd sat and read every word, something not one single concubine he'd selected in five hundred years had done. She had no way of knowing the changes he'd ordered Avery to make, or she wouldn't until she attended her studies. He'd planned for that and was prepared for the consequences.

Nevertheless—or likely because—after she finished reading it, her face pale, her eyes seething, she tossed it on the table, caught Lucien's gaze and announced, "Not on your life."

Thus had started Lucien's demands, her mother's pleading, Cosmo's chuckles and Avery's grins.

Not to mention Lucien's irritation.

Also on the table were the quill and the Joining Bowl, a small, oval, crystal plate that sat on four tiny crystal feet by the quill.

Both of which, Lucien decided, they would be using now.

Lucien's hand lifted to hers and his fingers wrapped around it. He forced her index finger straight and she fought that too. She knew she'd never win but she did it anyway.

He was, he found, finally enjoying this. "Keep fighting, my pet, I like it."

She stopped struggling immediately.

He grinned at her. She scowled at him.

He lifted the dagger to pierce her finger but stopped and looked at her. Her eyes flew from her finger to his.

He could see the pleading.

Yes, he was enjoying this.

He dropped the dagger on the table.

He felt her relief hit the room. Her heart had started beating wildly, tripping over itself. Now it began to slow.

His eyes moved to hers as he lifted her hand toward his mouth, finger still forced to extended by his thumb.

He felt her body tense, the fear invade, her heart picking up the pace as her hand resisted its ascent.

She was magnificent.

No! she cried in her brain.

He opened his mouth, put her finger to his lips and sucked it inside. She went completely still and her eyes dropped to his mouth.

With effort he fought back the arousal he felt at his first taste of her and the direction of her gaze.

Christ, she tasted fucking good.

He used a single tooth to tear open the pad of her finger.

Oh my God! she breathed in her mind as he sensed her registering the brief pain.

He'd been wrong, her skin tasted lovely, but her blood was glorious.

With regret he extracted her finger from his mouth, pushed her hand to one end of the Joining Bowl and pressed several drops of blood from the wound into the bowl.

She resisted this too and Lucien found this vaguely surprising. She knew she couldn't win. He had her trapped with his mind, and even if he didn't, she could never overpower him physically.

He found he liked her stubbornness when he had her at his command.

It was when he didn't he found it annoying.

When he was done, he returned her finger to his lips and his tongue darted out, lashing the cut. The bleeding stopped instantly. Through his saliva the wound would be healed within the hour.

He released her hand but demanded, *Dip the quill in your blood and sign the contract.*

Her body jerked, strained and, he was intrigued to see, she hesitated a second before she did as she was told. He watched as she did this, her face pale, her body trembling.

Could she possibly fight mesmerization?

It was, he knew, impossible. However, if she could, she'd be even more fun.

She put the quill down and turned to him.

I hate you.

He put a hand to her neck, his thumb resting along her jugular, her heart beating heavily against his skin and in his ears.

"That won't last long, my pet," he assured her.

Don't call me your pet.

"You *are* my pet."

She wrinkled her nose at him. It was meant to communicate her irritation and disgust. However, he found it adorable.

He had not, until she'd done it in The Selection, had anyone backtalk him while he was communicating nonverbally. He'd been surprised and pleased she had this heretofore unknown ability.

It would make things more interesting. Hell, it already was.

He turned to the table, took the dagger and pierced his own finger. Going through the same motions as she'd done, he signed the contract.

Once completed, he used the tip of the dagger to mingle their blood in the plate as she stood trembling beside him.

He moved into her and her body tensed.

"You can't fight it, Leah."

This can't be legal, she snapped.

She was right. It absolutely wasn't. If anyone knew he'd forced her signature through mesmerization, he'd be punished. Or they'd try to punish him.

They wouldn't succeed, of course. They'd have to kill him first.

She was, he knew without a doubt, going to be worth any risk.

He positioned her in front of him, one of his arms going around her waist holding her tight against his chest and his stomach. Her sweet ass pressed to his thighs.

Feeling her soft body against his hard one, he knew it would be a long week to wait for The Bloodletting.

He reached across the front of her, taking up the quill, and he dipped it in their combined blood.

Take my hand in yours, he commanded.

She did as she was told.

Together they wrote the word *Bound* between their names in their mingled blood.

It was done. She was his.

Triumph seared through him.

He hadn't felt that in a long time either and he liked it the best of all.

His arm tensed along her waist as he shoved his face into her neck, smelling her skin, her hair, the perfume that she didn't need, hearing the blood sing warm and moist through her veins. He heard the breath move out of her in a gasp and knew he was using too much strength.

He kept her pinned to him and didn't let go.

Mine, he declared.

Never, she returned.

His mouth moved to her ear and he murmured, "We'll see."

He felt her shiver.

Then he freed her mind and her body from his control.

She felt it immediately, turned in his arm to glare at him a moment before she tore herself free and ran directly from the room.

3
The Bloodletting

I stood at the window staring out at the night.

The sky was free of clouds, the moon full, its brightness frosting the dark, immaculate garden below in a way that was appropriately eerie.

My eyes moved from the garden and I caught my reflection in the glass.

I looked like an idiot.

I was wearing a pale-pink nightgown, simple, unadorned by lace or any other accoutrement. It was ankle length, slit up both sides all the way to my hips with spaghetti straps holding up the bodice and the back under my shoulder blades between a deep exposed V.

Some strange woman named Edwina had come in to do my hair and makeup. She'd been quiet and watchful, but smiling and obviously excited like I was about to be crowned queen of the world.

I let her have at it and stayed quiet too. I had too much on my mind.

I shouldn't have stayed quiet. She gave me way too much hair. She also gave me way, way, *way* too much makeup.

I was imminently going to get my throat gnashed open by that fucking vampire's teeth, he was going to suck my blood and then go home to his mate.

Why all the fuss?

After The Selection I told my mother what happened in the Contract Room and demanded she contact the Vampire Dominion and appeal the contract.

At first, she looked shaken. Then she called my aunts. My aunts called in my sister but surprisingly not my cousins.

They had a meeting I wasn't invited to which pissed me off.

Then they contacted The Dominion but not to appeal the contract, to get a copy of it.

As was my and their due, this we received. Avery delivered it personally. Behind closed doors, without me there, they'd perused it for hours.

Okay, more like *an* hour but it felt like a million of them.

My sister came out first, her face pale, eyes shocked. She said not one single word before she took off. This was surprising. Lana was chatty. She could chat anyone's ear off. I didn't think it was even in her not to say a single word.

This was not a good sign.

My Aunt Kate came out next. For some reason she looked shocked too, but determined. The oldest of the four Buchanan matriarchs, as tradition had ingrained in me for four decades, she had the final say. I just didn't like the final say.

It was this: "You'll abide by the contract."

"*What?*" I shouted.

"Every word," she returned. Then without one more word, as if she was scared of what those words might be and I swear Aunt Kate wasn't scared of *anything,* she took off.

So did Millicent and Nadia.

My mother stood before me and I demanded, "They can't be serious."

"If you go against us, you'll be banished from our family," my mother replied softly trying, I knew, to take the sting out of her awful words. "If you go against Lucien, with that signed contract, he'll have certain rights, Leah. Rights you won't want him to invoke. Rights I feel relatively certain he will."

"And those are?" I snapped, tired of the secrets and not scheduled to go to my Vampire Studies until the next day. Vampire Studies were two days of learning all things vampire and all things concubine, something I was not only *not* looking forward to, but had, at that moment, no intention of doing.

"He's allowed to hunt you and when he finds you, which he would, he's allowed to do as he wishes," Mom answered.

"And 'as he wishes' means suck my blood which is exactly what that contract allows him to do, amongst other things."

She blanched at my words—something I couldn't put my finger on right behind her eyes—but her next words forced my attention elsewhere.

"Feed, yes, and not stop."

"Sorry?" I asked.

"He has every right to feed and not stop. As his willing concubine, he's allowed to feed. Once he initiates you and you get used to the feeding, he can do it when he wishes as often as he wishes. But he must stop, not only before he kills you but before he unduly weakens you. If you challenge that contract, he can hunt you and he can feed from you *until you're dead.*"

I had nothing to say to that because it was downright terrifying.

Lucien hunting me down and sucking the blood out of my body until I was dead?

He'd do it. If I defied him, the bastard would not only do it, he'd love every minute of it.

"It's never happened. Not once. Not in five hundred years," Mom informed me, came close and grabbed my hands, both of them, fervently clenching them in her own. "Don't make the first be a Buchanan. Please don't," she beseeched me. "Our name is impeccable. We have the highest Selections, the longest Arrangements. The shame you'd create would mean no vampire would associate with us for years, decades, maybe *ever*. Your sister would be released and that would devastate her. Rafe adores her. He's lost no taste for her. She's set to challenge my accomplishment. Your cousins would be released too. And your cousins who haven't seen their Selections yet...but they want to, Leah...think of them."

"I can't believe you're asking this of me," I whispered and I couldn't.

It was hideous. *All* of it.

Her hands gave mine a squeeze. "You don't understand. Go to your studies, you'll learn. Go to Lucien. He'll be good to you, Leah. After he initiates you, I promise, you'll understand."

"Who *is* this guy?" I asked.

"He's Lucien," she replied as if that said it all.

"I think I need more information."

She nodded but said, "And I'll give you more, after your studies, after the first bloodletting, when you understand. Then I'll tell you about Lucien."

"Why after?"

"First, you must understand." She squeezed my hands again. "I've no doubt he'll make you understand. After that," she smiled, "you might not even care."

I doubted that then. I doubted it now, standing in this beautiful room, *my* beautiful room, in *my* new beautiful house, a room (and a house) that the Bastard Vampire Lucien had provided for me.

I hated him with all my beating heart.

On that thought, the door opened. I whirled toward it, and as I ended my whirl, I saw him close the door.

I hadn't seen him in a week.

He was again wearing a dark suit with a dark shirt open at the throat. His eyes never left me as he walked across the room to a chaise lounge where he shrugged off his jacket and threw it on the lounge.

Eyes still on me, he walked to the side of the bed where he stopped, stood and said, "Come here, Leah."

Again, I noted, he didn't even say "hello."

I didn't complain at his lack of greeting. Nor did I greet him.

I walked toward him.

Not because I had no control over my own body. *That* had been too humiliating to endure again.

But because I had no choice.

And that *sucked*.

He was just as huge and overwhelming as I remembered. More so in this smaller room standing by a bed with me in bare feet.

His eyes were more intense too. Far more intense. Scarily more intense.

I stopped a foot in front of him and tipped my head back to look at him. I didn't know him at all but he looked strangely disappointed.

I realized why when he spoke. "Not feeling stubborn tonight?"

I was stubborn every night. And every day for that matter. I just wasn't stupid.

"My mother says, if I run and break the contract, you can hunt me down and murder me."

His head tipped very slightly to the side.

Then he said somewhat hesitantly, "That's right."

"Well, even though the next however long I'm with you is going to stink, I kinda like breathing, and I definitely don't want *you* to get your kicks out of taking my life, so, no. I'm not feeling stubborn." I tilted my head back, exposing my throat, tensing my body and ungraciously invited, "Have at it."

I waited, slightly panicked and definitely scared, to be torn asunder.

Instead, I heard his rich shout of laughter before I found myself in his lap.

That's right. One second I was standing one foot in front of him offering him my blood as his lifeline. The next second (or maybe half a second), he was seated and I was in his lap, one of his arms tight around my front and hip, the other one strong along my spine between my shoulder blades, his fingers in my hair. My torso was pressed to the surprising warmth of his, my arms crushed at my sides.

His face was in my neck and he was still laughing.

He did this for a while. I sat stiff in his lap while he did.

Then his head moved, his mouth went to my ear, and he murmured, "I knew you'd be fun."

"I'm not trying to be fun," I told the wall behind him with total truthfulness.

He gently tugged on my hair to pull my head back and he lifted his own to face me. "I know. That's why you're fun."

I glared. He grinned.

He looked good grinning, or I should say *even better*, so I sighed.

"Can we get this over with, please?"

His eyes traveled over my face and hair. "Is this all for me?"

"What?"

His arm came from around my front and his hand gestured to my head. A hand, I might add, that was just as attractive as he was, all long tapered fingers and strong veins. Really, it wasn't fair.

"What?" I repeated, still not knowing what he was on about.

"You're far more beautiful without all that garbage."

I ignored him calling me beautiful. He wasn't going to be a domineering freak, telling me he was my master one meeting and then charm me by calling me beautiful the next.

"Or are you trying to turn me off?" he asked.

"Do you mean the hair and makeup?"

"Yes."

This genuinely confused me, so much so I didn't guard my answer. "Your lady did it."

"My lady?"

"Edwina. She came in earlier and gave me the works. I thought that was part of the deal."

"Edwina," he muttered, a smile tugging at the corners of his mouth. "Too many good intentions, not enough sense."

"Sorry?"

His eyes focused on mine. "Leah, Edwina is your housekeeper. She's not your lady's maid. Do what you wish with your hair and your face." He paused then said, "Or, I should say, do what *I* wish with your hair and your face, which means no more of *that*."

I decided instantly that Edwina was going to do my hair and makeup every time he came over.

He must have read my mind because he roared with laughter. He did this as he caught me in his arms again, pulling me close to his chest and shoving his face in my neck so his mirth tingled—unwanted (but also not unpleasant)—along my skin.

"I'm so glad you're having such a good time," I grumbled to the wall.

"I am too. Thank you." His gratitude was also expressed against the skin at my neck in a dry wit that only made *him* chuckle.

"Is this going to take all night?" I kept grumbling.

His mouth shifted from my neck to my ear where he murmured, "Impatient."

For once in my life I wasn't. Not really. There were two billion and five other things I would prefer to be doing. However, since this was my only choice, I was (kind of) ready to have it over with.

His face came out of my neck, he pulled back and looked at me.

"I see your studies didn't convince you this was something you'd take to."

"I was expelled," I announced.

His brows drew together before he said, "Pardon?"

"I was expelled," I repeated.

"You were expelled," he repeated after me.

I nodded.

"From Vampire Studies," he continued.

I nodded again.

His brows drew further together, ominously further.

"Why don't I know this?"

I ignored the ominous brow draw. "My Aunt Kate and Aunt Millicent went to talk to the instructor. They swore him to secrecy," I waved my hand in between our faces, "the whole Buchanan reputation and all that. They don't want it besmirched."

"What did you do?" he asked.

"Sorry?"

"To get expelled, what did you do?"

I decided to answer.

Why not? What could go wrong?

"I was texting my friends, you know, to say good-bye because I had to move here and it's not close. It was a quick thing for them. Obviously I couldn't tell them I was all of a sudden a vampire's concubine because they don't know you all exist and they'd think I needed a loony bin. So I had to tell them I had to quit work and care for an invalid aunt they'd never heard about. They were freaking."

Lucien looked angry though I sensed (shockingly) not at me. "They could have simply confiscated your phone."

"They did," I informed him. "Then I started passing notes in class."

His eyes locked on mine then they blinked *very slowly*.

"Why?" he asked.

"Why what?"

"Why did you pass notes in class?"

"I was bored." He made no reply so I explained, "We were in the vampire history part, that's boring. It went on forever. The other concubines weren't into passing notes. They acted like vampire history was their life's true meaning so they told on me."

He sighed and stated, "Leah, you're forty years old."

"Yes. So?"

"Isn't it a little juvenile to be passing notes in class at your age?"

I'd heard that before.

Being juvenile was yet another of my bad traits, or so others thought. Like my Aunt Kate. And my Aunt Millicent. *And* my Aunt Nadia (sometimes, most of the time Aunt Nadia thought I was a hoot). And my goodie-two-shoes, perfection-personified cousin Myrna.

I felt my body grow stiff and my nose, of its own accord, went half an inch up in the air before I declared, "I'll grow up when I'm ninety-three years old, not a day sooner. I made a vow to be a girl until then and I'm sticking to it." Lucien was silent so I finished with, "I have fifty-three years left."

He shook his head and dropped to his side on the bed taking me with him so my head was on the pillows but my bottom was tucked into his lap, my calves hanging over his thighs. His big body was at a right angle, his legs were still partially over the side of the bed, but he cocked a knee so his thigh was deeper into my bottom and he went up on his forearm beside me. He was towering over me, all huge, bulky vampire, and he rested his other arm at a slant across my abdomen, his fingers casually curled into my hip.

"That still isn't terms for expulsion," he announced while I concentrated on not hyperventilating at this new intimate position.

He was acting like we lay in bed, physically touching, nonchalantly discussing the weather, my frequent antics and the meaning of life every freaking day!

Not like we barely knew each other, which we didn't.

Not like he wasn't an overbearing vampire who'd made my life a living hell with his mind games.

Not like he was a being I hated with all my heart.

Not like he was there to suck my blood from my body to make him immortal and superhuman.

No.

Like we were *something else entirely.*

"I didn't get expelled for that," I said and it came out breathy.

I watched close up as his tongue wet his lips then he pressed them together. I didn't know for certain but this didn't seem like a good sign.

Finally he said, "Let's skip all of your other mischief and get to the part that got you expelled."

I decided that was a good idea. I was, I should note, wrong.

I didn't know that so I informed him, "Instead of taking the essay test at the end of the first day, I wrote my will."

"Your will?"

"My last Will and Testament. It freaked out some of the girls. It took the instructor a while to calm them down. I didn't mean to—"

I was so busy explaining, I missed his narrowing of the eyes. I should have paid attention.

His voice sounded angry, this time definitely at me, when he cut me off by asking, "Why in *the fuck* were you writing your will in Vampire Studies?"

Oh my.

Maybe I shouldn't have admitted to being expelled. It was clear I definitely shouldn't have explained why.

It was too late. I had to finish it.

"You're a vampire," I stated the obvious.

"Yes. And?"

"You suck people's blood."

"If you'd paid attention in class, my pet, you'd know we prefer to call it feeding."

"Whatever," I waved my hand between us again, "it's still my blood. Things can go wrong. What if something goes wrong?"

His eyes narrowed further. "Nothing will go wrong."

"You don't know that."

"I've been doing this for a long time."

"What if you get really hungry?"

"I'll repeat, if you'd paid attention in class, you'd know the answer to that."

"Well I didn't so maybe you should tell me."

"I don't have the time, or the inclination, to tell you."

At his words, my body froze and I felt my blood begin to race. "So you're going to su...I mean, feed? Now?"

He stared at me then closed his eyes and pulled in a deep breath. When he opened them again they were at my throat.

My heart started beating so fast I could feel it.

"No," he said softly. "Not now." His hand at my hip moved, sliding down the side of my thigh to my knee. Then up again. Then back again. The slit of my gown having opened, this meant his gentle movements were skin against skin.

This felt nice. I didn't want to admit it, but my body wasn't letting me deny it.

I ignored my body and whispered, "Why not now?"

"Your heart is beating too fast, my pet. If something *could* go wrong, which it won't, *that's* what would make it go wrong."

"How do you know my heart's beating too fast?"

"I can hear it."

"Really?"

He nodded.

Of course he could. I would have probably learned that in class too.

"What could go wrong?" I asked.

He studied me, likely weighing the wisdom of answering.

Then he said, "After you've had enough, I have to stop the blood from coming so I can heal the wound. If it's pumping too much, I might not be able to do that."

"That doesn't sound good," I whispered.

"It wouldn't be," he replied, his hand still stroking my thigh. "That's why we need to calm you down."

"I'm not sure that'll work," I admitted. "Me calming down, I mean."

He slid his arm out from under his upper body but bent his elbow and put his head in his hand. This pressed his warm chest against my side and brought his face a whole lot closer to mine.

"Let's try, shall we?" he suggested.

I didn't want to try. In fact, I felt hope for the first time in a week. Actually, for the first time in four weeks, since I got my invitation to The Selection.

"Maybe we shouldn't do this tonight," I tried. "Maybe we should try tomorrow night. Or," I hesitated, "next week."

Or never, but I wasn't going to go that far, not yet.

My very weak hope was dashed.

"I can't," he replied.

"Why not?"

He sighed and his hand stopped stroking my thigh. His fingers curled into my hip again and he rolled me to my side facing him as his legs came out from under mine and he stretched out full-length beside me. His arm moved around me, his hand sliding up my back to catch a tendril of hair and start playing with it.

"I'll give you a little lesson you *should* have learned in studies," he began with a disapproving tone before I could give in to hyperventilating at our newer, far more intimate, position.

I pulled my lips between my teeth and nodded.

"Five weeks ago, I informed The Council I would be releasing my concubine and I'd need to attend a Selection. A week ago, three hours before I arrived at your Selection, she and I officially ended our Arrangement. By law I'm not allowed to feed until I have my new concubine. Not even at a Feast. This means I haven't fed in a week. That's a long time, my pet," he finished on a whisper and then went right on whispering, "I need you. Tonight."

I ignored his admission of need, which made me feel strangely aroused. What helped that arousal (too much), was the way he whispered, his deep voice soft and low and somehow physical.

Instead, I asked, "What's a feast?"

His hand went from playing almost tenderly (all right, so it *was* tenderly, I couldn't deny it) with my hair, to sliding down my back and drawing circles at its small.

That felt nice too, both my body and mind admitted it without delay or quarrel. It just felt nice. *Really* nice.

"That I'll let your mother or Edwina explain," he told me, still talking low.

"So you're hungry?"

He nodded and answered, "Very."

"Why do you have to wait? That seems stupid."

Something passed across his face—annoyance, definitely, impatience also, frustration too, I was pretty certain. Then there looked to be defiance, but that was so fleeting I couldn't be sure.

"It isn't smart, you're correct, however it's also the law," he answered.

"Wouldn't that make the first bloodletting, the initiation, rather dangerous if the vampire is hungry?"

I thought he'd lie.

Instead he agreed by saying, "Yes."

"That doesn't make sense," I whispered and I could feel my heart, which had been slowing, start to speed up again.

"I was there when they wrote the law and I still don't understand it." He stopped speaking because I wasn't listening.

I was panicking.

His head cocked slightly then his fingers ceased drawing on my back and his hand flattened, moving over my bottom and up to my hip.

"Leah, your heart," he warned.

"I can't help it!" I burst out. "You even admitted you were hungry. What if you can't stop!"

"I'll stop."

"What if you can't?"

"Leah, I'll stop."

I shook my head and started to pull away, but his hand slid down my hip, over my bottom again but this time to cup it, and he pulled me closer, pressing my hips into his.

He was aroused too, very aroused. I felt it immediately. And his arousal made me even *more* aroused. It was insane but it was true.

Oh my God. What was wrong with me?

I stilled against his body and my eyes caught his in shock.

His face came close, his mouth barely a breath from mine before he promised, "I won't hurt you."

"You can't help it."

"I can."

"Please don't do this," I whispered my plea.

He drew a breath in his nostrils and his black eyes, so close, lost focus.

"God, you smell sweet," he murmured.

"Lucien."

When I said his name, his eyes came back into focus and they were more intense than ever.

"You'll like it," he told me softly.

I shook my head. My panic was keeping pace with my arousal. He was turning me on and scaring me to death at the same time. How, I didn't know, but he was doing it.

It was as if he sensed this and he liked it. He liked it *too* much, I could tell because his eyes started burning and that turned me on too.

"In a week, you'll be begging me for it," he said quietly.

My pulse spiked and my breath went ragged. His eyes flared.

"Calm, my pet," he murmured, his hand pressing into my behind, his hips starting to grind against mine.

That felt good too.

My lips parted, my breasts swelled and my nipples went hard, all at the same time a rush of warmth flooded between my legs.

In a second I was going to kiss him. I *had* to. It wasn't even my choice. I wasn't in control of myself. This wasn't mind games. This wasn't even head games. This was all me.

My eyes dropped to his mouth.

"Leah," he called but I couldn't tear my eyes from his mouth and my hips started moving against his.

"Leah, stop, you're making this harder on me," he warned and his hand at my ass moved up my back.

But I couldn't stop. I was driven, for some reason out of control.

It was then I made a near fatal mistake.

In an effort to get closer, I hooked my leg over his hip.

The instant I did, his head jerked down nearly colliding with mine, and he glanced down between our bodies in the direction of my lap.

I heard him draw another breath through his nostrils. This one seemed urgent, primal, animal.

When his head shot back up, I saw his eyes were blazing.

Hungry.

Hungry.

Hungry.

Hunger was written all over his face.

"Fuck," he growled, rolled over me, pinned my upper body with his colossal weight, one of his arms wrapped around me creating a warm, tight cage, and two things happened at once.

The first, his mouth was at my throat. I felt excruciating pain there as his teeth tore through my flesh and my blood burst forth into his mouth.

The second, his other hand went between my legs, cupping me over my nightgown, my panties, superhumanly strong fingers pressed in, invading.

I gasped, grabbed his broad shoulders and pushed with everything I had.

He didn't budge.

I lost track of what his hand was doing between my legs because the pain at my neck was agonizing, unbearable, my lifeblood rushing out of me in a warm, hideous flood.

"Lucien!" I cried, bucking, pushing, fighting.

He didn't move, he just drank.

It hurt. Killer hurt.

Intolerable.

I felt the strength leave me as my blood poured into his mouth, weakening me.

"Lucien," I gasped, still pushing, blackness penetrating at the sides of my eyes. It was my body's response either to the terrible pain or the loss of blood or both.

I welcomed the loss of consciousness. I could take no more.

My hands fell away from his shoulders as the blackness crept closer, my strength vanished, and I lay limp in his arm.

Before the blackness permeated, I felt his head rear up away from my throat and the last thing I remembered was saying in a frail whimper, "You promised."

Then there was nothing.

4

The Day After

I opened my eyes and saw it was morning. The sun shone weak around the edges of the heavy, drawn curtains.

I felt a moment of confusion, not knowing where I was, my surroundings unfamiliar.

Then I remembered.

My body froze stiff.

There was movement behind me, and before I could register this, I was gently rolled to my back. Lucien, fully visible but shadowed in the feeble light, was up on a forearm towering over me.

Stark terror surged through me. I tensed, preparing for escape.

The next second I was crushed in his arms, my face tucked in his throat, his big hand cupping the back of my head, one of his heavy thighs thrown over both of mine.

"Leah," he whispered.

My name sounded tormented on his lips.

I didn't care. He could feel as badly as he wanted. He could be tormented *forever* by his actions and forever was a freaking long time for a vampire.

Promising he wouldn't hurt me and then inflicting the worst pain I'd ever felt.

Promising he'd stop and then nearly killing me.

I assessed my options.

I couldn't fight him, I'd never win. Even if I did get away, he could control my mind, my movements.

Therefore, I had no options.

God, I really hated him.

"Please, let me go," I demanded to his throat, my voice sounded raspy, brittle, and that scared me too.

"Leah, you must listen to me."

I shook my head. This didn't hurt. I felt no pain at my throat where he'd torn my flesh apart, just an odd but profound numbness, like getting your gums shot with Novocain. I decided not to think about that bit of weirdness at that moment.

I decided to focus on something else.

"The contract didn't say word one about me having to listen to you. You feeding on me, yes. You fucking me, yes. Me listening to you, *no*."

His hand left my head and went to my jaw. His thumb under my chin, he pressed up cautiously as he tilted his head down to look at me.

"I'll explain," he declared.

I had no idea this was a remarkable declaration. Since I'd been expelled from Vampire Studies, I had no idea vampires didn't explain themselves. Even if I had an idea, I wouldn't have cared about that either.

"Are you hungry?" I asked.

"Leah."

"Well? Are you?"

"Of course not," he said on a sigh.

"No, of course not," I shot back. "Had your fill last night, did you?"

His face grew dark as his arms grew tighter, just to the edge of pain but not quite there. "Listen to me, pet."

"Stop calling me that," I hissed and watched his face grow even darker.

This should have scared me.

It didn't. I knew the worst he could do, outside actually finishing the job.

Ignorance was not bliss. Ignorance was torture.

"Are you going to fuck me?" I snapped in the face of his anger.

His head jerked before he asked, "Pardon?"

"Fuck me. You fed last night, you're no longer hungry, but you're still here. I'm wondering why? I'm wondering how I'm meant to service you now, master."

His arms tightened again, going over the edge of pain for a fleeting second before he rolled me to my back and settled some of his solid weight on me.

His hand went to the side of my head, his fingers curling into my hair there, not gentle, not entirely painful either.

I looked into his face and it was carved from stone but his eyes were blazing like last night, but not with hunger or desire.

With fury.

Okay, so maybe now I was a little bit scared.

His eyes burned into mine for long moments before he pulled in a deep breath.

On his exhale, he said, "Considering what happened last night, Leah, I'll let your behavior go this morning."

"Well, thank you," I returned with deep sarcasm.

His hand tightened in my hair. The not entirely painful part became a little more painful but not unbearable.

"Don't try your luck," he warned.

I really wanted to try my luck. Every bad trait that was me screamed at me to try my luck. Instead, my eyes slid to the side then I closed them so I didn't have to look at him even in my peripheral vision.

"I hate you," I whispered. It sounded weak, even scared, and I didn't care about that either.

His fingers loosened in my hair and he replied softly, "That's understandable."

With my head mostly freed, I turned it on the pillow away from him.

"Please go," I begged.

He began sifting his fingers through my hair at the side of my head. It felt good. I didn't want it to feel good and I hated him for that too.

His deep voice cut through my thoughts. "I'll go, Leah, but I'll be back tonight."

My eyes flew open and my head jerked back to facing him.

"Tonight?" I croaked, my voice broken with fear.

His middle finger touched my temple gently then his hand flattened carefully against the side of my face. "Tonight."

"But, you can't need—"

"I'll not be feeding."

Oh my God. That meant we'd be...

"I'll not be fucking you either," he went on.

I shook my head. "Then why are you coming back tonight?"

"We need to talk."

I stared at him a second before shaking my head again. "No, we don't."

"We do."

"We don't."

He sighed again and his face dipped closer to mine. I sucked in my breath.

"We *do*," he repeated.

Now I was angry, freaked out, hating him, terrified of him and confused.

"But I thought—" I started.

He cut me off. "Tonight."

"Lucien—"

His face dipped even closer, so close I didn't suck in breath. I quit breathing altogether.

His lips touched mine, briefly, softly. Then he moved from the bed.

I got up on an elbow. This took it out of me, my head swam alarmingly, and I fell back down.

Whoa.

What was that? What *the hell* was *that*?

Before I could process this, he was back, dressed completely except his suit jacket was bunched in his large hand.

He leaned in, put a fist in the bed on either side of me and got close. "You need to rest, pet. All day," he ordered.

"But—"

"Rest."

"But—"

"All day."

"But—"

His mouth touched mine but he didn't kiss me and he kept his eyes open, boring into mine.

I quieted.

"I took too much from you last night," he murmured against my lips. "You need to rest."

My mouth opened under his and I began to speak, "I—"

I stopped speaking when his tongue darted in and touched mine, startling me. It was a fleeting touch, but even so, his open eyes kept mine captive and I registered a distinct, excited flurry in the region of my belly.

Now.

Exactly.

What was *that*?

A flurry? Caused by a kiss from my near-murderer?

That proved it. I was deranged.

"Rest," he whispered against my mouth.

Before I knew it, he was gone.

I opened my eyes again when I sensed movement in the room.

It was light, I could still see the sun shining around the curtains so it was not yet "tonight" which meant, I hoped, the movement wasn't Lucien.

It wasn't. It was Edwina tiptoeing around the bed.

"I'm awake," I announced, cautiously getting up on an elbow.

She jumped at the sound of my voice and whirled to face me.

"You're awake," she repeated.

I nodded, focusing on her. She was a beautiful, older woman, older than my mother. How I knew this I didn't know because her face was nearly unlined, but I guessed it to be true. Her hair was thick, long and white and it looked soft. It was pulled back in a pony-tail at her nape. Like yesterday, she was wearing a gauzy outfit, a swirly, peachy-pink skirt and beige-pink flowy blouse cinched with an equally flowy scarf belt low on her waist.

She looked like a stylish hippie. Strange but true.

"Lucien spent the night," she declared on a strangled whisper.

I kept staring at her.

Then I asked, "What?"

"Lucien," she said then spoke no more.

"Yes, Lucien..." I prompted.

"*Spent the night*," she breathed in what sounded like deep surprise.

God, she was weird.

"Yes, he did," I replied slowly.

"Why?" she asked, still in a breathy, stunned voice.

Why did Lucien do anything? Because Lucien wanted to, that was why.

"He just did," I answered.

"I don't...he never..." She stopped then pivoted jerkily and walked briskly to the windows, throwing open the curtains as she wittered on. "This is unheard of, unprecedented. I don't know what to say. I can't even—"

"Edwina," I cut her off.

She turned again. The minute her eyes hit me they grew so big, they nearly popped out of her head, and she gasped. Loudly.

At the same time her hand flew to her mouth.

I knew I'd passed out before I'd been able to pull a comb through my hair and take off my heavy makeup but even what I knew was the sight of me the morning after her fervid ministrations couldn't induce *that* response.

"What?" I asked in a frightened voice.

"Your throat," she whispered from behind her hand.

My hand flew to my throat. It still felt that weird numb and Edwina's horrified stare was making me strangely embarrassed.

I covered the area Lucien fed from last night and pushed up from the bed. I was still lightheaded but I fought it, put my feet on the floor, got up and headed to the bathroom.

My bedroom...

No. Strike that.

Lucien's bedroom (I wasn't going to claim *anything* he gave me) was the biggest bedroom I'd ever had.

Painted a warm blush it had a king-size bed covered in a decadent, fluffy, down comforter with a slightly darker blush, cotton-sateen cover with beautiful embroidery heavy at the bottom of the coverlet and snaking to lighter up the bed. Stacks of downy pillows of all sizes from king, to European, to standard in cases and shams that ranged from the deepest to the most delicate blush adorned its head, some of them smooth, some of the embroidered.

There was a chaise lounge in a corner covered in cream velvet, edged with gleaming dark, intricately carved wood. Positioned strategically next to its only arm was a small, ornate, circular table. Matching stately but comfy-looking armchairs, each with their own tall, plush, round, tassel-bottomed, button-topped ottomans were arranged in another corner. The chairs shared a carved wood table. A charming writing desk with a laptop computer and stylish desk accessories faced the room from the opposite corner to the chairs.

I didn't see any of this.

Yesterday afternoon after I'd arrived, I'd inspected the entirety of the lavish cage Lucien had provided for me. I perused the six-bedroom house from top to bottom. Why he thought I'd need six bedrooms with a gigantic kitchen including breakfast nook and comfy seating area, a formal dining room, a sitting room, a living room, a family room, a study, four and a half baths—the list went on—I'd never know.

At that moment I didn't want to know. All I could think about was my throat.

I went into the bathroom. Another huge room with two sinks, a big mirror, a large, blush-marbled tub set in a platform under a stained glass window (if you can believe), separate shower cubicle with multiple heads (some *on the walls*), and the toilet had its own room.

I turned to the mirror and slowly, wincing slightly to prepare myself for the mutilation I'd see, took my hand from my throat.

Then I blinked.

There was only an insignificant, inch long, slightly glistening, pinkish scar.

"What on earth?" I whispered.

"I know," Edwina said, materializing behind me. "Can you believe it?"

"No," I gaped at the non-wound, remembering the tearing sensation last night, the pain, the powerful suction from Lucien's mouth, "I can't believe it."

"I can't believe it hasn't healed," Edwina breathed.

My eyes flew to hers in the mirror. "What?"

"It hasn't healed. How can that be? They always heal before morning. Usually sooner."

My mouth dropped open.

I snapped it shut moments before asking, "Are you joking?"

Her head quirked to the side. "Of course not. You know that."

No, I didn't know that.

I'd been expelled from blinkety-blank Vampire Studies and the time I'd been there I didn't pay a lick of attention.

I moved away from the mirror, walking toward the huge dressing room that was on the opposite side to the bedroom.

This room was also enormous, the walls filled with rails, shelves, drawers and a full-length, three-way mirror. There was enough space to house the wardrobes of a family of five. It even included a extravagant, built-in dressing table with dozens of drawers, a big mirror surrounded by Hollywood starlet lights, and was fronted by a blush-velvet padded stool. No kidding, the place was out of a movie.

Most of it was unutilized as I'd only brought two suitcases and a carry-on with me. My mother and aunties were packing up whatever else I'd need to be shipped. Even when they did, it still wouldn't fill the space and Lucien was seeing to the renting of my place while I was servicing him.

As I stormed into the dressing room, I announced, "I need to call my mother."

I walked to the dressing table and had to put a hand out to steady myself. I was still feeling woozy and weak. I needed food. And, as much as I hated to give it to the guy, Lucien was right, I needed rest.

"Um...dear..." Edwina said behind me as I caught my breath, controlled the dizziness, and reached for my purse to get my cell phone.

I ignored her and started digging through my purse.

"Dear..." Edwina called from closer.

"Where is it?" I muttered. "I'm sure it's—"

"Leah," Edwina said from beside me. "Lucien told me you weren't to phone anyone."

My head snapped up and I looked at her. "Sorry?"

"Direct orders. No calls."

"Why not?" I asked.

She shrugged, looking uncomfortable.

I looked back down at my purse and kept digging. "Well, he can order all he likes. I'm still going to—"

"You won't find it. Lucien took your phone."

My head snapped up again and I stared.

All I could do was stare. My heart had stopped beating which was pretty strange since my blood was boiling.

Finally I found my voice. "He *took* my *phone*?"

"Yes, and he told me to lock away all the others."

"Did you?"

She nodded.

I straightened and faced her. "Well, unlock one."

"I can't."

"You can."

"Lucien would be angry."

"I don't care," I snapped.

Her face grew pale. It didn't take a mind reader to know she didn't want to do anything that would make Lucien angry.

I could understand that. He could be a pretty freaking scary guy. And, I didn't know her, but I still didn't want to scare her.

Thwarted again by the hated *Lucien.*

"I'm going to *kill* him," I bit out, my emotions got the better of me, and I had to lean against the dressing table to stay standing.

"You need food. Lucien said the minute you woke, I needed to feed you."

"Lucien can go to hell," I clipped.

She studied me a moment, surprise behind her eyes, her head angled to the side like a bird's.

"I think something's not right here," she announced.

"You *think*?" I asked sarcastically.

"Why are you angry with Lucien? No one is ever angry with Lucien. Well, not no one. He has enemies, of course. But not his concubines. Never his concubines. They all love him."

Oh please.

"I'm not like the others," I proclaimed.

"I'm sensing that," she agreed on a comprehending nod.

I dropped my head and lifted my hand to my forehead.

"I think I need space," I told her, not wanting to be rude, but I did.

In this moment of tumult in my life, I hated to admit it, but I really needed my mother even though she and her ancestry of rabidly adoring vampire concubines had gotten me into this mess.

Suddenly, I felt Edwina's hands gentle on me as she pulled me away from the dressing table.

"What you need is bed and food, in that order," she declared.

I went with her because I didn't have the strength to fight.

I blamed that on Lucien mainly because it was his fault.

And I filed it away in my Why I Hate Lucien Vault.

Edwina put me to bed. She came back with a tray covered in food half an hour later, time I spent organizing all the many, *many* files in my Why I Hate Lucien Vault. A stack of light, fluffy, buttermilk pancakes drenched in melting, real butter and warmed syrup. Crisp bacon. Succulent berries. Grilled sausage links.

I ate it without complaint.

Normally I would never eat that much food as food like that, especially in those amounts, magically expanded to ten times its size and weight before it settled on my ass.

But I needed my strength. For tonight, I would be battling *Lucien*.

5

That Night

Lucien drove toward Leah's house feeling a welcome sense of anticipation after a not very good day.

She was, he knew, going to be cold or furious, but he couldn't care less.

Whatever she was, it would not be eager. It would not be sycophantic. It would not be adoring. And it would not be complaisant.

It would be something different. Something he relished. Something he had not had in a very long time.

That morning after he arrived at the home he shared with his mate, Katrina had been waiting for him.

The minute he closed the door behind him, she unleashed the fury that he knew she'd kept pent up all night waiting for his return.

Even though he was still furious with her for the plot she'd attempted to unleash at Leah's Selection, she had every right to be angry. A vampire did not sleep with his concubine, not in any sense of that word. He or she didn't spend the night.

Goodly portions of it, maybe. The entirety of it, never.

Vampires slept with their vampire mates in every sense of that word.

Things might, and often did (and The Dominion turned a blind eye), get out of hand at Feasts, but not with concubines. The lines were drawn, the boundaries understood, and no one, not even Lucien, could break them.

He ignored his mate, something he'd been doing a great deal for the past decade, walked upstairs straight to their bedroom, disrobed and got in the shower.

She followed, not ceasing for even a breath in her blistering tirade.

Lucien was angry with himself for losing control with Leah and nearly taking her life, something which he would miss, even knowing her such a short time. Not only because her blood was heavenly but also because she didn't intend to grow up until she was ninety-three years old. *That* was a concept he found intriguing and very much wanted the time to explore.

He was also angry that he'd caused her to experience such unadulterated terror.

Fear was delicious, especially when it was mingled with excitement.

Terror, or at least the terror he'd witnessed from Leah that morning when she woke, was revolting.

Last, and most importantly, no matter how much he tried, he could not get the sound of her saying, her eyes filled with pain and accusation, "You promised," out of his head.

Therefore, he was in no mood to deal patiently with Katrina.

He stepped out of the shower dripping wet and put a hand to her throat, silencing her invective. He lifted her clean off her feet and slammed her against the wall, her skull cracking against the plaster, and held her there, his fingers squeezing.

She clawed at his forearm with her nails to no avail.

He held her squirming against the wall, deftly avoiding her kicking legs until he felt she understood his meaning. Then he dropped her.

She landed lithely on all fours in a graceful crouch, her head snapping back, her cloud of long black hair falling over her back, her ice-blue eyes glaring at him. Her stunning face was contorted with rage.

She was preparing for attack.

"Don't even think of challenging me." His demand was quiet and it was lethal.

Indecision flickered in her eyes which was a strategic mistake. She should have long since learned to master any situation and indecision showed weakness.

She was a young vampire, only two hundred years old.

Even so she would never learn. She never had. He'd been trying to teach her for fifty years.

In the beginning she was quite like Leah, young, amusing, challenging, beautiful, and perhaps most importantly, unbelievably sexy.

The minute they finalized The Claiming she'd changed. Became possessive—intolerably so—jealous, even of his concubines, and until Leah he'd never given her reason for this ridiculous emotion. Demanding to go with him to Feasts (this he did not allow). Resistant to his teachings.

She'd been full of promise when he'd met her.

She'd become a disappointment.

He saw the fluid line of her shoulders fall in defeat, an action that defined his discontent with their pairing, and without a word he turned and strode back to the shower.

In the shower, he came to the swift decision to file for Severance. He'd been toying with it for years. Now was the time.

It was not unheard of for vampire mates to sever. It was also not nearly as commonplace as the mortals' divorce. Vampires, the vast majority of the time, mated for eternity which, being immortal, meant literally.

Although it was frowned upon, Severance was also never denied. It was not a good idea to force two vampires to live together. It was, they discovered centuries ago, deadly.

When he exited the shower, Katrina had calmed down. He found her curled in a ball on her side in their bed, a bed, at the sight of his defeated and sulking mate, he made the instant decision he would never share with her again.

"You must know I deserve an explanation," she whispered.

He didn't answer mainly because he knew nothing of the sort.

"No one spends the night with their concubines," she went on. "You'd lose your mind if I spent the night with Kyle."

This wasn't true. There was a good possibility he wouldn't even notice.

Her voice dropped below a whisper when she asked, "What *is* it about her?"

Lucien had been dressing while she talked.

Finished, he turned to face her and answered simply, "She's life."

He watched her body jolt as if struck.

Then she came up on an arm, her face filling with disbelief and twisting with bitterness. "*Your* life? You barely know her."

He crossed his arms on his chest and looked down at his mate. "Not my life, Rina. Life."

She shook her head. "I don't know what that means."

She wouldn't.

Katrina didn't know the difference between inexpensive champagne and the finest vintage and no amount of instruction or consumption would make her grasp that distinction.

He knew this because he'd tried for fifty years to teach her that exact lesson.

There was blood and there was Leah Buchanan's blood. It was the difference between eating dust and allowing the finest Belgian chocolate to melt on your tongue.

Feeding from Leah was like drinking in heaven.

Doing it with his hand between her legs, her soft body pinned under the weight of his, enveloped in the smell that was all her mingled with the scent of her sex in a heightened state of arousal, was nirvana.

He was looking forward to Leah's taming.

Regardless of how it happened, if the beauty of last night was any indication, feeding from her while they were physically joined and she gave herself wholly to him would be rapture.

"Lucien," Katrina called.

Torn from his thoughts and not appreciating it, Lucien announced, "We're finished talking."

He watched her body go taut as his words penetrated.

"Now what does *that* mean?" Katrina asked on an irritated snap.

He didn't answer. He left and put her out of his mind.

This was not difficult.

He met with Stephanie that day. And Avery.

There were plans to be made and he was making them. He had been making them since he received word from his informant that Leah had extricated herself from yet another of her hideously ill-suited boyfriends. The end of her mortal relationship opened her up for Selection. With vast and frustrating experience riding the tempestuous waves of Leah's love life, he had not delayed in taking his chance and he, amongst others, had placed her name on his list to receive an invitation to The Selection.

Lucien knew The Council would not be blinded to what he was doing for long. They'd find out. Likely, once he filed for Severance, Katrina would tell them. Possibly Leah's family would too, although he knew they'd demanded to examine the contract, and she'd not only gone to Study, but the Buchanans dispatched her for Homing.

If not those, undoubtedly The Council would hear of his actions somehow.

And he was ready.

Stephanie had always been impatient with the Immortal and Mortal Agreement. She'd even been indecisive on which side she would fight before The Revolution.

She was a definite ally.

Avery was a surprise. He'd been working in his role for The Council of The Dominion for centuries. Lucien had only sensed his willingness to turn traitor.

And Lucien had been right.

Cosmo, on the other hand, he'd been avoiding since Leah's Selection, something which he failed to do that day.

Late in the afternoon, Cosmo had pressed into Lucien's office, Lucien's secretary, Sally hot on his heels.

Sally halted when Cosmo hissed, "Are you planning a revolt?"

Lucien nodded at Sally who withdrew.

Once she closed the door behind her, he leveled his eyes on his friend and answered, "No."

"Then what's this all about?" Cosmo clipped. "I was there, Lucien. Leah refused to blood your contract. The next thing I know, it had been signed, Avery had filed it, you'd Homed her, and The Bloodletting was last night."

Lucien didn't speak.

Cosmo continued, "Katrina told Nestor who told Jordan who told Hamish who told *me* that you spent the night with her."

Lucien knew his secret wouldn't last long. "I did."

"*Have you gone mad?*" Cosmo bellowed.

Lucien stood, shaking his head. "Cosmo, calm down."

"The Council will hear of this," Cosmo bit out.

"They probably already have. Katrina was in a state this morning. She'll not be thinking before she acts."

Not that she ever did, he thought.

"They'll pull you in," Cosmo warned.

"It's likely."

Cosmo straightened and took in Lucien's composure before asking, "What happened? Did you fall asleep?"

"Yes, after the initiation, I fell asleep."

This was true. After he nearly killed her, he stopped the blood, soothed the wound, waited, watching and impatient for long minutes as the healing began. Then he watched for long hours as the healing progressed. When he was satisfied all would be well, only then did he pull Leah in his arms and fall asleep.

However, he had every intention of spending the night with Leah even had he not lost control necessitating that he wait for the healing. And he had every intention of spending *every* night with Leah until he lost interest in her and released her.

Cosmo continued to study him before he remarked dubiously, "So, it was all innocent."

"No," Lucien replied honestly. "It was far from innocent."

Cosmo closed his eyes.

In a low voice that held a vein of steel, Lucien declared, "I'll not live like this for another day, Cosmo."

Cosmo opened his eyes "You *are* planning a revolt."

"It might not lead to that."

"You know it will."

Lucien shrugged. "Then it's war."

Cosmo pulled in breath through his nostrils at Lucien's words, but his face and eyes went blank, hiding his thoughts.

Katrina could learn from Cosmo.

Quietly, Cosmo spoke. "I've seen her, Lucien. I've smelled her. I like her. She's fascinating. She's funny. She's different. But," he paused before finishing, "she's not worth war."

"You haven't tasted her," Lucien returned decisively.

Cosmo's head cocked to the side, intrigued despite himself. "She's that good?"

"Better."

Cosmo's brows went up before he muttered, "Jesus." Then he continued in a low voice, "Did you fuck her?"

"Not yet."

"You intend to?"

"Absolutely."

"Christ, Lucien—"

Lucien lost patience. "If I remember correctly there was many a night, for seven years, you left her mother and went direct with me to a Feast. Not to feed, to fuck, the way you wanted to fuck Lydia. If I remember correctly, for seven years, you wanted Lydia in a way you couldn't have her because the Agreement said you couldn't. It nearly drove you mad. You had to release her before you wanted just to end the torment. Do you remember?" Lucien demanded.

"I remember," Cosmo answered, his jaw clenching.

"That is not going to happen to me," Lucien stated. "I want Leah, *all* of Leah, and I'll damn well have her. I'm tired of these ancient, absurd edicts ruling my life, your life, Stephanie's life. We're vampires for fuck's sake and everything that is our essence has been stripped away. No more. I'm taking it back. If they try to punish me, I'll fight."

Cosmo's face again lost all expression. Because the time might come where he'd need allies, and Cosmo would be an excellent one, not to mention he was a trusted friend, Lucien continued to explain.

"It's been over five hundred years since I caught a scent as extraordinary as Leah's."

Understanding lit in Cosmo's eyes.

"Maggie," Cosmo muttered.

It took an extreme effort of will, even after all of these years, for Lucien not to flinch at her name.

He ignored his friend's muttering and carried on, "I caught Leah's scent twenty years ago. I should have had her then. I should have been able to take what I wanted. But I had to wait. Twenty years, Cosmo. I've lost twenty years. Or, more to the point, she's *aged* twenty years and I've lost that. My time has come, as has Leah's, and there will be no barriers, no boundaries, no fucking *laws* that tell me I cannot do what I wish."

"You intend to tame her," Cosmo surmised.

"I've already started," Lucien announced.

Cosmo's hesitation was brief before he sighed and shook his head. "I suppose there will be those who'll champion you."

"I'd like you to be one of them."

Cosmo went still, his face remaining blank, before he asked softly, "You doubted I would?"

Lucien didn't answer.

Still speaking softly, Cosmo said, "I'd burn for you, Lucien. I've proved that before."

"You have," Lucien agreed.

They locked eyes for long moments before Cosmo broke their silent renewed vow of allegiance by saying, "She'll not be easily tamed."

For the first time since seeing his friend, Lucien smiled. "This is very true."

Cosmo smiled back. "How was she last night?"

"Untamable."

Cosmo threw his head back and laughed.

Thus ended their tense conversation.

Lucien turned into the driveway of the home he'd purchased for Leah three months before, just weeks after she'd ended her last relationship.

He'd broken his own practice and searched for it himself. He gave Sally his requirements and attended the viewings personally, twenty of them, before he found what he wanted to provide for Leah. Then he'd hired a team of decorators to fit it to his exacting specifications.

When he'd met Edwina there just days before to give her the keys to her new home and place of employment, she'd been stunned at what she saw.

Edwina had been housekeeper to his acting concubines for forty years. She knew Lucien had a reputation for being particularly generous with them. He kept them well while they serviced him and left them well when he'd released them. All vampires did the same, but either miserly or unable financially, they didn't do it as Lucien did because he was not miserly and he was far from financially unable.

But a six-bedroom mansion on a fifteen acre plot was beyond even Lucien's pale.

He hit the garage door opener on his visor and slid his sleek black Porsche Turbo next to the equally sleek black Cayenne he'd purchased for Leah.

Edwina, likely curious at hearing his car pull in the garage, met him by the kitchen door, her face startled.

"Lucien," she breathed.

"Edwina," he replied in greeting, not pausing but moving beyond her.

"You're here," she noted unnecessarily.

He stopped in order to ask where Leah was as he had no desire to go in search of her and turned back to Edwina. "Yes, I am. Where's Leah?"

He watched her eyes go round before she blurted, "She's not ready for another feeding! And *you* can't be ready for another one either."

Lucien's gaze leveled on hers and he watched the color run from her face.

"Sorry. I'm so sorry," she mumbled, looking away.

"Where's Leah?" Lucien repeated with ill-concealed impatience.

"In her room."

Lucien turned immediately toward the stairs.

"Lucien!" Edwina called and with reluctance Lucien turned back. "She's..." She paused, her face still ashen, her fear fragrancing the room.

"She's what?" Lucien asked when she did not carry on.

Her body twitched then she continued, "She's..." and she stopped again.

"Edwina," Lucien's voice was a dangerous hiss.

"She's in a...a..." He watched her swallow before she finished, "She's in a *mood.*"

Leah was in a mood. This was excellent news.

Slowly, Lucien grinned.

Edwina gawked.

Lucien turned back to the stairs.

As Edwina said, Leah was in her bedroom, though he knew this since he heard her heart beating and smelled her scent the moment he entered the downstairs hall.

When he walked through the door he saw her sitting on the chaise, her back to its arm, her legs bent in front of her. She was wearing faded jeans, a pale pink camisole, and a lightweight pale green cardigan. Her feet were bare, but her toes were polished a new color. Last night it was a sheer pink, tonight it was a bright fuchsia, evidencing the fact that she obviously disobeyed his command to rest and instead gave herself a pedicure. Her long, layered blonde hair fell around her shoulders in soft flips, the tendrils at her neck curving in, framing the graceful line of her throat in an invitation she likely didn't know she was giving, but one he savored.

Her head shot up when he arrived and he noted she was reading a book which she had opened on her thighs.

He turned to close the door. When he turned back, her head was again bent to the book. He watched her as he walked into the room, shrugging off his suit jacket. He continued to watch her as he threw it on the foot of the bed and moved closer. And he continued to watch her as he walked past her to the small table at the arm of the lounge.

She kept her head bent to her book the whole time, ignoring him, but her heart was racing and he smelled her fear.

He bent and picked up the bookmark that was resting on the table next to a cold drink and walked to the lounge, seating himself an inch away from her feet.

Then he twisted his torso, reached out and pulled the book from her hands.

Her head snapped up and she cried angrily, "Hey!"

This time he ignored her, put the mark in the book and leaned into her.

She cringed back against the arm of the lounge, her head turning slightly to the side, the pace of her heart escalating.

Lucien ignored this too.

He deposited the book on the table, leaned in farther and put a hand in the chaise on either side of her hips, his stomach and chest brushing her calves.

His eyes caught her wary ones and he demanded, "When I come to you, Leah, I want you to greet me."

He watched her jaw tighten and the flash in her eyes and he waited for her reply.

She gave it to him. "I'm sorry, oh Great Master. Hello. How was your day?"

He smiled right before he moved.

He'd decided not to hide his heightened abilities from her. He would be nothing but what he was with Leah.

In a second he had her out of the lounge and resituated in it, stretched out on her back, Lucien at her side up on his forearm leaning over her, his lower body pressed against hers.

When he was done, her dark-blue eyes were wide, her full lips parted and her breath had stopped.

"You don't have to use the 'great' part, pet. 'Master' will do," he teased her, still smiling.

She wrinkled her nose and glared. He threw his head back and laughed, barely controlling the urge to bury his face in her throat to get closer to her scent, her pulse, *her*.

Instead, when he stopped laughing, he put his hand at her fully-healed neck and ran his thumb down her jugular while his eyes watched its movements.

Then his gaze caught hers. "How are you feeling?" he asked quietly.

"Full," she replied in a sharp, unfriendly voice. "Edwina isn't skimpy with her portions."

His brows went up. "You've eaten?"

"Yes."

His thumb continued caressing her throat and his eyes moved back to it as he murmured, "I would have liked to share dinner with you."

He felt her body give a small jolt, his gaze went to hers, and he caught her wonder before she could hide it.

"You're surprised?" he asked.

She briefly struggled with something before she nodded.

"Why are you surprised?" he went on. "Because I eat or because I wish to eat with you?"

"Because you eat." Her voice was still short, clipped, hostile.

Even so his body relaxed, pressing closer to hers, settling in. Hers tensed.

"I eat. I drink. I sleep. I bathe. I do everything you do," Lucien told her.

She made no comment to this, although her face was filled with curiosity.

She hid the curiosity and decided to change the subject, demanding, "Are we going to talk?"

"We are talking."

She lifted her hand and waved it around. "No, not talking-talking. Talking about whatever it was you wanted to talk about this morning."

"We'll get to that."

"Can we do it now so you can go?"

"That has a two part answer," he explained and her brows knitted.

"It's a yes or no question," she informed him.

"Then no, to both parts."

He watched her jaw clench again and he heard her teeth grind together. It took another enormous effort not to laugh.

"Why can't we get this over with?" she insisted.

"Because I'd like a moment to relax and get a drink."

She made to move and he allowed more of his weight to settle on her until she stilled.

"If you let me up, I'll get you a drink," she offered with false courtesy.

He ignored her attempt to get away from him and his gaze moved to her glass. "What are you drinking?"

She didn't answer as he took his hand from her neck and reached for the glass. He brought it to his nose and inhaled its scent. It was diet cola and rum.

His eyes moved to hers. "You shouldn't be drinking spirits," he admonished.

Her head tilted to the side and her blue eyes grew darker. "Is that an order?"

"For tonight, while you're still recovering, yes. Any other time you can drink what you wish."

"I just don't believe you," she whispered angrily under her breath.

This was something else he ignored while he took a drink from her glass. For some reason, this caused her to protest, her hand shooting out, fingers wrapping around his wrist and jerking to no avail.

"Hey! Don't drink from my drink!"

He replaced the glass on the table and looked at her. "Why?"

"It's *my* drink!"

"Yes. And?"

"You can't drink my drink!"

"And why not?"

"Because it's *my* drink."

He sighed her name, "Leah."

She mimicked his sigh sarcastically. "Lucien."

He could bear it no longer. She was, quite simply, enchanting.

He burst into laughter again, burying his face in her neck this time while he pulled her to her side facing him, his arms wrapping tight around her, pressing her torso deep against his chest.

"Stop hugging me," she grumbled over his shoulder, her hands between them pushing against him.

His hand slid down her back to its small, right above her ass, and he pressed in. "I can't help it, pet, you're entirely huggable."

"I'm *huggable*?"

He lifted his head and smiled at her. "Entirely."

Her eyes narrowed. "You know, Lucien, you need to make up your mind. Either you're this guy or you're the jerky controlling guy who I met at The Selection or you're the near-miss murder guy last night. Pick one. I'm getting confused."

He pulled slightly away, bent his elbow and rested his head in his hand, looking down at her.

"I'm all those...guys."

"Can we make a deal that I get to pick which one I want?"

He was still smiling when he asked, "And which one would you choose?"

"None of them, in a perfect world." He chuckled and she talked through it. "But this one, since we don't live in a perfect world."

"Lucky for you, you have this one now."

"Then this one would give me back my phone."

His smile died. "I'll not be giving back your phone."

"Okay then," she shot back, "I don't have the slightly tolerable one. I have the jerky controlling one."

He disregarded her heated words and said, "There are things you need to learn."

"Yes, and if I could *phone* my mother, she would teach me."

"*I'm* going to teach you."

Her mouth snapped shut and she stared before she asked in a soft, stunned voice, "You?"

"Me."

"Why you?"

It had been a boon she'd been expelled from Vampire Studies even if the reason why annoyed him. She had no idea her role or his limitations. All she knew was the contract, which flew straight in the face of the law. Until he knew why the Buchanans sent her to him even after examining the altered contract, she would have nothing to do with them or anyone.

In the meantime, his path was cleared—at least with Leah.

And that was all that was important.

He, obviously, didn't tell her any of that.

"Because the idea of doing it amuses me."

She rolled her eyes.

"Leah," he called and her gaze came to his. "I'll take your instruction seriously and I expect you to do the same."

"In case you hadn't noticed, there's no one to pass notes to here and I don't have a phone so I can text my friends."

He reached up a hand and slid his fingers through the soft hair on the side of her head. A mortal man might have missed the delicate shiver that slid across her skin at his touch. And a mortal would definitely miss the sudden racing of her heart.

Lucien didn't.

This pleased him.

Greatly.

He made no mention of it nor did he give her any indication he felt it.

His eyes locked with hers. "Good, then I'll have your undivided attention."

"Can we get started?" she snapped.

"You're very impatient," he told her, fighting a smile.

Her eyes darted to his mouth then away while she announced, "I'm a lot of things, none of them good."

"I've noticed you're a lot of them, pet, but I beg to differ. I think all of them are good."

She closed her eyes in despair while muttering, "Great."

He chuckled and slid under her, pulling her over his body until she was mostly on top of him, part of her settled at his side against the back of the lounge. He kept his arms locked around her waist as she came up on a forearm and looked down at him. Her thick hair fell in a curtain around her face, its fragrance enveloping him in an intoxicating mixture of peonies with a hint of grapefruit.

He tamped down the urge to pull her hair and her closer and instead offered, "We'll start with last night, shall we?"

"Finally," she breathed and he gave her a gentle but unmistakable squeeze.

"Leah," he added a verbal warning to his physical one.

She drew in a breath and exhaled loudly.

Then she invited, "Begin, oh Great Master."

He again fought back a grin. "You're about to earn another hug."

"You're already hugging me."

He let the feel of her, the vision of her and her divine aroma penetrate.

He lost focus and one of his hands roamed up her spine as he murmured, "Indeed I am."

"Lucien," she called. "You were going to impart great vampire wisdom on me?"

He'd rather kiss her. He'd also rather peel away her clothes and taste her skin, her breasts, the heat between her legs.

He did none of that no matter how much he wanted it.

Instead he told her, "Last night didn't go as I planned."

He watched her press her lips together in an effort to bite back her own words.

"You made it get out of hand, pet," he said quietly and her brows shot up as she reflexively pushed against his chest, again to no avail.

"Me?" she snapped when she'd stopped pushing.

"You," he returned.

"How was *I* responsible for last night?"

"You got too excited."

"Too..." she paused and repeated, "too..." Then she made a strangled noise, unable to continue.

His hand slid farther up her back, caught a lock of her hair, and he started twisting it around his finger.

"You wanted me," he murmured and she swallowed.

"Did not," she whispered her lie.

"You did, I smelled it."

Her eyes widened and her lips parted. Lucien decided that was his favorite of Leah's many expressions.

"My senses are far more acute than yours," he explained.

"I know that."

"So you know I could smell your excitement."

Her eyes slid away and she muttered with embarrassment, "I didn't know *that*."

He found he was surprised at her embarrassment, delighted but surprised. Even so, he sought to alleviate it.

"I wanted you too," he told her softly.

Her eyes slid back fleetingly, he saw pink rise in her cheeks and he heard her heart trip over itself. Then she moved her gaze to study the arm of the lounge.

His arm gave her a squeeze at her waist. "Look at me, pet."

She hesitated and then did as he commanded.

"Vampires are human," he informed her and instead of her lips parting, her mouth dropped open and she gaped at him. He continued despite her astonished reaction. "The theory is, we mutated from homo sapiens a long time ago. As the millennia passed, we developed necessary traits, instincts, abilities for our survival and for the survival of the species that would keep us alive."

She continued to stare at him then whispered, "You're human?"

"A kind of human, yes, the immortal kind."

"It's not dark magic?"

He shook his head and said, "No."

"Supernatural?"

"No."

"Paranormal?"

"Leah, I'm just like you, except different."

"Yes, you're *way* different! You suck human blood!" Her voice had risen and she tried to pull away but he stopped twisting her hair and drew her closer with both arms wrapped around her.

"We feed on human blood, yes."

"That's wrong."

"It's natural."

"It's crazy!"

"It's been happening since time began."

She shook her head looking anywhere but at him, visibly unable to process this information.

"This is nuts," she muttered with an edge of hysteria.

"It isn't."

Finally she looked at him. "It's sick."

His arms tightened further and he held control of his temper, but his voice betrayed it when he explained, "You should know, that's offensive, pet."

Her eyes skittered away and she accused his shoulder, "You move faster than anyone I've ever seen. That is *not* natural."

"You've never been with a vampire."

"You smell things, hear things—"

He cut her off, "Leah, this isn't difficult to understand."

Her eyes shot to his. "Easy for you to say!"

"Species have been evolving since the planet formed. It's entirely natural, what I can do, how I feed. It's who I am. It's the way of my people."

"I can't believe this," she whispered.

"It's true."

She studied him briefly, her eyes working, her thoughts shifting, wildly different expressions swiftly drifting across her features, settling on one. Distrust mingled with horror.

"So, what, we're your prey? *My* people, that is. In this 'natural world' of yours."

He didn't hesitate with his reply. "Yes."

She went still and stared at him, clearly stunned at both his answer and his honesty.

He took advantage. "What I haven't explained yet is there's more we can do. Something I didn't do last night. Something that would have made things go far better for you if you hadn't made me lose control."

She gritted her teeth at another mention of her responsibility for last night's events before asking, "And that would be?"

"I can anesthetize your skin."

Her body jerked before she said, "Pardon?"

"Before feeding, only before feeding, my saliva has a numbing agent that releases. Not only does it anesthetize, it has healing properties. Strong ones. The healing begins even before I finish feeding."

Leah blinked, the distrust and horror gone, confusion and disbelief in its place.

Lucien went on, "If I'd have prepared you before we started, you wouldn't have felt the tearing, just the feeding, which is highly pleasurable for mortals."

Her face instantly assumed the look he enjoyed, the one filled with wonder.

Then she said, "You're joking."

He shook his head. "Your people find it a sensual experience."

"No," she shook her head, pushed up again, got nowhere and gave up, collapsing against him. "I was wrong about what you said before. That wasn't nuts. *This* is nuts."

"It isn't."

She ignored him and her eyes narrowed. "So why didn't you... prepare me?"

His arm at her waist circled further. His other hand slid up her neck and into her hair, bringing her face closer.

Quietly, he explained, "You were excited, moving against me, agitated, aroused. You felt good. You smelled good," his voice dipped lower at the memory, "so fucking good I lost control."

Her head pressed against his hand and didn't stop even if her effort was futile.

"Tomorrow night, when we do it again, I'll prepare you," he murmured, his eyes dropping to her throat.

She halted her struggles and he listened to her pulse as it raced.

"No," she whispered.

He lifted his gaze to lock on hers. "You'll like it."

Her voice held a tremor when she said, "You said that last time."

"Tomorrow, I won't be so hungry. Tomorrow, I'll take care of you."

"I'm supposed to trust that?"

His voice was deadly serious when he replied, "Yes, Leah. With feeding and with everything, you're supposed to trust me."

Her head jerked against his hand and his fingers curled into her hair until it stilled.

"I don't trust you," she snapped.

"You will," he returned.

"I won't."

"You will."

"Never," she hissed, losing her shock and getting angry.

Damn, she was stubborn.

"I'll have to prove it to you," he promised her.

"I'm never doing that again," she announced and his fingers in her hair twisted slightly as his patience slipped.

"You will, tomorrow night." His voice was implacable.

"Over my dead body," she bit out, her eyes flashing, her insult crystal clear, and he felt it slice agonizingly through his gut.

"Not a chance," he clipped in return.

She glared at him. He scowled back.

She gave in first when she demanded to know, "Are we done with my lesson now?"

"Yes," he growled.

"Good, then you're going to go?"

"No."

Her body jolted again and she asked, "What?"

"That's answer to part two of your earlier question. I'm not going. I'm spending the night here."

Her eyes widened again when she asked, "Why?"

"I like the smell of you when I sleep."

"*What?*" she cried in horror.

"And the feel of you," he continued.

She rolled her eyes toward her forehead and muttered, "Oh my God. It just gets worse and worse."

He ignored her verbal non-prayer and called, "Leah." Her eyes snapped back to his face and she was back to glaring. "I'll be here every night."

Her nose wrinkled before she mumbled, "Yep. Gets worse and worse."

Lucien decided he was done and it was time to move on. Therefore he did so.

"Now, you have three choices," he informed her.

Her head tilted and her jaw clenched before she gritted from between her teeth, "And those are?"

"You can share a drink with me while I have dinner, yours being non-alcoholic."

"Next," she snapped.

"You can get changed into your nightgown, get into bed and read."

"That sounds doable."

"I'll be joining you."

"Next," she demanded immediately.

"Last, you can begin your next lesson."

"And that would be?"

"I'll be teaching you how I like to be kissed."

Her face paled and her body froze.

After a long moment, she whispered, "I'll pick door number two."

He lost his annoyance and his impatience instantly for that was his choice. Although his choice was actually number three but he knew she wasn't ready for that yet.

His fingers unclenched in her hair and his hand cupped the back of her head, bringing her face closer to his.

"I said I picked door number two, Lucien," she breathed, pushing her head against his hand.

He pressed her ever forward until her mouth was a breath away from his.

"Get changed. I need food, a word with Edwina, and I'll meet you in bed."

"Righty ho, oh Great Master."

At her words, Lucien changed his mind and decided her next lesson would be right now. And that lesson would be that you always respect a vampire.

He brought her head forward a breath so her lips were light on his.

"This is your only warning, pet. If you call me 'oh Great Master' again, I'll be forced to punish you."

She held his gaze defiantly, her mouth soft against his, her head pressing against his hand.

Seconds slid by.

Then, Lucien was disheartened to see, she stopped her struggles and he watched her eyelids slowly drop in defeat.

A scant second later, her lids lifted, her eyes flared, and she whispered passionately against his mouth, "God, I hate you."

He smiled against her lips.

Yes, he was right, she was utterly enchanting.

6
The Kiss

My eyes opened to a wall of sleek skin over the hard muscle of a massive chest.

I stared at it, confused.

Justin had chest hair. Did he shave his chest?

And was he working out, like, *a lot*?

Then I remembered that this wasn't Justin. Justin was long gone. Four months gone.

This was Lucien.

Lucien who had left me last night to get food and have a word with Edwina. Lucien who had come back half an hour later carrying an expensive looking black leather bag that appeared full. Lucien who had disappeared into the bathroom and come out ten minutes later wearing nothing but a pair of black, drawstring pajama bottoms, giving me the first-ever view of his bulging biceps, sinewy forearms, broad shoulders, defined collarbone and honed chest which narrowed into a six pack.

No kidding, he was perfect from the top of his head to his waist. Every inch.

I quit breathing and tried not to drool.

He totally sensed my reaction. I knew this because his eyes went hooded and he grinned.

My first reaction was to pant when his eyes went all vampire sexy like that.

My second reaction was vastly different. I resisted (barely) the urge to throw my book at him.

He got in bed beside me. I ignored him, turning my back to him and concentrating on my book, one page of which I read fifteen times before it sunk in.

I didn't know what Lucien did. I didn't look. I think he read because I heard pages turning. He didn't touch me, though, and finally I turned out my light and tried to sleep.

He didn't. He kept doing whatever it was he was doing for a good long while, keeping his light on.

Eventually this forced me to ask irritably, "Are you ever going to turn out your light?"

"In a minute, my pet."

God, I hated it when he called me his "pet." It was way too close to the bone.

"I can't get to sleep with the light on," I informed him waspishly, still with my back to him, speaking to the opposite wall.

"You'll learn," he replied casually.

I clamped my mouth shut. Then I lay there and seethed. Lucien took his time, which I thought was incredibly inconsiderate. Finally, he turned out his light.

I began to force myself to relax.

This effort was immediately rendered futile when he pulled me into him, the length of my back pressed to the length of his front and his arm tight around me.

"I'm not a cuddler," I shared.

"You'll learn that too," he returned.

What a jerk!

"Lucien—" I started.

He cut me off. "Quiet, Leah, I'm tired."

He said this like he expected me to obey without question. Which I supposed he did. And worse, I had pretty much no choice but to do so.

"My life sucks," I announced into the dark.

He chuckled into the hair at the back of my head.

I didn't know when he fell asleep. I didn't even know when I did. I just knew I did because now I was facing him, staring at his glorious chest.

I had to get out of there.

My body tensed for flight. The instant it did, his hand came up, grasped a handful of hair and tugged it down, forcing my head back. I looked up into his still-drowsy face and caught my breath.

I hated him but there was no denying he was gorgeous, especially in the morning with that still-drowsy face.

His head was tilting toward me, and before I could process the meaning behind his movement, his mouth was on mine.

This surprised me. Not that he would kiss me because the detail to my job description was pretty freaking clear.

No, what surprised me was that the kiss was soft, gentle, exploratory, not hard, demanding and invasive.

I was so surprised I didn't even think to pull free.

His lips moved on mine in sensual discovery, his head slanting ever so slightly to press deeper. It was nice, stirring me but not frightening me.

I felt him then, the heat from his body, the soft skin over strong muscle of his chest under my hands. That was nice too.

His hand at my hip slid to the small of my back, just above my bottom, and it pressed in.

More heat, more hardness, more pressure on my mouth, all of it controlled but delicious. Without a thought I helped, wriggling to get closer, liking what I was feeling.

His mouth opened over mine, and as if it was the most natural thing in the world, mine opened under his.

His tongue slid inside.

In a flash all gentle exploration was gone. The minute his tongue touched mine, my body exploded. My stomach dropped, my toes curled, my nipples hardened, and I felt a wave of fire rush between my legs.

It was fantastic.

Helpless to stop myself and not even trying, I pressed into him full body, trying to get as close as I could. Even though I was lying down, both of my hands slid up his chest and held on to his shoulders tightly like if I didn't, I would fall.

At my touch, he growled low in the back of his throat, the power of it vibrating through my mouth, against my tongue, and I lost it. Not that I had much of "it" to lose.

One of my hands pushed under his arm, wrapping an arm around his back. The other one curled around his neck and up, gliding into his thick, soft hair.

He rolled into me, slanting his head further, deepening the kiss, his hand at my back sliding over my bottom, cupping me, pressing in. Our tongues tangled and he tasted beautiful. I'd never tasted anyone (especially in the morning) that amazing.

I liked it. I craved it. I wanted more and I took it. I took it like I needed it, like my life had a limit and if I didn't get as much of it as I could, I'd quit breathing the next instant.

He felt my urgency and rolled me fully to my back, his weight pinning me, his hips grinding into mine so I could feel his arousal. My body answered with another luscious belly drop and rush of warmth at my core. My hand clenched in his hair and I didn't care if it hurt. I was going to hold him to me for as long as it took me to get my fill of that mind-blowing kiss.

Suddenly his mouth tore from mine. His head went up and cocked slightly to the side.

I did not like this.

I held his hair clenched in my fist, my body squirming under his to resurrect our contact, my breath coming in fast pants.

"We've company," he murmured, his eyes dark and unfocused, a strange look of annoyance on his features.

"What?" I breathed.

He looked down at me and when he did his face gentled.

"Company," he repeated and I didn't process this. I couldn't. My concentration was entirely centered on his mouth, his eyes, his face, his body, his hardness, his heat and the intense, altogether too pleasant feeling between my legs.

His face dipped closer and my mind and body rejoiced.

But he didn't kiss me (alas).

Instead, his hand came to cup my jaw and he muttered, "I can't tell you how much it pleases me that you need no instruction on how to kiss me like I like it."

This pleased me too. Intensely. Considering I hated him with every fiber of my being this also confused me. Just as intensely. And, considering I hated him with a depth that was scary, this also pissed me off, at myself. Even *more* intensely.

Before I could come to terms with any of this, his mouth brushed mine then he whispered, "I'll be back."

In a flash, he was out of bed. He hesitated at its side, looking down at me.

I blinked, still not used to how quickly he could move, not to mention the sight of his chest.

I watched his face grow hard and he ordered, "Don't move."

Then he was out the door.

I lay in bed wondering what in the hell just happened.

My body didn't wonder. It knew what happened. It liked what happened. It wanted *more* of what happened.

"Oh my God," I breathed aloud.

I *was* deranged.

I liked being kissed by a vampire. Worse! I liked being kissed by Lucien, the Big, Bad, Jerky, Controlling Vampire.

I'd lost my mind.

Then it hit me that I had company.

How could I have company? No one knew where I lived. Even *I* wasn't certain where I lived considering a driver picked me up at the airport and brought me here. I was too busy lamenting my sucky life to pay attention to where we were going.

Ignoring his order not to move, I threw back the covers and stood. This caused me to feel a wave of dizziness. Clearly, I hadn't fully recovered from his onslaught at The Bloodletting.

I let my head adjust and then I hurried to the bathroom. Grabbing my short, creamy-colored flannel robe off the hook on the back of the door, I shrugged it on and rushed out of the room. Tying the belt as I went, I ran as fast as my legs would carry me without passing out and doing myself bodily harm.

I flew around the landing. As I was descending the last flight of stairs, right in front of me at the door, I saw Lucien's powerfully muscled back exposed, his lower half covered in his pajama bottoms. I also saw he was holding himself rigid, why, I didn't know. Probably anger or frustration.

I also saw he was facing my aunties Kate, Millicent and Nadia, all of whom were standing just inside the door.

Hallelujah!

Before I was all the way to the bottom and opened my mouth to speak, Lucien's torso twisted so he was facing me. I caught the look on his face and realized it wasn't anger or frustration.

It was fury.

I didn't get to greet my family. Lucien spoke first.

"What did I tell you?" he demanded, his voice so harsh it was a whiplash.

"Sorry?" I asked, stopping two steps from the bottom in an effort at self-preservation. I hoped distance would help me avoid the almost physical lash of his tongue.

"What did I tell you?" he repeated, turning slowly to me.

My eyes flickered to my aunties who were looking pale and concerned, their own gazes moving between Lucien and me.

"Get back upstairs," Lucien went on when I didn't reply.

I looked back to him and said, what I thought was logically, "But, my aunts are—"

I didn't finish.

I found myself over his shoulder and in the bedroom where he tossed me on the bed. This happened so fast the only thing I could feel was the wind created by his movement.

I bounced on the bed once, twice, staring up at him.

Then I said in a furious whisper, "You did not just—"

Lucien interrupted me. "Don't move."

Rage engulfed me, I got to my feet, standing on the bed, and shouted, "Don't you *dare* tell me—"

He cut me off again, this time using mind control.

Lie down, Leah.

I fought it. Well, my mind did. This lasted about three seconds.

Humiliatingly quickly, I lay down on the bed.

Get comfortable, he ordered and I did as I was told as best as I could when I was struggling against my mind which was in his stranglehold.

Don't make a noise and don't fucking move, he finished, and without further ado, he left.

I lay on the bed motionless but comfortable as the minutes passed. There were a goodly number of them before he returned. I had no idea where my aunties were or why they were even here. I had no idea what was going on.

The only thing I knew was that I hated him now more than ever.

He sat on the side of the bed. My eyes watched him do this and I screamed my hatred at him in my head as he tugged me across the bed and into his lap.

I didn't struggle. I didn't because I couldn't move.

His eyes locked on mine. "You must learn to mind me."

Go to hell! my mind shouted.

He shook his head and cradled me closer, speaking softly, "You need to learn this lesson, pet."

Fuck off and don't call me pet! my mind shrieked.

He held my body in his arms and my glare with his calm gaze as I tried desperately to shoot laser beams out of my eyes and annihilate him.

This, unfortunately, did not work.

"I'll not countenance disobedience." He kept speaking softly.

No duh? my mind asked sarcastically.

He sighed then stated, "Leah, if you defy me again, especially if you do it in front of others, you'll be punished."

Do your worst! my mind challenged. *It can't be worse than what you've already done.*

He stopped using his voice and instead spoke directly to my mind. *You've no idea.*

Dazzle me, my mind snapped.

Our eyes locked for long moments before he took up my challenge. *As you wish. Tonight, I feed. Then your punishment begins.*

I can't wait, I lied.

I could definitely wait. This whole thing was freaking me out.

He looked angry but resigned as he muttered, "Stubborn."

My mind stayed silent.

"Your punishment will be just as difficult for me as it is for you, Leah."

Good! my mind ground out.

His eyes moved over my face, the anger drifted out of his, and I could swear he looked almost pleased.

"One thing about you, pet, you aren't a disappointment."

I had no idea what he meant by that and thus didn't have a retort.

I felt my mind freed, my body at my command again, and I didn't hesitate. I scrambled off his lap and backed swiftly away as he rose from the side of the bed.

"Can my lesson tonight be how you kill vampires?" I asked in an ugly voice.

Shockingly, Lucien replied instantly, "Burn to nothing but ash then scatter the remains."

"Well then, Lucien, you better get Edwina to hide the fucking matches," I retorted, and without another word, I turned on my heel and ran into the bathroom, slamming the door and locking it.

I put my back to it, drifting down to my ass.

I rested my forehead to my knees and realized I was in full-body tremble.

God, I *hated* him.

This was the rest of my blinkety-blank day:

First, I had to come out of the bathroom. I couldn't live there, as much as I wanted to at that moment. There was water but there was no food and I was hungry.

When I did the bed had been made and Edwina was setting the table between the armchairs with plates and cutlery.

She turned to me, all perky housekeeper, and smiled, asking, "And how are we this morning?"

"Murderous," I replied.

Her body twitched and her head tilted to the side in that weird birdlike manner of hers.

She took a moment to study me. "I see you're not in a very good mood again," she observed.

"No. I. Am. Not," I retorted. "Where's Lucien?"

"Here," he declared, sauntering in coolly like he hadn't just humbled me, kept me from my family, shackled me with his mind.

"You haven't left yet?" I snapped out my question.

"I'm showering, we're sharing breakfast then I'm leaving."

It was on the tip of my tongue to tell him to get a move on when I realized Edwina was still in the room. Not wanting a repeat of twenty minutes ago, I pressed my lips together and wrapped my arms around my middle.

Lucien watched me do this then, as he walked to the bathroom, he mumbled, "You're learning."

I turned to Edwina and asked, "Do we have any lighter fluid?"

Edwina's brows shot up to her hairline as I heard Lucien's bark of laughter from the bathroom cut off in mid-rumble as he shut the door. This made my hands clench into fists.

"I don't think so, dear," Edwina answered, confused at the question and the byplay.

"Maybe you should put it on your grocery list," I suggested.

"Are you planning a barbeque?" she asked.

"Yes," I answered. "A *big* one."

That's when I heard Lucien's *second* bark of laughter.

Damn the vampire.

Lucien and I shared breakfast.

We sat in the armchairs in my bedroom and he calmly ate while reading the paper as I made another attempt to get laser beams to shoot out of my eyes.

It goes without saying I failed in this endeavor.

Unable to take the silence, I asked, "Why are we eating in the bedroom?"

"Because I want to," he replied.

"But why?" I pushed.

His eyes locked on mine in a way that said I was testing him and I definitely shouldn't.

"Sorry for questioning you, my lord and master," I muttered, shoving more of Edwina's delicious French toast into my mouth, deciding if I gained one hundred pounds (which I could, no sweat), he wouldn't want me anymore.

"I think I explained how I feel about your sarcastic titles, Leah," Lucien reminded me.

I looked at him and chewed.

After I swallowed, I informed him, "You said I couldn't call you 'oh Great Master.'"

He watched me for a long moment before he spoke.

"You are correct," he allowed. "So now I'll tell you I won't tolerate *any* of your sarcastic titles."

I twirled my fork in the air, looking down at my plate, saying, "Whatever."

More silence then Lucien folded the paper and threw it on the table. I looked up, hopeful he was finished so I could put in action the plan I'd hatched in the bathroom.

He was watching me. "A package will arrive today," he started and I nodded because his plate was clean and I took this as a good sign. "You'll be wearing what's in the package when I arrive home tonight."

My mind was skittering across a thousand images of me in different types of bondage gear. Therefore I missed his swift movement from seated to standing and pulling my chair around so he could lean into me, a hand on each arm.

"Did you hear me?"

I glared at him and replied acidly, "Yes, darling."

Something flashed in his eyes, something strange—something that looked like exhilaration.

His eyes dropped to my mouth and he murmured, "I like that."

"What?"

"You calling me 'darling.'"

What an idiot I was!

I decided instantly never to call him that again.

He read my mind, his hand came to my neck, and he ordered, "I want you to call me that from now on."

"You're *ordering* me to call you 'darling?'" I asked with disbelief.

"Yes."

"That's crazy!" I protested.

"You'll do it," he demanded.

I looked to the ceiling and muttered, "I'm *such* an idiot."

Since I was looking at the ceiling, his mouth brushing mine came as a surprise. When my eyes rolled to his, I could see close up his were smiling.

"You're adorable," he whispered.

And with that, he left.

And with that, I was left with wondering how I could detest a being so much and still feel a little thrill at his calling me adorable *and* his giving me a brush on the lips.

My plan to escape was thwarted.

See, I'd decided to let Lucien hunt me down and kill me.

I didn't want to die. I also didn't think he'd do it.

Kill me that was.

It seemed, weirdly enough, he actually liked me in his freakish vampire way.

When he found me (and he would), I was counting on the fact he'd give in to me pleading for my life, figure out I was more of a pain in the ass than I was worth, he'd release me, and I'd be on my way.

It was a ludicrous plan hatched in a hysterically angry frame of mind.

However, my day turned out rather busy and I never had the chance to put it into action.

First up, I tried to get Edwina to tell me if she knew what happened with my aunties. She said she didn't know. I didn't know her enough to know if she was lying or not but I let it go.

Next, I started to plan my getaway.

Obviously, I'd need cash, credit cards and identification. So, logically, I started with my purse.

There I found the dread, detested Lucien had not only confiscated my phone; he'd also taken my wallet and my passport.

The bastard.

That was okay. I had a few pieces of jewelry that were worth some money. I'd pawn them to get some cash.

I went to the drawer in my dressing table that had an inbuilt, velvet-lined jewelry section.

My jewelry was gone.

Damn!

What? Did he read my mind at breakfast?

Undeterred, I decided just to go. Upon examining the house two days ago, I'd also examined the garage and saw the Cayenne which Edwina told me Lucien had bought for me. I could sell the Cayenne for a shed load of money.

Upon thoroughly searching and eventually asking Edwina, I found there were no keys. Lucien had taken them.

"He's concerned about you, dear," Edwina explained what *she* thought was the truth. "You weren't steady on your feet yesterday. You need a bit of time to get settled in and it won't help to go gallivanting around the countryside."

After offering that pearl of wisdom, she'd flitted away.

I was glaring at her back while considering loading the silver in a pillowcase and hitchhiking to the nearest town when the next thing happened.

The doorbell rang and Edwina and I both reached it at the same time. Me hoping it was my aunties or better yet, my mom. Edwina knowing who it was.

It was two men who came bearing lots and lots of boxes.

Edwina was obviously expecting this, and although she acted a little bit weirded out about it but didn't share why, she started to order them around as to where the boxes went.

When the men took some into the bedroom, I followed them and Edwina was waiting for them in the dressing room. Without hesitation she tore one open and started to pull out the things in the box.

The things in the box, by the way, were men's clothes. Expensive, well-tailored, designer-label men's clothes that looked like they would fit Lucien.

There were a lot of clothes.

I wandered out of the dressing room and down the stairs and saw other boxes were being placed in other rooms. Mostly the study.

I stood amongst this hubbub, perplexed.

Was he moving in?

I mean, I was pretty certain Rafe didn't live with Lana. I was equally pretty certain that Duncan didn't live with my cousin Natalie.

By the way, I'd learned Natalie's (my favorite cousin) vampire's name was Duncan after my Selection, when I learned all my cousin's vampire's names. I had six cousins, four of them Selected, two of them not yet.

All of them, I was pretty certain, didn't live with their vampires.

Furthermore, I was *sure* my mother didn't live with Cosmo.

As I was standing in the hall watching the men go back out to their truck to get even more boxes, Stephanie waltzed in the opened door.

She looked fantastic in a royal-blue satin blouse and matching skirt that fit her like a second skin and hit her at her knees. Her high-heeled, royal-blue, strappy sandals were—no other words for it—*the bomb*.

As a woman, regardless of my current tumultuous state-of-being, I couldn't stop myself from crying, "I love your outfit!"

She put her hands out and smiled. "Fab, isn't it? We'll get Lucien's card and I'll take you to the shop where I got it, kit you out."

My pleasure at her outfit disappeared and I wrinkled my nose.

"I don't think so," I said.

She got close, her brows drawn, a small smile playing at her mouth. "Why's that?"

"I don't want anything from Lucien," I announced grandly.

For some unhinged reason this made her laugh out loud like I was hilarious.

Then, eyes on me, she whispered, "God, I envy him."

Boy, vampires were weird.

Suddenly something occurred to me and I looked out at the blazing sun Stephanie had just walked through to get to the house.

"You can't be in the sun!" I shouted and it sounded like an accusation.

She asked through a chuckle, "What?"

"You," I stated, pointing at her, "just walked through the sun." I pointed out the door before dropping my hand. "I thought sunshine was deadly to vampires."

Confusion washed through her face before she muttered to herself, "Vampire Studies aren't what they used to be."

"I was expelled," I divulged.

Her beautiful blue eyes widened then she threw back her head and laughed, uproariously I might add, all the while coming toward me and sliding her arm around my waist. She moved me forward into the family room where she seated us facing on the couch.

"Vampires are human," she told me.

I waved my hand between us and said, "I know that. Lucien explained that last night."

"Sun isn't deadly to us."

I didn't know that but I didn't share mainly because she already knew I didn't know that from my reaction.

She went on, "We *were* nocturnal, back in the day. That's how that rumor got started."

"Oh," I said just for something to say.

This made sense. Actually it all made sense which was a little disappointing. I'd prefer it was dark magic or something sinister and evil. It would give me something else to put in my Why I Hate Lucien Vault.

"So, you obviously aren't nocturnal now," I remarked.

"Some still keep to the old ways." She leaned in and grinned. "Personally, I never wake up before at least noon." We heard the men come back in. She looked over her shoulder at the door then at me and asked, "What's with the boxes?"

"It appears Lucien is moving in," I replied, unable to hide my distaste for this idea.

She looked over her shoulder at the door again and again mumbled under her breath, "He sure doesn't waste any time."

"Waste any time what?" I asked.

She looked back to me and answered, "I'll let Lucien explain it."

I shook my head. "Stephanie, no disrespect, but I'd rather you did the explaining."

Her eyes softened and she said quietly, "I take it things aren't going well between you two."

"Nope," I replied instantly.

"Did he not feed?" she asked, sounding slightly incredulous.

"Yep. He fed," I shared. "Things got out of hand and he forgot to anesthetize me," I waved my hand in the air, "or whatever."

I watched her face shut down and realized it was to mask her reaction.

Then her hand came out and grabbed mine before she whispered in a voice that dripped compassion, "Oh, honey."

At her words and the tone in which they were uttered, I wanted to cry. I really did. She obviously understood even if it was from her viewpoint, not the victim's. It was good sitting across from someone, even someone I barely knew, who understood.

But I didn't cry. I felt the tears welling but I held them back. It took a lot out of me but I fucking well did it.

She watched my struggle, and when I'd come out victorious, she gave my hand a firm squeeze.

"You need to get drunk," she declared, taking her hand away.

I thought that was an *excellent* idea. Then I remembered why it might not be an excellent idea.

"Lucien said he's feeding again tonight."

She stood and pulled me up with her. "Good. It'll serve him right to get some secondhand alcohol in his system," she commented with feeling and leaned into me while she walked me from the room. "Feeding from someone inebriated," she gave a mock shudder, "tastes crap."

At learning that knowledge, I liked her plan all the better.

Stephanie and I were hanging off the stools that sat around the huge island bar that separated the enormous kitchen from the breakfast nook and comfy-kitchen-living-area. Yes, I had a comfy-kitchen-living-area with a big fluffy couch, an attractive low coffee table and a gigantic round beanbag that two small adults could pile themselves into. Who needs all that? I already had a living room *and* family room for goodness sakes!

Both Stephanie and I had consumed more than our fair share of vodka martinis under the watchful and reproachful (I might add) eyes of Edwina when the next thing happened.

More boxes arrived.

These weren't cardboard boxes filled with Lucien's clothes. These were glossy black boxes of all shapes and sizes, each of them tied with a blood-red satin bow.

The minute Stephanie eyed the delivery man carrying a tower of boxes, she cried, "Yippee! Lucien's been shopping."

This news did *not* make me happy.

"Oh, my dear. You may be moody, but you must have pleased him somehow," Edwina pronounced having lost her stern glare and donning a gleaming smile. She was following delivery man number two.

I ignored Edwina and watched Stephanie, who was already digging into the stash with an abandon that was slightly scary.

He'd said a package would arrive. *A* package.

Did he expect me to wear all this stuff at once?

Stephanie pulled out a flash of material, swinging it around and then smoothing it against her front.

"This is stunning. Come here, Leah, try this on," she demanded.

I looked at what she held.

She was right. It was stunning. It was the most exquisite thing I'd ever seen.

An evening dress, black matte silk, flowy skirt with a slit up the front lined in aubergine satin, halter-topped and backless.

Both delivery men came in again, each bearing another tower of boxes.

"More?" I whispered.

Stephanie didn't hear me or ignored me, likely the second, she was on a mission.

"Come here, Leah. This first," she was shaking the black gown at me, "then this." She picked up what looked like a cream-colored skirt lined in pale blue and it had a kick pleat.

I slid off my stool and drunkenly wobbled into the comfy-kitchen-living area.

I touched the fabric of the black gown. It was glorious.

Stephanie let it go to turn her attention to another box and I caught it before it fell to the ground.

I held the dress up in front of me.

I really wanted to enjoy this. I really, really did. But instead it made me feel more trapped, more suffocated, more *owned*.

Lucien was dressing up his pet. And I was his pet.

It made me feel somehow dirty.

"Why on earth would he buy me this stuff? I'll never wear it," I mumbled, or I should say slurred. We'd had a lot of martinis.

Stephanie paused in her gleeful activity and looked at me. "What do you mean, you'll never wear it?"

"I live in a house in the middle of nowhere. My job is to hang around until a vampire wants to feed from me."

Stephanie straightened and caught my eyes. "Yes, that's part of your job. Another part of your job is to play escort should he want to show you off. At the opera. Or a dinner party. Or a Feast."

God, I hoped Lucien didn't like opera. That would suck because I loathed it.

I decided to latch on to something else she said, something Lucien had mentioned before. "A feast?"

She nodded. "A Feast. Some vamps take their concubines to Feasts. I don't but I know on occasion that Lucien does."

"What's a feast?" I asked.

Edwina made a little pip noise and both Stephanie and I swung our eyes to her.

"You don't approve?" Stephanie asked, not dangerously, curiously.

"Not to his taking the girls there, no," Edwina answered softly then started to gather up discarded tissue, ribbons and boxes. "They can get dangerous."

"What's a feast?" I asked again, but Stephanie was still studying Edwina.

"Lucien would never let anything happen to one of his concubines."

"I know," Edwina said and straightened. "It's just..." She hesitated, looked between us and finished, proclaiming, "*My* girls are *good* girls."

This made me even more intrigued, so I asked, louder this time, "What's a feast?"

"She may need another martini for this," Edwina mumbled, dropped the detritus and headed to the martini shaker.

I was no longer intrigued, I was now concerned. So much so I plonked down on the fluffy couch amidst a mountain of tissue paper as the two delivery men added two more towers of boxes to the plethora.

Stephanie plonked down beside me and Edwina fetched us fresh martinis.

Then Stephanie explained. "Vamps can feed from two places, their concubines and any mortal who attends a Feast. That's it. That's the law."

"So why are they dangerous? Do they round up the victims...?" I stopped speaking when Stephanie's face grew scary hard.

"They aren't victims, Leah. They choose to be there." Her voice was as hard as her face.

I ignored her voice mainly because I couldn't imagine what she said was true.

She studied my expression and her face softened.

"It's not like it was with you and Lucien," she said under her breath so Edwina, who was tidying my new, extravagant wardrobe, couldn't hear. "Most mortals love it. Some even become addicted to it. There are even ex-concubines there."

I felt my eyes grow round.

She nodded and continued, "It's frowned upon, of course. A concubine will lose her or his reputation by attending Feasts after they've been released. Their families are normally shunned. Their line will henceforth go unchosen at Selections. They usually don't attend once a concubine falls mostly because they aren't invited."

"Why?" I asked.

"Feasts are where common mortals go." She put her hand on mine. "You, honey, are anything but common."

This sounded sickeningly superior.

She must have read my face because she went on, "They love it, the mortals who attend. They don't care. They build their whole lives around it, traveling from Feast to Feast. They're like groupies."

And *this* sounded simply sickening.

"I still don't get why it's dangerous," I pressed and Stephanie leaned back.

"Because anything goes," she replied. "Lots of liquor, loud music, dancing and bodies. Any mortal is fair game. Some have two, three, even more vampires feeding on them at once. There are some Feasts, not the ones Lucien attends, mind, where there are drugs. Sex. Orgies."

"Wow," I whispered and she smiled.

"The good ones are fun. You can take your fill of as many mortals as you want. It's great."

It didn't sound great but that was just me.

"Why would you take a concubine there?" I asked.

She shrugged. "To share another part of your life with her. If you've got a good one, to show her off to other vampires."

Something struck me. "If anything goes, and a concubine is mortal, is she fair game?"

Stephanie hesitated a moment before answering. "At the wilder ones, with vamps who don't take good care of their girls, yes." I sucked in breath and she hurried on, "But Lucien doesn't go to those."

"So, that's why it's dangerous," I whispered and Edwina made another pip noise. Again Stephanie and I looked at her.

"Not entirely," Stephanie replied, glancing back my way.

"What is it, entirely?" I pushed.

Stephanie sighed before saying, "Even at the good ones, things can get out of hand. Vampires are what we are. It isn't unheard of for there to be bloodlust. In the throes of bloodlust a vampire will go for anything mortal. It's not unusual for concubines to be used by other vamps, even offered by their own vampire to his friends."

"Oh my God," I breathed.

"Lucien wouldn't do that," she rushed to assure me.

"Oh my God," I breathed again.

She leaned toward me. "Leah, seriously, Lucien would never share. Ever. You have to believe me. I'm being very serious."

I just stared at her.

She kept talking. "He'd sense if things were deteriorating and he'd get you out of there. It wouldn't matter. No vampire is stupid enough to touch what's Lucien's. He'd burn. Lucien would make sure of it. He'd do it himself. He's even done it before."

"Done what before?"

"Burned another vampire. If memory serves, he's done it twice. Once was after something happened at a Feast. The other vamp didn't even feed from his concubine, he just touched her. Lucien went mad, hunted him down, made him burn. The second was—"

She didn't finish, I interrupted her by whispering, "Made him burn?"

Stephanie nodded. "Lucien killed him without a thought and he'd been within his rights. You don't touch another vamp's concubine. Most vampires cover it up, make a monetary agreement. They don't take it that far. Any money that exchanges hands they give to their concubine to buy her silence. But Lucien would take it that far, no doubt about it. If it happens, it reflects on her vampire. He'll seek vengeance and it'll be granted. And she can demand immediate release and that too will be granted."

"You can demand release?" I was too drunk to mask the hope in my voice.

"Yes," Stephanie answered. "It's tantamount to neglect which is grounds for unconditional release."

My inebriated mind recalled reading that in my contract.

Why hadn't I thought of that before?

There were grounds for unconditional release. Neglect, which Lucien had definitely not done, and extreme cruelty, which he *could* have done.

My brain was drunkenly churning so I didn't catch Stephanie getting close.

"That doesn't count," she said softly, reading my drunken thoughts. "It happens to us all, not often, but it does. I'm surprised it happened to Lucien, but not surprised at the same time, considering it's you. We lose focus or control. We're vampires, you're concubines. It's the nature of the relationship."

There it was. My hopes were dashed.

Again.

"I don't like anything about the relationship. Not. One. Thing," I announced and then took a huge sip of my martini.

When I was done swallowing, I caught her sly grin. "I'll call you tomorrow morning after he feeds tonight and we'll see what you say about the relationship then."

I rolled my eyes. Stephanie laughed.

"Don't you have more boxes to open?" I asked tartly.

She looked down at the boxes on the coffee table, her eyes narrowed, and she reached out to grab one.

"This one has a note on it." She yanked off the bow using the thick, cream card that was attached. "It says, 'This is for tonight.'" She turned it to face me. "That's Lucien's handwriting."

I looked at the bold, slashing, powerful black scrawl that, in itself, was a command even if I couldn't make out the words that seemed to be moving under my eyes. Of course it was his handwriting.

She thrust the box in my hands. "Open it. I have to see this."

"No," I thrust it back, "you open it."

She pushed it back to me. "No, I want to see your face when you see what's inside."

I glared at her. She had eternity to live; she could play this game forever. I had only another forty, fifty years, if I was lucky.

I pulled open the box. It was, to my relief, not bondage gear.

It was, to my surprise and secret delight, something even more exquisite than the black gown.

A rich taupe camisole with dusty, lilac flowers imprinting the silk jacquard, trimmed in delicate taupe lace. The cups were half-jacquard, half-lace. The body was jacquard as were the thin straps. There were matching Brazilian-cut panties, the front was jacquard with lace trim, the back almost entirely lace except a tantalizing triangle of jacquard at the top. There were sweet little rosettes at the waistband of the panties under the navel and at the juncture of the bodice where it met each of the straps of the camisole.

Stephanie eyeballed the camisole and panties as she took a sip from her martini. "Lucien always had good taste." Her gaze moved to my face, a smile lit in her eyes, and she repeated, "Always."

I decided, yet again, I really liked Stephanie.

"Thanks," I whispered.

She gave me a wink and nodded to the lingerie. "New order. Try *that* on first. Then the black gown."

"We'll have a fashion parade!" Edwina shouted enthusiastically from the kitchen where she was cooking dinner. I jumped because I forgot she was there.

A fashion parade didn't seem like a bad idea. Or, at least it didn't after four martinis.

I jumped up, wobbled then righted myself and announced, "I'll change, you open more boxes."

Stephanie didn't need to be told twice.

I started to run to the powder room but skidded to a halt and asked Edwina like I was a tweenie and Stephanie had come over after school, "Can Stephanie stay for dinner?"

"Of course, dear." Edwina smiled and I smiled back.

Then I whirled to Stephanie. "Will you stay for dinner?"

She was still digging through boxes and didn't look up when she answered, "I'd like that."

Happy for the first time in weeks, I took my pretty lingerie, deciding not to think of it as a gift from Lucien as that would spoil the fun, and ran to the powder room to start the fashion parade.

7
The Punishment

Lucien walked into the kitchen from the garage and halted. Edwina was busy at the sink scouring pots and pans. The living area looked like an exclusive boutique exploded in it. Red tissue paper, ribbons, and black boxes were scattered everywhere, mounds of the clothing Lucien purchased for Leah were smoothed out on the backs and arms of furniture. On the countertop of the island bar were three used martini glasses all with silver toothpicks resting in varying states of martini remains. One still had a half-eaten olive on it.

Edwina turned to him with a bright smile on her face and he instantly knew she was intoxicated. He saw it *and* he smelled it.

This surprised him.

In the forty years she'd worked for him he had never, not once, come to his concubine's home to find it a mess, to find the kitchen not sparkling clean, to find Edwina inebriated while on duty.

He'd seen her that way, of course, during parties or celebrations where she attended as a guest. For instance the birthday parties he threw every year for his concubines past and present. And the first anniversary of The Bloodletting which it was a tradition to celebrate.

Any other time, never.

"You're here!" Edwina greeted happily, a huge drunken smile on her face.

Lucien's eyes scanned the room again and went back to Edwina. "What happened?"

She glanced over her shoulder at the mess, lifted a hand from the sink and waved it around, slopping soapy water and bubbles on the floor, the counter, her shoulder.

"We had a fashion parade," she explained bizarrely, ignoring the mess she made and went back to scouring. "Leah's up in your bedroom." Her voice dropped to a happy murmur. "Such a sweet, beautiful girl."

Lucien studied his housekeeper.

Leah was hardly a girl. She was forty years old, for God's sake.

She was, of course, beautiful. But sweet?

"How is she?" Lucien found himself asking and he had no earthly idea why.

He had also, in the years he'd employed Edwina, never requested such information.

Then again he'd never needed to.

"Oh, she's fine. Settling in. She's so cute. You should have seen her tonight. She was hilarious."

Fascinated by the idea of a cute, hilarious, sweet Leah "settling in," Lucien tired of the discourse with Edwina and headed for the stairs.

"Good night!" Edwina trilled gaily behind him.

Lucien didn't reply.

Five strides into their room, Lucien saw Leah exiting the bathroom. He again halted.

She was wearing the lingerie he'd sent.

He saw he'd been wrong in his thoughts when he'd watched the stick thin model sashaying down the short runway displaying it at his personal showing when he was ordering Leah's wardrobe the day after her Selection.

He had, in his mind, expected it to look far better on Leah's generous curves.

However, he had not anticipated it looking *that* much better.

She was wearing her robe over it, but the robe had fallen open at her sides, exposing the camisole and pants. The cups of the camisole hugged her full breasts, the silk ending just above the nipple so a tantalizing hint of the aureole peeked through the lace, a chill in the air obviously causing her nipples to harden against the silk. It hugged her midriff and stomach like it had been made for her. The hem of the camisole left only a glimpse of smooth skin above the underwear. Her long legs went on forever beneath the lace of the panties.

He felt his body's immediate response to the sight of her and he liked it.

Her face had been averted when she walked out of the bathroom, but it snapped around, she focused on him and cried, "Lucien!"

Lucien only had a moment to brace before she flew at him, running flat out across the room, and at the last instant, launched herself full body at him.

Stunned and unsure of her intent, he caught her in his arms, his hands cupping her ass as she wrapped her long limbs around him.

Instead of attempting, however pointless such an effort would be, to tear him limb from limb, she caught his gaze and he noticed she, too, was under the influence.

Very much so.

"Hello, darling, how was your day?" she purred cheerfully, if drunkenly.

"Interesting," he replied truthfully, this exact moment being indicative of his interesting day.

He was on guard, not certain what her game was.

His day *had* been interesting. Starting with the roller coaster ride of their morning and ending with Leah's current behavior, it included an afternoon meeting with her aunts. A meeting where they explained their concern that they hadn't heard from Leah after The Bloodletting. A meeting where he declared his intentions and ascertained their tentative allegiance. They were hesitant, considering what it might mean to the future of their family, indeed to the future of all concubines. But they were also not willing to defy him.

He wasn't entirely surprised at this. They were Buchanans and obedience had been ingrained in them for centuries.

Leah's hand moved to fiddle with the collar of his shirt, bringing his attention back to her.

"Mine was too," she shared.

"Is that so?"

Her eyes went from his collar to his and she nodded. Fervently.

"And what did you do today, my pet?" he asked softly, reading her mood and relaxing into it.

"First off, I tried to escape."

His relaxation fled and his body went solid, but she didn't notice and kept talking.

"I couldn't, of course, you took my wallet, my passport, my jewelry, the keys to *the car*." Her eyes narrowed on him and she declared, "It was very vexing."

Her words, informative and not accusing, caused him again to relax.

He struggled with the desire to laugh and won before he repeated, "Vexing?"

She nodded, smiling at him, and he felt his frame go solid again, "Yes. Vexing. Very."

He wasn't listening to her words. He was staring at her mouth.

He'd never seen her smile.

This wasn't strictly true. He had, from a distance, many times in the last twenty years. He'd just never had it directed at him.

His body reacted to that too, in a way he very much liked.

He could remain standing holding her body to his for eternity (literally). But he walked her to the bed and sat on its edge, settling her into his lap, her soft curves pressing against his hardening cock.

He liked this too.

She was still talking. "Then the men arrived with the boxes. Lots of boxes. Lots and lots and lots." She tipped her head to the side and queried, "Are you moving in?"

"Yes," he replied and she nodded again, apparently perfectly content with this idea.

Her hands went to his shoulders and she started to tug off his suit jacket. He reluctantly let her go to assist her with getting it down his arms. All the while she did this, she was still babbling.

"Then Stephanie came over and, Lucien, you should have *seen* her *outfit*. It was *the bomb*." Lucien felt his mouth twitch against the effort of smiling, her eyes dropped to it, and she announced, "I like it when your mouth does that."

He blinked at her slowly and asked, "Pardon?"

She threw the suit jacket unceremoniously to the end of the bed then touched the corner of his mouth with her index finger too briefly and her eyes came to his. They were dancing.

"When you fight a smile. I like it. It's sexy," she explained.

Fucking hell, but she was magnificent.

He thought she was magnificent when she fought him and when he felt her fear of him and attraction to him. The challenge was exhilarating.

But she was even more magnificent now. He wouldn't have believed this was possible but the evidence was sitting in his lap.

He didn't like to feed when the mortal servicing him was inebriated. Tipsy, perhaps, downright drunk, no. And Leah was beyond inebriated, she was hammered.

She'd brushed her teeth, however, obviously very thoroughly. And her scent was strong enough to overpower the vodka he also caught mingling with her essence. Not to mention, she was, as Edwina described her, hilarious, cute and definitely sweet.

Therefore, he decided to break his own rule and feed, regardless of the fact that she was smashed.

His hands went to her robe, pushing it wide over her shoulders, and she didn't hesitate with dropping her arms in an effort to aid him to rid her of it.

She also kept chattering. "Then Stephanie and I had a natter then we had some martinis then your other boxes came and we had a fashion parade. After that, Stephanie stayed for dinner, we talked Edwina into having martinis with us, and, because you sent a lot of boxes, we had *even more* of a fashion parade." She stopped when her arms were loose from the robe and he let it drop to the floor. Both of her hands came back to his shirt and she began fiddling with his buttons but her eyes never left his as she continued happily, "I like Stephanie. She's funny."

His arms circled her waist, one hand drifting down over her ass, one drifting up to capture and play with a lock of her soft, thick hair.

"So you had a good time?" he asked softly. She nodded again fervently and he went on, "Did you like the clothes?"

This time her eyes grew wide and her nodding became fanatical. "Especially this." Her head tipped down so quickly it nearly collided with his nose and he had to jerk his head back. She pointed to the camisole. When she was done, her head snapped back up, her hand went directly back to his shirt, this time slapping flat against his pectoral, and she kept speaking. "I *love* this! It's perfect for me. And the black dress. The black dress is *divine*. Everyone thinks so!"

"I'm glad you liked them, pet," he murmured on a smile.

"Oh, I do. With your and my stuff, the dressing room is going to be almost *full*," she declared as if this was a feat akin to climbing Mount Everest. Then her face fell before she informed him, "You forgot shoes."

His hand twisted, capturing a fistful of hair, and he told her, "Those are arriving tomorrow."

Her body jerked as she threw both arms straight up in the air and shouted, "Yay!"

With such an enchanting opportunity exposed to him, he released her hair, both of his hands curled around her waist and drifted up the silk at her sides. He did this as he chuckled.

He felt a tremor slide through her, her hands settled on his shoulders, and she declared, "I like that too."

His eyes moved from her torso to her face, "You like what?"

"When you chuckle. It's all rumbly. I especially like it now when I can *feel* it."

A wave of desire tore through him so strong if he'd been standing he'd have gone down to a knee. His fingers tightened reflexively against her ribs and he had to concentrate so as not to snap them.

She began fiddling with the buttons of his shirt again and he realized she was releasing them.

"Leah," he called, attempting focus and finding, just as at her Bloodletting, which had been the first time in his very long life, the effort was difficult.

She was biting the side of her lip in concentration, her eyes on her task before she asked, "What?"

"What are you doing?"

Her head came up and she answered, "Taking off your shirt."

"Why?"

She grinned playfully. "I like your chest. It's *way* better than your chuckle."

After imparting this information on him, she wriggled her bottom in his lap.

As much as he was enjoying her, he was done.

He had her on her back in an instant, his torso covering hers, her legs still wrapped around his waist so his crotch was seated against the heat of her. His mouth at her throat, he slid his tongue along the length of her jugular, preparing her.

He did this carefully, savoring the taste of her but keeping a rigid hold on his control.

"It freaks me out when you do that," she whispered and his head came up.

He slid his hand down her side, around, over her ass, pulling her up as he pressed his groin to hers.

"Do what?" he asked.

"Move so fast."

His mouth went to hers as he ground their hips together. When he did, without hesitation she reciprocated the movement and the effect was staggering.

"You'll get used to it." His voice betrayed his heightening arousal.

She opened her mouth but didn't get a chance to speak because he kissed her.

He dispensed with the discovery he'd used to initiate their first kiss. His tongue swept inside her mouth and her reaction was delightfully immediate. Her body bucked upwards seeking something more even though his weight was pressing her into the bed. Her head tipped to the side giving him better access and her tongue tangled boldly with his. Her hands tugged his shirt from his trousers and he felt them travel up the skin of his back.

Her touch sent shockwaves tearing through his system and he growled into her mouth, deepening the kiss. She welcomed it, taking from him at the same time she gave and invited...no, *demanded* more.

He gave her what she wanted and contentedly absorbed her moan when he did.

He broke their connection and his mouth glided to her ear.

"I like the way you kiss me, pet," he whispered there and he felt her head turn.

Her lips close to his neck, she breathed, no guard over the wonder in her words, "You're so big, heavy, strong. You make me feel tiny. I've never felt tiny. Not in my whole life."

He sensed this was important, something she'd always desired but never had, and he was pleased he gave that to her. His mouth went back to her throat, gliding again along her skin. He was suddenly intent to give her something else, something she couldn't imagine she'd long for, but she would, he'd see to it.

"Your mouth is going to tingle, sweetheart," he murmured against her skin before he used his tongue on her again.

Her neck arched, her limbs tightened, her nails curled into the flesh of his back.

"It already is," she whispered. "Why is that?"

"I'll explain later," he replied quietly, his hand at her ass moving around her hip slowly as his mouth drifted up her neck, to her jaw, back to hers.

He caught her gaze as he lifted his hips away from hers and his fingers trailed along the waistband of her panties.

"Are you ready for me?" he asked softly.

Her eyes grew wide and her lips parted.

Lucien loved it when she looked at him like that.

Especially now.

So much, he didn't wait for her reply and his hand dipped into her underwear. He touched her, finding her sleek, hot and very, very wet.

She was ready, and as if to prove this further, at his exploring touch, her neck arched in invitation. An invitation he gratefully accepted.

His lips went to her throat and his teeth tore through, her blood flowing into his mouth at the same time he slid a finger inside her.

She gasped and it wasn't in pain. It was a sound of sheer pleasure and her hips bucked against his hand.

He withdrew his hand even though he knew she wanted it and he wanted her to have it.

Tonight, however, her lesson would be only about the feeding.

She whimpered when she lost his hand but he drew her blood into his mouth. He heard her second gasp, this one surprised, excited. Her hands coming out of his shirt, and just like that morning but with both of them this time, they came to his neck, up, and then her fingers fisted in his hair. Not to pull him back, to hold him to her.

Her body arched, pressing into his as he heard her heart race, her blood scoring through her system, her breath coming in wilder and wilder pants.

"Oh my God," she breathed, her hands clenching tighter in his hair. "Oh my *God*," she cried softly, trembling underneath him.

He wrapped his arm around her low on her hips and he held her body tightly to the warmth of his. He stroked her wound with his tongue and reared up. Taking her mouth with his, he kissed her hard.

She kissed him back, her hands still clutching his hair, her mouth greedy.

He broke the kiss and her eyes slowly opened, alluringly foggy with desire.

"Do you see why I like the taste of you?" he asked, his voice a low growl.

"Yes," she whispered her admission, her voice a soft moan.

He buried his face in her throat again, reopening the wound, and drinking deep.

"Lucien," she whispered.

He sucked fiercely, thrilling at the sound of his name on her lips when her blood, just as delicious, surprisingly even more so with the vodka mingled with it, was pouring down his throat. This caused her to gasp yet again and writhe underneath him.

She was done, he knew it. He'd taken enough. Even though he wanted more, his mouth detached and he swept his tongue along the wound. The bleeding stopped instantly. The healing had already begun.

He pulled his body over her and rolled to his side, gathering her in his arms and taking her with him. He tucked her face in his throat, cautious with the still healing wound.

Her breathing was heavy as was her pulse and she whispered with a mixture of disappointment and marvel, "You're done?"

He shook his head and tightened his arms, drawing her deeper into him.

"I'm not done, pet. *You're* done."

She wasn't done. He knew it the way she moved restlessly against him.

It wasn't the feeding she wanted, it was the climax he'd brought her so very close to and didn't let her have.

Her head tilted back and he tipped his down to face her.

"You can't be done," she whispered and it was a soft demand.

"I'm done," he declared.

"You're not," she returned, her voice getting stronger as were her movements, her hands sliding over his body, her own body pressing into his.

"Be still, Leah," he commanded.

"No," she refused.

"Leah."

She pressed closer, her hands moving over his ass, pulling in as she returned, "Lucien."

He reached behind him, wrapping his fingers around her wrists and pulling her arms around to the front. He rolled to his back, bringing her with him so she was on top, her arms cocked and caught between them. The deep red of her wound was blazing but the skin was closing.

Her eyes narrowed and she pressed her soft hips into his still hard ones, demanding, "You can't seriously think we're finished."

"I know it."

"You're in a state!" she observed angrily.

"It'll pass."

"*I'm* in a state," she informed him, her anger escalating at her need to point out her condition.

He left her hands trapped between them and he circled her with his arms, giving her a small shake before he held her tightly.

"Do you remember this morning?" he asked softly and her brows knitted over ever-narrowing eyes.

"How could I forget?" she snapped.

"This is your punishment."

She pulled in a sharp breath as understanding dawned.

Then she said on a heavy exhale, "You're joking."

"You'll go unfulfilled until you learn your lesson, pet."

She blinked, hard and fast, her lips parting in shock and anger.

All vestiges of cute, hilarious, sweet, intoxicated Leah had vanished and Lucien uncharacteristically felt doubt about his decision to carry through with her punishment.

This was mainly because he liked cute, hilarious, sweet Leah and he wanted her back.

This was also because she wanted him. She made this abundantly clear without any evasion. Even if she hadn't, he could smell it.

This was also because he wanted her. He wanted to bury himself inside her slick, wet core. He wanted to fuck her so hard he felt her body jolt under his with his thrusts. He wanted to listen to the noises she made, feel her sleekness clench around him, smell her sex in his nostrils and watch her face as she came.

He wanted her more than he'd ever wanted a female, vampire or mortal.

Even Maggie.

And the power of his desire caused him to doubt the wisdom of carrying through with her punishment.

She tried to tear free of his arms but he moved swiftly.

He exited the bed, taking her with him, standing her on her feet. She swayed a moment then moved to flee but he caught her wrist in an unbreakable grip, ripping his shirt open at the same time, the buttons flying. He released her for less than a second, taking his shirt off. Then he tossed her back into bed, and as she scrambled to get her limbs in order, he finished disrobing. Before she could escape, he had her on her side, her back to his front, tucked into the bend of his body, his arm holding her captive.

"Let me go," she demanded, her breath straining, exposing her body's inability to keep pace with his.

He settled behind her. "Leah, sleep."

She struggled. "Let me *go*."

He gave her a shake and repeated, "Sleep."

She kept struggling and he contained it effortlessly. This went on for quite some time.

Suddenly she stilled.

He listened to her heavy breathing and felt her legs move, still wrestling with residual desire.

After some time, she settled.

He thought she'd conquered her body and finally fell asleep.

Instead, in a fierce, tortured whisper, she declared, "This morning, if you told me there was a way I could hate you more, I wouldn't have believed it. But it's true."

Yes, he *seriously* doubted the wisdom of carrying through her punishment.

"Leah," he murmured into her hair.

"I'll *never* stop hating you," she vowed, her voice scratching with her passionate assertion.

He pulled her closer and made his own vow. "Yes you will, my pet. I'll find a way through."

"Impossible."

"Nothing is impossible."

"We'll see," she said, her voice dripping with doubt at his words as well as conviction to her oath.

Yes, Lucien thought but didn't speak aloud, *we'll see.*

Lucien woke before Leah.

His first act was to pull back her head gently to check her wound. Fully healed.

His next act was to lie beside her watching her sleep. Her face was relaxed and expressionless, not one of his preferred looks, but appealing all the same.

After some time, her eyes fluttered open, and as she had the day before, her expressionless face became bewildered.

Shortly after waking, as she had the day before, she tensed in preparation for flight.

He caught her close. Her head jerked back, her eyes narrowed and her mouth opened to protest.

He brought his down on hers, hard and demanding her response.

She withheld and began her vain struggles, as usual stubborn to an extreme.

So stubborn, this carried on for long enough that Lucien was forced to try a different tactic. Rolling her to her back and pinning her, his hands moved on her, down her sides, across her belly, up her midriff, all the while his tongue engaged in its sensual duel with hers.

Then his hand moved over her breast, cupping it gently before he snagged her nipple with his thumb.

Her body stopped bucking against his in protest and melted underneath him.

"That's it, sweetheart," he whispered against her mouth at her capitulation and he took advantage, his finger met his thumb, and he rolled her nipple between them.

A delicious noise slid from the back of her throat into his mouth. Her legs opened, one calf wrapping around his hip and he caught the scent of her excitement.

He smiled his triumph against her mouth and slanted his head for another kiss. She met his intent, her own head tipping to the side, her lips pressing against his, no longer resistant, but hungry.

He fed her with his hands and his mouth and he kept doing it as she continued to demand it, insatiable, magnificent.

After a time, his hand was in her panties, finger pressed deep and swirling, her mouth against his, breaths sharp and sweet against his lips. She was so deep in her need she was unable to concentrate on kissing him or bear the further sensation of his tongue in her mouth. Her hand was clenched in his hair, her other arm wrapped tight around his back.

"Lucien!" she gasped urgently and he saw it on her face, he smelled it.

He knew she was right there.

He withdrew his hand.

"No!" she cried, her hand going to his, fingers wrapping around his wrist.

Her cry sliced through him like a blade. He had been incorrect in what he'd told her the morning before. Even as tortured as her cry was, he suspected this was far more difficult on him than it was on her.

However, he'd chosen his path and he had to continue his efforts at her taming. She had no way of knowing but he knew the reward at the end would be worth the battle.

"Will you mind me?" he queried, his voice was harsh, not with anger, but with regret.

Her hazy eyes struggled to focus on his face. "Lucien."

"Will you mind me?"

He watched the haze clear, his words penetrating, incredulity flooding her face, quickly chased by anger.

"I fucking *hate* you," she hissed, but even as she did, her hips sought his, her body agitated, struggling with her desire.

Lucien sighed impatiently. "I'll take that as a no."

"You're damn right it's a no!" she snapped and wrenched unsuccessfully against his hold.

After this failure, she let out an enraged, strangled scream.

"Leah, you can end this now," he told her.

"Go to hell!" she flashed.

"Do you want my mouth on you?" he asked.

"Go to hell!" she repeated.

"Do you want me inside you?"

She froze and shrieked, *"Go to hell!"*

He threw a thigh over her legs and captured her moving body against his. With a hand in her hair, he tucked her face in his neck.

"You're very stubborn, pet," he murmured into the hair at the top of her head.

Her entire frame gave a mighty flex then went limp.

She grew silent. He held her closer.

After long moments, he said softly, "I'll be leaving soon."

She made no reply.

"While I'm gone, if you touch yourself, Leah, I'll know and I'll have to deal with that too."

He could hear the pace of her heart increase but her body tensed only briefly before she subdued her reaction.

"Do you understand me?" he pushed.

She remained silent.

"Leah, I asked, do you understand me?"

"Yes," she gritted between her teeth.

"I'll be home at ten. We're going out tonight. I want you ready."

She didn't speak.

"Leah, when I talk to you, you acknowledge what I say."

"I'll be ready," she bit out.

"I want you wearing the black dress."

She made an angry noise, but whispered, "I'll be wearing the black dress."

His hand moved from her head to her jaw and with his thumb under her chin he tilted her face up to receive his soft kiss.

Then he left her in bed and went to shower.

After he turned off the water and stepped out of the shower, while he was reaching for a towel, in the sudden silence, he heard it.

His head shot up and cocked to the side.

Quietly, likely muffled in her pillow, he heard her sobs.

Good Christ. He'd broken her.

He'd fucking broken her.

He'd taken a huge step closer to her taming.

He'd expected to feel elation at this moment.

Instead, his eyes met his reflection in the mirror and he growled a low, slow, agonized, "Fuck."

That night when he arrived home promptly at ten, he opened the door from the garage and found her there, waiting for him in the kitchen.

Her hair was swept back from her face to tumble in a mass of curls down her exposed back. She wore no jewels because she didn't have any.

She didn't need them.

The dress was spectacular—elegant and enticing. The spike-heeled, aubergine satin, strappy sandals were delicate, sexy and significantly lengthened her already tall frame, making her striking and, he suspected, to any other man but Lucien, even intimidating. Her makeup was smoky and dramatic, heightening the mystery behind her stunning but expressionless face.

Her eyes caught his and there was no flash, no dancing, they were completely blank.

"Hello, darling, how was your day?" she asked as if she was a robot and this was a prerecorded message set to play at appropriately programmed times.

Suddenly angry, he stopped five feet from her and commanded, "Come here, Leah."

Without hesitation she moved to him.

His body tensed at her uncharacteristic acquiescence.

"Put your arms around me," he went on.

She did as he demanded but her eyes remained at his throat.

"Look at me, pet."

She immediately tipped her head back and caught his eyes.

Trying to read her mood, Lucien sought patience, wrapped an arm around her and cupped her jaw with his other hand.

"You're angry with me," he murmured and she shook her head.

"No, darling, why would you think that?"

His patience slipped. "Leah, stop it," he ordered.

Her head tilted to the side in an unnatural movement. "Stop what?"

His eyes narrowed as her intent came clear. "So, this is your game now?"

"My game?" she asked with what sounded like genuine confusion.

He watched her carefully empty face. Then he decided, so be it.

He could work with this.

In fact, he had a feeling he'd enjoy it.

"I need to change," he informed her and she made to move away but his arm tightened and he said, "No."

She stopped and regarded him.

"Kiss me before I go upstairs."

Without delay she got up on her toes, pressed against him and touched her parted lips to his.

She pulled away and asked, as if she sincerely cared about his answer, "Was that okay?"

He thought she'd have trouble with that.

She had no trouble with that.

She was good.

Therefore his tests would need to be more challenging.

"It will do," he let her go, "for now."

He walked away but she called to his back, "What do you want me to do while you're changing?"

"Whatever you want," he replied and imagined her first thought was to search the house for gasoline and matches.

Upstairs he changed his shirt and was walking back through the bathroom to join Leah when his eyes caught on something.

He halted.

Looking in the trash bin, he saw taupe wisps of shredded silk and lace, the lilac-flowered imprints barely nuances in the tatters. He reached down and allowed the obliterated material of the lingerie Leah wore the night before to sift through his fingers.

He straightened, his mouth tightening at the same time he felt a similar sensation in his gut.

Then something profound cut through him. He didn't understand it and he didn't fucking like it. It was a feeling he'd never felt in his very long life and a feeling he never wanted to have again.

Last night, wearing that lingerie, she had run to him. Flung herself in his arms. Told him she liked it when he bit back a smile. Rejoiced in the gifts he'd given her, particularly the camisole and panties. Smiled at him for the first time. And passionately enjoyed her bloodletting.

Now, that lingerie—what would have been a physical reminder to both of them throughout their Arrangement of the splendor of last night—lay shredded and discarded in a trash bin.

And he, and his unwise decision to carry out her punishment even after she'd given glaring indication of what Edwina called "settling in," was solely responsible for the bleak emotion evidenced in that fucking bin.

"Fuck," he swore, his stare riveted to the scraps, his mind consumed with what they meant.

Then he cleared his thoughts and walked downstairs to Leah.

8
The Feast

I sat in the Porsche as Lucien drove us to wherever the hell we were going. Ever his new obedient concubine, I hadn't asked and he hadn't shared.

It was taking a lot out of me not to turn and claw out his eyes or throw open my door and toss myself bodily from the car.

The reason for this was not only because my Why I Hate Lucien Vault was so full.

That morning, he came fully dressed from the bathroom. This was luckily after I had plenty of time to dry the tears from my face and pretend to be sleeping. Still, even though he at least should have *pretended* to believe I was sleeping after he was such a big, fat, vampire jerk, he'd kissed the nape of my exposed neck softly before he left (the bastard).

I then spent the whole day mentally moving everything to a far, far, *far* bigger vault.

It was also because, ten minutes into our drive, Lucien's hand had come to my leg. He'd slowly slid the gorgeous material aside, exposing my thigh, then, when he wasn't shifting, he stroked the skin on the inside gently, leisurely, enticingly, and worst of all, *constantly.*

It was driving me mad.

It was driving me mad because it felt so *fucking* good.

What was worse was that wherever the hell we were going was a long, long way from the house Lucien provided for me.

Which meant my torture seemed to last an eternity.

During that eternity, I decided I'd never forgive him.

I'd never, *ever* forgive him for forcing my body to betray me again and again thus making me hate myself more than I hated him.

We were deep in the bowels of the city (and "bowels" was an aptly descriptive word), when he turned into an alley.

I didn't normally hang in alleys but if I were to choose one this one would be near the bottom of the list.

Lucien slowed to a stop and all of a sudden from out of nowhere a man jumped toward the car.

I couldn't control my surprised gasp.

Lucien's hand flexed on the inside of my thigh and he murmured, "It's all right, pet."

I forced myself to turn and nod at him as if I trusted him with my very life even though I did *not*. His latest maneuver of driving me down a dank alley was proof positive why I shouldn't.

My door was flung open and a hand was shoved through.

I shrank from it as I heard a stranger say, "Milady."

"Take his hand, Leah," Lucien ordered, and I didn't want to, I *really* didn't want to, but I did.

The stranger helped me out of the car. He was shorter than me, wiry to the point of being gaunt, and I guessed he was younger than me by at least a decade.

He was paying me no attention even as he cautiously steered me clear of the door before he slammed it to.

His eyes were hungry on Lucien who had alighted out the other side. Very hungry. *Creepy* hungry.

How incredibly *weird*.

"Wats," Lucien said before he casually tossed the keys to his absurdly expensive sports car to a man who resembled a tramp who had just had a clean at the shelter where he'd been given ill-fitting clothes and a not-so-good haircut.

"Master," the man panted upon catching the keys, his eyes glued to Lucien, and I felt a sick feeling crawl through the pit of my stomach.

Faster than a flash, Lucien was at my side, his fingers firm at my elbow, drawing me away from the stranger. The man's eyes flickered to me before moving devotedly back to Lucien.

"Like they're all saying, she's beautiful, master," he breathed, leaning into Lucien but holding himself back, quite obviously wary, excited, petrified, all at the same time.

I looked up to Lucien to see he was regarding the man with barely concealed revulsion.

"Take care of the car, Wats," Lucien ordered.

Wats nodded, still panting while he backed away, slightly bowing like a mad scientist's deformed lackey in a bad horror movie.

Lucien moved me toward a door and I followed.

I wanted to ask about Wats, but I didn't. I wanted to run screaming into the night, but I didn't.

Crazily, I also wanted to throw myself in Lucien's arms and beg him to fuck me against the wall in the alley.

I most certainly didn't do *that*.

The door opened before we arrived, a similar character to Wats but rounder, older, with a thick beard and a mess of long, tangled hair was holding the door wide.

"Master," he whispered reverently, his eyes dropping as if he was too lowly a creature to gaze upon the magnificence of Lucien, and my stomach twisted nauseatingly.

"Breed," Lucien murmured his greeting not even glancing the man's way, leading me by him and into a dark hall that almost immediately led to stairs going down.

The door closed behind us and I barely controlled my desire to jump or cry out. We started descending the stairs side by side and Lucien still hadn't taken his hand from my arm.

"We get to The Feast, pet, you aren't outside touching distance from me unless I specifically allow it. Am I understood?"

Oh my God.

He was taking me to a Feast. I wasn't ready for a Feast, I was pretty sure.

"You're understood," I mumbled regardless of my newfound terror, making an attempt to instill in my tone the reverence Breed used, thinking this would annoy him greatly.

Apparently, it worked. His head turned sharply to the side and his fingers dug into the flesh around my elbow painfully.

When I looked up to him, forcing my face into what I hoped was innocence mixed with eagerness (Wats and Breed had given me a *great* idea), I saw his eyes narrow and his mouth grow tight.

He, and thus I, remained silent as we descended the first staircase. And the second. And the third.

At the end of the fourth, Lucien guided me into my first Feast.

I saw immediately there was a reason Wats and Breed weren't down here. The place was a crush of beautiful people. Not thin. Not gaunt. Not heavy. Not ill-kept.

Perfect.

I didn't know where the vampires ended and the mortals began.

And all of them were dressed impeccably. The men in tuxedos or well-cut suits, the women in evening gowns. There was no one there that looked hopeful and desperate to be chosen. No overabundance of jewels and finery. The people here were too cool, too elegant, too polished to exhibit themselves in a way that would cry for attention.

The people were the only thing about the place that was elegant.

It looked like it was made out of cement, all of it, including the bar that ran along the length of one side. The shelves at the back were glass, however. Covered in bottles of liquor and different shaped glasses and backlit with red lights, as was the rest of the place, all of it illuminated by very dim, red lights.

The music was loud. Not rock 'n' roll but slow, throbbing and seductive.

As unassuming as it was, the room seemed alive as a hum of conversation ran low under the music. People were standing and talking or moving gracefully between the tightly-packed bodies.

There was what amounted to a dance floor but the dancers weren't exactly dancing. I found my attention riveted to them as I watched the bodies move, pressed close, swaying against each other suggestively, hands moving, reaching, touching. Faces tucked into necks, lips, and, even from my distance I saw a few glistening tongues gliding along jaws, cheekbones, temples, shoulders, other lips. It didn't seem there were couples but like the group was one, a whole, anyone who joined it would be pulled into what amounted to mass foreplay.

No wonder Edwina, who thought of her girls as *good* girls, didn't want them to come here.

I couldn't believe Lucien brought me here.

Not that I had any problem with this kind of thing, it just wasn't my scene.

It was on the tip of my tongue to ask him if this was also part of my punishment when he dropped my arm, caught my hand in his and drove forward, propelling us through the bodies.

His grip was sure and strong as he pulled me through.

I saw people turn to him and nod acknowledgement. A few mouthed greetings.

I also saw people studying me, faces impassive, eyes scanning, too sophisticated to be overt, but still betraying their curiosity.

Lucien stopped at the bar, and with a tug on my hand, yanked me through the final throng. In a tiny patch of free space, he curled his arm, whirling me so my back was plastered to his front, his arm tight around my waist, his hand still in mine, and he didn't let me go.

"What are you drinking tonight, pet?" he asked, his mouth bent to my ear and it pissed me off his deep voice sounding against my skin made me shiver.

I twisted my head and his came up to give it room to move.

I got up on tiptoes and sought his ear where I answered, "What do you want me to drink?"

Reflexively his arm tightened at my waist as his head shot up and his eyes scanned my face in the red light.

Then he looked away, clearly angry, and jerked his chin at the bartender.

It was then I decided maybe I was laying it on a bit thick.

He looked back down at me, dipping his face close, his forehead touching mine, his mouth a breath away.

"I like you best when you're drunk on vodka," he declared, his words invoking a memory that made my stomach pitch in a way that wasn't sickening but it hurt all the same.

I didn't know what came over me the night before.

That wasn't entirely true. I did.

I was drunk and my inhibitions were swept away.

They said you act most honestly when you're drunk which gave me something else to spend my day fretting and getting angry at myself about. And last night, for the first time, I enjoyed my time with him before the bloodletting, not to mention the bloodletting itself, which was, I couldn't deny it, *unbelievable.*

By the time I'd drunk my last martini, I'd listened to both Edwina and Stephanie talking about what a great man he was, how generous he was with his concubines when they were with him and after he released them. Apparently, he not only took care of them, he still saw most of them, even the ones who were now old and frail. It didn't hurt that the evidence of his colossal generosity was scattered around me, the clothes, the house, the housekeeper.

Sometime during the fashion parade, I'd forgotten my Why I Hate Lucien Vault and instead only remembered the good parts about him. The way a smile tugged at his mouth. The way his eyes went hooded when he knew I was watching him and I liked what I saw. The way he thought my worst traits were amusing. The way he could sometimes be gentle and patient. The way he kissed.

Good parts he showed upon arriving home, cementing in my inebriated mind that I'd been wrong about him.

Until he proved me right, that was.

He pulled his face away, wrenching me from my thoughts.

I watched him glance again to the bar and order, "Two martinis, vodka, olives."

After this, Lucien was silent and motionless until our drinks arrived. Once they did, he passed a bill to the bartender. I took my drink and he repositioned us. Lucien with mostly his side but also his back to the bar. Me turned to the room, my back still tight to his front, my body snugly, possessively, even protectively held in the curve of his arm.

His mouth came back to my ear, and apropos of nothing, he murmured, "Breed and Wats are hangers."

I hadn't asked but I was curious to know. I turned my head to face him and when I did I saw his expression was guarded and watchful.

Yes, I'd taken it too far.

Damn.

While doing my hair for the night (Edwina wanted to do it but I put my foot down this time), I'd come up with my plan.

He wanted to instruct me?

Well, I was going to teach *him* a few lessons too.

But I'd gotten carried away.

I determined to rectify that.

"Hangers?" I asked.

He nodded.

"What does that mean?" I went on.

He looked to the room. It was a gesture I was meant to follow which I did, and when I was facing the room his mouth came back to my ear. "They want to be down here."

I stayed facing forward, something I sensed he wanted me to do, and asked, "Have they ever been down here?"

"Never, and they never will," he answered. "But they don't give up. Obsessed with vampires and our culture, especially The Feasts. Obsessed in an unhealthy way. They've made themselves servants, unpaid unless someone gives them a gratuity."

I felt badly for Breed and Wats, to want something so badly, to be so close, but never to have what you want.

"How do they know about vampires?" I queried since I thought no one but those in the life did.

"They sense us," Lucien answered. "I've no idea how. Very few mortals do. And those who do always become hangers."

I found this interesting.

"Do people tip them?" I asked.

"Rarely."

"Why?"

"They're filthy, ill-bred, unkempt. Most vampires have the capacity to procure the finer things in life and they do, without fail. They don't have patience for reminders that there might be something less." I felt my body stiffen as he continued, "And they're hangers, Leah. Zealots. They make people uncomfortable, vampires, but especially the mortals. They're not only uninvited, they aren't wanted."

I looked across the room, taking in the beautiful people who could afford the finer things in life who wouldn't tolerate the not so beautiful people who had next to nothing.

Then I remembered Lucien tossing his keys to Wats and Wats's fanatical toadying.

"Do *you* tip them?" I whispered, thinking he might not hear me, my voice was so low, and forgetting he was a vampire, so of course he'd hear me.

"Always," Lucien answered and I twisted my neck to look at him.

"Really?" I breathed, not knowing why his answer, which was the right answer, meant so much to me.

His eyes roamed my face and I watched the guard go down as they gentled.

"Really, my pet. They wouldn't eat if it wasn't for Cosmo and me."

Without my permission, my body relaxed into his and I faced forward again.

His arm grew tighter around my waist as his mouth went back to my ear. "It doesn't make us terribly popular with our kind, however."

"Screw 'em," I muttered before I could stop myself and I felt his body shake with laughter as I heard his throat roar with it.

Automatically, my entire being tuned itself to his laughter. Something I hadn't heard since yesterday morning. Something that seemed to feed me, not like chocolate or some other forbidden treat, but like essential nourishment.

I felt my throat close with fear at the very thought.

In all the time I was with him, a vampire who drank human blood, who was vastly stronger than me (hell, than anyone I knew), who hurt me and humbled me and played my body against me, I'd never felt more fear than at that moment.

He felt it or sensed it, I knew this when his mouth at my ear called questioningly, "Leah?"

I noticed it then. Something else. Something that had been playing at the edge of my consciousness since we arrived.

Actually, two things.

The first wasn't so much real as it was an undercurrent.

The eyes. The ears. The senses. The attention. Surreptitiously people were watching us, listening to us, probably, as some of them were vampires, hearing our words, smelling my perfume mingled with his woodsy cologne.

I wasn't the sole curiosity, being new to this crowd.

It was also Lucien. In fact, it seemed to be mostly Lucien.

It was like we were movie stars...

No.

It was like *he* was a wildly famous movie star, I was his arm candy, and we'd gone out to a regular club amongst the common people.

The second thing was what I'd felt at The Selection. The weird drugged feeling. The feeling Stephanie explained was him tracking me, marking me.

"Are you marking me?" I whispered.

His arm at my waist slid up, his hand stopping at the side of my breast, his thumb stroking over my dress there.

I felt his head move, his mouth no longer at my ear but his lips were against my neck.

"Yes," he answered.

I forgot our audience, who were now getting a show, turned slightly to him, and his head came up.

I got close to his face and asked, "What *is* that?"

He answered without delay. "I've tuned myself to you."

I didn't know what that meant.

"What does that mean?" I asked.

"You know I can hear your heart?" he asked in return.

I nodded.

He hesitated before he went on, "You know I can control your mind?"

I swallowed before I nodded again and asked, "Are you reading my mind?"

"I can't read your mind unless you're speaking to me with it."

Wow. That was a relief.

"So what are you doing?"

"I've adjusted you to me and me to you. At the same time I've attuned my senses to you, so every breath you take, every slight movement, I know it almost before you do it."

I didn't get it but whatever it was, it was freaking me out.

"What does that mean?"

"It means our hearts are beating in tandem. It means I'm anticipating your movements. It says to the vampires in this room who can hear it and feel it, that you're mine."

"Don't they already know that?"

"Yes."

"Then isn't that overkill?"

For some reason his face got hard before he replied, "No."

"Don't you think you holding me pretty much sends the message?"

"Holding you is a message I'm sending to the mortals."

I was surprised at that answer. "What do they care?"

"I don't give a fuck if they care. I care. But it says I'm not here to feed. I'm not here to play. I'm not here to fuck. I'm here to be with you."

Oh my God.

What did *that* mean?

I didn't ask because I didn't want to know.

And why did my heart skip a beat when he said that?

I didn't even answer myself.

Instead, I asked something far, far more stupid and definitely more dangerous. "Do you do this with all your concubines?"

Then I got the answer to my very stupid, very, *very* dangerous question.

"I've never done it with another concubine."

I felt my mouth drop open. I knew I was gaping at him and I knew I had an audience. I was just too shocked to care.

Finally, I squeaked, "Why me?"

"You're Leah."

He felt this was an answer. I didn't feel the same but I decided not to push it because I sensed innately that I wouldn't want to know the answer to that either.

Even though I really wanted to know the answer.

My eyes skittered around the room and came back to him. "Is anyone else doing it?"

"No."

"There are no other vampires here with their concubines?"

"Yes, there are."

"But they aren't doing it?"

"No, Leah."

"Why not?"

"Because they can't."

I felt the martini glass slipping through my fingers but I didn't notice he caught it by its stem before it even cleared my hand. It also didn't register that he placed it and his on the bar and he turned me full-frontal into his arms.

I tipped my head back to look at him, put my hands to his chest and stared.

Then I asked, "Why can't anyone else do it?"

"Very few vampires have the capacity to mesmerize. Those that do don't have the control I have. None of them, or none that I know, have anywhere near the potency of my ability."

Oh my God!

"This is crazy," I whispered.

"You're correct, in a way. What I can do is very unusual."

"I'll say!" I cried.

He grinned at my outburst. I ignored his grin.

"Is that why everyone is staring at you like you're a movie star?" I blurted, his head cocked and he examined me inquisitively for a long moment.

Finally he asked, "You noticed that?"

"It's hard to miss."

He leaned back against the bar and pulled me with him so I was on my toes, my body flattened against his. His hand came up and twisted in my hair like he did when we were alone, not like we were the focus of hundreds of eyes and mammoth amounts of vampire extra sensory perception.

Then he spoke. "It's part of it."

"What's the other part?"

His hand twisted deeper into my hair and his mouth came to mine. "We'll leave that for later, shall we?"

I wanted to say no, we shall not.

But far more agreeable, acquiescent, hopefully annoying Leah wouldn't have demanded an explanation.

And anyway, I didn't get a chance.

He kissed me.

He did this too in the same way he'd do it when we were alone.

In other words, it was a deep, open-mouthed, tongues tangling, make me breathe heavily, fiery shot right between the legs kiss.

Further, there was something different about it, better, more intense, almost overpowering, but in a really good way. I knew intuitively it was because he'd marked me. I knew it was because our bodies were attuned. I didn't know how and I didn't understand what that meant, I just knew it affected me physically in a way that shook me to my soul.

When he lifted his head, I found I was hanging on, beyond my toes, straight to my tiptoes. My front was pressed deep to his, the fingers of one hand curled on his shoulder, the other wrapped insistently around the back of his neck.

"I fucking *love* the way you kiss," he growled again like we weren't in a jam-packed, vibrating, vampire club. The almost feral rumble of his growl slid through me, making my toes curl.

That's when I felt it, the buzz, the undercurrent that was focused on us had shifted, intensified, become rapt. I felt eyes on us now and I knew they weren't furtive.

The heat hit my face just as the danger permeated my consciousness.

"Something's wrong," I breathed.

His face took on that inquisitive look again as he studied me then he replied, "Yes."

"What is it?"

His eyes lifted, moving across the room.

I registered impatience, frustration, then stony resignation in his expression before he answered, "It's time for me to be good, pet."

This made no sense whatsoever, but before I could ask another question, he'd moved us again to our original positions, his hand with my glass coming in front of me.

I took it, lifted it to my lips and sucked back a healthy sip mostly because I needed it.

I should have taken a larger sip because his mouth came back to my ear and he asked, "Do you want to dance?"

My eyes shot to the writhing dance floor and my legs wobbled.

There it was. To be Obedient Leah, I was going to have to do something I really didn't want to do.

"If you want to." I tried to sound respectful and subservient like his wish was my command but I wasn't sure I accomplished this feat.

My fears were proved correct when I felt his body move with his chuckle at my back.

"We don't have to do anything you don't want to do, Leah."

We didn't?

Boy, *that* was a first.

I stared at the undulating bodies on the dance floor, trying and failing to imagine Lucien's powerful frame among them, and gulped before asking, "Um, do, you, er, dance?"

"Not publicly, no. However, privately, yes."

I twisted my neck to look at him. "Privately?"

He grinned. "Drink up, pet, and I'll show you The Feast."

I felt my brows knit. "I thought we were at The Feast."

His fingers wrapped around my wrist and lifted my glass to my lips. "Drink," he ordered.

I drank and he took my glass, put it next to his on the bar, and then captured my hand.

Again, he moved us through the crowd, his hand secure in mine, anchoring me to him as he pushed through. The bodies seemed to close in this time, the eyes no longer averted, the curiosity now explicit.

Lucien either ignored it or didn't notice it (likely the first). He led me to a back wall where there was an open doorway that led to a shadowed hall. What looked like an overdeveloped bouncer was standing just outside the doorway.

Without hesitation or even glancing at the bouncer, Lucien guided me in.

The hall was long and snaking, turning this way and that, not with corners, but with curves. There were no doors, which I thought was weird. It was shadowed, creepy and strangely threatening, and if I wasn't with Lucien there was no way I'd have been there. The music and the hum slowly died as we moved forward and followed the snake.

Finally, with the club just a soft, nearly indistinct buzz behind us, we turned an actual corner.

And I was confronted with a Feast.

My first instinct was to look away.

But it was like a car crash and I couldn't, no matter how much I wanted to.

It was different here, like night and day. The walls weren't cement but painted a deep, rich red. The floor was covered in thick pile carpets and pillows. Some of the pillows huge, the size of double beds. Some of them smaller. All of them covered in velvet in different rich shades, plum, scarlet, sapphire, ruby, forest green, wine and blood red. There were enormous mirrors on the wall framed in heavily carved, dark wood, reflecting the activity on the pillows, against the walls, on the floor.

Feeding and lots of it.

On a double-bed-sized pillow was a woman so stunning she looked like a model, her alabaster skin exposed in a low-cut black dress. Three vampires were attached to her. One at her neck, one at her ankle, and one whose mouth was at her cleavage suckling at the side of her breast.

My gaze floated, horrified at the raw, brutal sensuality of it. It was everywhere. I couldn't escape it.

I tore my eyes free, trying to find a safe place, but caught an image in a mirror, a vampire nearly as big as Lucien had a tiny woman pinned to the wall. Her head was lolling on her shoulder, her arms limp. He was holding her to his mouth with his hands under her armpits, her feet clean off the floor, legs dangling. Her face was a picture of ecstasy as blood dribbled down her neck, escaping his mouth.

With nowhere to put my eyes, I turned into Lucien and shoved my face in his massive chest. My hands lifting, fingers curling into his lapels, I pulled the fabric to my cheeks so no vision could penetrate even accidentally.

His arms came around me, a hand drifting up my naked spine, under my hair to rest warm on my neck. I felt his body bow so his mouth could be at the top of my head and my face and torso arched into his to keep the contact.

His voice was low when he asked quietly, "You don't think it's beautiful?"

Oh my God.

He thought this was *beautiful*?

A thought occurred to me, and panicked, my head snapped back and his jerked up to avoid a collision.

"Don't feed from me here," I blurted out my plea.

I felt his body jolt then saw his eyes narrow before he asked, "Pardon?"

"Please. I'll do anything you say. Just don't feed from me here."

"Leah—"

I shook his lapels roughly and pressed closer, going up on my toes, so much in a state I didn't measure my words. "Promise me, Lucien. What happened last night is something special, something that should be between us, not reflected in a *fucking* mirror for anyone to see."

At my words, his face gentled, his fingers came to my hairline at the side of my head and slid in, stopping, curling and holding me there before he whispered, "Sweetheart—"

I was too rocked by what I just witnessed, knowing how it felt, seeing what was likely *my* ecstasy of last night on that woman's face, I didn't let his actions register. Or his tone. Or the endearment he'd used last night and this morning which I thought, regardless of the outcome of both events, was achingly sweet.

It was too humiliating by half. Or it *would* be if he did it to me.

"Please," I begged on a frantic whisper.

"I won't feed from you here," he murmured and with his agreement my relief was so great, my body collapsed into his. My arms went tight around him and I pressed the side of my face to his chest.

He bent again, his words stirring the hair on top of my head. "Do you want me to take you away?"

I nodded, my cheek sliding against his chest and his hand, still in my hair at the other side of my head, tensed reassuringly then slid away.

He took my hand and we were away, leaving the scene behind us, quickly snaking back through the hall.

I found my heart was beating wildly. Without my panic overcoming my being I felt it. In fact it was beating so hard I fancied I heard it.

Then I realized what I'd done and a new panic surged through me.

The panic was so strong I yanked at his hand, planted my feet and stopped.

Lucien stopped with me and looked back at me. "Leah—"

I cut him off yet again, saying, "I don't want you to think I'm a Miss Priss."

He didn't respond. He just stared at me.

I continued, taking a step closer, tipping my head back to look at him. "It *was* beautiful. Those things always are. But they're also raw. That, particularly, was raw. And revealing. And I don't want anyone to see me that way."

"Leah—" he started but I kept on talking.

"It's private and it's okay if they," I looked behind me, throwing my arm toward the hallway we'd walked through for emphasis before I turned back to him, "want to give and share and...whatever... but, if you do it in front of others, you give it away and it's not just yours anymore. And I'm yours, you said so yourself, and I don't want anyone to have me, not even a little piece of me, not anyone, just you."

I was so panicked, desperate to give him my explanation, not wanting him to think I was a prude, or worse, to offend him by casting aspersions on his culture, I didn't even realize what I was saying.

And furthermore, I didn't mean for it to come out the way it did.

But it did.

And Lucien took it a certain way.

I knew this because one second I was standing with my hand in his.

The next second I was against the wall, his body was pressed to mine, his hand in my hair yanking my head back in an arc that was painful not only at my neck but in my hair, and his mouth was on mine.

This wasn't like the kisses we'd shared before. This one was demanding, bruising, possessive, branding and undeniably savage.

And, it might make me a freak, but I loved every fucking second of it.

His mouth tore from mine and before I could even take a breath, he asked, "You're mine?"

I tried to salvage something, anything. "I didn't mean—"

He cut me off with a growl. "You're mine."

Now what had I gotten myself into?

"Lucien—"

He had an arm around my waist and it coiled so tight, forcing me so deep against his body, it cut off my breath.

"All. Fucking. *Mine*," he whispered fiercely.

I felt my legs go weak and I knew it was not only fear at his ferocious proclamation but also an unhinged desire that I did *not* want to feel.

"Lucien, I can't breathe," I wheezed in all truthfulness but I'd lost his attention.

His head shot to the side and his mouth got tight right before his hold dropped away. I nearly collapsed but his hand seized mine again and he started striding swiftly back toward the club. Not long after, I saw a couple coming our way down the hall and I knew Lucien heard their approach.

As they got closer, I noted it was a man and a woman. They were both so gorgeous I had no idea which was the vampire or if they both were (or weren't).

"Lucien," the man called from several feet away.

"Jordan," Lucien replied.

It was clear Lucien didn't feel like conversing.

It was just as clear Jordan did for he stopped, halting the striking redheaded woman at his side.

Her gaze flickered nervously over Lucien right before she gave me the once-over, and to my shock, right in front of me, the haughty bitch let her lip curl.

I returned the favor but without the lip curl.

Instead, when Lucien stopped, I moved into him. That alone was going to make my point, but Lucien went one better.

His arm slid around my shoulders, brushing my hair with it so it all fell to the front where he mindlessly grabbed a tendril and started twisting it on his finger. Even in the dim light, I saw her eyes focus on Lucien's hand and her face went pale.

I just stopped myself from giving her a "so there" grin.

I looked up at Lucien and saw his eyes were on Jordan. I looked at Jordan and saw Jordan's eyes were on me.

"So this is Leah," Jordan noted.

What?

How did he know me?

"It is," Lucien agreed.

Jordan's eyes gave me a once-over too. When they did, the air in the hall went thick and the animosity rolling off Lucien was the cause of it.

The redhead took a step back, my body involuntarily braced, and Jordan's gaze swung to Lucien.

"Easy, Lucien," Jordan said in a low conciliatory voice.

"Don't tell me easy, Jordan," Lucien returned in a low, anything but conciliatory voice.

"You're amongst friends," Jordan noted and I might have been wrong but it seemed there was deeper meaning to his words than the one that seemed obvious to me.

"That might be put to the test," Lucien retorted.

"I'll pass or I'll burn," Jordan replied.

They locked eyes and the redhead and I were powerless to do anything but look on and hope they didn't tear each other limb from limb.

Jordan broke the macho vampire staring contest and he looked again at me. I didn't think this was a good idea but I couldn't tell him that.

"I can see she's worth it," he muttered, his eyes going back to Lucien even as his words made the redhead's face twist into a pout that I wish I could say wasn't pretty but it made her look damnably cute as a button.

What I wanted to know, but didn't ask, was what I was worth.

It was like they were talking code!

Lucien didn't respond to Jordan. Instead he looked at the redhead.

"Cecile," he murmured.

"Lucien," she whispered in a breathy voice.

"Now, Lucien, you released her, remember?" Jordan said and his tone was lighthearted but his words felt like a kick to my gut. The redhead looked like she felt the same and this look was not cute as a button at all. It was anguished.

She recovered before I did, damn the woman.

"*I* remember," she spoke up.

Jordan turned to me. "He always gets the best ones. Luckily, sometimes the rest of us can pick up the scraps."

Everyone tensed then.

Me in an all of a sudden feeling of camaraderie for my female brethren.

Lucien because he could be a jerk but I suspected he was a gentleman.

Cecile because his insult wasn't veiled, not in the slightest.

"Perhaps you should be on your way," Lucien suggested from between clenched teeth.

Jordan, clearly a new kind of vampire to me, the *demented* kind, grinned in the face of certain peril (namely Lucien). "Perhaps I should." His eyes came again to me. "Leah, it was a pleasure."

I didn't know what to do so I simply lifted my chin. This made his grin widen to a smile, he nodded to Lucien, and he took Cecile's arm and moved to pass us.

Lucien moved too. Keeping me to his side with his arm around my shoulders, he shifted us around and his hand shot out and wrapped around Cecile's upper arm.

Jordan and Cecile stopped.

"Cecile's going home," Lucien declared and I felt my mouth drop open as Jordan's eyes narrowed on Lucien's hand then on Lucien.

We were almost home free and now foiled by Lucien, who was also obviously of the demented vampire sort.

"I beg your pardon?" Jordan asked Lucien.

"It's okay, Lucien," Cecile whispered.

"Don't do this," Lucien clipped to Cecile.

"It's okay," she repeated.

Lucien dropped his hand but he didn't admit defeat. "Your family won't agree."

I watched as her face paled again.

"I'm not sure this is your business," Jordan butted in, coming closer to the threesome that included Lucien, Cecile and me.

"I've selected three of her line, not including her. It's my business," Lucien returned.

"You released her just over a week ago," Jordan snapped. "You had your fill, you're out."

My eyes turned to Cecile.

This was Lucien's last concubine.

I didn't want to meet any of Lucien's concubines, but *definitely* not the gorgeous willowy redhead that was his *last* concubine.

Why did my life suck so much?

Why?

However at that moment I suspected Cecile's life sucked more, which made my heart go out to her, regardless of the earlier lip curl.

Lucien ignored Jordan and kept focus on Cecile. "You know what you lose if you walk down that hall."

"Lucien—" she started.

He cut her off. "I'll take it from you."

Her eyes fell to the floor and she whispered, "I know."

"Go home," Lucien ordered.

Her eyes lifted and they were pleading when she repeated, "Lucien."

"Go home."

Her gaze flitted to me then back to Lucien and she pulled her arm free of Jordan.

"I miss it," she whispered.

"You'll find someone to give it back to you but not here," Lucien replied. "Go home."

"I don't believe this shit," Jordan hissed.

Lucien's eyes cut to Jordan. "Janette's at the feeding. If I'm remembering correctly, she's your taste."

"I've *had* her," Jordan returned.

"Have her again," Lucien clipped back.

Another macho vampire staring contest ensued and this one was far, far, *far* more dangerous and definitely scarier than the first.

"Um..." I butted in, proving beyond a shadow of a doubt that I was indeed deranged as all eyes swung to me and all six of them (including Lucien's) were incredulous. "Can I just say," my gaze went to Cecile, I swallowed and sallied forth, "you're beautiful. Gorgeous. Change can suck. Trust me, I know. But, honest to God, you'll find someone the minute you start looking. All you'll have to do is snap your fingers. Sure, he won't be able to move at the speed of light and he won't feed on human blood but there are always problems in a relationship. Am I right?"

For a second there was complete and total silence and I thought maybe I might have stepped over a line I should never, ever, ever, *ever* have crossed.

I really should have paid attention in Vampire Studies. I was seeing the error of my ways now.

Then I was curled forcefully into Lucien's body, his hand in my hair shoving my face in his chest, a chest that was moving, rocking deeply, weirdly, until I figured it out. And I figured it out right before he let out a shout of amused laughter.

I relaxed into him and peeked over my shoulder at Cecile and Jordan.

Cecile had lost her haughty disdain and was watching me with a look that was astonished at the same time it was sad and confused.

Jordan was watching me too, a grin playing on his lips, and also, to my shock, he looked amused.

Cecile turned to Jordan and asked quietly, "Will you be angry if I go home?"

Jordan sighed. "It'll be a loss, dearest, but by all means, scurry home and save your reputation."

Her look became grateful. It swung to Lucien then even to me before she turned and swanned down the hall.

My eyes moved to Jordan when he spoke and I realized he was speaking to me.

"I hope to see *you* at another Feast. The next time, heading in the other direction."

"I wouldn't hold your breath," Lucien remarked dryly.

Jordan didn't take his eyes from me when he asked, "She didn't fancy it?"

"Not even a little bit," Lucien answered.

"Shame," Jordan muttered, I shivered, Lucien's arm tightened, and Jordan lifted a hand and then he was gone.

Just like that.

Whoosh.

One second there, the next second he disappeared.

Lucien uncurled me from his body and walked me down the hall. This time he didn't take my hand but kept his arm around my shoulders.

At the top of the stairs when Breed opened the door for us, Lucien slipped him a bill. I tried to see what it was but didn't succeed.

Wats was standing sentry by the car right where we left it.

"Everything's fine, master, no one even looked at it," he panted, bowing and holding the keys out to Lucien who held his hand up and Wats dropped the keys in.

Lucien held the door for me and Wats scampered out of the way for him to do so.

After Lucien closed my door, I spied the one hundred dollar bill Lucien slid into Wats's waiting hand. I also saw the shiver of excitement that shook Wats's body and I had the feeling it had nothing to do with the fact that Lucien just made him the highest paid car watcher in history, but because Lucien had almost, but not quite, touched him.

We were well away, Lucien's hand back on my thigh after he'd pulled the material away, but this time no stroking, just proprietary resting.

After a while, I couldn't help myself, so I requested, "May I ask a question?"

"Of course," Lucien replied instantly.

I pulled in a breath and before I could lose my courage, I asked, "You said to Cecile you'd take it away from her. What would you take away?"

Again he answered without hesitation. "Her house, her car, her money, everything I give her to keep her. Everything I'll keep giving her until she dies. If she falls, which, you should know, Leah, any concubine does if they attend a Feast after they're released, I'm within my rights to cease her keeping."

"You'd do that?" I whispered.

"In a second," he answered. "My concubines, current or past, don't participate in Feasts."

I was confused. "But you took *me* to a Feast."

His hand squeezed my thigh. "To see, to watch, to experience, to be with me amongst my own, *not* to participate."

My head turned to look at him. "You were never going to feed?"

He glanced at me briefly then back to the road before he stated implacably, "Never."

This caused me to feel an extreme sense of relief.

Then I felt an extreme sense of fear that I felt so relieved.

Then I felt the extreme desire to cover his hand with mine.

Then I mentally kicked myself.

Shortly after, the sleek, high-performance sports car eating the miles serenely beneath me, I fell asleep.

9
The Lesson

I woke for the first time since I'd been in my new bedroom know-ing exactly where I was.

But something wasn't right.

I opened my eyes and saw the big wide bed empty in front of me. Lucien wasn't there.

Elation and disappointment crashed against each other and they caused a very strange sensation that I didn't like one bit.

Then my mind traveled back to the night before.

I thought about The Feast and all I'd seen.

Then I thought about Lucien's behavior and the conflicting emotions it made me feel. Most specifically that I liked being out with him. It wasn't what I'd call a fun date, but it was interesting and being on his arm was weirdly thrilling. He acted a complete gentle-man (well, mostly) and I hadn't had that in a *long* time (as in, never). Not to mention his possessive-protective streak, which made me feel safe and if that wasn't enough to screw with my head, nothing was.

Lastly, I thought about falling asleep in the car after Lucien assured me he was the kind of vamp who didn't...

I went solid and then whipped up the bedclothes. I stared at my semi-naked body before pulling the covers back down.

I was wearing nothing but a pair of black lace panties. I fell asleep in the car and that damn vampire carried me upstairs, took off my clothes and put me to bed.

In all that he'd done, and there was *a lot* that he'd done, taking off my clothes while I was asleep seemed like the worst (well, at that moment it did).

Only *I* was allowed to show my body to who *I* wanted to show it to when *I* was in the mood to show it.

Okay, so it could be argued that he'd had his tongue in my mouth (more than once), and his hand in my pants (again more than once), and he'd sucked my blood (also more than once), and he controlled my mind (way too many times, which meant twice, which was two times too many).

But this was taking it too far.

While my head was preparing to explode, the bedroom door opened and Lucien strode in.

When I saw him, I was so shocked, my fury vanished and I came up on a forearm to get a better look.

He was wearing faded well-worn jeans and a tight-fitting, long-sleeved, white T-shirt.

I'd never seen him in anything but a suit (and his pajamas, of course). And I'd never seen him in anything but dark colors.

I didn't think he was the type of guy *to* wear something as everyday normal as jeans and a tee.

And he looked good in them.

No, great.

Even better than the suit.

Phenomenal.

My mouth started watering.

His eyes went lazy and he grinned.

My heart skipped a beat at seeing that look I liked way too damn much about one second before I remembered I hated him and he'd taken my clothes off me the night before.

"You're awake," he commented, walking around the bed while I watched him.

I remembered my plan and Obedient Leah kicked in instantly.

The game was afoot.

"Yes," I answered, clutching the covers to my chest.

He stopped at my side and in a flash he'd plucked me out of the bed, sat on the edge and had me settled in his lap.

Seeing as I still wasn't used to his incomprehensible speed, not to mention I was mostly naked, this freaked me out.

Luckily, his arms were around me and he was pressing my torso to his chest, hiding my nudity.

"Did you sleep well, pet?" he asked softly in my ear.

I nodded.

His lips went to my neck where he muttered, "Good."

Then they slid around to my throat.

His mouth felt nice, too nice. So nice, I couldn't control my tremble.

"I like that," he muttered against my throat.

"What?"

His lips came to mine, his eyes open and watching me as he answered, "When you tremble in my arms."

What did you say to that?

I didn't know so I just mumbled, "Oh."

I felt his mouth smile against mine.

With him in his gentle mood I was losing my will to play games. My will preferred to throw itself bodily at him and rip his fantastic looking jeans and tee off his equally fantastic looking body and have my way with him.

In an effort at control, I asked, "Did you sleep well?"

His head moved back a couple of inches and one hand came up, fingers sifting through my hair at my temple and back, pulling it away from my face while his eyes watched.

When his fingers had glided the length of my hair down my back, his arm curled around me again, and he said, "My first good night's sleep in the last week."

This admission surprised me. I couldn't imagine anything causing the Mighty Lucien to lose sleep.

It surprised me so much my head tilted to the side and I inquired with genuine curiosity, "Why haven't you been sleeping well?"

His arms grew tighter before he answered, "At first it was anticipation for your Bloodletting. After your initiation, it was concern because the wound wasn't healing swiftly. Then, my pet, I found it difficult sleeping beside you."

My heart lurched even though my brain reminded it that it should be rejoicing. Another collision of sensations that wasn't exactly pleasurable.

"You have difficulty sleeping with me?" My question was a whisper.

His hand slid up my naked back to capture a lock of hair and I felt him start twisting. This felt nice too.

It always did when he did that.

"It's your scent, Leah. It's intoxicating." His mouth came to mine and brushed my lips before he pulled back again, a grin tugging the corners of his mouth as he continued, "Especially when you're aroused. Your natural scent mixed with the scent of your sex is overpowering." My body went stiff and his arms gave me a squeeze before he finished, losing the fight with his smile, "In a *good* way."

I examined his arrogant, self-satisfied smile while briefly considering karate chopping him on the shoulder.

However, this would probably be as effective as a gnat landing on him.

Instead, I asked solicitously, "Would you prefer if I bathed before going to bed, darling?"

I saw his eyes flash, I wasn't certain if it was anger or amusement, before his head bent to the side and his mouth was again at my neck.

"Only if I'm bathing with you," he answered.

Damn. That was a good comeback.

"Whatever you want," I replied dutifully.

"Mm," he murmured effectively, so effectively the timbre slid across my skin, making me shiver. "I like that idea. Maybe I'll only allow you to bathe when you're with me."

Oh my *God*.

Now what had I done?

I had no choice. I had to go with it.

Trying to keep my voice even, I inquired, "Do you want to do that now?"

I felt his tongue touch my neck and that made me shiver too.

Then he said, "Not now. I'm hungry."

A sudden bolt of electricity slammed between my legs giving me an off the charts happy tingle.

He wanted to feed. And I wanted him to feed. I despised that I did but I also couldn't deny it.

"You're hungry?"

"Yes," he said against my neck and then lifted his head to look at me. "Your choice today, Leah, in here or in the kitchen."

He wanted to feed in the kitchen?

Really?

That was crazy! What if Edwina walked in?

"If we do it in the kitchen, what if Edwina walks in?"

His brows drew together. "She'll have to be there, unless you intend to cook for me."

"Cook for you?" I parroted stupidly, finding that idea both intriguing and terrifying.

I mean, I knew how to cook. And the idea of cooking for Lucien was kind of nice even though that admission further proved my insanity. But what if I messed it up? This I did a lot, especially when I tried something fancy, and I doubted Lucien ate non-fancy food.

And anyway, why were we talking about cooking?

He studied me while these thoughts chased themselves through my head before saying, "You *can* cook, Leah. You can do what you like. It's your house, not Edwina's. Are you saying you want to cook?"

Oh. I got it.

"You're talking about *breakfast*," I breathed in a voice that denoted my mental heel of hand to head slap.

He smiled another arrogant, self-satisfied, now even so far as smug smile before he said, "You thought I wanted to feed."

"Erm..." I wriggled in his lap then remembered I was mostly naked so getting away from him would expose my upper body and I wasn't ready for that, so I stilled.

His large hands slid to my hips and tensed. "I can't feed, pet. Not until tonight."

That was news to me.

"You can't?"

He shook his head saying, "You aren't used to me yet."

This further confused me.

"I'm not?"

The smug smile came back before his face disappeared in my neck again. "We could try."

Oh my.

"But you'd be weak all day and it's Saturday. I have plans for you today."

He had plans for me. Plans that required me not being weak.

I didn't know if that was good or not.

"Plans?"

One of his hands came up to cup the back of my head and he looked at me again. "First up, another lesson, this time about feeding."

"Okay," I breathed, trying but not quite achieving the feat of not sounding disappointed.

He grinned.

Damn the vampire!

I tried to look dutiful. It was hard.

He studied my face then burst out laughing while he stood, putting me on my feet.

He began to set me away from him, and panicked at the idea of baring myself, I latched on to his shoulders and pressed my body against his.

His head tilted down to look at me.

"Leah?"

"Close your eyes," I whispered before I could stop myself

"Pardon?"

"Um..." How to do this and be submissive? "Would you please close your eyes, darling?"

His hands at my waist gave me an impatient squeeze.

"Why?"

"I'm nearly naked," I explained softly and, I thought, unnecessarily.

His hands gave me another squeeze, this time also pulling me even deeper into his body as his head dipped closer.

"I saw you last night, pet."

"I know."

His face came even closer.

"You have a beautiful body, Leah."

My eyes slid to the side.

"Look at me," he demanded.

My eyes slid back to his.

"I don't want you hiding yourself from me," he ordered.

"Is that an order?" I asked just to confirm.

"Not unless you make it one," he answered.

What the hell did that mean?

"So, what you're saying is, you're not going to close your eyes?"

"No."

Really, he was a jerk.

He must have read my thoughts, or since he couldn't do that unless I was speaking to him *in* my thoughts, he must have read my face.

Therefore he kept talking, "I'd like to understand why this is an issue."

"I'm naked," I explained, again unnecessarily.

"And I saw you last night," he repeated, his tone stating clearly he thought this was unnecessary too.

"It isn't last night anymore. It's this morning."

"And?"

"The sun is shining," I went on.

"The sun?" he asked

"Yes. And I'm awake," I continued.

His hands slid around to my back as he murmured, "I see."

"You see what?"

Instead of answering, he said patiently, "I've had my tongue in your mouth."

"Yes, but—"

"And your blood has filled *my* mouth."

"Yes, but—"

"And I've had my hand in your pants."

This was all sounding familiar.

Still.

"Yes, but—"

"And my finger in your—"

"*Yes!*" I snapped, cutting him off. "But this is different!"

"How?"

"It just is."

"Explain it to me."

"I can't."

He sighed before stating, "You're standing mostly naked in my arms. I can feel your skin, smell your scent, touch your hair. You're pressed against me and you're saying the thought of me seeing your breasts makes you uncomfortable even though I've seen them before?"

That made it sound stupid.

I dropped my eyes and looked at his throat.

"That makes it sound stupid," I said in a small voice.

"Show yourself to me, Leah."

My eyes snapped back to his. "What?" I breathed.

"Do it," he ordered and it was definitely an order. I could see it in the hard set of his jaw and the intensity of his eyes.

I really had to make certain lighter fluid was on Edwina's grocery list.

Doing my best to be Obedient Leah, I pushed against his arms at my waist to take a step back. He didn't let me go. He kept his arms around me so I was forced to arch my back.

I looked away the minute his eyes dropped down. It was only a second before I was again pressed against him, his hand in my hair, cupping my head and putting pressure there so my cheek was against his chest.

He bent so he was talking into the hair on top of my head when he spoke again softly, "That wasn't so hard, was it?"

Actually, it wasn't.

But I'd never give him that.

So instead, in my most obvious, well-behaved voice, I agreed, "No, darling. It wasn't."

I felt his body go solid and his hand in my hair twisted before he noted, "You try me, pet."

Good, I thought.

His hand tugged back, taking my head with it so I was looking up at him.

"You're lucky I enjoy it." His voice was a warning.

Great. He enjoyed it.

Boy, I *was* lucky.

"Put on a robe, meet me downstairs. We'll have breakfast in the kitchen," he commanded before he touched his lips to mine and let me go.

I nearly flew to the bathroom and it took all my effort not to slam the door.

"Is there something particular you want for breakfast?" he called through the closed door as I slid on my robe.

"Whatever you want," I called back and then stuck my tongue out at the door.

"I saw that, Leah." I heard him say and he didn't sound like I was trying him anymore. He sounded amused.

I didn't care if he sounded amused.

My mind and body froze.

"What?" I called between stiff lips.

The door opened, I jumped, and Lucien crossed his arms on his chest before he leaned against its frame.

"I saw it," he repeated.

"But...I thought," I stammered then breathed, "You can *see* through *doors*?"

"No, I can't see through doors. You were speaking to me."

"I was *gesturing* to you."

He grinned. "Same thing."

I stayed silent.

This was not good news.

"This new game is fun," he noted, freaking me *way the hell* out. "Almost better than the other one."

I tried innocence. "What game?"

He shook his head, his hand shot out, curled around the back of my neck, and he pulled me in so he could kiss the top of my head.

When he let me go, he said, "Time for your lesson. I'll meet you downstairs."

Without another word, he turned and was gone.

I stared at the still open door of the bedroom.

Then I screamed.

But only in my mind.

And since I was screaming because of Lucien, I really hoped he couldn't hear.

I took my sweet time doing my morning business and sauntered downstairs to the kitchen.

Edwina was at the stove. Lucien was nowhere to be seen.

"Hey, Edwina," I called.

"Hello, dear." Edwina threw a smile over her shoulder. "Did you have fun last night?"

I wrinkled my nose.

She smiled then shook her head, muttering with distaste, "Feasts."

She turned back to whatever she was doing and I strolled to the coffeepot.

"You want a refresh?" I asked, reaching for her empty mug.

"Please."

"I'll take one too, Leah," Lucien said, striding into the kitchen and I just barely controlled my glare.

"Of course, darling," I murmured to the cabinet with the coffee mugs, taking two down.

"Black, three sugars," Lucien continued.

He took *three sugars*?

It really was too bad that vampires didn't get diabetes and at that moment I didn't care how unkind that thought was.

I measured three gargantuan heaping teaspoons of sugar into Lucien's coffee, splashed mine with milk, asked Edwina her preference and then passed them around.

I took my mug and went to sit on one of the stools.

"Lucien's ordered poached eggs on toast, Leah. What would you like?" Edwina asked.

I avoided looking at Lucien and replied, "I'll have whatever Lucien's having."

I felt Lucien turn to me but I continued to ignore him.

Edwina stayed busy at the huge, stainless steel, restaurant quality stove and offered, "It's no bother. I'll make whatever you like."

Finally I turned to Lucien, "What would you like me to eat, darling?"

Lucien's gaze locked with mine but he didn't speak. I tried to keep my face attentive and expectant like his decision on my morning meal was the reason for my being.

Finally he inquired, "Do you like poached eggs?"

"Do you *want* me to like poached eggs?" I returned on a breathy exhale.

"I want you to tell me if you like poached eggs," he retorted.

We had a short staring contest but his black eyes were too much for me and I turned away.

"I like poached eggs," I replied demurely.

Lucien looked at Edwina. "She'll have poached eggs."

Edwina's gaze was drifting back and forth between Lucien and me. Then she bit her lip (and I could swear it was to hide a smile) and turned back to the stove.

Lucien took a sip of his coffee. I watched him under my lashes as I took a sip from mine.

"The grocery list is on the counter, dear, right in front of you," Edwina was saying. "I have Saturday and Sunday afternoons off as well as all day Monday. So anything you want to cook or have in the house, write it down. I'm going to the store after breakfast."

I was wondering if they sold gallon jugs of gasoline at the grocery store (or flamethrowers) when Lucien walked to the sink, poured out his coffee and walked to the coffeemaker.

I just stopped myself from grinning.

Edwina stared at him in horror, a stainless steel spoon any television chef would give one of their kidneys for held aloft. "Is it too weak?"

Lucien poured himself another cup. "It's fine. But Leah has a heavy hand with the sugar."

"Oh dear, I didn't do it right?" I chirped, sounding devastated, like someone ran over the beloved cat that I'd had since childhood.

Lucien turned to me. "Do you remember what your behavior bought you when you disobeyed me?"

Oh I remembered all right.

Boy did I remember.

I clenched my teeth and nodded my head once.

"You could get more of that before breakfast," Lucien went on. "Would you like that?"

Lucien turning me on to the point my body screamed for release and then leaving me wanting?

No. I didn't want that.

I shook my head.

He calmly took a sip of his coffee.

Edwina thankfully pretended she hadn't heard a thing.

I pulled the grocery list to me and started to read it.

All of a sudden I felt Lucien behind me, the heat from his chest against my back as he leaned over me.

I detested a lot of things about him. His recent behavior was one shining example. When he went all nearly breaking the sound barrier vampire was another.

"Tonight, I want you to make your fried chicken for me," he ordered and my mind cleared of the latest Humiliating Lucien Encounter.

I twisted my neck to look up at him, dumbfounded.

"What?"

His eyes caught mine. "Your fried chicken."

My fried chicken?

I did, of course, make great fried chicken. The best. It was one of my only real talents.

But how the hell would he know that?

A weird chill ran up my spine.

"How do you know about my fried chicken?" I whispered.

His chin motioned to the pad of paper on the table and he didn't answer my question.

Instead he commanded, "Put the ingredients down."

"How do you—?"

"Just write down the ingredients, Leah."

I gaped at him.

Then I considered my recipe, which required at least overnight marinating of the chicken in my famous buttermilk marinade.

It wouldn't be near as good without time to marinade.

"I can't," I told him.

His eyes narrowed.

"No, really, I can't. It's the marinade. It needs at least..." I looked at the clock on the microwave. It was nearly ten. "Eight hours of marinating!" My voice was rising dramatically, but what could I say? I had a fried chicken reputation to keep up. Every woman knew how important that was. "And even that isn't optimal. Anything less just isn't worth it. I don't even have eight hours!"

He grinned, I caught it close up and my heart skipped.

But he was relentless. "Put the ingredients down."

"Lucien!"

"You can make it for me tomorrow night."

Oh. Right.

Tomorrow night would give me plenty of time. I could do that.

I wrote the ingredients down.

Edwina served up poached eggs on toast with crisp fried bacon. Lucien had three eggs. I had only two. I wanted to ask for another egg (or two), seeing as I was still on course to gain as much weight as possible to turn Lucien off my "beautiful body," but I felt I'd tried his patience enough for one morning.

He sat beside me and we ate while Edwina tidied the kitchen and I wrote stuff down on the grocery list. I omitted the flamethrower. When the laptop in the bedroom had broadband, something I discovered the day before it didn't, I'd see if I could order one online.

Edwina whisked the plates out from under us when we were done, rinsed them, put them in the dishwasher and did a rub down of all the countertops while Lucien and I sipped at our final drops of coffee.

It was weird having a housekeeper.

It was even weirder living in a rambling mansion in the middle of nowhere.

In my ex-life I lived in a two-bedroom condo in the city, and although I didn't do too badly career-wise, I didn't have a housekeeper. I had been a media specialist, a field in which I'd never get a job again considering I gave them two whole days notice. Though I didn't have to worry about that since Lucien would be taking care of me for the rest of my natural born life, something else that sucked.

My condo was excellently situated. I could walk anywhere to get anything I needed. Bars, takeaway pizza, movie theaters, grocery stores. My condo had enough room not to feel like I lived in a cave but not too much where it would take all weekend to clean or I could accumulate too much stuff which I had a habit of doing.

Luckily, although Edwina was a bit strange, I liked her and her living with me made the big house seem less monstrous.

Still, I missed my little place. I'd lived there for ten years. I'd made every inch of it mine.

I *liked* it.

On that thought, I heard the back door close heralding Edwina's departure (further heralded by her calling out "good-bye"), and I came back to the room.

"Time for your lesson, pet."

I looked at Lucien in time for him to take my hand. He pulled me off the stool and walked me to the comfy seating area. With me standing in front of him, he sat on the big fluffy couch then grabbed my hips, pulling me off my feet. He fell to the side, twisted to his back with me on top, partially falling off his side, my back to the back of the couch.

Why we needed to be lying pressed together on the couch for my lesson, I didn't know.

Obedient Leah also didn't ask, even though she wanted to.

I just looked at him expectantly like whatever wisdom he was about to share would soothe my savaged soul.

His eyes roamed my face.

Then he whispered, "You're adorable."

Not that again. I was *trying* to be annoying. It just wasn't working.

"My lesson?" I prompted.

He smiled.

My heart skipped another beat.

His smile grew arrogant.

With effort I contained my frustrated growl.

He burst out laughing, his arms closed around me, and he hugged me close.

"Are we going to hug or are you going to teach me vampire knowledge?" I asked, trying not to sound as annoyed as I was.

"We're going to do both," he replied, his arms loosening but not letting go.

Whatever.

I lifted my head again and looked at him. His eyes caught mine.

"Feeding," he started and my ears perked up because I was interested in spite of myself. "Do you remember the other night when I kissed you and your mouth tingled?"

I nodded.

"That was the anesthesia," he explained. "It releases when my body prepares to feed. If I'd kissed you harder, longer, more frequently, your mouth would have gone numb."

I didn't like the sound of that. He was a good kisser and if my mouth was numb I'd miss all the fun.

He kept talking. "Also, when my body prepares to feed, the healing properties in my saliva release. They permeate your skin when I prepare it for the wound and they infiltrate the wound while I'm feeding so it's healing even as I feed."

As with all things vampire, this made sense so I nodded again.

Lucien continued, "Those healing properties stay in your bloodstream. They help your blood regenerate. Even after your first bloodletting, they were working. No mortal could have lost that much blood without a transfusion, but after a couple of days rest, you were back to normal. The longer I feed, the more healing agents are released into your bloodstream, the quicker you recover. In a week, I can feed once a day. In two, I can feed more than once a day. In three weeks, I can feed whenever I like."

This also made sense.

However, I was stuck on the idea of him feeding whenever he liked.

"How much do you need to feed?" I asked.

"The same as anyone. Three times a day."

I felt my eyes grow wide and my lips part. Through my shock, I also saw his gaze scan my face, and for some reason, his face gentled when he caught sight of my expression.

"Food, the food you eat, gives me nourishment," he went on to explain. "Just as it does for you, and my body needs it, just as yours does. However, the nutrients in mortal's food aren't near enough to sustain my body's energy, to keep it functioning. Therefore, I need something more."

"But you're feeding every other day," I whispered.

"Yes."

"Are you saying that, right now, you're fasting for more than a day?"

"Yes."

Oh my God!

I'd tried fasting when I was on some crazy diet years ago. I couldn't last until dinner. I couldn't imagine going for more than a day!

"Are you hungry?" I asked.

"Not as much as when I fasted for a week, but yes, I am."

I couldn't believe this. "I don't understand. Why would the rules do this to vampires when they change concubines?"

"The rules only state I can't feed between the release of one and the initiation of another. Once you're initiated, I'm free to attend Feasts."

I felt my stomach twist at the idea of Lucien going to a Feast. Feeding on some random mortal. Touching her. Making her feel what he made me feel. Giving her what he gave me (before he took it away).

But last night at The Feast, he didn't feed.

I swallowed hard before asking, "Are you going to Feasts, um, in between—?"

"Normally, I would, however, with you I haven't."

"Why?"

His arms gave me a squeeze. "If you taste the finest wine, Leah, you want another glass, and if it takes a while to get it you're content to wait. You don't switch to lemonade no matter how sweet that lemonade might be or how thirsty you may get."

It was the weirdest compliment I'd ever been given.

It was also, somehow, the most profound.

I really didn't know how to respond, so I said, "Oh."

His hand slid up my back and started to play with my hair. "There's more."

I tilted my head to the side, trying not to dislodge his hand from my hair. I knew I shouldn't like him playing with my hair, but I did.

He went on, "As time passes and the healing properties stay in your bloodstream, they do other things to you as well."

I felt my body tense. "Like what?"

"It takes a while, years, but they'll start regenerating your body, your organs, your skin, your hair, everything. They help you fight off infection. They help any injury you should sustain to heal swiftly. They even ward off disease. It's more but, to put it simply, in essence, you'll be aging backward."

At his words, I gasped.

Finally, a bonus for being a concubine!

"You're joking," I breathed but I hoped he wasn't.

"No. For it to happen, a vampire has to keep his concubine for some time and feed regularly. It takes at least a year before this process begins, sometimes two or even three." His eyes locked on mine and he asked, "Didn't you ever wonder why your mother and aunts look so much younger than they really are?"

I just thought it was the strict skincare regime they forced on my sister and me and all the cousins. I had no idea it was vampire saliva regeneration.

How weird.

How cool!

He must have read my face because he chuckled. "I see you like that."

I couldn't hide my exuberant response. "What's not to like?"

His chuckle stopped but his handsome grin stayed in place as his hand twisted possessively in my hair.

"Nothing. There's absolutely nothing not to like," he murmured.

I didn't know for certain what he was referring to, but I felt it essential to stay on target. I was liking this lesson, liking it a lot.

"How much age will I lose?"

"That depends on how long our Arrangement lasts, how much I feed. It's important to note the healing heals. It doesn't start a regression to childhood. It doesn't undo growth or mental capacity. You'll lose years of cell and organ aging, maybe more. But you'll always be an adult."

This was getting better and better. I didn't exactly want to go back to my teen years. They sucked enough the first time.

He slid out from under me and to his side so we were face to face. I caught his expression and it had grown serious.

"Before The Revolution," he paused and asked, "Did you at least learn about The Revolution before you were expelled?"

I had. The Vampire Revolution was where this concubine business, and the rules and laws that governed vampires, all started, which was pretty much where the Vampire Studies syllabus started.

In a nutshell, in 1665 the vampires revolted in a bloody, year-long (and then some) battle which was almost fully contained in London. History knew it as The Great Plague which was a story Parliament, King Charles II and The Vampire Dominion agreed would be spread. It was, instead, vampires fighting their own, an offshoot vampire sect who had allied themselves with mortals. I was fuzzy on the details of *why* the vampires revolted, but they did and it wasn't a pretty scene.

The offshoot sect won.

The Great Fire of London didn't herald the end of the plague. It was an enormous vampire execution that got out of hand and burned down a lot of London. It also heralded the official end of The Vampire Revolution and the beginning of the Terms of Agreement between Immortal and Mortal.

"Yes," I answered Lucien's question.

He pulled me closer and his voice dipped lower. "Before The Revolution, it wasn't unusual for vampires to take mortal mates."

This was shocking news as another thing I'd caught in the moments I paid attention in class was that vampires mated—as in pledged their troth—with vampires, period, dot, the end. Not mortals. Never.

"Really?" I asked.

"Yes."

"How did that work, considering vampires are immortal? I mean, it would stink to be forever young and your partner..." I trailed off and my eyes grew wide.

He noticed my dawning comprehension and pulled me even closer. "That's right, Leah. Back then, it wasn't unusual for vampires to keep their mortal mates alive for centuries. The healing is strong, and if constant, meant a vastly elongated life for the mortal, even going so far as making a mortal *immortal* should it have continued indefinitely. If feeding ceased, it would take years before the properties were fully expunged from the mortal's system. They wouldn't age for some time. Once they did, their normal aging process would begin again as usual."

"Oh my God," I whispered, overwhelmed by this stunning news.

Lucien ignored my reaction and kept with his lesson. "After The Revolution, the Immortal and Mortal Agreement prohibited inter-cultural unions. All vampires who had them where ordered to release their mortal mates."

I stared at him in renewed, now horrified, astonishment.

I couldn't believe it. I couldn't imagine being with someone, maybe for centuries, and all of a sudden being forced to part.

Something about this made tears sting my eyes. "That's terrible."

"It was," he murmured, his tone stating eloquently that he agreed. "It also didn't go over very well. All of them refused. Thus began The Hunt, which is an ugly piece of our history they don't teach you in class."

I didn't think I wanted to know.

Lucien told me anyway. "All vampires and their mortal mates were hunted. Every last one. When caught, they were tortured until they denounced the relationship. If they didn't, which was most often the case, they were executed."

I couldn't process this. It was too hideous.

"Both of them?" I breathed.

He shook his head, but answered, "Sometimes, yes. Sometimes it was just the vampire, other times, it was the mortal."

The tears in my eyes clogged my throat and I forced them down in a painful swallow.

Lucien continued, "It has served for centuries as a powerful lesson to any vampire who might wish to cross that line."

As it would!

"I don't like this lesson," I whispered.

"It isn't a nice lesson, pet," he agreed.

"I don't understand why they did that," I returned hotly. "Why would they do that?"

"Survival of the species, both mine and yours. We can't survive without you. And a vampire and mortal cannot procreate. Further, at the time, vampires hunted for their food. Mortals were prey, literally, and vampires were feared greatly. For millennia, vampires lived underground, not out in the open, many mortals didn't even believe in us. We were considered unreal monsters, too vile to allow the fragile mortal mind to believe existed. It was in a time where many fed without stopping, leaving their victims dead, so there was a great deal to fear. We were largely nocturnal. We were entirely predators and most were highly content with this life."

Okay, it was safe to say he was freaking me out.

He either didn't notice or didn't care because he continued.

"Then there was a shift of sensibilities that led to The Revolution. There were vampires who were growing tired of living in the shadows, saw the advantages of eternal life and wished to exploit them. Those vampires over the centuries acquired great wealth, sophistication and started to move within the mortal world. They became vastly more civilized than the predatory vampire, even going so far as having what are now concubines, without contracts of course and without the limit of one at a time. Many of those vampires had several concubines, sometimes dozens."

"Is *this* covered in class?" I interrupted and Lucien shook his head in answer to my question and kept telling his story.

"Other vampires preferred their life as hunters and felt this growing section of our culture who wished for something more was threatening their way of life. And they were correct. This was the reason for The Revolution. The vampires who wished more from life allied themselves with mortals and fought the predatory vampires. The Union of Vampires and Mortals, the one that orchestrated the Agreement after The Revolution, felt there needed to be strictures governing the interaction between our cultures. Their intentions were sound, even just. The priority was to protect our prey and protect our species by facilitating Vampire Claimings, or in mortal terms, marriage. Even vampires don't often procreate, it's difficult but it's impossible with a mortal. For our species to thrive, they thrust these edicts on us."

I had a million questions. Maybe even a million and two.

As was necessary, I started with one.

"Why do you need to procreate when you don't die?"

"We die. Sometimes accidentally, a house fire, for example. But usually, it's suicide. Eternal life isn't for everyone." I sucked in a shocked breath and Lucien continued softly, "It's an honorable death, Leah. Not frowned upon in any way. Eternal life can get trying."

I nodded because that, too, made a weird kind of sense.

He kept going. "Then there are the executions for those who break the rules, mostly if they hunt. This doesn't happen often. And lastly, there are the rights vampires have against their own. For instance, if a concubine is misused by another vampire, her vampire can exact retribution, which can come in the form of assassination."

I knew that last already. Stephanie told me, including the fact that Lucien had conducted two such assassinations himself.

Something occurred to me then. Something I knew but hadn't thought about. Something that made me feel like my blood had turned to hot lava, an intensely uncomfortable sensation.

I didn't want to ask, I really didn't, but I found myself doing it anyway.

"Do you and your, er..." I tried not to choke on the word and luckily succeeded, "mate have any children?"

For some reason, I hated thinking about him having a mate. Essentially a wife somewhere out there staking claim to him on a level I would never have. Why I felt this way, I had no clue and it scared me most of all.

He shook his head but I didn't feel relief. His next words, spoken so casually they were careless, cemented this feeling further.

"Not with Katrina, no. From two separate unions long ago, I created a son, Julian, and a daughter, Isobel, both live in England."

Oh my God!

Lucien was a father.

I couldn't wrap my head around that concept at all.

My eyes shifted away from him when I queried, "Do you talk to them?"

"Frequently."

I kept my eyes averted. "Are you close?"

"Very."

"Do you, um...keep in touch with their mothers?"

Why was I asking these questions?

He didn't hesitate with his reply. "Isobel's mother took her life thirty years ago."

My eyes snapped back to his face but there was no expression there, no sadness or remorse.

He continued, "I still speak with, and sometimes see, Cressida, Julian's mother."

I didn't want to be talking about this anymore. And in hopes of ending the discussion and my lesson, which had started out great but took a turn for the worse, I asked no further questions and simply said, "Okay."

For a moment, Lucien examined my face.

Then he asked quietly, "Have you had enough, pet?"

I'd had enough.

Boy, had I had enough.

I nodded.

"Do you have any questions?" he offered and I shook my head.

This was a lie. I still had a million questions, none of which I wanted answers to at that moment. The top of the list was the existence of *Katrina*. Who she was. Where she was. What she thought about me. How long they'd been together and why Lucien was in my bed at night, his clothes in my dressing room, his body lying with me at this very moment on the couch he provided for me.

Though I knew I *definitely* didn't want the answer to any of *that*.

As I was sorting through this new mess in my brain, his head lifted and his face disappeared in my neck. "All right, sweetheart. Lesson over."

I shivered mainly because his deep voice sounded against the sensitive skin of my neck and that felt nice. Also because, after he stopped speaking, his tongue tasted me there and that felt nicer. Finally because he called me "sweetheart" and I liked it when he did that.

In an effort at self-preservation, to end my body's betraying response and in an attempt to take some control of the situation, I asked, "Can I get dressed?"

"No."

I blinked.

"No?" I queried and my voice sounded breathy.

His mouth traveled up my neck, over my jaw to meet my lips.

"No. I've decided you'll be naked most of today."

What? my mind screamed.

"What?" my mouth whispered.

I felt his smile against my lips. "You'll be naked. Obviously you've learned your lesson and decided to mind me. That deserves a reward." His voice dipped lower when he informed me, "And I'm going to spend all day giving you that reward."

Oh my God.

Now what had I done?

The game I'd instigated had taken a nasty turn. And this was because he played it far better than me.

Damn the vampire!

"Lucien..." I started but his hand hit my bare thigh, roving upwards under my robe to cup my bottom.

He interrupted my concentration on the movement of his hand by demanding, "Kiss me, pet."

"Kiss you?" I whispered.

"I want your tongue in my mouth."

Oh my *God*.

"Lucien—" I started again, but he cut me off.

"You intend to disobey me?" His tone sounded like a gentle threat or possibly a challenge.

What did I do now?

My choices were to be Obedient Leah and kiss him or be Real Leah and likely get punishment.

I was screwed!

"Can we—?" I began yet again only to be interrupted again.

"Kiss me, Leah."

"Just give me two—"

His hand pressed my hips against his and I could feel he was hard. My body registered that I liked it that he was hard, that I could make him hard just by lying beside him and talking.

That may have been what my body registered but my mind registered complete and utter fear.

I watched his eyes grow dark and intense.

Then he growled, "Do what I say or—"

I cut *him* off this time and kissed him.

The minute my tongue touched his, per usual, I wondered why I'd struggled against it. Both our heads slanted to opposite sides. Our tongues dueled, both fighting for supremacy, taking, taking, taking, so hungry, at the same time giving so much I felt my body consumed with the gift of his kiss.

It was glorious.

My back arched, pressing my torso into his, seeking maximum contact, but he pulled away. His hand moving between us, he yanked at the tie on my robe, shifting it aside. His hand slid across my waist, up my back, pressing in, my sensitive naked torso flattened against his massive, hard, tee-covered chest.

It felt *great*.

His mouth broke from mine and he demanded in a husky voice, "Wrap your leg around my waist. I want to smell you."

His demand caused my belly to dip and a rush of heat to surge between my legs.

I did as I was told, biting my lip, feeling both desire and embarrassment all of this mingled with fear, of him, of what we were doing, of what it meant that I responded to him so strongly even though I despised him so thoroughly.

When my calf curled around his ass, his eyes grew unfocused.

"Fucking hell," he muttered and his gaze caught mine, still fogged. "I can't wait to have my mouth on you, to have the taste of you on my tongue, to have that scent take over my world."

That was the second weirdest, yet most profound, compliment I'd ever had.

I had no time to let it sink in. He was kissing me, harder, more demanding, more beautiful than the last.

His hands moved on me, mine moved on him, yanking up his tee so they could move skin against skin.

His body felt amazing beneath my touch. Hard, silken, strong, massive, defined.

His mouth tore from mine but his lips slid down my cheek, scoring a delicious path over my jaw, neck, down, making me tremble.

"Offer your breast to me," he ordered, mouth at my chest, and I was so deep in my own sensual fog, his question confused me.

"Sorry?"

His lips moved away and he pulled up, his eyes locking with mine.

"I want you to offer me your breast."

His command sliced through my arousal. I didn't know what he meant. Was he going to feed on me there like I'd seen the vampire do last night? Or was he going to do something else?

Both of which I wanted. Both of which terrified me.

I swallowed.

His eyes scanned my face before he asked softly, "What's this?"

I stared at him and it hit me that he looked strangely hopeful.

"Maybe this is going a little fast for me," I tried.

And failed.

His expression shifted, not angry or impatient, but pleased. Very pleased. Even, if it could be credited, relieved.

And stimulated. Or, *more* stimulated.

"You deny me?" he whispered sounding like he hoped I did.

"Um..."

"Offer me your breast, Leah," he repeated.

"Er..."

"Cup it in your hand and offer it to me."

"Couldn't we just, you know, carry on like before, natural-like?" I suggested.

He shook his head and his arms stole around me, tensing fiercely, crushing me to him.

"Today, if it takes all day, if it takes into tomorrow, if it takes the next month, you'll learn to submit to me. You'll learn to give me what I want when I ask for it. You'll learn to offer me what I desire when I demand it. You'll learn to beg me for your own release when I require it."

I felt my temper rise. Really, he was *such* a jerk.

"I don't think—"

"Give me your breast, pet."

"Lucien, seriously."

"*Do it!*" he snarled, his voice turning dangerous, his patience waning.

Obedient Leah evaporated and Real Leah glared.

"You want it, take it! I'm not giving you *anything,*" I snarled back.

He rolled into me, his massive weight crushing me to the couch, and for some unhinged reason, regardless of the fact we were locked in our usual battle, I found I was wrong about his patience waning.

It had been a test. A test I failed. A battle he won.

And he looked triumphant.

"I was hoping you'd say that," he muttered.

Great!

Then it began, my punishment for disobeying—his hands on me, his mouth on me everywhere, hard, hot, ravenous, demanding my response and getting it in spades.

He lit me on fire. I fought it but I didn't win. My defenses were puny and they collapsed within minutes.

I pulled up his tee and he took over, arching away from me, tearing it over his head and tossing it aside. With all his delicious skin exposed, a craving so intense it felt like it would shatter me tore through my system. My mouth sought anywhere it could touch, taste, lick, bite, suck, and I liked the way he tasted.

No, I *adored* it.

When we kissed again, my fingers curled into his hair, holding him to me like I'd never let him go.

He broke our kiss and his mouth traveled the length of me, pushing the robe wide, exposing me to him, and I didn't try to hide. I kept my fingers in his hair as he explored, tempting, pressing for a reaction, taking it when it happened but not giving that first thing back. He blew against my nipples; they hardened, peaking with a beautiful pain. His tongue swept along my skin, under the swells of my breasts, across my midriff, circling my belly button, lower, until it teased the edge of my black lace panties.

Then his mouth was on me between my legs, sucking for an instant, hot and hard, over my panties.

The pleasure seared through me, rocking me to my soul, and my hips surged upwards, an instinctive demand for more.

His mouth disappeared and all of a sudden his body was on mine again, his lips against my mouth, the flavor of me a hint on his.

"You want my mouth between your legs?" he growled, even his voice, rough with desire, trilled through my system, making me squirm.

I did. I wanted his mouth between my legs. I wanted *him* inside me, his tongue or anything else he choose to put there.

I didn't answer, instead I panted against his mouth.

"Do you want me?" he pushed.

"Lucien—" My voice was a breathy plea for release.

"Beg me," he demanded.

It would be so easy to give up, to give in, to take what I wanted knowing it would be—by far—the best I ever had. It would be so easy to humble myself and deal with the consequences later.

But I couldn't. If I did, I knew I'd lose myself, all that was me. The mass of bad traits, stubbornness, impatience and sometimes fumbling idiocy, and all the good traits too, my loyalty, sense of humor and compassion. I wouldn't hold on to me anymore. I would be giving it to him and I didn't trust him to take care of it.

And I knew that even if he kept it safe, he wouldn't keep it long. He'd release me as he did Cecile and countless other concubines. By then, everything I was would be gone. He'd retain it for centuries, likely uncaring he held such a precious gift, but for me, all would be lost.

Instead of explaining any of that, or giving him the demand he asked for, I gave him another kind of entreaty. "Don't make me do that."

His face grew hard. "I have eternity, pet, to teach you this lesson."

"You won't last that long. You'll give up," I told him, my body still burning for his touch, wriggling underneath him.

At my words, he looked a mixture of amused and surprised.

His head cocked to the side and he asked, "Do you think that's true?"

I nodded, being honest for once. "You're a vampire but you're also a man. You'll need to get it elsewhere and you will. Eventually you'll tire of me."

He grinned and I didn't like it. It was his smug grin and I reckoned it foretold very bad things for me.

I wasn't wrong.

"Oh, I won't tire of you, Leah. But, you're right. If you force me, I will indeed get it elsewhere."

At the thought of him getting anything elsewhere, a different kind of heat slashed through me, washing away my desire in a wave of pain. This was unexpected, not only the reaction, but the excruciating intensity of it.

Before the razor-sharp edge of this sensation could subside, his head snapped up. He drew in a deep breath through his nostrils and his eyes narrowed, focusing on something but not me, not something close.

I sensed the danger instantly.

Our current situation forgotten, I whispered, "Lucien, something's wrong."

His eyes locked on mine.

For some reason communicating nonverbally, he replied straight into my brain, *Yes, pet.*

Without further reply, his body knifed off mine and he moved away. He was holding himself tense, his powerful musculature standing out, more defined. The way he held his body was menacing, even sinister. I could sense he wanted to move with vampire speed but was forcing himself to go slowly.

I heaved myself up and followed him, closing my robe, tying it tightly. The doorbell rang, but he was already pulling the door open as the bell sounded. I stopped five feet away.

A woman stood there. Gleaming black hair, ice-blue eyes, her beauty so extraordinary, her sexuality so explicit, I couldn't stop myself from sucking in a stunned breath at the sight of her.

This was a mistake.

When I gasped, her eyes, which were fastened on Lucien, sliced to me.

She, too, pulled in breath through her nostrils.

In an instant, her face contorted with primal rage.

In the next instant, she attacked.

Her target?

Me.

10
The Confrontations

She flew at me and when I say that I mean it literally.

She was a streak, a blur, my mortal eyes couldn't make out the lines of her body.

She didn't get close.

Three feet away from me, she came into definition.

This was because she was halted, Lucien's arm around her waist.

Then Lucien twisted, executing a near-blur, full-on, powerful hurl that would have been awe-inspiring if it hadn't been so freaking scary. She was a streak again, going backwards with tremendous velocity until she slammed against the wall. The plaster behind her buckled in a body-like shape, white dust and paint chips raining down around her as she fell to a graceful crouch, completely unharmed.

Her head snapped back, her seething eyes pinned on me. With only a moment's delay, she sprang toward me again in another blurry attack. And again she was stopped, this time when she was, her whole body still swayed toward me.

Her whole body, that was, except her head and her neck.

Lucien had her by her throat. Just one hand at her throat, the muscles in his arm and back bunching as he took two steps and slammed her against another wall, more plaster breaking, more debris falling.

Lucien got close to her and I saw his fingers squeeze.

"You just made a fatal mistake, Katrina," he gritted from between clenched teeth.

His fury matched hers, maybe surpassed it. I knew this because his jaw was working so hard a muscle leapt there.

I stood frozen, not only from what I just witnessed, but that I was just almost attacked by what amounted to Lucien's wife.

His wife!

And she was stunning. She was the most beautiful creature I'd ever seen. I had to admit that even if she wanted to tear me limb from limb.

Her incensed gaze slid from me to Lucien.

"You've fucked her. I can smell it." Her voice was deep, throaty, seductive. It wasn't throaty because her husband held her by the throat, but just because it was.

"I haven't fucked her," Lucien replied truthfully and I thanked God at that moment that it was, indeed, the truth. Then, presenting more evidence he was the demented sort of vampire, Lucien finished with, "Yet."

Her fisted hands slammed into the walls at her sides, breaking clean through the drywall before her body started thrashing wildly to gain release.

In a delayed effort of self-preservation, I took several hasty steps back.

Settle, pet. I'll not let her hurt you. You're safe. Lucien's voice sounded in my head and it was just his voice, not a command, my body was at my will.

Even so, I stopped moving.

Suddenly, Katrina tensed from the top of her head to her toes. She tilted her head back and let out a wild screech that hurt my ears and felt like it even shook the windows.

After she was done, her eyes sliced to me.

"*I'm going to kill her,*" she screamed.

My body grew tense but I stayed still.

Lucien's voice was a snarl. "You touch her, fuck, Rina, after this you even *look* at her, you'll fucking *burn.*"

Her gaze moved to Lucien and she changed her threat. "Then I'm going to kill *you.*"

Instantly, to my shock and despair, he dropped her and stepped back. His hands went out to his sides and he issued a one word invitation.

"Try."

A roar of fury tore from her throat and she lunged.

That was pretty much all I saw with any clarity.

They were too fast, too powerful, all their movement was a blur. Every once in a while Lucien would pin her and they'd come into focus but she'd escape and their movements would become indistinct.

The table in the hall was turned over, the vase on it shattering into pieces, those pieces kicked wildly about as they moved.

I took two more steps back, these up the stairs, when I heard Lucien again in my brain, *Still, pet.*

I stilled. I didn't want to. I didn't even know *why* I did. I just did.

Even though I didn't see it, I knew it was brutal, savage even. The noises they made, her grunts of pain and effort, Lucien's grunts solely of effort, the sounds of fists against flesh, the noise of bodies colliding, all of this slashed through the air.

I had felt a great deal of fear in the last few weeks but I'd never been so terrified in all my life than I was at that moment.

This was because I was witnessing something extraordinarily vicious.

This was also because I was witnessing, no matter how indistinct, Lucien beating *the shit* out of his wife.

If he ever got physical with me in that way he'd kill me in seconds.

My body started trembling and I wanted to run, I really did, but my fear rooted me to the spot.

Finally, Katrina came into focus, her body slamming against the door making its heavy, solidness shake.

She stopped, as did Lucien facing her, but slightly turned to the side. I could see bloody, angry scratch marks marring his chest and neck.

She was far worse for the wear, her nose bleeding profusely, her lip cut, angry red marks at her neck and wrists.

At the sight of what Lucien had done to her, a violent tremor shook through my body nearly bringing me to my knees.

"I got the Severance papers this morning," she spat at him as she wiped the back of her hand under her nose, smearing the blood across her face.

Her words confused me.

"You don't say?" he retorted carelessly.

Her face twisted with rage. "You'd throw me away for *a mortal?*"

My astonished, frightened eyes moved to Lucien.

"Look at her, Rina, she's no mere mortal," Lucien clipped.

Katrina didn't look at me, instead she snapped, "Yes, I forgot. She's *life.*"

What did that mean?

Any of it!

Lucien took an ominous step closer to her and I watched her quail, her bravado slipping. She'd learned her lesson far faster than any he'd ever taught me.

"I lost you the minute you laid eyes on her," she accused, her voice turning small.

"You lost me two seconds after The Claiming and you know it," he returned sharply. She flinched because clearly, whatever the hell that meant, she did know it.

I flinched for her. It was hard not to feel sorry for her. She wasn't pathetic, she was just broken.

Her gaze shifted to me and it narrowed.

"Are you enjoying this?" she asked, her voice dripping with sarcasm.

It was safe to say I was *not.*

I was saved from having to reply when Lucien gritted out, "Look at me, Rina, don't look at Leah. She no longer exists for you." When she didn't obey immediately, he thundered, *"Fucking look at me!"*

She did, so did I, *anyone* would.

"Keep her safe, Lucien," she whispered, her tone disturbing, so disturbing it sent a chill straight through me.

"You touch her, you'll burn." Lucien's voice was just as disturbing, more so.

I didn't know Katrina, her threat could be empty. I knew Lucien, his threat was not.

"Yes, but you don't get it, Lucien. I'll be happy to burn because while I burn I'll know you'll be facing eternity without your precious *life.*"

Lucien's body tensed the way it had done earlier, his muscles coming into sharp relief, menacing, sinister.

I held my breath. Then I heard the back door open.

"Yoo hoo!" Edwina called. "There's a car in the drive! Do we have...oh!"

Edwina stopped speaking. The back door had a direct shot to the front door down a wide hall off of which four rooms led. Edwina couldn't see me but she could likely see Lucien and Katrina. And you didn't have to have extra sensory perception to feel the crackling animosity in the air, not to mention Katrina's face was a bloody mess.

"You backed a losing horse, Edwina," Katrina called apropos of absolutely nothing. "Everyone knows about Leah. He kissed her at the bar at a fucking *Feast* for all the world to fucking *see.*"

This too confused me and I heard Edwina's shocked gasp from not too far away so I knew it surprised her, which confused me all the more.

"The Council will investigate," Katrina went on and I saw Edwina come into my vision at the side of the stairs.

Her face was pale.

"Investigate?" Edwina asked the question on the tip of my tongue.

"You know they will," Katrina stated, her eyes sliding to Lucien. "I'll make sure of it."

Lucien was standing with his arms crossed on his chest like he was watching a vaguely annoying street performer who had roped him into his routine.

"Another threat," he drawled derisively.

"I'll call them from your fucking driveway. You're kissing her at Feasts. You've moved in with her. You intend to—" Katrina retorted and Lucien cut her off.

"Be my guest," he invited and Katrina's eyes went wide then they swung to me.

"You've lost your mind," she breathed toward me, even though she was talking to Lucien. Her gaze moving back, she studied him a moment and all of a sudden her lip curled. "Though I shouldn't be surprised. You've always had a taste for sweet smelling pussy."

I gasped. Edwina gasped. Lucien moved.

He crowded her back into the door, his powerful frame cutting her off from view.

I looked nervously at Edwina. Edwina looked nervously at me. Then she gave me a shaky smile, which I did *not* return, and we both looked back at the scene.

"The Council will grant me this," Lucien was saying.

"Never," Katrina returned.

"I'm calling in my marker," Lucien announced.

I heard Katrina's sharp intake of breath. I looked to Edwina who was staring fixedly at Lucien's back, her face the picture of shock, and I knew at least she knew what this meant.

I had no idea what was going on. None of it.

"They'll still not allow it." Katrina didn't sound so sure now.

"They owe me," Lucien retorted.

"They do, but a mortal?" Katrina shot back. "They won't even consider it. Not even for you."

"They've no choice," Lucien stated.

There was a hesitation then softly, with some kind of weird understanding in her voice, Katrina said, "I've heard of this but didn't expect it of you. Her scent has driven you insane."

Lucien didn't hesitate with his reply. "If that's the case, I'm happy in my insanity."

That was the third weirdest, yet most profound, compliment I had that day, even though I had no idea what was going on. I also had the distinct feeling I wanted no more compliments from the Mighty Vampire Lucien who'd beat the crap out of his wife in his concubine's foyer while insisting said concubine watch.

"You want war," Katrina whispered.

"I want my life back," Lucien replied. "If to get it that means war then I want war."

Um...

War?

"I'll not fight on your side," she informed him, the bravado back in her voice, her words a challenge.

"I never expected you would," Lucien returned.

I couldn't see all of her but I saw parts of her body twitch as if she'd been struck.

"You don't think much of me, do you?" she asked.

"I haven't for the last thirty years," he replied with frank cruelty.

She stepped out from in front of him and I could see her now. Her eyes looked to me then back to Lucien.

"I'm beginning to feel sorry for her," Katrina commented.

"You shouldn't. She's everything you're not," Lucien responded.

That hurt. I could see it in her flinch and I felt her pain. Any woman would.

He was harsh and he was heartless, and honest to goodness, I never thought I could hate him any more, but I did at that moment. It was lunacy, his wife had tried to do me bodily harm, but I felt for her. I couldn't help it.

"What did I do to make you hate me so much?" she whispered.

"You, like all of them, tried to cage me. I can't abide that, Rina, you knew it. You knew how I felt about it and you did it all the same."

"I loved you." She was still whispering.

Even at her soft words, Lucien remained remote. "Love is a blanket that keeps you warm, not one that traps and suffocates you. You never learned that lesson, Rina. You never paid it any attention no matter how many times I explained. You kept pulling that blanket over my head."

Silently, she assumed the posture of defeat and it was so heart-breaking, my eyes swung to Lucien, thinking he'd relent.

He didn't. In fact, as he took her in, his lip curled in a contemptuous sneer.

My heart started beating faster. I didn't know why, hatred, fear for my future life as this man was going to factor largely in it, or both.

He heard my heart. I knew this because his eyes cut to me, his face lost its disdain and his brows drew together in puzzlement.

"Edwina," Katrina said in a soft farewell and I tore my gaze from Lucien, but before I could focus or Edwina could respond, Katrina was gone.

"See to the groceries," Lucien ordered Edwina. I looked back to him to see him striding with purpose toward me.

I started backing up the steps.

"Clean up this mess," Lucien continued his instructions, his gait wide and determined, and I started backing up double time. "You don't need to say good-bye when you leave," Lucien finished his commands to Edwina.

At those ominous words, I turned on the landing and ran.

In a second, I was cradled in his arms and in the next we were in the bedroom and I was bouncing on the bed.

Lucien was looming over me, fists to his hips, eyes dark and glittering.

"You run from me?" His voice was dangerous.

I felt my fear escalate at a slightly lower rate than my temper flared.

"Down there, I trusted you." Those five words were an accusation.

His head cocked to the side. "And how, exactly, did I betray that trust, pet?"

"You told me to stay," I informed him.

"Yes?"

"I stayed."

"And?"

"You can't possibly need me to explain!" I snapped.

"I'm afraid I do," he clipped back.

I got to my knees, hands balled into fists at my sides, and I leaned toward him.

"You just beat your wife in front of me!" I shouted.

"It wasn't the first time, but fortunately, it was the last," he replied indifferently.

I drew in a sharp breath, reared back in horror and fell to my bottom.

"You disgust me," I hissed, meaning every word.

His body did that thing again, that menacing sinister change where his muscles came into sharp relief.

"I disgust you?" he whispered.

I ignored his stance even though he had to know my fear. My heart was beating so wildly I could, indeed, actually hear it.

If I could, he certainly could.

"Yes," I retorted with more bravery than sense.

"You don't have any fucking idea what you just witnessed." His voice was still a low outraged whisper.

"I do and it was nauseating."

All of a sudden his rage filled the room, clogging my throat, expanding my lungs, and he was leaning over me, his fists in the bed beside my hips.

I scrambled backwards up the bed.

He followed, faster, crawling along with my body.

My head hit the headboard and he retreated, only far enough to rise up, using my legs to yank me back down the bed between his thighs and then he settled his heavy weight on me.

"You've demonstrated another appalling trait, pet." He was still using his scary whisper.

"And what's this one?" I shot back. "I thought you'd seen them all."

"You're quick to judge, not even asking that first fucking question," he retorted.

"And how could you explain bloodying your wife's nose in front of your supposed to be lover? Hunh? How about humiliating her in the same company? How about wanting a lover at all when you have *a wife.*" I made a snorting noise that was slightly embarrassing but I was too furious to care. "I shouldn't be surprised. You've forced me to humble myself more than once. Why I trusted you and didn't run so I wasn't forced to witness that I...will...*never...know.*"

His body went solid and his eyes bored into mine. This lasted what felt like an eternity.

Then he pulled in a breath sharply through his nose.

When he was done, I sensed the patience he was seeking eluded him.

I wasn't wrong.

"I've risked everything for you," he told me quietly.

"Your marriage?" My voice was dripping acid. "It didn't seem you prized that overly much."

It was like I didn't even speak.

"Everything," he repeated. "And what do I get in return?"

It was beginning to dawn on me that I was in a very bad situation.

Firstly, Lucien could and did in a fury beat the crap out of his wife. Secondly, if he did that to me, I wouldn't survive. Thirdly, for whatever reason, he was angry. No, he was infuriated. Beyond anything I'd ever experienced from anyone before in my life. And lastly, I couldn't fight him. I had absolutely no way to defend myself against anything he chose to inflict on me.

All the tissues in my body petrified as fear paralyzed me.

"That's the smartest response you've had today," Lucien informed me and I knew I was in trouble.

He grinned and it was not one of his handsome grins. This was a grin I'd never seen before.

It was ruthless.

His grin disappeared because his face disappeared in my neck.

"Listen to me now, Leah. I *will* break you. Do you understand me?" he vowed, his voice rumbling against my skin.

I didn't, but at the same time I did.

He continued, "And, right now, I'm taking a taste of what I'm risking everything for." His head came up and his face came close, so close I could feel his breath against my lips. "But don't worry, pet, you don't have to beg for it."

Oh no.

My body burst into a flurry of frenzied motion, a futile effort at escape.

I knew this would have no effect and it didn't.

My robe was gone in nary a second. My panties whisked down my legs in a blur of his arm. He spread my legs with his large hands and I opened my mouth to scream.

The scream died in my throat as his mouth touched me.

The sudden shock of his mouth moving on me killed my scream. His obvious talent subdued my struggles. He'd lived a long time and in that time he'd obviously learned *exactly* what to do between a woman's legs.

In fact, it was pretty clear he'd made an art of it.

In an instinctive reaction to the pleasure rippling through my system, my hips rose to meet his mouth.

He was not gentle. He was voracious. Lips, tongue, suction, he used it all. My fingers curled into the covers as my neck arched and moans of sheer pleasure purred from my throat.

His hands went up the back of my thighs to my knees and pushed them high, until they were at my sides.

This gave him better access which he utilized to his definite advantage.

I was close, so close, right there, and it was going to be beyond anything I'd ever experienced. Beyond anything *any* woman had ever experienced (unless she'd been with Lucien, obviously).

My hands went from the comforter to his head, holding him to me as I prepared to topple over the edge.

His mouth disappeared and I was yanked right back.

"*No!*" I cried as his big body settled on me and his strong hand cupped me between my legs, keeping me warm but exerting no pressure which was a cruel tease.

"Now, you beg, Leah," he said against my mouth.

With effort, my eyes focused on him and I screamed, *"I hate you!"*

He disappeared, but only for a moment, then his mouth was back at me. The advantage I'd gained over my body's reaction was lost in seconds. This time he teased as I fought my rising desire. When I lost, he made me go after it. He gave me enough to keep me squirming. And when my fingers clutched his hair in defeat, he gave me all of it again.

Then, right at the golden moment, he was up over me and covering me again.

"Beg," he demanded.

It took everything I had but I focused on him. "Go to hell!"

He rolled to his back taking me with him, pulling me up over his body. Spreading my legs, he settled me in a crouch on his mouth. Hands strong on my hips, he pulled me down and kept at me.

It was delicious. It was divine. It was ecstasy.

I grabbed the headboard and moaned deep in the back of my throat, no longer conscious of the sounds I was making. I rocked my hips against his mouth. He pulled down on them, going deeper, using his tongue in new and astounding ways. He took me there again, to that glorious place, and right before I felt it coming, he pulled me away from his mouth and yanked me down his body.

"Beg me for it, Leah." His voice was husky and near to a plea on its own.

He had an arm tight around my waist, fastening my squirming body to his. His other hand was working between our bodies but I was too much in a state to notice what he was doing. Every centimeter of my skin was sensitized beyond being bearable. I could even feel the air around us causing agonizing pleasure.

His hands went to the backs of my knees and jerked them up. I was straddling him and for one beautiful moment, I felt the hard hot tip of him enter me.

In triumph, I ground my hips down but he was faster than me. He caught me at my waist before I gained half an inch.

My head snapped up and my eyes flew to his.

"You want my cock inside you?" he asked, his voice hoarse.

I did. I wanted it more than oxygen.

I remained silent.

He inched up what felt like a millimeter and I felt my lids slowly close in rapture. Then he stopped and my eyes shot open.

"Beg me, pet," he whispered, his voice now tortured.

I had no voice so I shook my head.

"Beg me," he ordered harshly.

"No," I breathed.

"You want me," he stated.

I stared at him then I nodded.

"Then beg me."

Finding a strength inside me that *I* didn't even know was there, I pulled up against his hands, my body straining against my brain's demands and I couldn't believe it, he let me.

I felt the small but hard and thick and unbelievably magnificent piece of him that I had slide out of me.

It felt like I'd lost a piece of *me*, not him, when I pulled free.

Regardless, stubborn to the last (and now hating myself for it), my eyes locked on his, and I declared, "You won't break me."

His arms wrapped around me, crushing me to him, I was hoping in defeat so he'd give me what my body was aching for.

Instead, he rolled us to our sides, his arms still holding me close, and into the top of my hair, he said, "You've forced my hand, Leah."

Fear pierced through me because, without any attempt to hide it, his voice was filled with regret and I didn't know why. What was worse, even though I didn't know what he regretted, I had a feeling whatever it was it was something I'd regret more.

He kept talking. "I'm leaving and when I return, if I find you've touched yourself, you'll have a week of what you just had and you can beg me until you're hoarse to make me let you come, but I won't do it. Am I understood?"

"You're understood," I mumbled into his chest where he'd pressed my face.

He tensed as if to move and I didn't want him to go. Not because I forgot he disgusted and terrified me and I detested him, I only could forget those when his mouth was between my legs and other times besides, but because any movement made my body feel like it was going to shatter.

I felt his body relax right before he sighed.

Then he asked, "Why do you fight me, sweetheart?"

I didn't answer. To answer was to trust him with a piece of me, and after all that he'd done to me and what he'd done to his fucking *wife*, I knew he was not someone I could trust.

Ever.

No matter how gentle he could seem.

Like right now.

Or when he called me sweetheart. Or when he laughed like I was the funniest person he'd ever met in his centuries upon centuries of life.

He went on, "You must know it will be good."

Oh, I knew that.

I still didn't answer.

He sighed again before he murmured, "You don't understand."

No.

I.

Did.

Not.

And I didn't want to.

I still didn't speak.

"My pet, it'll be so much better when you submit to me. That, I can promise. Not just here, in bed, but all of it, everything that will be you and me. I promise you, Leah, I'm trying to give you something beautiful. I can't explain it, you have to feel it. But to feel it, you must trust me."

Fat chance of *that*.

I still didn't speak.

For a while, he didn't either.

Then, as if he wasn't talking to me (which he wasn't), he muttered, "I'm the one who wanted a challenge. I need to get my fucking head examined."

I didn't understand that either.

There was a lot that I didn't understand.

But I didn't ask.

And I was never going to. Never, never, *never*.

Gently, he pulled away from me. The loss of his hard warmth meant the cold hit my sensitive nudity like a slap. He adjusted his jeans and had me beneath the sheet in a blur of motion, faster than he'd been before even when he was being Speedy Vamp.

Obviously, he'd been holding out on me.

He pulled my hair away from my shoulder and I shoved my face in the pillow to escape his action, even though I allowed his touch.

"Stubborn," he murmured but I could swear there was pride mixed with the frustration in his voice.

And I didn't understand *that* either.

Then he was gone, but within five minutes he was back, this time dressed in a suit.

He sat on the edge of the bed and I glared up at him as he gazed down at me.

"It's been a long time that, on some level, I didn't look forward to attending a Feast," he informed me and my body grew rock solid.

He was going to a Feast.

Unbidden, unwanted, but undeniable anguish scorched through me, hot and biting.

He bent forward, brushing my cheek with his lips. "Have a good day, pet, and sleep well."

Oh my God!

He wasn't even coming home.

Even though my mind screamed, neither my mouth nor body moved.

He did. In an instant, he was gone.

I hate you, my brain whispered.

I heard you, sweetheart, he whispered back.

His endearment burned into me like a brand.

I know, I told him.

Stubborn, he told me.

I turned off my mind, turned my face in my pillow and put every effort into making absolutely certain I didn't cry.

After a long struggle, at last, I finally succeeded at something.

It was an empty victory.

II
The Betrayal

Lucien's eyes scanned the heaving dance floor and he saw her. Although he didn't often attend this particular Feast, he'd seen her before. Each time she'd enticed him, long dark-blonde hair, blue eyes, curvy body, alluring scent.

Tonight, she did especially as she was wearing a black dress almost like the one Leah had worn last night. Not the same quality, but close enough.

Everything about her was not the same quality, but close enough.

He knew she captured his attention because she reminded him of Leah. It had been the reason he'd never taken her. He was anticipating the real thing, not an oft-used imitation.

But tonight, she'd do.

Her eyes caught his and she smiled beguilingly, an open and eager invitation. It was clear she was his to do with as he wished, and this Feast, as he wished had very few boundaries.

He looked away, allowing his aversion to show.

Eager and willing were not what he wanted. Spirit, personality, passion, defiance, fear, challenge, those were what he wanted.

After centuries he finally had all of that, a great deal of it. It was just that he was finding it maddening to an extreme.

And excruciatingly frustrating.

Lucien attended Feasts often, even if he particularly liked the taste of his concubine, and it went without saying he particularly liked the taste of Leah. He was a vampire with a healthy appetite and Feasts allowed him diversity in that appetite.

However, over the last several centuries, he'd grown weary of them.

All the mortals who attended Feasts were registered with The Council. They were safe, healthy, willing, well-bred, from well-to-do families and their time was limited. They had two years to attend Feasts, any Feast they wanted, as many as they could attend before they were retired.

Fallen concubines were a different story. They came to Feasts, and out of respect for their legacy families, they were reluctantly allowed to attend but they weren't registered. However, The Council tracked them and after a few years the fallen concubines were eventually banned.

There were times when vampires had a taste at a Feast that they exceptionally enjoyed, one they didn't wish to share. If this was the case, they could petition The Council. If The Council found the mortal suitable, the family would be approached for recruitment. If accepted, that mortal could become the vampire's concubine. But also that new concubine's line would forever be in the life.

The mortal never refused. Every mortal there hoped to be claimed into the life, ensuring their own continued feeding and their line's future.

It rarely happened that a vampire made this petition but it was encouraged by The Council. More choice at Selections meant happier vampires.

The concubine lines detested it when this happened, more choice meant less opportunity for their own line to be chosen.

Surveying the crush of bodies in the room, Lucien couldn't imagine petitioning for such a mortal. Although he enjoyed Feasts on a variety of levels, most especially being with his brethren in a place where they could be who they were without hiding, without secrets, he didn't enjoy the mortals they drew. They were, for all practical purposes, whores without any money changing hands. He fed from them, naturally, but he'd never chosen from a line recruited from a Feast. The very idea of entering an Arrangement with such a mortal was repugnant.

This attitude, Stephanie told him, was alarmingly superior, but he didn't give a fuck.

To take his mind off the woman on the dance floor and his thoughts, he started to sip his martini and noticed the glass was drained. He turned away from his position facing the room to the bar, caught the bartender's attention and jerked up his chin. The bartender acknowledged his order and started to work on another martini, leaving the drinks he was preparing sitting on the counter unfinished.

Lucien looked at the three women whose drinks had gone wanting. Mortals. All looking at him. All smiling at him. All smiling the same smile the blonde had tossed him.

His eyes raked over them in revulsion and their smiles wavered, one went pale and turned away. Lucien did as well.

And his thoughts went instantly to Leah.

It had been difficult to shut her from his mind, but he had succeeded in doing so the last ten hours, mainly with work.

There were many vampires who amassed their fortunes and happily lived their eternities managing them and living off the interest.

Lucien was not such a vampire.

Unlike everything else in his life, his business never ceased to be a challenge. There was always a new mountain to be tried, tested and conquered. New inventions, new technologies, new strategies and more and more money to earn. If it hadn't been for that, he would have gone mad ages ago.

The bartender served his martini. Lucien paid for it, turning back unseeing to the room and allowing his thoughts to travel to Leah.

His fury had cooled considerably since their confrontation. Although, the thought of her declaration of him "disgusting" her still made him clench his teeth.

However Lucien had to admit that she didn't know male and female vampires were vastly different from her kind. Females were just as strong and skilled as males, many more so. For instance, Stephanie, who was known to be a fierce and cunning fighter.

He further had to admit there was no way for Leah to know the way of vampire mates. This would not even have been covered in Vampire Studies had she managed not to be expelled.

She had no way of knowing that, because of the matched strength and the way of their culture, vampires, especially mates, did not settle arguments by having heartfelt chats or seeking counseling.

They challenged then they battled physically with no rules and no holds barred.

This had the benefit of settling the order of vampires, who was strongest, quickest, sharpest and smartest.

In the case of mates, this had the additional benefit that, more often than not, physical duels led to something vastly more pleasurable.

He also had to admit that there was no way of Leah knowing his history with Katrina. Her frequent and misguided jealous rages. Her phone calls, sometimes a dozen a day. To check in, she said. To check up, she meant. Her constant suspicion, rifling through his things, listening in to phone calls.

And then there were the times—infrequent though they were, they happened far too often for Lucien's liking—when she would appear at a Feast that Lucien was attending. She'd done this twice. Then he'd had to break her of this habit which he'd done by more than bloodying her nose. He'd also broken her femur and five ribs, all of which healed within an hour and obviously it had not led to something more pleasurable. This happened after she'd entered his private chamber and appeared at his side when he was actually *feeding*. Suggesting, during those times, with false sensuality, that they share the mortal morsel. That such an activity would bring them closer together.

Katrina knew he didn't like to share.

During these two times, she had also infiltrated his privacy, something he required even at a Feast. He meant it when he told Leah he "danced" privately. He didn't simply not share the mortal on whom he was feeding, he didn't share the experience. Therefore, he always took a private room, leaving the group feeding to others. He disliked the idea of other mortals, or vampires for that matter, getting off on watching him with his meal.

And they would, he'd be the center of attention. He always was.

It wasn't that he thought it was a private activity. He too enjoyed watching others feed. He also meant it when he told Leah he thought it was beautiful.

It was just his nature.

Even if for only one feeding, that mortal was his and his alone, and in any way the word could be defined, he didn't share.

And lastly, Leah didn't know what he was risking for her. To have her in every way meant he was challenging his culture, his people's way of life *and* hers, and putting his own life at risk.

Even though he had to admit all those things, the simple fact of the matter was, she hadn't asked.

Not a single question.

She instantly thought the worst of him, judging him through the acceptable behaviors of her own culture, never considering there might be a difference in his.

Not only that, he had saved her from Katrina's attack, which would have been deadly.

He had also, very blatantly, shown his preference for Leah over his own mate. This was not something she could know was completely unheard of in the vampire realm, but any woman of his experience would have had a vastly different reaction to Leah's.

Not to mention, with all of this, in addition to his clothes in her closet, his body in her bed, the rather luxurious roof over her head and opulent wardrobe he had provided her, he had made it abundantly clear she had his continued protection, his undivided attention and his profuse generosity.

None of which, considering her reaction, seemed to penetrate that obstinate fucking brain of hers.

It was high time, Lucien decided, that Leah learn these important lessons.

"I didn't expect to see you here," Cosmo said, appearing at his side, smiling at Lucien and taking him from his thoughts.

"I could say the same," Lucien replied. "This isn't normally your scene."

Cosmo murmured, "Vodka, rocks," to the bartender and turned his attention back to Lucien. "It isn't yours either." Then he looked around while asking, "Where's Leah? Is she in the restroom?"

"She's home," Lucien answered and Cosmo's head swung to him.

"Home?" he repeated.

"Home," Lucien stated firmly. "She's having some difficulty adjusting to her new life. I'm giving her space to sort herself out."

Cosmo threw his head back and burst out laughing. Lucien watched his friend thinking that not the first damn thing was funny. Cosmo's laughter became chuckling as he paid for his drink and took a sip.

"You're losing your touch, my friend," Cosmo noted, his eyes scanning the crowd also unseeing, his attention was on the conversation. "It's been a whole week. Back in the day, within a week, you'd have them gagging for it."

"Perhaps, considering it's been centuries, I'm out of practice."

"Perhaps?" Cosmo was still smiling broadly. "Or perhaps you've met your match."

"She'll break," Lucien said low, meaning every word and taking a sip from his drink.

And she would.

After he'd heard her weeping and later discovering the shredded lingerie, he had thought she already had, albeit briefly.

Having it confirmed that day that only her game plan had changed had not only been invigorating, it had been a relief.

Indeed, the sense of relief was so strong it was vaguely alarming. It was as if he didn't *want* her to break. As if he didn't want the taming. As if he didn't want her to submit to his control, instantly acquiesce to his demands, all of which would be for her own good or her pleasure, even though she didn't understand this. As if he didn't want to show her that her life, entrusted in his care, would blossom beyond her imagining.

It was as if he wanted things to remain as they were; the constant battles, contests of will, and bickering interspersed with her quirky sweetness and immense humor.

Which was absurd.

"Well, how long do you think it'll take?" Cosmo asked. "Maybe Stephanie and I can place bets. It would be amusing."

Lucien leaned back against the bar and didn't answer.

Cosmo was undeterred. "It took you three weeks with Maggie. Do you think Leah will break Maggie's record?"

"At the rate she's going," Lucien drawled, "it'll be the next century before either you or Stephanie see a return on your bet."

Cosmo again burst out laughing but Lucien's mind turned to something about their conversation that was unsettling.

Cosmo had mentioned Maggie, and for the first time in hundreds of years, the mention of her name had not felt like a knife twisted in his gut.

He scanned his memories, all of which, over eight hundred years of them, stayed sharp in his mind.

He remembered Maggie's taming. It had been the sweetest moment in his life, both up until that point and since. The submission, the gift of her trust, the laying of her life in his hands for his safekeeping. He'd rewarded her and she'd flourished immediately. He could still feel her underneath him, her legs opening of their own accord, her welcoming of his body in hers, the taste of her blood in his mouth, the scent of her filling his nostrils.

He could also see her smile, hear her laughter, taste her skin and feel her warm body pressed against him in sleep.

Every second with Maggie was burned on his brain, none of it was forgotten nor was it any less sweet.

It was just that the familiar pain of the memory which fused with the memory of her loss had vanished.

"Lucien?" Cosmo called and Lucien focused on his friend. "Maggie," Cosmo murmured, his face grew concerned, and he continued in a soft voice, "Sorry, that's twice I've—"

"Don't worry about it," Lucien cut him off, not about to share his revelation.

Cosmo nodded, taking another sip, his eyes on the crowd, letting the matter drop as he had learned to do with a good deal of practice over the years.

"I hear Katrina is causing troubles," Cosmo noted and Lucien sighed.

"I filed Severance," Lucien shared.

"I know. *Everyone* knows. I'm pretty certain her phone is fused to her ear, she's been so fucking busy."

This didn't surprise Lucien. It annoyed him, but it didn't surprise him.

"She tried to attack Leah today," Lucien disclosed. He heard Cosmo's sharp intake of breath and felt Cosmo's eyes turn to him.

"Please tell me you're joking," Cosmo whispered.

"I'm not."

Cosmo continued to stare at him. "How did that happen?" Cosmo asked, still sounding shocked, as he would be.

It was not done to go visiting a mate's concubine, no matter what you might suspect was happening.

Concubines were sacrosanct. They were under the protection of their vampire and only allowed in the company of other vampires with their vampire's permission. To arrive on one's doorstep with or without the intent to harm was not only not done, it was against the law. To attempt to harm the concubine was warrant for deadly retribution.

Katrina had likely come to confront Lucien and Leah had gotten in the way of her rage.

It mattered not that Lucien was flying in the face of the laws that ruled all vampires. It was Leah's safety that mattered. Katrina's behavior had been condemnable, and even though Lucien was breaking the law on his own, and flaunting it, he was within his rights, even if she was his mate, to hunt her and make her burn.

"She arrived on our doorstep this morning spoiling for a fight," Lucien answered his friend's question.

"And she attacked Leah?"

"She tried, yes. Twice."

Cosmo let out a low whistle before inquiring, "Good Christ, what are you going to do?"

"If she continues to be just a nuisance, I'll let her burn out her temper and move on, which is what I'm expecting she'll do. If she ever gets near Leah again, I'll see she burns a different way," Lucien answered calmly but with deadly seriousness.

"You know The Council has heard all of this. Not only from Katrina but from Nestor, who was there last night when you kissed Leah," Cosmo told him.

Lucien was not surprised about this either mainly because he'd seen Nestor watching them.

"I'm prepared to talk to The Council," Lucien stated.

Cosmo turned fully to his friend, putting his drink on the bar and leaning closer.

In an effort not to be overheard, using his mind to communicate, a capacity that Cosmo had as well, he asked, *And what will you say to them?*

They owe me, they'll allow me Leah, Lucien replied.

Yes, I believe they will. The debt has gone unpaid too long and they're uncomfortable with it. However, they won't like it or the idea it may give to others. It'll be the only such dispensation since the Agreement was signed. And they only will if you intend to feed and to fuck. They'll have a problem with you taking her as your mate, Cosmo returned and Lucien's head snapped around to look in surprise at his friend.

What makes you think I intend to take her as a mate?

Everyone thinks that's your intention.

It fucking well isn't, Lucien clipped.

And it wasn't. However, Lucien thought wryly, it might take eternity to break her, which would be the same thing.

I hope to God you're serious, Lucien. Cosmo cut into his thoughts. *Because you attempt something like that, it won't only mean war, it'll mean hunting. They'll torture you, which you've endured, but they'll also torture Leah...*

Involuntarily, at the thought of Leah under torture, hot brands held against her smooth skin, her fingernails ripped out at the roots, acid dripped on her beautiful body, Lucien's midsection rocked back violently as if he'd been kicked in the gut.

His burning black eyes locked with Cosmo's green ones. *I mean to feed and to fuck. I mean to indulge in a taming. And I mean to have her how I want her, however long it lasts after the taming. Not as mates, not for eternity,* Lucien stated clearly and went on, *Cosmo, hear me. You set straight anyone who says otherwise. If The Council intends to investigate, they investigate me, not Leah.*

Cosmo studied his friend and nodded.

"Did Katrina start that rumor?" Lucien asked out loud deciding, if she did, he'd hunt her that night, not wait for her to do something else immensely stupid.

"I've no idea where it started," Cosmo muttered, shaken, not at Lucien's denial of the rumor, but at his unconcealed reaction to any harm coming to Leah.

First, because Lucien did not have open reactions, unless he was in a position of complete trust with the person with whom he was talking and all those around him. Which would mean not under the hundreds of watching eyes at a Feast.

Second, because his reaction betrayed his feeling for his concubine, which went beyond a desire for a simple taming.

This was familiar. Cosmo had experienced this emotion from Lucien once before. When Lucien took Maggie as his mate, expecting to live the rest of eternity with her only to have her captured by their enemies during The Revolution, tortured, then executed.

They had not known it at the time but this, for Lucien, had been a boon. He and Maggie both would have died during The Hunt. Neither would denounce the other, Cosmo knew it to the depths of his soul. Further, Maggie's murder had inflamed Lucien to the point where he was an unstoppable killing machine during the war, albeit controlled and strategic, but nevertheless immensely successful and exceptionally deadly. Avenging Maggie's murder had made him a hero of The Revolution to such an extent, with his added mesmerizing abilities and his unparalleled wealth, centuries later he was now an idol.

If she had lived to see it, Maggie would have laughed.

Back then, Lucien had been content with modest wealth (for a vampire, for a mortal, he was fabulously wealthy).

And he had been more than content with Maggie.

Being a hero, and definitely an idol, would not have been something he would have sought, although he didn't. It also wasn't something he would have allowed, although he had no choice.

He would have found a way to return them to their simple life, just the two of them, for eternity. No hopes for children, but no disease, no death, just Maggie's oft-used dry wit, excellent cooking skills, flashing gray eyes, and Lucien's complete devotion.

Not for the first time, nor likely the last, sorrow for his friend and his loss gentled Cosmo's tone.

"Maybe you should feed," Cosmo suggested.

Lucien didn't hesitate. "Excellent idea," he murmured his reply.

Lucien's eyes moved to the blonde on the dance floor. His mind sought hers and he called to her.

Come to me.

She had her back to him and he watched her body twitch, then she whirled around, her eyes seeking his.

She looked surprised, even anxious. It wasn't something that happened, hearing someone else's voice in your head.

Then her anxiety melted and she smiled smugly. Without hesitation, she moved toward him, slithering adeptly through the crowd.

As he watched her move, Lucien made a decision. He didn't make her come to him, he moved with the intent to meet her at the doorway to the maze that led into The Den.

He wanted to be done with this and get home to Leah.

He had intended to return tomorrow evening for a feeding and another attempt at her taming. However, he decided he'd talk to her, not instruction, but explanation. And he also decided to do it without delay.

Perhaps that would hold some sway, or at least enough for her to beg him to take her.

All day his body had reminded him of his own unfulfilled need to be buried inside Leah's silken wet warmth. It had been an error of judgment to give his cock even the hint of a feel of her. It had taken a supreme effort of will to set those thoughts aside during the day. No matter how little he had of her, what he had had been exquisite.

"Lucien," the blonde breathed when she made it to his side.

He didn't greet her nor did he touch her.

He walked into the hallway, knowing she'd follow.

She did.

This hallway didn't snake to The Den—or feeding room—of this Feast. Instead, it was a maze, the center of which held The Den. Every vampire knew the layout, none of the mortals did. A mortal could only go to The Den in the company of a vampire at his or her invitation. If they wandered back in hopes of melting into the feedings, at this particular Feast, they could be lost for hours, even days.

Lucien moved swiftly, surely, feeling her struggling to keep up, not allowing her to get her bearings, and within minutes they were in The Den.

Lucien's eyes went immediately to the steward who noticed him and jerked his head toward another door. Lucien wended his way through the bodies on the floor, feeling her behind him, smelling her scent, which was nowhere near as delicious as Leah's.

Most definitely lemonade. And not good lemonade.

"Master Lucien," the steward murmured as he inserted a key and opened one of a half dozen doors leading off The Den.

"Clive," Lucien returned the greeting and walked into the small room.

It was much like any Den, decorated in rich colors, the furniture comfortable and inviting, meant for lounging, covered in soft plush fabrics.

Lucien had intended to lead Leah to a room off The Den they visited last night, not to feed, to indulge in other pleasurable activities. However, her extreme reaction stopped him from doing that. He'd been disappointed, but only until she'd explained. Then he'd been elated.

The door closed behind them and Lucien turned to the woman.

"I'm Kitty," she said in her breathy voice.

Lucien regarded her for a moment then he gave his honest dispassionate opinion. "What a perfectly ridiculous name."

She blinked both in surprise and, he noted instantly, stupidity. She had no idea if he was being serious or teasing, and with the way the wheels churned behind her blue eyes, it would take far longer than he intended to spend with her to figure it out.

"Come here," he ordered and she stopped the taxing effort of thinking and moved forward.

When she was inches away, she leaned in, going up on her toes. "You should know I'll do anything you want." She hesitated and gave him her slightly effective but obviously practiced alluring look before stressing, "*Anything.*"

"If you'll give me anything then please do me the favor of not speaking." He gave her an altogether different highly effective look before stressing, "At all."

She blinked again, confusion filling her face, and Lucien was through.

In less than a second, he had her in his arms, his tongue lashed her neck, and he pulled her head back roughly by her long hair. Then he tore into her, her blood spurting into his mouth.

He smelled her excitement immediately.

Neither assuaged the ache in his belly or the throbbing he felt in his cock.

Her head rolled back, giving him better access and further tearing open her own wound, something which he was certain was also practiced.

Her arms started to steal around him and he lifted his head without stroking her wound with his tongue to stop the bleeding. The blood poured down her throat, staining her gown.

"Don't touch me," he growled.

Her eyes caught his and he saw uncertainty before his mouth went back to the wound.

He fed beyond what would have been healthy for Leah this early in their Arrangement, but where he knew he could take this woman. She'd regenerate by the time she wandered into The Den, once invited, open to feeding by anyone.

Then he swept his tongue along the wound, the bleeding stopped and the skin started knitting together. His arms fell away from her, she sagged to her knees in front of him and he made to move to the door.

"Is that it?" she whispered, her hands shooting out to hold him at his hips, her head tilted back, her eyes beseeching, her desperate need to service Lucien in more than just feeding written all over her face.

His eyes dropped to her cleavage and his body responded in spite of his thoughts.

He'd misused her. Even with the mortals at a Feast he had better manners. Hell, even with Wats and Breed he had better manners.

It was Leah and his frustration with her that he was taking out on this creature and it was inexcusable.

Therefore, his tone gentled when he asked, "And what would you like, pet?"

Her eyes flicked to his trousers then back to his. "Anything you want to give me," she breathed.

Lucien thought of Leah, her stubbornness and the likely weeks of torture ahead for them both.

Lucien was a vampire. Vampires weren't even expected to be faithful to their mates (another frustration Lucien had with Katrina), certainly not their mule-headed concubines.

He shrugged off his jacket.

"Stand up and take off your dress," he commanded.

At once, she did as she was told and Lucien was far later getting back to Leah than he'd recently decided he would be.

It was an hour away from dawn when he arrived home.

Upon entering the kitchen, he heard the television and saw the flashing lights coming from the family room.

He moved in that direction, entering the room, seeing a late night movie playing, the volume turned low.

Leah was asleep on the couch on her side, her hands in prayer position tucked under her cheek. She was wearing a pair of drawstring pajama bottoms in a paisley of muted colors intermingled with bright pastels with a tight-fitting camisole in robin's egg blue, one of the colors in the pants.

She looked innocent and adorable, the latter of which she was some of the time, the former, only in her sleep.

Laid out on the coffee table with some of it escaping onto the floor were the remains of what had been an eating orgy. Microwave popcorn, open chip bags, cookies, candy wrappers, and a small tub of ice cream, half-eaten and now fully melted.

Lucien was not one to partake in junk food, except, as tonight, at a Feast.

A delicious, finely-crafted dessert, definitely.

An orgy of chemically saturated savories and diabetic coma-inducing sweets, never.

He decided he'd have a word with her later about this, if he found the right time, which would likely be in the next decade.

He lifted her, and as had happened last night, she didn't wake. She simply settled into him, her temple on his shoulder, her forehead pressed into his neck.

He walked with a mortal's slowness, taking the time to savor her scent. His eyes moving over her profile, his arms curling her soft body closer, enjoying everything that was her after having his fill, several times, of her poor relation tonight. This enjoyment strengthened his resolve to be far more patient while he made her understand and brought about her taming.

Carefully, he pulled back the covers and put her in bed. Swiftly disrobing, he joined her there.

Then he did what he'd decided to do in the car on the way home. It would, he thought, make Leah infinitely more agreeable.

Not delaying, his hands sought her, one at her breast, the other went straight into her pajama bottoms. His mouth went to the skin on her neck below her ear and he tasted her with his tongue.

His fingers worked and she woke on a soft, low moan.

"Lucien?" she whispered, her voice sleepy and sweet and entirely unguarded.

"Yes, sweetheart."

She drew in a breath, her body stilled, then it bucked as if to get away.

He expected this, kept her where she was and continued to work her.

"Lucien!" she snapped, an edge to her voice he hadn't heard before.

His hand at her breast moved up to her jaw, twisting her head as he lifted his own. He took her mouth in a kiss, his tongue sliding inside as his finger slid inside her.

God, she felt and tasted magnificent.

On that thought he decided, no matter the frustration, he'd not take another meal, or anything, outside of Leah for some time.

Maybe years.

To his surprise, her head reared back into the pillows in order to break their kiss.

It was rare she'd break a kiss. Very rare. She was usually as hungry as he was for that connection. Even more.

Her lips parted, her eyes were wide, and he watched them flare with an intensity he'd never seen before from her, which was also surprising. She didn't mask her reactions and she was extraordinarily passionate.

"You've—" she started and he withdrew his finger, found her, exerted pressure and circled.

She stopped speaking, her face softened and her eyes grew dazed.

"That's it, sweetheart," he murmured, his mouth capturing hers, her head reared back again, but she pushed her hips into his hand. He gave up on the kiss, opting for something more intimate. He moved his lips to her throat, sweeping his tongue against her skin then biting her there, a small wound opened, but the blood didn't flow.

He had to suck. Which he did.

She liked it as he knew she would.

He heard her moan and her body melted back into his. He drew the blood out of the small wound, heightening her arousal in measured, controlled increments. His hand went back to her breast, fingers rolling her nipple, and her head fell back to his shoulder.

He knew she was his when she started bucking her hips, riding his hand.

He felt his cock grow hard at her movements, his mind filled with visions of her riding him, and alternately and no less enjoyable, visions of him riding her.

He carefully opened the wound further and drew more deeply at her blood.

She gasped, her body tightening, he slid a finger inside then another one, both of them stroking deeply all the while his thumb circling her. Her hips were now moving in desperation, her breath coming in pants.

His tongue swathed her wound and he lifted his head to watch her face. He wanted to see her climax.

It didn't disappoint.

Her neck arched gracefully, her face flushed gorgeously, her eyes slowly closed and her lips parted in a silent moan as her hot wet sheath closed around his fingers deep inside her.

God, she wasn't just magnificent. She was so stunning he stopped breathing, feeling it in his gut, lungs and cock, watching her come.

He pushed her orgasm further with his thumb. Her fingers circled his wrist in protest then imprisoned it as she drew in another breath and the shudder tore through her.

He ceased his movements, cupping her breast in one hand, stopping his thumb, but allowing himself to keep his fingers inside her with the other. She trembled once, again, then again, before she stilled, spent, her body leaning heavily against his.

He held her close, his face in the hair at the back of her head, listening to her racing heart as it settled and breathing her scent, letting it consume his senses.

After a while, his hand left her breast and he curled his arm around her stomach, pulling her closer as his fingers slowly slid out of her and he cupped her between her legs.

He lifted his head and touched his lips to the now-pink wound.

"How are you feeling, pet?" he murmured there.

She didn't move or speak.

He lifted his head to look at her profile. Her eyes were closed, her head tilted slightly forward.

"Leah? Are you asleep?"

When she spoke, she didn't open her eyes and her voice was both very quiet and completely dead.

"You did that to me and I can smell her perfume on your skin." His body froze and she kept talking. "And when you kissed me, I could taste her blood in my mouth."

"Leah—"

She cut him off. "You forced me out of my home and my life. You've made me leave my friends and my job. During my initiation you caused me more pain than I've ever felt in my life. You've controlled my mind and my body. You've humiliated me. Today, you betrayed my trust. Tonight, you betrayed *me*."

"Leah—"

"You win," she whispered in her dead voice. "I can't fight you, Lucien. You win."

Remembering his oath to be patient with her, he rolled her to her back and got up on an elbow to get a better look at her.

"You don't understand the way of my people, pet—"

He stopped speaking when she closed her eyes slowly in a gesture of defeat that seemed foul when done by Leah.

"Please give me one thing. Just one." She opened her eyes and he was alarmed to see they were dead too. "Don't call me pet and please, never, ever again call me sweetheart."

"Leah—"

"May I go back to sleep?" she asked with genuine, not false, consideration.

In spite of his earlier vow, his temper was rising and with it the feeling he'd had when he saw her discarded lingerie.

"Leah, I'm within my rights to attend a Feast."

She turned her head and looked over his shoulder. "I know you are. Of course you are," she said wearily. "You're within your rights to do anything."

He decided to try a different tactic and his hand moved to cup her jaw.

Gently, he said, "I wanted to give you something tonight, sweetheart."

When he uttered his endearment, she winced, her head jerking as if he'd struck her.

At this reaction, the strange vile feeling was overtaking his temper and he didn't like it. It felt like pain. Twisting, burning pain and it was magnifying quickly.

He lost hold of his patience but held tight to the anger. If he didn't the pain would begin to be unbearable.

"Leah, goddamn it, look at me."

Without hesitation she did.

"We need to talk about this," he went on.

She shook her head and asked, "Why? I promise to be good, do as you say. Anything you want, I'll do it. Isn't that what you wanted?"

No, it wasn't what he fucking wanted.

He wanted her trust, her acceptance of his power, his dominance, not to wield it against her, but to use it to keep her safe, protected, nurtured, thriving.

"You don't understand," he told her.

"Do you want me to understand?" she asked.

"Yes, I fucking do."

Her eyes locked on his, hers were still lifeless. "Then of course I'll listen. Whatever you want, Lucien."

Blinding rage wrenched through him. At that moment, he didn't know if he was furious at Leah or himself. This mingled with the bizarre twisting pain and it took every effort not tear the room apart.

He watched her waiting expectantly and pulled in breath through his nose.

He knew he didn't have the control to deal with this tonight. He needed to seek calm and deal with this rationally, not when he wanted to throw the lounge through the window.

"We'll talk about it tomorrow."

She nodded and asked, "Do you mind if I go back to sleep?"

He drew another breath into his nostrils, attempting to keep a tight rein on his temper, which, fortunately worked.

"You don't have to ask me to sleep."

She nodded again, whispered, "Okay," then rolled to her side, tucking her hands under her cheek again and closing her eyes. "Goodnight, Lucien," she told her pillow.

His hold on his temper slipped and he growled. Her eyes snapped open and her head started to twist to look at him but he buried his face in her neck as his arms wrapped tight around her.

"You undo me, pet," he muttered there, seeking solace in her warm soft body, anything that might subdue that twisting pain.

He felt her grow still before she relaxed then, softly, she admitted, "I don't know if I can redo you."

Her words were so absurd, in spite of his anger, he smiled into her neck.

She kept talking. "But I think to redo you, I'd have to figure out how to redo me and that ship has finally sailed."

His smile died and her head tilted forward, not to refuse him access to her neck but settling into sleep.

"It's for the best," she whispered as he lifted his head to watch her tired face. "I was always driving everyone crazy with my personality defects. Aunt Kate's going to be thrilled."

Her words made the burning pain intensify considerably.

"Leah, stop talking," Lucien ordered.

"Okay," she said then her eyes flew open and to the side. "That's speaking. Sorry. No, I mean...sorry!" She pressed her lips together and turned her face into the pillow.

Lucien didn't know whether to laugh or to shout.

What he did know was that Kitty was a very bad idea.

He settled behind her, pulling her deeper into his body, something she didn't resist, and pressing his face into her thick soft hair.

He had thought Leah had been broken before and he'd been wrong. He took in a deep breath deciding that he'd see what tomorrow might bring.

When he knew she was asleep, he carefully pulled away so as not to wake her and took a shower.

12
The Understanding

I woke up and pretty much saw nothing but the wide expanse of Lucien's smooth, defined chest. This was because my cheek was resting against his pectoral. How I slept cuddled up to him like that, I'd never know. I wasn't a cuddling type of girl.

Memories of the night before and yesterday flooded my brain, but regardless of the pain, or maybe because of it, automatically I shifted closer to his hard warmth.

Yesterday, after taking a very long, very cold shower and then just barely stopping myself from breaking everything breakable I could find, I'd found myself in a huge rambling house with nothing to do. I'd finished the only book I'd brought with me. There was no company. No phone. No car keys. No books. No Internet. No cleaning to do. No dirty laundry. No ironing.

Nothing.

I realized too late I should have asked Edwina to buy a few magazines. I only had the television and my thoughts and I didn't want to spend time with either of them.

I avoided the television as I'd found over the years (with vast amounts of experience) that there was rarely anything on. Plus I usually ate like a pothead with the munchies when I sat in front of the TV, so I made the decision to take a walk.

This was a very stupid idea mainly because I forgot my stinking iPod. There was nothing to do but think when you walked without your iPod.

Too lazy to go back, I forged on, and as they do, things occurred to me as I walked.

For instance, the fact that Katrina had marked Lucien. It wasn't something that registered on me at the time seeing as I was freaking out, but looking back, the scratches were ugly and savage. His skin had been broken. Katrina not only had not held back, she had the power and speed to get a bit of hers back.

And she hadn't responded in any way shocked at their fight. It had been like it happened all the time.

Even Lucien's baiting, "Try," sounded, in retrospect, as if it wasn't the first time he'd ever said it, but as if he'd said it lots.

And lots.

And Katrina hadn't hesitated to attack.

Katrina had attacked *Lucien*, not the other way around.

She had also attacked *me*, something which Lucien not only protected me from (easily), but also it infuriated him (greatly).

Then there was their conversation, Katrina saying I was "life" to Lucien.

I still didn't know what that meant.

What I did know was that something important was going on. Something I didn't understand, told myself I didn't *want* to understand, but something that was happening regardless.

It was Katrina who left and Lucien didn't go after her. As far as I knew, he didn't give her a second thought before he'd turned to me.

This all made me distinctly uncomfortable or more uncomfortable than normal.

Mainly because I was afraid Lucien was right. I'd jumped to conclusions.

I had a lot of bad qualities but I'd never been judgmental. I *hated* people who were judgmental. They were the worst.

But I feared I had been with Lucien.

Regardless of Katrina's words, it was clear that Lucien wasn't sending her "severance papers" (it wasn't hard to figure out what severance meant) because of me, but because of something that had been going on far longer.

And, no matter how much I tried to stop it, his deep voice saying that love was a blanket that keeps you warm kept playing over and over in my head.

He said this *not* like he'd read it somewhere and liked that quote or as if he was simply explaining what he thought love should be. He said it like he'd felt that before, like he *knew* it to be fact.

This fascinated me, scared me and for some reason made me very sad, because whoever taught him that lesson was not Katrina.

The house Lucien gave me was surrounded by woods except for the huge yard, immaculate garden and the pool (yes, pool, with a small pool house, no less). During my house inspection the day I arrived, I'd noticed a path leading into the woods and I took it.

Upon realizing I was a judgmental person and that I probably owed the Mighty Lucien an apology (which sucked), the winding woodsy path led out onto a lake.

And what a lake.

It was huge. The day was warm and sunny, a gentle breeze blew, but it didn't disturb the glassy surface of the water which went on forever, the wooded hills around it rising to the blue cloudless sky.

It was gorgeous.

There were big beautiful homes nestled in the hills with paths or steps leading to the water. There weren't many of them though. I counted five.

Seriously exclusive real estate.

I could see at the bottom of the path a long, wide, sturdy pier. Not rickety and ill-kept, of course not. It was the kind of pier you tied a fancy speed boat to (or a small yacht).

I walked out to the end of the pier and sat in the sun, staring out at the tranquil beauty of the lake, wondering if Lucien provided such luxurious locations for all his concubines. If he did, it must cost him a whack. He had to have dozens of concubines still alive. If he didn't, this had still cost him a whack.

Either way, it didn't change the fact that he'd provided *this* for *me*.

"I am *so* fucked," I told the lake.

The lake, not surprisingly, had no reply.

I sat staring at the water and tried not to think of Gentle Generous Lucien or the fact that, in all fairness, I should open a Why I *Might* Like Lucien Vault, even if it was only a small, fireproof safe. I also tried not to think about my many bad traits, which maybe got my fool self into this mess in the first place.

Being a vampire's concubine was my family's legacy. It was their business, as it were, and had been for five hundred years. In fact, this whole practice had been going on for centuries and people *liked* it. It was their way of life.

Who was I to buck the trend?

Cosmo's money had kept my mother, sister and I clothed, fed and housed rather nicely, I had to admit, until Lana and I moved out. Lana and I shared the same dad, or I should say, we shared the same sire. Our sire, from what little I remembered, drank a lot, yelled a lot and got kicked out on his ass by my mom backed up by the arsenal of my aunties. Then he took off, sending birthday cards for the first couple of years before giving up. I hadn't seen him since I was six.

Cosmo still kept my mother in manicures, pedicures, a three bedroom ranch-style house, designer handbags and martini lunches with my aunties.

I should have thanked him when I first met him, not been cold to him.

And then there was Lucien.

Well, of course he was pathologically controlling and a pain in the ass, but when he wasn't being those two things he was other things. I couldn't help but think about the way he was with me when I was drunk (before he became a jerk, I hasten to add) and the way he was at The Feast (and he never became a jerk then).

In fact, when he wasn't being a jerk, controlling or a pain in the ass, he looked at me...

He looked at me...

Oh hell, he looked at me like I was life.

Like I was beautiful. Like I was beyond sexy, whatever that was, but Lucien looked at me that way. Like I was funny, interesting, and he didn't know what I'd do next, but whatever I did, he was going to enjoy it on some level and therefore he was looking forward to it.

He was looking forward to *me*.

No one *ever* looked forward to *me*.

I could barely credit it.

I'd spent years looking for some guy who would keep me away from the concubine life. There wasn't a lot I knew before my Selection and I didn't know a lot more now. One thing I knew was that vampires could not invite the Uninitiated to go to a Selection if the Uninitiated was in a relationship with a mortal.

Therefore, I made sure I was in a relationship most of the time.

Which meant I'd been in and out of relationships since I became eligible for my first Selection at eighteen.

Out of desperation, because I didn't like to think I was an idiot, but that was more likely the case, I'd picked all the wrong guys. Justin, the last, was the most wrong of all. And I stayed with them longer than I should in order to keep myself safe.

Maybe, just maybe (and I wasn't putting a lot into that "maybe"), I'd been wrong.

Which meant two things.

One, I'd have to apologize to Lucien for being a judgmental bitch. Two, I'd have to ask him to speed up his instructions so I understood more about the life I was meant to be leading.

Then I'd make my decision.

The one thing I knew was that, however it went between Lucien and me, I wasn't going to let him break me.

I'd meet him halfway.

If he wasn't willing to do that then we were back to square one.

Obviously, even the tranquility of the lake didn't stop me from thinking about Lucien.

I heaved myself up and walked back up the path. When I got to the house, I made the marinade, slid the chicken breasts in and put it in the fridge.

Then I decided to spend the rest of the day drowning my sorrows in food and numbing my mind with television.

My unfocused sight cleared and Lucien's chest, and incidentally, Katrina's scratch marks were completely healed, became defined again as my thoughts turned to last night.

Why I had that reaction to him feeding on someone else, to smelling her perfume, I didn't know. But there was no denying it. I did.

In all the hateful feelings I'd had for the last two weeks, having Lucien touch me while he smelled and tasted of another woman was by far and away the worst.

Because it hurt. A lot. Too much.

I knew it shouldn't, I had no claim on him.

But it did.

And I got it then. I understood. I knew why there was always this hint of sadness in the very backs of my mother's eyes. And I knew the minute he told me I didn't understand the way of his people that I couldn't live this life.

Not as Leah Buchanan.

I'd have to be A Buchanan from The Premier Family of Vampire Concubines. Not impatient, not short-tempered, not stubborn, not immature, not anything that was *me*.

I'd have to be the good, perfect, dutiful concubine like my annoying cousin Myrna.

For what could be years, I was going to have to channel goody-two-shoes "I'm gonna tell on you" Myrna.

And that totally and completely *stunk*.

But, I told myself, I could live with that in the beautiful house close to the beautiful lake with my beautiful clothes, and it must be said, with Lucien giving me mind-boggling, body-rocking, *unbelievable* orgasms if last night was anything to go by, and feeding all the time which, I had to admit, was sublime.

And he would do whatever he wanted to do which he would anyway.

Then he'd release me and I could go on.

But not with that sadness. He wasn't going to get me to like him (or worse) and then break me *that* way.

I didn't even know if I liked him and the pain of having him touch me, make my body feel like it was vibrating with life, his big solid warmth surrounding me, making me feel precious, fragile, and above all, safe while I could smell *her* and taste *her* was bad enough.

If I actually *did* like him, I'd be really screwed.

Luckily, I didn't like him so hopefully I'd be safe.

It was on this thought that his hand, which was curled at my hip, drifted up my back and tangled in my hair.

"Are you awake, pet?" he asked in a sexy, rough, drowsy voice.

I tried not to shiver and failed. I also tried not to let him calling me "pet" feel like it was lacerating my heart and failed at that too. Then I tried not to wonder if he called the nameless, faceless *her* of last night "pet" and I failed at that as well.

I nodded my head, my cheek sliding against his skin. His hand fisted in my hair and he gave it a gentle tug. I looked up at him and his eyes caught mine.

"I'm hungry," he murmured.

He wasn't talking about eggs and bacon for breakfast hungry, therefore I felt a rush of heat between my legs and my nipples contracted.

His eyes went lazy and he whispered, "Come here."

I was about as "here" as anyone could get but I knew what he meant. I slid up, my body rolling deeper into his as his other arm came around to assist, hauling me up further and pulling me over him so I was mostly on top.

His hand guiding my head, my lips hit his and he kissed me.

I closed my eyes and all of a sudden I wanted desperately to cry.

He was a really good kisser but this wasn't our flat-out, fight for supremacy, hungry, sexy duel. This was a soft, sweet, morning kiss that felt nice and wonderful.

It was then I began to see the flaws in my new plan.

His lips broke from mine, traveled to my cheek, down to my jaw then to my neck. My legs moved restlessly as a really good kind of warmth tingled through my system.

His hand at my waist slid up my back to my shoulder, over it then, using only his middle finger to touch me in a whisper-soft caress, slowly, unbelievably slowly, it traveled down my arm. I felt the goose bumps rising on my skin and they were the really good kind too.

"Do you want me to make you come while I feed?" he muttered against my neck and the answer to that was a big old *yes*.

But I couldn't believe he was asking me.

Was this some kind of test?

"Can we see how it goes?" I asked and my voice sounded breathy.

His hand in my hair tugged my head back so he could look at me. The fingers of his other hand curled around my wrist as he studied my face, his eyes thoughtful and maybe even a little wary.

"If that's what you'd like," he replied, and I started to nod my head when he went on, a smile tugging his handsome mouth, "But I know how it'll go."

He didn't wait for me to reply. His hand brought my wrist to his mouth while he kept his eyes locked on mine. I felt his tongue lash against the pulse at my wrist in a way that was so sensual, my breath caught.

His long fingers slid down, curling into my palm, dwarfing my hand in his much larger one. His mouth moved and all I felt was the flow as he began to feed.

It's impossible to explain how beautiful this feeling was. If I hadn't felt it, I wouldn't believe it. Perhaps it had something to do with giving another being sustenance, nourishment, life. Perhaps it was lips locked and sucking. Perhaps it was bodies touching and other connections besides, both physical and emotional, both intimate.

Whatever it was, it felt *great*.

His black eyes held mine captive as he drew my blood into his mouth and I squirmed, the fire building, the need turning hungry.

I saw his tongue sweep my skin and then he let my hand go. I couldn't help it, I felt and heard the mew of complaint escape my throat.

He grinned, rolled me away and his hand went to the drawstring on my pajama bottoms.

"I've decided I want you to come while I'm feeding." He said this like it was some sort of tender challenge.

I was okay with that. Way okay.

"Okay," I whispered.

His grin spread into an arrogant smile.

He swept the covers aside and my bottoms and panties were gone in the blink of an eye. He pulled me over him, yanking my knees so I was astride him, open and bared.

I felt extreme discomfort at this exposure.

For about two seconds.

Then he was kissing me and his hand was between my legs.

This kiss *was* a ravenous duel, both of us taking, which meant, weirdly, both of us giving.

Then I thought nothing at all and everything I felt was beautiful.

His mouth went to my neck. I felt his tongue as I registered my own mouth was tingling.

Then he was feeding and his fingers were inside me, his thumb manipulating me, and it built fast. My heart started tripping, blood singing through my veins. My head tilted back to give him better access, my hips rocked into his hand demanding more of what he was giving me, and all of it was good.

It built fast, it built huge, before it happened I knew it was going to be overwhelming.

But it wasn't. It was *consuming*.

My climax was like nothing I'd ever felt before. It was beyond beautiful. Better than even the night before, straight to life-altering.

I gasped then stopped breathing, my neck arching back, my hips grinding into his hand as it hit me in a wave of pure, perfect, toe-curling, breasts-swelling, moan-inducing bliss.

I felt his hand in my hair position my head, but I didn't know he watched until the pleasure slowly subsided and my eyes refocused.

"Beautiful," he whispered, his gaze soft on my face.

Yes, there were definitely flaws in my plan.

So I didn't have to look at his handsome face gazing at me with such rapt attention, I gave a gentle yank against his fingers in my hair. I didn't try to escape but settled on top of him, my forehead in his neck as his hand carefully moved out from between my legs and both his arms circled me.

"Did you like that, sweetheart?"

Clearly, he wasn't going to do me the favor of not calling me endearments.

I decided to let this go and nodded. I mean, the answer was obvious.

"Good," he murmured as his arms grew tighter.

It occurred to me my body was exposed and I didn't like it much about a nanosecond before he rolled me to my back, yanking the covers over the both of us.

He put his head in his hand, his elbow in the pillow and shifted his weight so it was resting against my side, but he tangled his heavy legs with mine. I looked up at him as his other hand came up, fingers curling around my neck, thumb stroking against the now numb wound.

"What would you like to do today?" he asked quietly.

His eyes were both languid and alert, as if he liked what just happened but he needed to be prepared for whatever happened next. I thought this was strange but I was focused on his question.

Lucien was asking *me* what I wanted to do that day? Was this another test?

Clearly, I'd passed the last one but I didn't want to try my luck. I'd always been terrible with tests.

"I'm not sure," I answered. "What are my choices?"

His response was immediate. "Anything you want as long as it includes me."

No man would do anything a woman wanted. He might say he would then you'd somehow end up drinking beer, eating hot wings and watching a game at a bar where the waitresses wore short-shorts and skintight tank tops.

"Um..." I thought about it, my eyes sliding to the side. I felt his body start moving so my eyes slid back to see he was silently laughing, his lips tilted up in an attractive smile. "What's funny?" I asked quietly.

He shook his head, didn't answer, and still grinning, he repeated, "What do you want to do today?"

"I don't know," I answered.

"What's the first thing that comes to mind?"

"Um..."

"Leah, think. The first thing."

"Um..."

His voice dipped low, sultry and amused, an effective combination. "It isn't hard, sweetheart."

"Books," I blurted, and he blinked slowly.

"Books?"

"Yes, books," I replied. "My stuff isn't here yet and without a telephone or Internet or a house to clean or a car and with Edwina gone, there wasn't much to do yesterday. I don't like TV, nothing's ever on and whenever I sit in front of one I start eating like my stomach's a bottomless pit, so I need to go buy some books."

His face changed. The amusement fled, it went blank, and I wondered if this was an overshare. His eyes shifted away and stared unfocused at my pillow. This would have been all right except I saw close up a muscle jump in his cheek.

I didn't think this was good.

I had momentarily forgotten that men, on the whole, weren't really fond of shopping, even for books. Big, bad, male vamps were probably *seriously* not fond of shopping.

"We don't have to buy books," I went on hurriedly and his eyes sliced to mine, no longer blank, but now broody and intense. Regardless I sallied forth, "We could—"

He cut me off and freaked me out by saying, "I'm sorry, Leah."

Now, hang on a second.

Lucien was sorry? And he admitted it?

It was my turn to blink.

Then I asked, "What?"

His face dropped closer and his voice dipped lower when he repeated, "I'm sorry."

I felt my heart start racing and Lucien did too or he heard it because his fingers tensed on my neck.

"You're sorry about what?" I whispered, finding I was having trouble breathing and finding this was because I wanted to hear what he said next.

"I'm sorry I left you with nothing to do yesterday. I was so angry, I didn't fucking think."

I didn't know what I expected to hear or wanted to hear, but whatever it was, that wasn't it.

Still, I said, "That's okay."

His head bent and he touched his lips to mine briefly before he lifted it again.

"We'll get you some books," he said softly.

I nodded.

"And I'll see that the broadband is activated tomorrow."

I nodded again.

"And, if you promise you won't attempt to drive to Panama, I'll give you the keys to the Cayenne."

Boy, I must have passed the second test too.

"I promise I won't drive to Panama," I whispered.

The broody intensity went out of his eyes and he said, "Good."

"I couldn't anyway, I don't have my wallet," I told him. His eyes went broody intense again. "Or," I went on quickly, "a map to Panama." He stared at me and I continued, "Can you actually drive to Panama?"

He studied me a moment, his face softened and his lips twitched. Okay then. Crisis averted.

Thank God.

"I'd rather you not find out," he said.

"I don't really think I want to," I shared. "Panama isn't one of my preferred on the run from a vamp locations."

The lip twitch happened again and his hand shifted from my throat to my cheek, then his fingers slid into the hair at the side of my head.

He cocked his head deeper into his hand and asked, "What is?"

"What is what?"

"Your preferred on the run from a vamp location."

My eyes moved to his naked shoulder (this was a mistake, by the way, he had a nice shoulder, but I had to power through it), "I don't think it's a good idea to tell you that."

His body moved when his head jerked back and he let out a shout of laughter. Half a second later, his arms were tight around me and he was hugging me again, his face stuffed in my neck.

"Probably not," he said against my neck, his voice still shaking with hilarity.

It was time for this to end. I could easily find things to put in my Why I *Might* Like Lucien Small Fireproof Safe when he was like this.

For instance, how good it made me feel when I made him laugh.

And that (I hated to admit it but it was undeniable) I liked it when he hugged me. He gave good hugs, tight and warm and with him being so big, I felt snugly and cozy and safe.

"I think I'm hungry," I told his ear and his head went back.

His eyes were still amused when he looked at me and that look had to go in my little safe as well.

He brushed my mouth with his, pulled back less than an inch and rested his forehead against mine.

"Let's get you fed and take you to town," he murmured.

Oh hell.

That had to go into my safe too. All of it, the mouth brush, the forehead rest and him taking me to town.

Damn but it was getting freaking crowded in there.

He rolled over me, exited the bed, but pulled the covers to, not exposing my lower half at all.

He leaned in, put fists into the bed on either side of me and said, "Take your time, sweetheart. Edwina's likely gone. I'll see what I can do about breakfast."

Then he was gone, *zoom*, out of the room.

I looked at the clock and noticed it was nearly noon. Then I looked at the ceiling. Then I wondered if Lucien could make breakfast. I figured, since he'd lived hundreds of years, during *one* of those years he'd have to learn how to cook. At least make toast (or something).

Then I sighed because I couldn't escape it.

If he kept acting like this, there was a big, ugly, gaping flaw in my plan.

This was going to be hard. Really, *really* hard.

Lucky for me, one of my bad traits would come in handy. I was crazy stubborn.

"I can do this," I mouthed to the ceiling, not wanting Lucien to hear and hoping I wasn't lying to myself.

I stood at the stove and slid the big spoonfuls of vegetable shortening into the skillet, the shortening melting as it hit the hot iron. As I did this, I considered the many mistakes I'd made that day and began to prepare *not* to make anymore that evening.

I didn't discover if Lucien could cook. But I did discover he could toast a mean sesame bagel and put the exact right amount of cream cheese, smoked salmon and capers on it.

As we ate our bagels and drank our coffee, we didn't talk. This was not companionable silence, it was uncomfortable, or at least it was for me. I didn't know what to say, seeing as I couldn't be me. And I didn't know why Lucien wasn't talking. And I wanted to know why, like, a lot.

I tried to gauge his mood but failed.

What I did know was that he'd attuned himself to me. It wasn't that he marked me. It was something else, something new, it made me feel less like I was drugged and more like I was pulsating. It was like he was trying to figure me out, source my mood.

I didn't know if he succeeded but I guessed no as his quiet watchfulness lasted all day.

I was terrified he'd want to take a shower with me, or worse, a bath, but he let me take a shower alone.

My first big mistake was when I was sitting at my dressing table, blow drying my hair.

Lucien had disappeared while I showered but I heard the shower go on as I was doing my makeup. While I was doing my hair, Lucien walked into the dressing room in nothing but a towel.

My mistake was I should have looked away. But I caught sight of him in my big Hollywood starlet mirror and my mouth started watering.

Then he tugged off the towel with me sitting right there, and at the sight of all that was Lucien, and there was a lot of it, my mouth went dry.

He was, it must be said, perfect from head to toe. Utterly perfect. Strong, heavy thighs. Muscled, well-formed behind. Bunched, defined calves. He even had handsome feet!

And there were other parts of him that made me wonder if he was not a vampire but instead a living god.

I jerked my eyes back to my reflection as Lucien dressed.

He chose jeans, boots, a great belt and a tailored shirt that was stripes of white, baby blue, midnight blue, light gray and charcoal gray. He wore this untucked.

It was pretty much casual wear on any other man.

Lucien looked like he'd stepped alive out of a magazine.

I decided from what Stephanie had said during my Selection, and how Lucien behaved at The Feast, that he'd want me to make an effort so he could show me off.

This wasn't tough for me. I was a girlie girl. I made an effort even if I was running to the store to buy eggs.

I decided on nice low-rider jeans, high-heeled, ultra-strappy tan sandals, a matching belt and a great blouse, almost see-through, white, with buttons that stopped at my cleavage. The neckline went out to a V, it was collared and had half a dozen thin pleats running along the sleeves and down the spine from collar to waist. It was a killer shirt.

I did my makeup subtle and left my hair long, in smooth flips.

I had no jewelry to put on so, being done, I just tucked my lip gloss in my back pocket as I had no wallet or phone, thus taking a purse was unnecessary. Then I left the room.

By the time I was ready, Lucien had disappeared and I went in search of him. When I found him, he was plugging the phone into the jack in the kitchen.

I didn't know what this meant to him but I knew what it meant to me. Thus I nearly threw myself at him and gave him a big kiss.

Instead, I called, "Ready."

His head came up, he looked at me, his eyes went lazy, and my stomach pitched pleasantly.

Then he asked me, "Do you have any idea how beautiful you are?"

My body rocked to a complete halt.

It was safe to say, no. I didn't know.

I mean, I knew I was nothing to sneeze at. No mothers had pulled their children away from my grotesqueness and I could somewhat easily get a date.

The way he said it, the fact that *Lucien* said it—a man so rugged, so compelling, I'd likened him to a living god not twenty minutes before; a man who'd probably seen his fair share of women in his time—that made it another compliment which was profound and I was definitely not sure I could handle it.

"Leah?" His voice calling my name jerked me out of my Lucien Profound Compliment Stupor.

I didn't know what to say. What *did* you say?

I decided on, "Thank you."

He walked right up to me, his eyes thoughtful. When he stopped (in my space, by the way), he used both his hands to shift my hair over my shoulders and he curled his fingers around my neck. The whole time, his eyes were locked on mine.

"You have no idea, do you?" he asked quietly.

"I count the fact that I've reached forty and no one has asked me to join a circus as a good sign," I told him, his head cocked sharply to the side and he burst out laughing, pulling me to him roughly and giving me a stand-up hug.

I endured this hug. It was hard. A stand-up hug from Lucien wasn't as good as a lying down one, but it wasn't far off.

Eventually, after what felt like an eternity (but wasn't, obviously), he pulled away. "Let's get you some books."

He drove us in the Cayenne to a mall in the city. Not any mall but an exclusive one that was surrounded by streets and streets of luxurious boutique shops and classy restaurants, cafés and bars. These were all nestled in between wide clean sidewalks with lampposts on which hooked hanging planters and big stylish pots on the walks all dripping colorful flowers.

He valet parked and we went to an enormous bookstore. There, he bought me ten books.

I thought we'd walk right back to the valet, but he steered me into the boutique streets and seemed perfectly fine with wandering the sidewalks on a sunny day, hand in hand.

I saw a particularly gorgeous outfit in a window and my heart must have leaped because his head turned to me before he walked me right in. Then he went directly to the shop assistant, told her we wanted the outfit in the window and gave her my size.

I was staring at him and I was pretty sure my mouth was hanging open when the assistant asked me, "Would you like to try it on?"

I looked at her and was about to speak when Lucien said, "No. We'll take it."

I watched in horror, mainly because I could see the prices on the register display, as she rung it up and it took all my willpower not to freak out.

I stood dutifully beside Lucien as he paid, the shop assistant looking at him probably like I did when he yanked off the towel and at me definitely like I was the luckiest woman in the universe.

As we walked out, Lucien carrying both my bags, I felt it important to say something.

"That wasn't necessary."

His hand gave mine a squeeze but he didn't look at me.

"You're correct, it wasn't," he replied.

Well, what could you say to that?

Except nothing. So I said nothing.

I was careful to moderate my heart and I did this by not looking into any more windows so that Lucien wouldn't again go spending hundreds and hundreds (and *hundreds*) of dollars on one single outfit.

It didn't matter. This happened twice more with things Lucien wanted me to have. A pair of delicate, antique, silver and coral Navajo chandelier earrings and two pairs of outrageously expensive but undeniably gorgeous high-heeled shoes.

I tried the shoes on. Both pairs, Lucien, lounged back in a chair like he owned the joint and staring at my feet, asked me, "Do they fit?" Before I said a word, he looked at my face (which was probably rapturous, what could I say, they were great shoes) and then said to the salesperson, "We'll take them."

I was struggling with the supremely peculiar fact that it appeared that the Mighty Vampire Lucien, who was most definitely a male of his species, didn't mind shopping when I noticed something.

It was the same on the street and in the shops as it had been at The Feast. People were looking at him, even some of them staring at him.

They didn't know who he was. They only saw a tall, vital, unbelievably good-looking man who was clearly wealthy and held himself with a raw but restrained power.

They had no idea he could move faster than lightning and haul me *and* my fat ass around like I weighed as much as a pencil. They had no idea that, for whatever reason, he was revered by his people, a race of superhumans who lived forever.

And they'd never know.

The Mighty Vampire Lucien was walking down a sunny street, but he was forced to live a secret life hiding who he really was.

Memories hit me like sledgehammers. My behavior at The Selection. My response to my first lesson, telling him the way his people fed was sick. When I was talking to Stephanie, assuming the people who went to Feasts were victims. Telling Lucien yesterday he disgusted me.

This was when I made my second mistake.

I stopped walking down the sidewalk but I did it like my body had slammed against a brick wall. Lucien kept walking for a stride but turned his head when he felt resistance from my arm. His eyes went to our linked hands then to my face. Whatever he saw made him turn to me and take a swift step back.

"Leah, sweetheart, what is it?"

My head had tilted back to look at him and for some reason I again felt like crying.

Before I could think better of it, I blurted, "You can't be you."

He got closer. "Pardon?"

I lifted my hand and waved it around. "Out here. You can't be you."

"I don't understand."

"*You*," I repeated, pointing at him. "You can move like a rocket and you can probably lift up that car and throw it across the street." I gestured to a shiny Audi parked next to us and Lucien looked at the car, then back at me. "You can, can't you?"

"Throw a car across the street?" he asked like he thought I might be mental.

"Yes," I answered.

"I've never tried," he replied, his brows drawing together and he got even closer. "What's this about?"

I gestured again in a vague way. "Everyone's looking at you. They look at you and they can see you, but they don't have any clue what you are."

His jaw got tight but I was too much in my tizzy to notice it.

Then I said, "I was a bitch and I've said some pretty unforgivable things, and for that, I apologize. It won't happen again."

His brows unknitted but they went up. I'd surprised him.

His gaze turned wary. "What brought that on?"

I didn't answer him.

Instead I asked my own question, "If you tried, could you throw that car across the street?"

"Leah—"

"Please answer me," I requested softly.

He sighed before saying, "Without a doubt."

Wow. I'd just guessed.

Holy crap.

He even made it sound like that wouldn't be too much of an effort.

All of a sudden I wanted to know how strong he was. I wanted to know how old he was. I wanted to know how he could walk and move like a normal person and not shatter glasses in his hand or crush my bones to dust when he hugged me.

It was at this point that I was seriously lamenting my behavior in Vampire Studies.

"Would you like to tell me what this is about?" he inquired, taking me out of my astonishment.

I didn't. But I'd started this; I had no choice but to end it.

"It seems," I hesitated, not knowing what to say, found the word and carried on, "wrong, that you can't be you. There aren't a lot of people you can be you around and I'm supposed to be one of them. That thought just occurred to me and I've said some nasty things about you and your people. You deserved an apology, so I gave you one."

I tried to pass it off as nothing, a simple apology. I was wrong and admitted it.

It clearly didn't come out as a simple apology.

In fact, looking into his face, which had changed again to a look I'd seen a glimpse of before, right before he slammed me against the wall at The Feast and kissed me with savage possession, that he took it as something far, far more.

I took a step back.

Lucien's arm twitched. It was a simple movement for him, barely there, but I staggered forward, crashing against his hard body. His hand dropped mine, his other hand dropped the bags and both arms came around me in a crush. He kissed me with a savage possession that was highly inappropriate on a Sunday afternoon on a street filled with boutiques.

It also curled my toes, sent fire straight between my legs and had me melting into him.

"Yeesh, get a room," someone who seemed far, far away said.

"Randy, shush!" someone else who seemed far, far away shushed the first someone. "They're probably on their honeymoon or something."

Lucien's mouth disconnected from mine and I found I was on tiptoes. I had one arm wrapped around his neck, my other hand was fisted in his hair, and I was plastered against him from chest to knees.

My foggy mind snapped to and I tried to shut down my systems, my response, the way I liked it far more than was healthy when he kissed me.

Especially when he kissed me like that.

My hand left his hair and went to his shoulder, but he kept me close, his eyes hooded but examining my face.

And he said something that freaked me out.

"I want to believe this is you," his voice was low, soft, quiet, "but this isn't you."

He was wrong and he was right.

It wasn't me. It was the new, improved me.

Or at least the new, improved, perfect concubine me before I could go back to the old, faulty, real me when he released me.

"You don't think I can apologize?" I asked, giving his shoulder a testing push.

He didn't move a centimeter.

I stopped pushing.

"No," his voice was still low, "that was you. The kiss was you. The rest of it is not."

"What rest of it?"

He changed subjects. "We should talk about last night."

I felt my body begin to stiffen, but I fought it and stayed relaxed. "If you like."

His mouth grew tight as his gaze grew sharp.

"Not. Fucking. You," he declared, now angry, and I held my breath for what was next.

I couldn't fight with him. The new, improved Leah wouldn't do that, certainly not on a boutique street.

No. Not ever. I could never fight with him.

I was channeling Perfect Cousin Myrna when he let me go but grabbed my hand, snatched up the bags, switched our direction and headed back to the valet parking.

We walked in silence.

I decided to test his mood. "Do you mind if we get a latte for the road?"

He stopped and looked at me. "What would you say if I did mind?"

Old Leah would tell him it would only take ten flipping minutes, or at least she'd glare at him and pout all the way home.

New Leah didn't know what to say.

As I struggled to come up with a reply, he closed his eyes as if patience eluded him. Then he gave up, walked us into the nearest coffee house (there were a billion), got me a latte, him a double espresso with enough sugar to down an elephant, and we were away home.

My third mistake wasn't a mistake, as such. It was just being in the wrong place at the wrong time.

I was in the dressing room putting my fantastic new shoes on the tilted shelves that showed shoes to their strategic best when Lucien walked in and went directly to my purse that was sitting on the dressing table. I turned and saw him drop my cell phone and wallet in the purse, my passport beside it.

Throughout the ride home he seemed tense. He didn't anymore and I was unsure of his mood and further unsure what to do.

Was this another test?

The phone in the house was one thing but he'd put the keys to the Cayenne on the key holder by the back door. Now he was giving me back my freedom, in total.

Obviously, I couldn't run immediately from the house, he'd catch me. I also couldn't run at all because, again, he'd catch me.

Still.

He turned to leave, caught me staring at him and stopped.

"Italy," he said.

I blinked. "What?"

"Italy. That would be your preferred on the run from a vamp destination."

I felt my lips part and my eyes grow wide.

For some reason, my expression made his guarded face gentle and he walked into my space.

I tilted my head to look back at him and whispered, "How did you know?"

"Fiona," he answered without hesitation.

"Fiona?" I asked.

"Fiona Hawkins."

Fiona Hawkins? *Aunt* Fiona Hawkins? How did he know Aunt Fiona?

And why would she be telling him about me always wanting to go to Italy?

This was just bizarre!

"Aunt Fiona told you I've always wanted to go to Italy?"

"Fiona told me a great number of things. Fiona Hawkins was my concubine fifty-one years ago."

This information rocked me so much it was physical. I took a step back but his arm snaked around my waist and brought me forward so my stomach, hips and thighs were pressed against his.

"Aunt Fiona serviced you?" I breathed.

I mean, I knew she was a concubine. She wasn't a Buchanan but concubines were friendly (most of the time). I'd known her since forever.

"I throw birthday parties for all my concubines every year," he answered.

I felt my mouth drop open again as something occurred to me.

I went to Aunt Fiona's birthday parties.

Every year.

"Oh my God."

Lucien ignored my prayer and went on, "I try to attend. Sometimes I can't stay long. Sometimes I don't attend the party but visit with them before or after. Twenty years ago I was able to attend. She served fried chicken."

I felt the pulse of his words shaft through my body and it was physical too. My entire frame jolted with it so much I had to grab on to the sleeves of his shirt at his biceps to stay standing.

"Or," Lucien continued, "I should say, *you* made fried chicken for her guests. She told me before I went it would be the best thing I tasted...for eternity." I kept staring at him as his face dipped closer, his black eyes warmed, and he murmured, "She was wrong."

My mouth opened and then closed. I didn't know what to say. What I did know was that he'd just given me another earth-shattering compliment.

He kept talking. "After that I went every year. And every year, you made her your fried chicken."

"That's her favorite," I whispered.

"I know," he replied.

I put my hands on his chest and commented, "I didn't see you."

"I didn't want to be seen."

"You can do that?"

"When you can control people's minds, you can do anything. Even disappear."

I felt my body tense. "You controlled my mind?"

He nodded and said, "I also marked you."

Oh my *God*.

That was true!

I'd felt it. That weird drugged feeling, not as strong as he did it now, but I felt it. I always thought it was the oppressive heat of Aunt Fiona's kitchen. She had bad ventilation and frying chicken for seventy-five guests heated up a kitchen, believe you me.

"Why would you do that? There were no vampires there."

"Yes there were."

Wow. I didn't know that. I'd been in the presence of vampires before.

"Really?" I asked.

He nodded.

"Did Aunt Fiona tell you about me?"

"As much as she knew. She liked talking about you. She's very fond of you, thinks you have spirit. She also kept an eye on you for me."

Holy crap!

What on earth did *that* mean?

"An eye on me?" I prompted.

He nodded again.

"What does that mean?"

"She told me what you were up to," his face grew dark, "and who you were with when you were up to it."

He didn't look happy.

I figured I was less happy.

"Are you saying Aunt Fiona *informed* on me?" My voice was pitching higher.

"Yes." He was back to seeming unperturbed.

This was unreal!

"So, essentially, she spied on me."

"Not with that, no. Fiona listened, she watched, and she told me. She'd also tell me where you were. Then *I* spied on you."

My body jerked again.

"*What?*"

"It wasn't exactly spying," he continued casually, "more like watching. It was highly enjoyable. You'd get up to practically anything and you've a very expressive face, pet."

I couldn't take this in. The Mighty Vampire Lucien was a stalker!

"Why..." I spluttered. "Why would you do that?"

"It amused me. *You* amused me." He studied my face and muttered, "Most of the time, you still do."

"You stalked me!" It wasn't a shout. Cousin Myrna wouldn't shout. But it was pretty damn close.

"You can't stalk what's yours," he returned.

I looked at his shirt. "Yes, I suspect that's what all the stalkers say."

He threw back his head and shouted with laughter.

I didn't feel like putting *this* in my Why I *Might* Like Lucien Safe. This went straight into the Why I Hate Lucien Vault, pride of place.

"You're freaking me out," I informed him as I pressed against his chest to get away.

His other arm joined the one around me and he drew me closer as his face dipped lower. "The minute I saw you, twenty years ago, I knew you'd be mine."

Yes, totally freaking me out.

"Lucien—"

He cut me off. "Leah, I've been waiting twenty years to have you *right here*." He emphasized his last two words with a tight arm squeeze.

Nope, not freaking me out. I didn't know what beyond freaking out was, but whatever it was, he was making me do *that*.

"I don't know what to do with this information," I told him honestly.

"You don't need to know. *I* know," he returned.

I didn't think that was good.

"Are you going to, um...share?"

He shook his head and then bent to brush his lips against mine.

Pulling away a scant inch, he said mysteriously, "You'll know when it happens." Then his arms grew tighter and I was pressed against him from chest to knees. His voice turned rough and his eyes went intense when he asked, "Are you hungry for dinner or should we find something else to do for a while?"

I didn't think it would be healthy for me in any way to find something else to do with Lucien for a while.

Fried chicken wasn't healthy for you either, but I figured it was far healthier to my future than what Lucien might have in mind.

"I'm hungry for dinner."

He grinned. "Now why did I know that would be your answer?"

I decided my best course of action was not to reply. So I didn't.

He bent and kissed the pulse in my neck then shifted to my side. His arm sliding around my shoulders, he walked me to the kitchen. After he deposited me there, he disappeared.

Now, forty-five minutes later, I looked down and found I was whipping the potatoes.

Dinner was ready. A dinner I'd have to share with Lucien.

I looked across the room.

I'd tidied as I'd cooked which was something my mother taught me to do. The kitchen was relatively clean, the chicken in the oven staying warm, the green beans in their water, the warm homemade biscuits wrapped up in a clean tea towel. I'd set the breakfast nook for our meal.

Myrna would definitely have set the dining room table. She'd have a damask tablecloth, perfectly clean and unwrinkled, a silver candelabrum *and* fresh-cut flowers from the garden she tended, a bouquet that she'd arranged herself.

I figured Lucien would know that wasn't me and if I did something like that it might put him in a mood.

I had to get through the night before I got through the rest of my however many years with him trying *not* to put him in a mood. So I set the far more casual breakfast nook.

However, I was in a quandary. I needed him at the dinner table and I needed to set out the food.

Old Leah would just shout for him, louder and louder, until he appeared.

New Leah thought that wasn't seemly.

Myrna would go find him and likely give a low curtsy, begging the pleasure of his company.

I took a chance and tried something.

Lucien, if you can hear me, dinner is ready, I thought in his direction, wherever that was.

I listened, heard no movement in the house and sighed at how annoying it was that he couldn't hear me talking to him when *I* wanted him to hear me, only when *he* was eavesdropping. I threw another tea towel over the potatoes, deciding to go in search of him.

I turned and saw Lucien walking in, his eyes on me, his face blank, his posture strange.

It was, somehow, alert.

I went alert too.

He got in my space (again) and looked down at me, his face still blank.

"How did you do that?" he asked.

"Do what?" I asked back.

"You got in my head," he told me.

So it worked.

"Well, I didn't want to shout and you can hear me when I'm talking to you in my mind, so I tried it, and—"

He cut me off. "I can't hear you all the time, only when I'm listening."

That was news.

"Really?"

He waited a moment before stating, "No one has ever done that."

I felt my eyes go round as I repeated, *"Really?"*

His expression turned thoughtful. I suspected so did mine seeing as I wanted to know what in *the hell* was going on.

Then his expression went watchful again like he was denying something from me, which I thought was weird.

Eventually, he said quietly, "Really."

He studied my face, his eyes so intent I felt that pulsating feeling again, as if he was trying to source my mood, invade my thoughts.

I wished with all my heart I could do the same thing.

I wanted to ask what he was doing but I figured Myrna would let him do whatever he wanted to do without question, even if he was invading her mind. So I just looked at him.

Finally he declared, "Let's eat."

I put the potatoes in a serving bowl and carried all the food to the table while Lucien opened the wine and poured it. All the while this happened I had a freaky feeling about the whole getting into his mind business.

I added that to my very long mental Ask Mom Tomorrow List.

We'd served up the food and I was buttering my flaky, still-warm biscuit (it could be argued my biscuits were better than my fried chicken, or, at least, Mom and Lana could argue about it, and they did all the time) when Lucien spoke again.

"We need to talk about last night."

My mouth was watering for the biscuit. When he spoke those words, it went dry and my appetite took a hike.

Regardless, I bit into the biscuit and chewed, the biscuit like dust in my mouth, and looked at him with what I hoped was respectful inquiry.

He took in my look and his mouth got tight.

"And yesterday," he went on.

I decided to waylay the talk by announcing hurriedly, "I was wrong about yesterday."

His eyes locked with mine. "Yes, you were."

My mind seethed.

My mouth reminded him softly, "I already apologized."

"You apologized about some of it, not all of it."

I pressed my lips together.

Lucien kept talking. "Katrina and I have been mates for fifty years, Leah, but I've known her seventy-five. I filed Severance from her this week. Do you know what Severance means?"

I nodded.

He watched me nod and continued, "Our impending Severance had nothing to do with you and everything to do with you."

That didn't make any sense and I didn't want it to make any sense. I didn't want to be talking about this at all.

But as usual, I didn't get a choice. Lucien kept speaking.

"I knew things weren't right with Rina and you personify everything that isn't right about her. Being with you prompted me, finally, to make my decision."

His words didn't penetrate.

That wasn't true, one did. He called her *Rina*.

I heard him say it the day before, but now I *felt* him say it.

My stomach twisted.

"She loves you," I whispered through the pain in my stomach.

"She doesn't know what love is," he replied tersely. "Vampires don't have the same expectations when they mate, Leah. Eternity is a very long time. It isn't unheard of for there to be absences, sometimes for years, even decades. And fidelity is definitely not a requirement of vampire mating."

I had the sense he was explaining something about his relationship with *Rina*, but I also had the sense he was explaining something to me.

My dry mouth went parched.

Obviously, since my contract stated he had free use of my blood and my body, I couldn't expect him to be faithful to his mate.

Just as obviously, since he had a mate, Severance or not, I shouldn't expect that he would be faithful to me. Neither my blood nor my body.

It was then something hit me. Something so overpowering that stomach twist wrenched the other way, more acute, slicing through me.

I had enough experience with the wrong kind of men to know *exactly* what he was saying. The about-face with the orgasm business last night and this morning wasn't him wanting to give me something.

It was Lucien's act of contrition.

Regardless of this Vamp Non-Fidelity rule, he felt guilty.

I put my biscuit on my plate.

Then I whispered, "You had sex last night."

It sounded like an accusation and I wanted to kick myself. Myrna wouldn't make an accusation, never in a million years. And I didn't have any right to make an accusation. None whatsoever.

But I couldn't take it back.

His face went hard. "Leah—"

I waved my hand in the air, trying to undo the damage I'd done as the knife in my belly sliced a painful line straight up to my gullet.

"It isn't any of my business." I tried to make it come out airily but feared I failed.

"Leah—" he started again, but I began to carve into my fried chicken breast and talked over him.

"You just be you, do what you want, live your life like any vamp would. And I'll be me and do my job, no troubles for you, no expectations of you. Promise."

I was looking at my plate, surprised, even at myself, that I'd just let go of the game and came clean.

This was a mistake. I should have kept my eyes on him.

"Your *job*?" he asked in a silky voice I'd never heard him use before. A voice that was beyond scary. So scary, my eyes shot to his face.

It appeared I'd made some kind of mistake. A bad one.

He was angry. Belatedly, I felt his fury had filled the room and I found it hard to breathe.

I also found myself confused. I mean, it *was* my job being his concubine.

Wasn't it?

In an effort to calm his anger, I decided to explain.

"I figured it out yesterday, Lucien," I told him, and seeing as this was slightly embarrassing, my eyes went to a point over his shoulder before going back to my plate. I put a bite of chicken in my mouth then looked back to him.

He was silent through this, not eating, his elbow on the table, his wineglass in hand, his eyes scorching into me.

I kept going after I swallowed.

"I'd been an idiot." I thought he'd like that but his face didn't change. "You've been very kind to me, generous with me." I waved my fork around the kitchen in a lame effort to make my point. "I can't imagine all vamps are like this, and even if they are, it's not a bad life. I...I..." I stammered, losing my momentum when his face still didn't change, but I found the courage to sally forth. "I'd been wrong. So, yesterday, when I had all that time to think, I decided I'll do my job servicing you until you're through with me. No more fights. No more tantrums. I promise."

He finally broke his silence and said, "Servicing me."

I nodded.

"Servicing me," he repeated.

I nodded again, this time more hesitantly.

"Would you care to explain to me, in detail, what you think your job is, Leah?"

I didn't really care to, and anyway, he knew.

Didn't he?

"You know," I told him.

"Explain it," he said.

My head tilted to the side in confusion. "But...I don't understand. You know."

He leaned forward a fraction of an inch, his voice dipped danger-ously low, and he clipped, "Explain it."

"I...you, I..." I faltered then recovered, "I'm available for you to feed and...to...um, do other things, whenever you want." His mouth got tight and I went on, "And, you know, let you show me off, go with you to places and..."

"Stop talking," he demanded and I snapped my mouth shut.

Something was wrong.

I'd never expected to say any of this to him but I thought the time was right. Cards on the table. He won.

I thought he'd be happy. He won.

Why wasn't he happy?

Why did he look so...freaking...*mad*?

"Lucien—" I started but he interrupted me.

"So you think you're my whore," he stated, and I winced.

I wouldn't put it that way. I mean, it kind of *was* that way, but even my mind was shying away from that terminology.

"I wouldn't put it that way," I said quietly.

"How would you put it? You think you're here to service me. You think your job is to let me feed from you and fuck you whenever I want. Your *job*." He spit out the last word like it tasted foul and he couldn't bear it in his mouth. "So, how, exactly, would you put it, my pet?"

"I'm your concubine," I reminded him, thinking that said it all.

I thought this because it did!

He watched me a moment and I watched him back. Mainly I watched his eyes working and I didn't like the way they were working.

Then his arm moved, it was a blur and nearly instantly his wine glass shattered against the wall. The strength of the throw was so immense the glass was sand, the liquid in it splashed in a tall, wide mark against the wall.

I stared over my shoulder at the wall. Then I looked at him, mouth hanging open.

"Have you been paying attention," he growled, hesitated, then kept growling, "*at all?*"

I felt my body start to tremble at the ferocity in his gaze.

"Lucien—" I whispered, unsure what I was going to say, but whatever it was I didn't get the chance to say it.

"I've a mind," he talked over me—gone was the growl, his voice was back to silky smooth, "to show you what being my whore would mean."

I had the feeling this was *not* good.

My heart started beating so fast I could feel my pulse in my neck.

"Yes, sweetheart," his voice was still silky smooth, "you wouldn't like it."

My breath started coming in pants.

He stood, got close and looked down at me.

I tilted my head to look up at him.

"For the record, Leah," he said softly, "I didn't fuck Kitty last night." He leaned in and his voice dropped to a whisper. "She wanted it, even begged for it. She begged to touch me, begged for the chance to take me in her mouth, begged me to fuck her." He leaned in closer, his hand came up, fingers curling around my neck. I saw him hold his body rigid as if he was controlling an impulse and I held my breath. "I was tempted, I'll admit, but in the end she didn't smell like you and she didn't taste like you and she didn't look like you so I could scarcely bear to feed from her, which is all I fucking did."

Before I knew it, he was gone. *Whoosh.*

I heard the garage door go up, the Porsche roared to life and then the garage door went back down.

The entire time I sat there, not knowing what to do or how to feel, especially about the fact that he just gave me another weird, but extraordinary, compliment.

What I did know was that I, again, managed to screw things up. Even though I thought I was doing the right thing for myself, for my family, for Lucien even.

What I also knew was that I really, *really* needed to call my mom.

Shakily, I got up and left the fried chicken, the pulverized wine glass, and that's exactly what I did.

13

The Dream

I finally understood.

As my head lifted, my legs slid open, his hips fell between and my arms wrapped around him tight as if they'd never let go.

And I never *wanted* to let him go.

Never. Not for eternity.

My mouth sought his ear.

"I understand," I whispered, the budding beauty of it flowing through me.

Lucien's tongue swept across the wound where he was feeding.

His head came up, his beautiful eyes boring into mine, his blazing with triumph and searing into me like a brand.

His hands moved to my hips, lifting, his mouth came down on mine in a bruising, possessive kiss, and he filled me.

Through his claiming thrusts, my mouth against his, I breathed lovingly, "I'm yours."

"Leah."

Hands were on me, my lover's hands, but they weren't touching me in a loverly way.

"Leah, wake up."

"Say it again," Lucien snarled but I'd lost track.

I was so full of him I'd never been so filled. It was beautiful, so beautiful I started crying.

"Say it again," he demanded, his hand in my hair pulling my head back, not gently, the pain mingled with the pleasure of his claiming.

"I'm yours," I whispered, my eyes focusing on his. "Only yours. Always."

I was rolled, I felt weight on me, a hand on my arm shaking me.

"Leah, you're dreaming. Wake up."

He melted away. He wasn't inside me anymore. My arms held nothing.

Everything went black.

The loss of him was immense. I felt it through to my soul.

Fear filled me and I screamed.

"Leah, wake up!"

They were burning him.

And they were hanging me.

The sentence for his crime was to watch my death before his own.

My eyes were riveted to him as the flames curled around his powerful body.

I felt the noose go around my neck.

I love you, I whispered to his mind.

The hand shaking me stilled, but the fingers curled, biting into my arm.

I watched his eyes close, not with the pain of the flames with a different kind of pain.

I closed my own.

I love you too, sweetling. I heard his voice in my head.

My heart took flight.

Then the trapdoor fell out from beneath my feet.

I came awake with a jerk and a cry, yanking away from Lucien's warm heavy body, my own prepared to flee. From what, I didn't know.

I had my feet to the floor when an arm hooked around my waist and I was lifted up, back into the bed. Lucien curled me into his body, cradled in his arms. His back was to the headboard, I was in his lap.

I melted into him.

In all this bizarreness, the most bizarre of all was that I was trembling like a leaf and bawling like a baby.

"Ho-ho-holy *crap*," I whispered, my voice hitching. My arms were around him, holding tightly, and I didn't let go as I kept right on blubbering.

One of his arms left me and I felt his hand stroking my hair.

"Holy *crap*," I repeated, this time without the hitch. I burrowed closer, not knowing why, just that I needed to get close, as close as I could.

I actually *needed* it. I needed to feel his warm, hard, big body surrounding me, keeping me safe.

"It's all right, Leah, you've just had a bad dream," Lucien murmured to the top of my head.

Was that what happened?

I didn't remember. I just remembered the terror.

And the sorrow.

No, not just the sorrow. The *loss* and the sorrow.

"Holy crap," I whispered again, a fresh batch of tears overflowing, this time silently.

"Shh, sweetheart, it was just a dream," Lucien soothed gently, his words stirring my hair.

I burrowed deeper as the tears flowed. He held me and I held him back.

Finally, after I had control, I said quietly, "I don't remember."

His hand left my hair and his arm wrapped around my upper back, his long fingers curling around my shoulder.

It was then everything came crashing back to me.

Not the dream. Lucien and the wineglass incident. My body tensed, and when it did, so did his arms. My eyes took in what I could see, which wasn't much, mostly his throat in the dark.

"You're here," I said stupidly.

"Where else would I be?"

I didn't know. He seemed pretty pissed when he left. I didn't expect in a million years he'd come back at all, much less hold me tenderly after I had a bad dream.

My head tipped up so I could see his face in the shadows.

"You aren't mad at me anymore?"

I saw his chin dip down to look at me.

"I was," he told me, and I braced. "I shouldn't tell you this, pet, but it's difficult to stay angry with you when I can smell you." He gave me a squeeze and continued on a murmur, "And fucking impossible when I can feel you and hear your breathing and your heart beating in your sleep."

This made my heart start beating faster.

He went on, "Then you were moving, then screaming, then crying."

I felt my lips part. "I screamed?"

His shadowy head nodded.

"I *cried*?" I asked.

Another nod.

"In my sleep?" I went on.

Still another nod right before he moved us, sliding down the bed and rolling so we were facing each other. He pulled the covers over us and then his arms moved around me again.

"Do you remember any of it?" he asked, sounding more than mildly curious, and I shook my head against the pillow. "None of it?" he pressed, and I shook my head again.

"I don't think I want to," I told him. "It made me scream," I paused, then added, "and cry."

His arms gave me a squeeze. "Do you remember who was in your dream?"

I shook my head yet again. "I don't know. All I know is whoever it was, I lost them and it made me sad." I felt a shudder slide through my body and I pressed closer to him. "Unbelievably sad."

He gathered me tightly to his chest. "It was just a dream, sweetheart."

This time I nodded my head.

But it didn't feel like a dream. I didn't remember it but whatever it was, it felt real, or at least the pain it left behind did.

"Has that ever happened before?" Lucien asked.

I nodded again. "When I was younger I used to have dreams I didn't remember. My mom would have to wake me up, but it hasn't happened in a really long time."

"Did you ever remember those dreams?"

I shook my head and whispered, "I hope I never remember this one either. With those, I would wake up scared or upset," my voice dipped to nearly inaudible, "this one was worse."

He gave me another reassuring squeeze. "It's over."

It was then I realized what I was doing. And it was a second after that that I wondered if Myrna would snuggle close to her vampire after pissing him off royally.

"Lucien?"

"Yes, my pet?"

"Earlier," I started, he tensed, and even though I didn't want another wineglass incident, especially when the thing he was holding now and very able to throw and shatter against a wall was me, I forged ahead, "I didn't mean to make you mad."

He didn't reply so I got up on an elbow and looked down on his shadowed face.

"I'm sorry I made you mad."

He rolled to his back and pulled me on top of him, a hand in my hair pressing my face into his neck.

He still didn't reply. He simply started to play with my hair.

I decided it was time to get things straight.

Unfortunately, my mother wasn't answering her phone, which meant she was probably out at a movie. Mom liked movies, any kind of movies, mostly weepies and rom coms, but she wasn't avverse to an action film, the bloodier the better.

Aunt Nadia, who was always my favorite auntie and the one I could talk to about anything, wasn't answering either, which meant she was probably out with Mom.

I didn't want to call any of my other aunties or cousins because I didn't want them to know I was such a moron, or more of a moron than they already thought I was.

I called Lana who answered. But she said Rafe was going to be there any minute. She was in a tizzy of excitement. I could hear it and now I understood it, but she promised she'd call me back first thing in the morning.

So I was still as in the dark as ever about everything that was happening.

Therefore, it was up to me to get things straight.

"I thought I was giving you what you wanted," I told Lucien and his hand in my hair stilled for a few moments before his fingers started twirling a lock again.

Then he said something that threw me way off guard, "I want *you.*"

Me? He wanted me?

No one wanted me.

I was, as I just noted, a moron, amongst other not so good things.

This made my stomach feel warm at the same time it made my heart lurch and fear crawl up my spine.

This was just great. Instead of two contradictory emotions now I was having three.

"You have me," I lied before pointing out the obvious, "I'm right here."

I felt his head move, his lips touched my temple, before he settled onto the pillows again.

"I had you, sweetling," he murmured, using a different endearment, this one old-fashioned and way, way, *way* too effective. So effective it wiped out the heart lurch and the crawling fear and significantly intensified the warmth in my belly. "Every day and every night, I've had you. Until today and tonight. Now, you're gone." His hand clenched in my hair gently and he asked softly, "Why have you gone, Leah?"

Something stuck in my throat. I knew what it was but I swallowed it away and pretended it wasn't there in the first place.

I knew I was lying to myself now but I figured lying to myself was definitely the best way to go.

"I'm here," I whispered, "right here, where you want me to be."

His hand went out of my hair and he moved me. He slid me off his body and shifted me so my back was pressed to his front, his arm tight around my waist, elbow cocked, hand pressed flat between my breasts.

"Remember that," he said into the back of my hair when he'd repositioned me.

"What?" I asked.

"That here is where I want you to be. For twenty years, I've wanted you here." His arm tensed and pressed me deeper into his body as I felt his face press deeper into my hair. "You don't wait twenty years for a whore, Leah. You don't take her shopping for books. You don't move your clothes in her closet. You don't take her amongst your people. And you certainly don't put up with her when she's misbehaving."

I decided to focus on the last thing he said because it pissed me off. The other stuff made a lot of sense. It also made my belly feel warm again and I really didn't need *that*.

But Myrna wouldn't get pissed off. Never.

I tamped down the anger and decided to go with resigned.

"So, where does this leave us?"

"Where we've always been," he replied, his voice somehow lighter like he'd not only had some weight lifted, but also like he was amused. "But instead of you coming out fighting, you've retreated and put up your defenses."

Oh no.

He had me totally figured out!

He pressed closer and stated firmly, "But I'll get through."

Oh no he would *not*. Not if I had anything to do with it (which I did).

"You're already through," I lied, and he chuckled, which made me want to throw something at him.

Of course, I didn't.

"I'm not," he declared.

"You are."

"I'm not."

I pushed against his arm, surprisingly it loosened, and I turned to face him.

I looked up at him in the dark and I said my next in a whisper, "If you want me to beg you to fuck me, I will. I'll do anything you want me to do. Try me. I'll prove it to you. Lucien, you have me."

I held my breath, not really wanting him to make me do anything he wanted me to do but prepared to do it nonetheless.

His face dipped closer to mine but stopped a breath away giving me the impression he could see in the dark.

"I don't want you to beg, sweetling. It isn't about that. That was just a test, which you failed. If you'd let go, just a little bit, I'll show you what it *is* about."

"Tell me," I urged.

"There are no words."

"Okay, *try* to tell me."

He hesitated then he said, "Trust."

I blinked in the dark. "Trust?"

"I've told you this before, you need to trust me, Leah."

"With what?"

"With everything."

Was he crazy?

He wanted me to trust him? With everything? Then, when he was sick of me, he'd let me go and move on to his next concubine, doing this for eternity.

He *had* to be crazy!

He would, of course, throw me birthday parties and maybe, as decades passed, recruit me to help him stalk his next obsession.

Boy, *that* would be fun.

It took a lot out of me and it was really not a nice thing to do but self-preservation forced me to curl closer to him and lie yet again.

"You have my trust."

It was nearly imperceptible but I could swear I felt his body give a small jerk.

"You don't think I know how it feels?" he asked and his voice was no longer mellow and amused, it was edging toward anger.

I had, inadvertently, made a tactical error.

I attempted to salvage the situation.

"Lucien—" I started.

I failed to salvage the situation. He kept right on talking.

"When the taming is complete, Leah, it isn't completed with words or a ceremony. It happens through actions and feelings."

His words took the breath out of me. Or, I should say, one particular word.

"The taming?"

"The taming," he said calmly. "I'm taming you."

I felt Old Leah slipping back into place.

"You're *taming* me?"

His body tensed and his arm tightened around me in a way that felt like containment.

Even so, his voice was still calm when he replied, "Yes."

"Taming," I repeated.

Now he sounded like he was smiling when he repeated, "Yes."

"Does that mean what I think it means?" I asked.

"I'm guessing that's unlikely," he answered.

This did not make me feel any better.

"Have you done this..." I could barely bring myself to say it but I forced myself, "*taming* business a lot?"

"Not recently, no. But I used to do it before The Revolution on occasion. But only if my prey was special," he held me closer and his voice got softer, "like you."

I figured he thought that this was one of his profound compliments.

I did *not*.

"I'm tired," I announced suddenly.

And I was. Very tired. Of my crazy life!

Most especially the crazy vampire who was sharing my crazy life (against my will, I might add).

He was silent for several moments.

Then his body moved like he was laughing. I ground my teeth together when I realized he was, indeed, laughing. He must have heard my teeth grinding because his laughter became vocal.

I visualized myself kicking him in the shin. It was childish, but it worked.

"That wouldn't be a very nice thing to do, my pet," he whispered and my body went still.

He'd seen me visualizing.

God, I hated him!

I tried to pull away but his arm locked.

"Will you please let me go?"

"Why?" he asked, still chuckling.

"So I can get comfortable," I snapped.

Myrna would never snap but screw Myrna. If there was a snapping moment, this was it.

He settled his heavy weight into me, shifting me to my back, his legs tangling with mine, his arm still caging me in, keeping me close.

"This isn't comfortable," I declared on yet another lie.

"Mm," he murmured against my temple and a happy trill glided across my skin (something else I ignored), "I disagree."

Okay, I had to get control. As much as I detested asking it, I had to.

What would Myrna do?

I wracked my brain. Then I had it.

"Whatever you wish, Lucien," I mumbled obediently.

He chuckled low yet again, kissed my temple, then ordered, "Go to sleep, Leah."

I didn't answer. I also didn't go to sleep.

I decided to fume.

This lasted for about five minutes.

Then his heat, his heaviness, his soft breath stirring my hair, his large powerful body at rest by mine, a body which could likely keep me safe from just about anything in the world, permeated my subconscious, and a second later, I was dead to the world.

14

The Explosion

" **W**hat's happened to Leah?"

Even after hearing Stephanie's whispered question, Lucien didn't take his eyes from Leah as she slid away from them through the crowded room.

He heard Leah saying softly again and again, "Excuse me," as she moved amongst the crush of opera patrons on her way to the restroom. Sometimes she would give them a small polite smile.

As she moved and spoke, the patrons turned to look.

The men would keep looking. The women would either stare or glare.

She disappeared from sight and Lucien's eyes stayed where he last saw her.

Three weeks.

It had been three weeks since their Sunday together, a day that started unbelievably well and ended unbelievably badly.

And then she had her dream.

"Lucien?" Stephanie called, but lost in thought, Lucien didn't respond. He continued to watch the entrance to the hall where he'd last seen Leah.

He feared he'd broken her. Not how he'd intended, in a way he could never have imagined nor would ever have wanted.

For the first week, he saw her come through every once in a while. Often her eyes would flash. Other times she'd look painfully and hilariously undecided, as if she had one reaction but was forcing herself to display another. She also lost her patience while attempting to make him some complicated soufflé that went tremendously badly, however her foul-mouthed tirade after it collapsed was immensely entertaining.

The disastrous soufflé gave him hope.

So did the dreams.

She'd had four more, all the same. All of them starting with her moving, nearly writhing against him as if in ecstasy, but this would end abruptly in a blood-chilling scream.

Seconds later, he'd hear her words whispered in his head.

I love you.

Shortly after came the choking sobs, she'd wake and attempt to flee. He'd catch her and hold her until her trembling and tears ceased.

After the second dream they'd stopped talking about it. She would simply hold on to him in a way that felt desperate. He'd stroke her back or her hair until her body relaxed and she fell asleep in his arms.

Lucien closed his eyes tightly as the words sounded softly in his head.

I love you.

Those words, those three *fucking* words, whispered in his head.

It wasn't even the words, it was the way she said them. As if she'd pulled them out of her soul and offered them to him like a gift.

And he knew she was talking to him, dreaming of him. She wouldn't be in his head if she wasn't. He wouldn't be able to hear it.

He also knew she wasn't lying when she said she didn't remember. Something was blocking the memory, likely the power behind the emotion of whatever made her scream and sob in such a fucking heartbroken way it was difficult to witness.

Lucien didn't know what to make of the intensity of her dream and the aftermath or what they meant to him or Leah, except it was pretty clear her earlier hostility toward him, and now her deference to him, were defense mechanisms. He'd managed to establish a connection but she wasn't allowing herself to embrace it.

Even so, he didn't like that Leah had them.

Her terror was stark, her pain palpable, and he was powerless to stop them, a feeling he never felt and one he didn't much like.

But he had to admit, he was intrigued by the words and the intensity with which she spoke them.

Even if he felt somehow tortured by them.

It was the dream, and the soufflé, that made him think she'd never be able to continue her latest game.

However, the last two weeks, except for when she had the dreams or when he was feeding (and even then she seemed to hold herself back), all that was Leah had vanished. And it appeared not to be a struggle in the slightest.

None of his Leah came shining through even for a moment.

She was like every concubine he'd had for five hundred years. Perhaps not as worshipful as some or as obviously greedy for the feeding as others, but mostly just the same.

He missed her.

He actually missed their verbal tussles, her comical one-liners delivered when she was angry, her strength of will, her stubbornness, her curiosity, her spirit which filled the house.

All that was gone, including his anticipation of coming home to see what she'd be up to next.

"Lucien? Luce? Helloooo, Luce! Are you in there?" Stephanie called and Lucien's gaze moved to her.

"Sorry," he muttered and Stephanie's eyes narrowed on his face.

"Something's not right in Lucien and Leah Land," Stephanie noted.

Lucien took a sip from his drink before saying, "Everything's fine."

"Doesn't seem fine to me," Stephanie shot back. "Leah *looks* like Leah, gorgeous as ever. And she *smells* like Leah. And she walks like Leah. And talks *somewhat* like Leah. But she's *not* Leah."

Finally Lucien's eyes focused on his friend. "This isn't any of your business, Teffie."

Stephanie was one of the very few (in fact, there were only two, her and Cosmo) who would look at Lucien's face at that moment and issue a challenge.

And that was what she did.

"Well, I beg to differ. Leah's become my friend and I'm worried. I've been over there twice this week. It's like I drove into Stepford and it's *eerie*. I don't like it and Edwina is none too happy either."

"Everything will be fine," Lucien said, turning to look back toward the hall.

"I hope so, Luce, and I hope you make it soon. Because there is no way a woman like that can hold back that much without exploding and I'm not certain even *you* will want to be around when she lets it all out."

Lucien sliced a glance at her, the tone of his voice making his words crystal clear. "We're done talking about this."

Stephanie held his gaze for long moments then changed the subject to one that was only slightly less annoying.

"Rumors are flying," she informed him.

"Rumors always fly," Lucien returned dismissively.

"Not rumors like this," she retorted. "Heard word that The Council is going to open an investigation tomorrow into what you're doing with Leah."

Lucien glanced back at the hall with unconcern. "I've heard that too."

"Well, I bet you haven't heard that Rafe told Dante who told Hamish who told *me* that he's considering moving in with Lana Buchanan."

Lucien's narrowed eyes sliced back to Stephanie.

"Thought that'd get your attention," she muttered.

"Tell me you're joking," he demanded.

She shook her head.

"What's he thinking?" Lucien ground out.

"I'm guessing the same thing as you. He wants more than Lana's blood. The Buchanans are a tasty lot. I had one myself years ago, I know. You boys like different smells, though, and you want to get yourselves some of *that*."

Lucien's body moved, turning toward Stephanie in a way that made her tense.

"Are you bored, Teffie? Do you *want* me to challenge you?"

"I'm saying it like it is," she returned.

"If all I wanted was a piece of ass, I would have seduced Leah twenty years ago."

"Oh right," Stephanie scoffed. "You want *the taming*."

Lucien, who, these days with Leah behaving the way she was, had little patience, lost the little he had.

"What are you driving at?" he clipped.

"What I'm driving at, Lucien, is I'm all for this. Vampires being vampires. These ridiculous rules being shattered to smithereens. I want the hunt, just like we all do. I miss it. I *yearn* for it. The problem I have, right now, with you, is that you've gone off target. You're messing with Leah and things are obviously *not right*."

"Stay out of it, Teffie," he warned.

"She's changed," Stephanie shot back.

"She's changed before. You know how it is, how they fight it. She'll change again."

"I suspect she will, but are you prepared for when she does?"

For the first time in days, Lucien smiled. Stephanie growled.

Then she hissed, "You don't get it, do you?"

Lucien's smile grew arrogant. "Not right now but I'm going to."

Stephanie leaned in. "What, exactly, do you think she's working so damned hard to protect herself from, Lucien? Have you ever thought of that? You've tamed many mortals, what happened with the one who gave you the toughest fight?"

The smile died from his face and Lucien felt himself flinch. Stephanie saw it and went in for the kill.

Speaking quietly, she said, "That's right, she fell in love with you. Luckily for Maggie, you fell in love with her too and you could make her your mate. That isn't an option for Leah. So what happens to her when she directs all that feeling and life-force inside her at you then, when you're done with her, where does she go from there?"

I love you.

The words spoken in Leah's heartfelt whisper, like they did time and again, day after day, came unbidden into his head.

Lucien didn't like what he was feeling.

"Stay out of it, Teffie."

"I'm in it, we all are." She got closer. "If Rafe moves in with Lana, takes her as a lover, The Council is not going to look kindly on what you're doing with Leah. They might have before, to pay back their debt, but this is spreading. They'll want to nip it in the bud and the best way to do that is shut down its source."

"I'll talk to Rafe."

"Yes? And what will you say?"

Lucien held Stephanie's gaze and made a decision.

"I'll congratulate him on his new home."

Her eyes narrowed. "You're talking about revolution."

"Why are you acting surprised?" Lucien asked. "You knew that was a possibility from the beginning."

She threw up a hand. "This is happening too fast, Luce. We're not prepared."

"It already happened, Teffie. I drew the line the minute you and Cosmo sheltered Leah from anyone declaring their intentions at her Selection. Since then everyone's been taking their positions on their side of the line. The Council will have to take that into consideration when they make their judgment."

"You think they'll roll over?"

"I think they must understand on some level that their traditions are antiquated and I'm counting on them being forward-thinking."

"And if they're not?"

Lucien leveled his eyes at her. "You took your position on the line, Teffie, are you changing your mind?"

"When I chose my side, I didn't know Leah."

Lucien's brows drew together. "And what does this have to do with Leah?"

He watched, surprised, as Stephanie's face grew pale, her mouth went slack and her eyes slid from his.

"Teffie?" he prompted.

Her eyes slid back and she whispered, "You have to ask that? *You?*"

Lucien, unfortunately, chose not to respond.

So Stephanie kept talking. "What did the last Revolution have to do with Maggie, Lucien?"

Lucien felt every inch of his body stretch taut.

"We're placing her in danger," Stephanie went on.

"Leah will not be in any danger," Lucien clipped.

"You're so certain?"

Lucien moved forward a very threatening inch.

"Yes," he growled. "I'm *very* certain."

Stephanie watched him, her eyes not moving from his, something that looked like understanding finally flashing in hers.

Then, seemingly appeased, even now actually pleased, she nodded and looked over his shoulder.

"She's coming back," Stephanie noted, and Lucien turned.

Leah was moving toward them, squeezing between the bodies with more small smiles and murmured pardons. He noticed immediately she'd reapplied her lip gloss.

She was wearing an orchid-colored strapless dress. Simple. Elegant. No adornment on the dress, only a deep slit up the center front that stopped at the swell of her thighs and a short train, the weight of which dragged the skirt back exposing her shapely legs. She wore the pair of high-heeled, burnished gold sandals he'd bought for her when they were shopping.

Her hair was not simple however, it was elegant. She'd let it dry in natural waves, then pulled it up and back in a way that was stylish but messy, innocent-looking but sexy. Strategically placed in it, she'd affixed the dozen tiny gold-filigreed butterfly hair clips he'd bought her, and at her throat from a delicate gold chain hung another larger filigreed butterfly. The ones in her hair, the wings were near to closed, the one at her throat the wings where spanned.

He'd bought her the jewelry because he liked it, he thought it suited her and he wanted a reaction. He'd been cautious with her ever since the night he threw the wineglass and she'd had her first dream. He'd backed off and used extreme patience, attempting to draw her out gently. None of which, incidentally, was working.

He'd given the jewelry to her the night before, right before they went to bed when he told her they'd be going out that evening.

She had not been overwhelmed by this gesture. He'd received no radiant smile. In fact, she'd only ever smiled at him once and never repeated it.

Instead, she'd been only dutifully grateful. Nothing more.

He watched her get closer thinking he'd been absolutely right. The dress, the shoes and the jewelry all very much suited her.

The blank expression on her beautiful face very much did not.

She was less than ten feet away when a man's hand curled on her upper arm, stopping her progress.

"Leah?" Lucien heard the voice and his eyes moved to the man. He recognized him and without delay he moved.

He would have liked to have moved faster but he forced himself to go with a mortal's slowness and it was at that moment Lucien hoped there was revolution, that vampires would be freed to be who they were and do what they liked.

For instance, being at Leah's side in a split second, grabbing her and leaping across the room instead of having to wend his way excruciatingly slowly toward her.

"Justin?" Leah's voice was stunned and not in a happy way.

"Leah, girl, what are you doing here?" Justin's voice was also stunned, definitely in a happy way.

Lucien made it to her side in time for Justin to pull Leah into his arms.

She visibly stiffened. So did Lucien, a half a second before he moved closer in order to extricate her from an embrace with her ex-lover.

Leah got there before him. She put her hands to Justin's waist and pushed away. Her shoulder met Lucien's chest and her head jerked up to look at him.

And then she did something that stunned Lucien.

She turned to him, sliding her arm along his back, her fingers curling into his waist. She leaned the front of her body into his side, pressing close.

The act was smoothly done, as if she curled into him all the time. It was also immensely proprietary in a beguiling feminine way.

He liked it, a great deal, and therefore relaxed into it.

"Lucien, this is Justin." She gestured with her hand then turned from him to Justin. "Justin, meet Lucien."

Lucien looked at Justin who, Lucien was pleased to note, was now not looking so happy to see Leah. His eyes were darting back and forth between the two of them and his faced had paled slightly.

Unfortunately, Lucien had to break contact with Leah who'd burrowed under his right arm to shake the man's hand.

"Justin," he murmured.

"Lucien," Justin murmured back, shaking his hand.

It took effort but Lucien stopped himself from crushing all the bones in Justin's hand. Regardless, Justin winced behind the power of Lucien's grip.

The minute their hands broke, Leah moved back in, assuming the same position, but this time she rested her other hand on his upper abdominals.

It was a light touch, but it spoke volumes.

As with most moments with Leah, but especially *that* moment, Lucien had the raging desire to kiss her.

"What are you doing here?" she asked Justin, her voice not entirely friendly, not exactly unfriendly. She was testing the waters and Lucien decided to give her the lead in this uncertain situation.

"I just asked the same thing," Justin replied, his voice was entirely unfriendly, his pleasure at seeing her had evaporated.

"You first," Leah said, she'd read his tone and her words were frosted.

Lucien settled in to watch.

Justin looked between Lucien and Leah again, his eyes traveling down to Lucien's middle. Lucien slid his arm around Leah, cupping his fingers on her shoulder. Justin's eyes shifted, he watched this, and his mouth grew tight.

Then he spoke. "At the last minute, they changed their minds and instead of transferring me to Seattle, they transferred me here."

"You live here?" Leah asked and Lucien felt her body tensing.

Not good news, at least not for Leah.

"Yes, I do," Justin replied. "Now...you."

"I live here too," Leah told him and Lucien watched as Justin's eyes grew wide with disbelief.

"You *live* here?" he whispered.

"Well, not here, in the city," Leah explained. "I live in Dragon Lake."

Justin's eyes, already wide, went huge.

"Dragon Lake?" His voice had dropped even lower then he whistled before stating, "That explains it."

"Explains what?" Leah asked sharply.

"What would drag you away from that family and all those friends of yours. Obviously, if you can afford to live in Dragon Lake, you must have got a helluva job. That's a pricey neighborhood."

"We don't actually live in Dragon Lake." Lucien decided it was time to enter the conversation. "We live outside town, on the lake."

Lucien didn't put any emphasis on the "we," but then again, he didn't have to. Justin caught his meaning, his eyes narrowed on Lucien and his jaw clenched. He again looked between Lucien and Leah and Lucien heard his heart start beating faster.

Angry.

Lucien bit back a smile.

Finally Justin's eyes settled on Lucien and he asked, "Do you?"

"Justin—" Leah started, her tense body going solid, but Justin's eyes didn't move from Lucien.

"Do you know who I am?" he asked.

"Justin—" Leah began again but Lucien talked over her.

"Yes," Lucien replied.

"Then you know she broke up with me just five months ago."

"Justin!" Leah snapped but Lucien again spoke over her.

"Yes," Lucien repeated.

Justin's eyes shot to Leah. "You're a fast mover. Or were you with him before you finished with me?"

"Justin—" she started yet again, his name a shard of ice, but this time Justin talked over her.

"Nice necklace, Ley-lo." His voice was snide and it was Lucien's turn to go tense.

"Do we have to do this?" Leah asked, her tone hard, saying it was not a question at all and that they were not going to do "this."

Justin disagreed.

"Oh, I don't know," he drawled sarcastically. "Six months ago I was told I was being transferred, with a fucking great raise and a huge bonus. Not anything that would put me near Dragon Lake, but it wasn't anything to fucking sneeze at either. You said you wouldn't move, no way, no how. Guess you were waiting for someone who could put gold around your neck and your ass in a three million dollar house *on* Dragon Lake."

"I think you're done," Lucien told him and his voice made it clear Justin was, indeed, done.

Again, Justin didn't agree. "Oh, do you now?"

Leah pressed into his side as her hand came up to grasp his lapel. "Lucien, don't—"

Lucien looked down at her and saw her face had paled with alarm. But before he could reassure her, Justin was there.

"He's a big guy, Ley-lo, but you know I can handle myself," he announced.

Leah's body turned to marble and Lucien's eyes sliced to him.

Justin was dark-haired, dark-eyed and clearly fit, but even if Lucien wasn't a vampire, he had four inches and fifty pounds on him at least.

However, he *was* a vampire and without any effort at all, he could rip the man's head off, which was something he would have liked to do. Not because he was clearly an asshole but because Lucien knew he'd been an asshole to Leah for a very long time.

Justin, Lucien knew from Fiona, was ambitious. He was also callous with his ambition, not only in business, but often cancelling plans with Leah—sometimes important or special ones—in order to spend his time clawing his way to the top.

Justin was so ambitious that when he needed Leah to be available to charm associates at a business dinner or the like, regardless of the fact that he often chose work over her, he demanded her attendance. He did this even, on occasion, when she was ill or when she had other plans. The former, she'd done, according to Fiona, once. The latter she'd told him to "go screw himself" (Fiona's account, direct from Leah's mouth), which meant they fought, not cleanly or at least Justin didn't fight clean. In a fight, as he was always, he was insensitive, selfish and manipulative.

Justin, Lucien now knew, was also stupid.

Leah tried to salvage the situation. "We're at the *opera*," she hissed to Justin.

"So fucking *what?*" Justin hissed back. "You think you can stand there and hang on some guy, some guy you've known for what? A couple of months? Some guy you've *moved in with* when you wouldn't entertain the notion for even a second with me? Hang on him right in front of me when five months ago you were in *my* bed?"

Lucien prepared to move. "I see you're not done, but we are."

Justin, proving his immense stupidity, leaned in and snapped, "Listen up, *Lucien*, whatever fucking kind of name *that* is, take it from me. Trust me, I fucking know. Get out. Get out now. She'll twist you around her little finger, get you addicted to that toffee snatch of hers, then she'll—"

Lucien was done.

Instead of ripping his head off, which was something he now *really* wished to do, he did something else, which would likely not horrify Leah, the rest of their many onlookers and sentence him to be hunted down and burned by The Dominion. The last of which would put a world of hurt on his plans to tame Leah as he'd be dead.

Silence, Lucien commanded.

Justin's mouth clamped shut and his eyes bugged out.

Walk away, Lucien continued, and without hesitation, Justin's body jerking woodenly, he turned and walked away.

Lucien watched him go.

Then he heard Leah breathe, "Did you...?"

His head tilted down to look at her and she was staring at him, lips parted, eyes wide, faced filled with wonder. His favorite look. A look he hadn't seen in three weeks, a look he didn't realize how much he missed until that very moment.

She went on, "Did you just *mind control* Justin?"

"Yes," Lucien replied without hesitation, wondering what her reaction would be.

If he'd been asked, he would have guessed a variety of things. None of which was what he received.

She burst out laughing.

Laughing.

She threw her head back, exposing the elegant line of her throat, her face lit with mirth, her entire body shaking with it.

He'd never made her laugh. Not once.

In eight hundred years there were a great number of things he'd done, but at that moment none of them seemed as monumental as making Leah laugh.

She curled into his front. One arm was still holding him tight around the waist, her other hand still clenched at his lapel. The rest of her body collapsed into him as if the weight of her hilarity was too much to bear. She bent her neck and rested her forehead against his chest, still giggling.

"You...you...*mind controlled Justin*," she stammered through her giggles into his chest then her head snapped back and she cried with very loud glee, "Justin!"

Lucien felt Stephanie's gaze. He glanced at her to see her brows raised, a smile playing at her mouth.

He looked back down at Leah and made a decision. Half-leading, half-dragging her still-giggling frame, he guided her to the far less crowded hall that led to the restrooms. There, he pressed her to the wall and got close.

She put her hands on his chest and smiled up at him.

Lucien felt his chest get tight and this feeling wasn't unpleasant in the slightest.

"That's usually Justin's gig," she said through her smile.

"Pardon?" Lucien asked, smiling back, his arms sliding around her waist to pull her closer even as he leaned into her, pressing her back to the wall.

"Mind control. Justin was *the master*." Then she laughed again, out loud, her body sagging into his. When she controlled herself she told him, "If I'd have known you six months ago, I would have *paid* you to mind control Justin. He was such a shit, the master manipulator."

"You wouldn't have had to pay me, my pet. It would have been my pleasure." He was still smiling but his words were serious.

They also sobered her. Her body twitched and the smile died on her face.

Lucien wanted it back.

"Don't," he warned, his arms tightening.

She looked around, noticing for the first time where she was. Then her eyes locked at the entryway five feet down the hall.

"We should get back to Stephanie—"

"Look at me, Leah."

For the first time in weeks, he watched her struggling against her natural reaction before her eyes met his.

"For five minutes, I had you back. Don't go away again," he demanded.

"But you already—" she started, and he cut her off.

"If you tell me I've already got you, I swear to Christ, we're going home right now and I'll do whatever I have to do to drag you out of that fucking fortress you've built around you."

Her mouth clamped shut, her eyes flashed, and Lucien felt a bolt of elation rip through him.

Finally, he was getting somewhere.

"Can we talk about this later?" she asked quietly.

"There's nothing to talk about," he told her. "You're withholding from me."

"Am not," she returned.

"Leah." Her name was a warning.

"Well, I'm not!" Her voice was rising and Lucien welcomed it.

Because of this, his tone softened when he spoke. "You forget, sweetling, I've been watching you for twenty years."

Her eyes slid away and she muttered, "I haven't forgotten *that*."

His arms gave her a squeeze and her gaze came back to his.

"Therefore, I know the Leah Buchanan who I'm sharing a bed with is not Leah Buchanan."

"She is," Leah retorted.

Stubborn.

He nearly smiled.

He didn't.

"She isn't," he replied.

"What do you want from me?" she asked and there was the barest hint of a snap to her question. Regardless of her crumbling composure, he could hear her heart racing and he could smell her fear.

He'd missed that too.

He drew her even closer and her hands on his chest started pressing.

He ignored it.

"Everything," he answered.

"You've got it."

"I don't."

"Whatever you don't have you *can't* have."

Definitely a snap.

Yes, his Leah was coming back.

He couldn't help it, he smiled. Her eyes dropped to his mouth and he heard her pulse accelerate.

"You're saying you're determined to be nothing but my whore," he stated.

Her body grew still and her heart skipped. "What?"

"You have a choice. You can be with me as I want you to be or you can be my whore. Your choice."

He watched her face work as she struggled to find a way out of the predicament she'd placed herself in.

Then she said, "There's a third choice."

"And that would be?"

"You can release me."

He felt his chest tighten again. This time it was *extremely* unpleasant.

"That isn't going to happen."

She pushed against him. He ignored it.

"I refuse to choose," she hissed.

"Then I'll choose."

She stopped breathing and her face went pale before she whispered, "You can't *make* me do either one."

His hand slid up her back, fingers wrapping around her neck.

"Would you like to try me, pet?"

Her fear spiked, the scent of it filling the hall and he felt his cock start to get hard in reaction as he felt her heart tripping against his chest.

The bells sounded, announcing it was time for the patrons to take their seats.

"*Please* can we talk about this later?" she begged, and he studied her face.

She'd had enough. However, he was again getting through.

"Yes," he relented. "We can talk about it later."

She sagged in relief against him.

He dipped his face to touch his mouth to hers.

"But we *will* talk about it, Leah," he cautioned, his lips moving against hers. "Your new game ends and we begin." He watched close up as her eyes grew round, her scent enveloping him, her delicious fear coating his throat. "Tonight," he finished.

Leah sat beside him in the car, feigning sleep.

He knew she wasn't asleep. He'd slept a month of nights beside her. He knew exactly what her breathing and heart sounded like when she was sleeping.

That was not it.

Furthermore, she couldn't be tired considering she'd had a nap at the opera.

It was safe to say, even though Leah hadn't told him, she didn't like opera.

During the first act, he'd discovered this when he felt her subtle movements beside him. However, when he turned his head to look at her, her own head was bowed as if deep in contemplation.

He thought nothing of this, suspecting she was considering her options for their discussion later that evening.

His gaze moved to Stephanie who was sitting beside Leah, eyes glued on the stage, lips curved into an amused grin.

They weren't watching a comedy.

His gaze traveled back to Leah and he saw her suddenly pull an outrageous face. Chin jutted out so the cords in her neck strained, she flicked her tongue between her lips like a snake.

Lucien stared in disbelief, wondering if the pressure of his taming was getting to her.

Then he heard a child's giggle.

He looked down over the balcony railing and saw a little girl no more than six, who was completely uninterested in the opera. She was staring up at Leah, her face wreathed in smiles. After a moment she mimicked Leah's snake face and then rearranged her features, using her thumbs to pull out her mouth and her fingers to pull down her eyes.

Lucien looked back at Leah, who'd bugged out her eyes comically wide and was shaking her head in a subtle "no."

The child giggled again, practically jumping up in her seat, making motions with her hands that Leah was to follow her lead, something that had, apparently, been going on for some time. Her mother, sitting beside her, finally noticed her daughter's behavior and Lucien heard the mother's hushed rebuke.

His arm moved around Leah's shoulders, she jumped and her head turned to him. He caught a look on her face that nearly made him roar with laughter. She looked exactly like the six-year-old below who'd just been caught and scolded.

He sought her ear with his mouth and whispered, "Be good."

He felt her shoulders tense under his arm but ignored it, pulling her into his side, which she resisted pointlessly.

His eyes moved to Stephanie who was watching them, smiling broadly now before he tucked Leah firmly in his side and glanced back at the stage.

He, too, was smiling.

She managed to curtail her antics for the rest of the first act and chatted amicably, if pensively, with Stephanie during intermission.

The second act, he positioned her as he had the first and she promptly fell asleep with her head against his shoulder.

And *that* nap had not been feigned. She had been out, the entirety of her weight resting against him. Although he wished she'd told him she didn't like opera, he couldn't say he minded her sleeping with her head on his shoulder where he could tug a tendril of her hair free and twirl its silkiness around his finger, something he found that night he could do for hours.

His thoughts still on that tendril, Lucien saw they were home.

He hit the garage door opener and parked the Porsche next to the Cayenne. He was out of the car over to her side with her door open when she pretended to wake.

"We're home?" she asked in a false drowsy voice.

Lucien bit back a smile. "Yes, pet."

He helped her out and she started to wander sleepily to the door to the kitchen. He caught her and slid an arm along her shoulders, pulling her close and guiding her the rest of the way.

"Tired?" he asked with sham solicitousness as he halted them by the door so he could hang his keys on the hook on the kitchen wall.

She faked a yawn.

Then she answered, *"Definitely."*

"Let's get you to bed," he murmured, and she nodded.

He walked with her close to his side all the way to the bedroom where she pulled away. He moved to turn on the bedside light and she sat on the bed, bending double, her hands moving to the straps of her shoe.

He shrugged off his suit jacket and walked to the chaise.

"I take it you aren't fond of opera?" he asked, throwing his jacket on the chaise and sitting to take off his own shoes.

"Um..." she hesitated, sliding her shoe off her foot, setting it aside and then going after the straps of the other one, "no."

Pleased she hadn't attempted to lie in order to tell him what she thought he would want to hear, Lucien stood and unbuttoned his shirt. "I think I got that."

She rose from the bed without a reply or even looking at him and started toward the dressing room.

Using his natural speed, he slid off his shirt, dropped it on the chaise and was at her side before she walked three steps.

His hand caught hers, she quaked to a stop and looked up at him.

"Where are you going?" he queried.

"To take off my dress and put on my pajamas," she answered.

"No pajamas," Lucien replied, her eyes grew wide, and he turned her so her back was facing him before he continued. "I want to feel you against me tonight, pet."

Her body turned to stone as his fingers went to her zipper, but she didn't resist.

He slid it down and she stood ramrod straight. The material parted and then fell away. She was wearing nothing but a pair of sheer lavender-colored panties edged in the same colored lace. Her hands went up to shield her breasts as he turned her again and pulled her to him, her arms caught between their bodies.

"Take off my trousers," he ordered, his fingers drifting up the soft skin of her naked back.

She blinked.

Then she asked, "What?"

His fingers found a butterfly clip in her hair. He squeezed the wings gently and pulled it out.

Then he repeated, "Leah, take off my trousers."

She hesitated a moment then, stiltedly, her hands went to his belt.

His fingers found another clip and he carefully pulled it out.

"So, I take it you've decided?" she whispered, his belt undone, she moved to the fastening.

"Decided what?" he asked, taking out another butterfly and watching, with no small amount of fascination, as her shining hair slowly tumbled to her shoulders.

"That I'm to be your whore."

So deep in his study of her hair he was startled by her words and his eyes moved from her hair to hers.

"Why would you say that?"

She slid his zipper down. This, evidently, was her answer.

With one hand, he found more clips and also bobby pins which he pulled out as well. The other hand he wrapped around the back of her neck.

He didn't take his eyes from hers.

"Lovers disrobe each other, Leah," he said softly.

He heard her heart bump unevenly, she tore her eyes from his, looking at his shoulder as she slid her hands along his waist and tugged his pants down.

They barely hit the floor before he stepped out of them, had her cradled in his arms and at the side of the bed. He yanked back the covers, depositing her in it. He dropped her hair bobs on her bedside table, moved over her and settled at her side.

"Sit up and turn your back to me," he demanded.

She hesitated again before she complied, bringing the covers up to her chest as she did so.

His hands went back to her hair.

"How many pins do you have in here, sweetling?" he muttered as all the butterflies were out but there seemed hundreds of pins still in.

"I have a lot of hair," she whispered.

He stopped pulling out pins, his hand moving to her neck, across her throat and down. He curled his fingers around her upper arm and pulled her back to his chest, his face buried in her thick, soft, now wildly wavy hair.

"Mm," he murmured into the locks, "that you do."

Her hands came up, fingers sliding into her hair. "I'll finish it."

He pulled back, letting her go, and pushed her hands away.

"I'll do it."

She blindly batted at his hands. "It won't take me a second."

"I said I'll do it."

"Really—"

He leaned in deep, taking her with him and dumping the pins and clips on the nightstand. Then he caught her wrists in a tight hold and pulled them around, crossing them at her front.

Against her ear he repeated firmly, "I'll do it."

She stiffened a second before her body went slack.

"Okay," she whispered.

She pulled the covers up to hide herself and then sat still as he finished with the pins.

After some time, he slid his fingers through her hair, searching for any pins he'd left behind. Finding none, he deposited the last of them with the others. His hands going back to her hair, he gathered it all in his fists. Transferring it to one, he pulled it aside and kissed her bare shoulder.

She trembled against his lips. He smiled against her skin.

"Can I go to sleep now?" she asked.

"No," he answered.

Her body jerked and she twisted her head to look at him.

"But I'm tired," she lied.

"Yes, I know." He tried not to grin.

"You said we could go to bed." Her tone held a mild accusation.

"We're in bed," he pointed out.

"I thought you meant to sleep," she told him.

"I didn't."

"But—" she started but didn't finish. He moved her to face him, tugging the covers out of her hands at the same time lifting up to lean his back against the headboard and pressing her torso to his side.

"We're going to talk," he announced.

She tilted her head back to look at him. "I'm really tired, Lucien. *Really tired.*" She stressed the words vocally *and* by pressing her soft body deeper into his. "I don't think I have it in me to talk."

His hand came up to cup her jaw. "That's fine, sweetheart, you aren't going to be talking."

Her body grew tense.

"It's been some time since you've had a lesson," he told her and saw surprise slide across her features.

He watched her struggle with her reaction. Then he watched her lose.

"Have you come to a decision?" she asked, her voice edging toward a demand.

"About what?"

He heard her teeth grinding and controlled his laughter.

Barely.

"Earlier tonight, you said you were going to choose," she reminded him. "Have you come to your decision?"

As much as he was enjoying this, Lucien let her off the hook.

"That's what your lesson is about."

He watched her face working again, heard her teeth grinding again before he felt her weight settle into his side.

"I'm all ears," she muttered, now her voice held mild irritation.

His hand at her jaw slid into the side of her hair and he pressed her cheek against his chest. He then took her wrist, pulling it across his abdomen, resting her arm there. Finally, he placed his hand on her neck, thumb stroking her throat.

"Did you learn anything about the history of concubines while in class?" he asked.

He felt her head move, indicating a negative against his chest.

Of course she didn't.

Lucien smiled over her head and continued, "The role of official concubine started just after The Revolution when mortal and immortal representatives met to negotiate the Agreement, which would dictate how the two cultures would co-exist. Eleven Elders, or oldest living vampires, represented our culture. Ambassadors from eleven European countries represented yours. For mortals, the primary concern was to stop hunting. For immortals, the primary concern was to ensure safe feeding, but also to find a way that vampires could feed and still have a place in society, not in shadows. As I told you before, many vampires already had what amounted to concubines, women who shared their blood willingly. It was agreed that this would be the practice from that point on. The Agreement was written and both immortals and mortals signed it."

Lucien paused and Leah nodded that she understood and he should carry on, which he did.

"Concubines were recruited from the highest-born families in Europe, aristocrats, the daughters of wealthy merchants, even some lower-born royals. This was facilitated secretly by command of monarchs across Europe. It wasn't essential that the women came willing. Most often they were sold into the life."

He heard her take in a sharp breath and his hand at her neck gave her a reassuring squeeze.

"They might have been sold into the life, Leah, but once there, not one attempted to leave it."

"Okay," she whispered when he paused again for her to give indication that she accepted this fact.

"The first family to come forward and sign the agreement was yours," he told her and added, "The Buchanans came willingly."

"I knew that," she said softly.

"Did you know that they'd already been concubines for five generations?"

Her head tilted back and he met her gaze.

"I didn't know that," she replied softly.

He nodded. "Not only concubines to vampires but concubines to kings."

He watched her face pale, felt her body get tight, and she pushed up and away.

"Oh my God," she breathed, so appalled for once she forgot her own nudity.

"Leah—"

Expression still horrified, she talked over him. "I come from a family of whores."

His arms curved around her and he pulled her up his chest so they were face to face.

"You must remember, those times were different," he warned, locking eyes with her. "And the Buchanan women were different. They wanted something else from life. Strong women couldn't live their own lives back then, no women could. Your ancestors did what they had to do to guarantee themselves a certain amount of freedom, freedom that included safety and comfort, and they didn't care what people thought. These are traits to admire, then and now."

She continued to look horrified and dubious so he went on.

"I knew your Buchanan ancestors, pet, they made their own way without men ruling their lives. You have absolutely nothing to be ashamed of." His voice dipped low. "And they would have liked you, particularly you. You remind me of them, Leah."

She wrinkled her nose and Lucien thought it made her look adorable, so he smiled.

"I'm giving you a compliment," he informed her.

"Okay," she agreed without actually agreeing, clearly wanting to be off the subject.

He disregarded her nonverbal cue. "They ensured, for centuries, that all of their line would live safe and well, even you. And I don't mean now with me, I mean your whole life as provided by your mother."

"Seems to me men provided that life, or at least vampires did. In our case, Cosmo took care of us."

"Yes, but for seven years your mother took care of Cosmo."

She made a noise that sounded like a snort.

He gave her an impatient squeeze but softened his voice. "What your family does is no small thing. Without your blood, your mother's, your entire line, and all those like you, given willingly, we would need to hunt."

He watched as understanding dawned then her brows drew together and she replied, "All those people at the Feasts, Wats and Breed...you wouldn't go hungry and you wouldn't need to hunt."

"You're correct," he allowed. "But survival feeding is very different than partaking of an elegant repast. The vampires who remained after The Revolution as a whole crave the finer things in life. You saw them, Leah. Wats and Breed are *not* the finer things in life. Concubines definitely are. To find *that*, if not given willingly, we'd hunt."

Her eyes moved from his and she muttered, "Snooty."

"Look at me, pet," he demanded, and when she did, he went on. "That isn't it, there's more. You said three weeks ago that there were not many people I could be myself with and you're one. Do you have any idea what it's like, second to second for centuries, hiding who you are to live in the mortals' world?"

She squirmed uncomfortably against him and he stilled her with another arm squeeze.

She seemed to be searching for an argument, found one and retorted, "Lucien, you can totally be yourself at Feasts and around Wats and Breed. They'd love it. They'd do anything for you to be you. They live for it."

"It's different."

"How?"

Lucien sighed before explaining, "They don't want me to be me. They want me to be whatever their twisted notion is of a vampire, superhuman creature of the night, romanticized or demonized in their minds. They think they're playing with fire or living a novel. They don't accept me for being what I am. They're takers, users, all of them. You see it as them giving me something, but it's not. They're taking. I may be feeding off their blood but they're feeding as well. What I do is natural, giving my body what it needs. What they do is selfish and greedy. Not once from the likes of Breed and Wats or anyone at a Feast have I ever met a single mortal soul who knows what I am who's given one whit about me. Asked me about my day. Wondered aloud at my mood. Wished to discuss a book. Five hundred years, Leah, and not once. I'm not human to them. I don't exist outside whatever fantasy they've created about me. I'm their tool to manipulate to an orgasm or whatever the fuck they get from me."

As he spoke, he noticed her face soften before sorrow filled her gaze. Sorrow mixed with tenderness, a look so bleak yet intensely compassionate, it shook him.

Her hand drifted up his chest, lifted, and he held his breath because he thought she was actually going to touch his face in an act of affection.

Instead, disappointingly, she thought better of it and her hand floated down to rest lightly on his shoulder.

Regardless of his disappointment, his fingers captured a lock of her hair and started twisting

"Concubines aren't like that," he continued quietly when she made no reply. "Concubines understand and accept who we are, what we need, and they give us more. Not just blood. A safe harbor where we can be who we are. You," his voice dropped to a whisper and his face moved closer to hers, "are part of my life, my real life, not some romance novel or horror film. This is a relationship, sweetling, one in my world as it is today that is essential to me. Without it, I'd go mad."

The sorrow left her gaze, the compassion remained, and he felt her body melt into his.

Thank fucking God.

Finally, he was getting somewhere.

"Lucien—" she murmured.

He didn't let her continue, feeling the time was ripe to make his point. "I don't want a whore, Leah. I want you to accept who I am and what we are to each other."

"I accept you," she whispered and the way she did it he believed her.

Without hesitation he asked, "Do you accept what we are to each other?"

She bit her lip in indecision.

"Do you?" he pressed.

"What, um," she paused then went on, "exactly *are* we to each other?"

"I'd like us to be lovers."

Oddly, her eyes turned hopeful. "Lovers?"

Not certain of the reasons behind her hope, he replied cautiously, "Lovers."

"Just lovers?" she repeated.

His sense of caution escalated. "Perhaps you should describe to me what 'just lovers' means."

"Perhaps you should describe to me what *you* think 'lovers' means."

"I've made that clear," he told her.

"You want me to trust you."

"That and more."

Her pliant body stiffened.

"What else?" she asked.

He studied her for a moment, wondering if she was genuinely obtuse or stubbornly so. He decided the latter.

He also thought that perhaps he actually *wasn't* getting somewhere.

With waning patience, he explained, "Leah, my clothes are in your closet. My body is in your bed. I come home to you every night."

Her reply was swift. "Lucien, your clothes are in *your* closet. Your body is in *your* bed. You come home to *your* house every night."

He felt his brows draw together. "This is your house, Leah."

"You're wrong," she returned. "This is the house *you* provided for me to live in while all this is going on."

His eyes narrowed under his drawn brows and his patience slipped another notch. "You're correct, I was wrong. This isn't your house. And you're also wrong. This isn't the house I provided for you 'while all this is going on.'"

When she spoke, he sensed her patience was slipping too.

"Then what is it?"

"It's *our* house."

Her body jerked and she pulled reflexively against his arms. He held her tightly, not giving her an inch.

"There is no 'our,'" she snapped, her hand at his shoulder pressing to no avail. Still, she didn't stop.

"There will be," he declared decisively and he saw her eyes flash before they filled with anger.

She pressed harder while muttering irately, "Lucien, let me go."

No, he was definitely not getting somewhere.

At her attempt to retreat, his patience took another hit.

"What the fuck do you think this is all about?" he ground out.

She locked eyes with him and demanded, "Let me go."

"Answer me."

She didn't. Instead, she asked her own question.

"Is this what taming is?" Her voice was rising. "Creating an 'our' which means you'd be creating an 'us?'"

"Yes, that's part of it."

"It sure has a lot of parts," she retorted sarcastically.

"Yes, it fucking well does, and if you'd stop being so goddamned stubborn, you might open yourself up to learning them all and understand how beautiful it is."

"Right," she shot back derisively.

His arms gave her a gentle shake. "You don't have any idea what you're treating with such scorn."

"Oh yes I do."

"Explain it to me then."

She stilled and to his surprise, agreed. "All right, I will."

He held her defiant glare before muttering, "This will be interesting."

She shot him a look that would have been amusing if he wasn't so annoyed.

Then she spoke, clipping out every word.

"Beautiful house. Beautiful clothes. Beautiful path that leads down to a beautiful lake. Beautiful pool. Ritzy neighborhood. Going to the opera with gold butterflies in her hair. A housekeeper who launders her clothes and makes her breakfast. Hot, superhuman vampire with a great body who's good with his hands, not to mention his mouth, coming home to her every night. A girl could get used to that."

"That's the point," he returned.

"Okay then, what happens when you're through with me?"

"It's common practice for other vampires, including myself, to move their concubines into less lavish accommodation after the Arrangement is finished. But, if you'd have given me five minutes to explain in the last month, you would know that, given the taming, this is your life *until you die.*"

Lucien thought that was rather substantial.

Leah disagreed.

"Thanks, Lucien," she snapped back sarcastically. "That takes a load off."

He gave her another shake, this one far less gentle. "Explain yourself."

She gave him another look, this one far less amusing. She also started trying to pull away again but he held her close.

"I don't think I care to," she stated.

"Let me see if I understand you, my pet. What I told you tonight is that you're an important part of my life, meaningful to me. I intend to live with you, share my life with you, take you as my lover, something you want as badly as me and don't fucking deny it, *and* provide you with supremely comfortable life until you die and you're throwing that in my face?"

"Yep," she returned instantly, now irritatingly glib. "That's exactly what I'm saying. I don't want any of this." She threw an arm out, encompassing the room before it went back to push against his chest. "I don't want any of what you said. And most of all, I don't want *you*."

His patience fled, anger replacing it. A great deal of anger.

He yanked her over his body so they were chest to chest.

His voice was low and cold when he replied, "I've an urge to call you on that last lie."

He could see her anger was escalating at the same pace as his.

Therefore she ignored his threat and demanded, "Release me."

His arms grew tighter. "Not until you've learned tonight's lesson, my pet."

"I don't mean now!" she snapped. "I mean completely. Release me from our Arrangement. Find someone else's head to mess with."

Her words roaring through him, leaving behind that twisting vile feeling he despised, he sat up suddenly, and to accommodate him, she was forced to straddle his lap.

She gasped in shocked surprise then tried to pull away.

"Stop struggling," he demanded, his arm locking around her waist, his other hand fisting in her hair.

"Release me," she shot back.

"That's not going to happen, Leah."

"You want me to give you everything. My trust, my body, my time, and you think I should be grateful because of some pretty clothes and a fucking great house?"

"You missed some things," he returned.

"Oh yes, my blood," she clipped.

"Yes, your blood and a great deal more."

She stopped struggling against his hold and her angry face got close to his.

"Yes, I get that Lucien." Her voice was an enraged whisper. "You don't say it but I know what you want. And you can't have it because I know, eventually, you're going to throw it away. Therefore, it doesn't mean one *fucking* thing to you, no matter how you pretty up the words. So I'm keeping it."

Involuntarily, his arms tensed. He knew it was too much and he didn't care. He felt her pulse soar as her breath went out of her.

"How can you say that?" he hissed.

Breathing with difficulty, she went back to her earlier theme. "Release me."

"I've been waiting for you for twenty fucking years," he reminded her.

"Don't worry, Lucien." Her tone was cutting. "I'm sure another sweet-smelling pussy will happen along."

Controlling his fury by a very weak thread, he twisted. She landed on her back, him on top, his hips between her legs.

"You haven't listened or paid any attention to a fucking thing I've said or done," he grated.

"I haven't missed *one freaking thing*!" she shouted in his face.

"You've missed everything. So I'll say it so you can understand it. I've been waiting to have you since I knew you existed. But I've been waiting for someone *like* you for *five fucking centuries*."

"I doubt the earth is going to crash into the sun anytime soon. You'll get another chance."

Good *Christ* she was stubborn.

He growled.

"Release me," she demanded.

"No."

"*Release me!*" she yelled.

"*Never!*" he shouted back.

His last word made her face change. It twisted, contorting in a look of pain so raw, so severe, it caught him off guard and translated into a kindred slash of pain through his gut that was so intense he felt instant nausea.

Which meant her fist connecting with his jaw came as a surprise.

His head wrenched to the side on contact and he stayed that way, looking unseeing across the room.

It didn't hurt. She was a female mortal in a disadvantageous position on her back with him close.

But he was a vampire.

And concubines were meant to respect vampires.

He gave her her head in many things because he knew what he'd bought into when he'd selected her.

But she had just crossed the line.

Slowly, his head turned back to her. She was panting, her heart racing, rampant fear in her scent, but obstinacy and rage was in her eyes.

"You struck me," he said, his voice deceptively soft.

She ignored the danger in his tone, bucked and demanded, "Get off me!"

He did as she asked but only to sit at the side of the bed, pulling her roughly into his lap and locking her to his body with his arms.

She struggled. "Let me go!"

He shook her with enough force to get her attention. She stopped struggling, her eyes jerked to his and he heard her heart spike as her breath caught.

"Right now, Leah, you're going to learn to respect me," he whispered.

She opened her mouth to speak but he moved her so quickly whatever words she had died in her throat.

He twisted her so she was facedown on the bed, her hips in his lap, ass pointed to the ceiling.

She read his intent and reared up, screaming with terrified fury, "*No!*"

Silence, he commanded, her vocal denials stopped instantly but she kept fighting.

He thought it prudent to allow her struggles. She'd not thank him for this after and commanding her acquiescence through controlling her mind, he surmised, would be a tactical error. Silencing her cries was enough. He had enough of a battle on his hands, clearly not making any advances in the slightest, even after a head to head week followed by three of détente. He didn't need her sincerely hating him instead of telling herself she did.

He positioned one thigh over both hers and held her down to the bed with his hand in her back. She pressed, pushed and bucked, but he didn't allow her to make any progress toward freeing herself.

Then his hand came down on her ass, sharply enough to make his point, not enough to cause any real pain.

The instant the crack of his hand against her skin filled the room, she stilled completely.

He did this three more times. Each strike, her body jerked in response but she didn't fight.

The next time his hand went to her ass, it was not to strike, but to soothe.

"Do you get my point?" he asked quietly, his hand moving gently over her bottom, his gaze moving toward her head.

Her face was buried in the comforter, her hair splayed around her shoulders, arms stretched out before her, fingers curled into a pillow.

He watched her nod.

Now it was time to teach her another lesson.

His thigh lifted, and as he suspected she'd do, she immediately sought escape. Moving her legs just enough to open them, his thigh descended, trapping her now parted ones.

He watched her head jerk back and her fingers fist into the pillow.

He tugged down her panties, exposing her.

No, her mind called out to him.

Yes, sweetling, he replied.

As his hand moved between her legs, she tried struggling, but he held her down. She kept struggling as he worked her and with a swiftness that gratified him, but likely mortified her, she grew wet.

He continued working her until she dripped. Her movements turned from fighting to squirming, her hips lifting, her legs moving under his thigh, not for escape, but to move farther apart to give him more access.

He allowed this and carried on, her movements, the feel of her, wet and silken, and her scent making his cock grow hard and start aching.

With better access and weeks between orgasms, her movements quickly became urgent.

When he knew she was close, he lifted his thigh, pulled her out from beneath it, and swept her panties from her legs. Then he tugged her up and settled her straddling his lap.

Her arms immediately circled his shoulders, one hand fisting in his hair, her forehead dropping to his shoulder. Her hips moved, seeking his cock, which he withheld. Considering she'd latched on to him, it was unnecessary that he hold her captive with his arm around her waist, but he did so. He also pressed a hand between her legs, stroking, teasing, circling, fueling the burn, but not enough to relieve it.

He released her from her silence.

She felt it instantly and whispered with deep feeling, "I really hate you."

He buried his face in her neck to hide his smile.

Even his very stubborn Leah couldn't hate him at the same time her body moved in desperation to join with his.

His hand drifted up her back as he rubbed himself against her.

"Do you ever wonder at the intensity of your feeling for me, pet?" he asked her neck.

"No," she snapped back, but her voice was breathy and her head moved back to expose more of her throat, inviting his lips, tongue, or teeth, it was clearly his choice. "You're a big, fat, vampire *jerk*."

He decided to ignore her words.

"Do you want me to feed or do you want my cock?" He paused, pressing against her. "Or both?"

"I hate you," she whispered instead of answering.

His hand moved from her waist to her breast, his thumb brushing her rock-hard nipple. She caught her breath and her heart skipped a beat. She bucked against his hand between her legs and he smelled her rush of wetness even as he felt it.

God, she was magnificent.

If he ever lost sight of why he was enduring this torture, he only had to remember that moment.

Or the one where she melted against him with tenderness in her eyes.

"Answer me, Leah."

"Both," she breathed, her tone managing to be somehow defiant and defeated.

Tonight, he decided, Leah would get what she wanted.

And, finally, so would he.

He moved, shifting her to her back, his hips between her legs, hers rising instantly in invitation.

His mouth went to hers as he pressed the tip of his cock inside her. Tight and saturated.

He couldn't fucking *wait* to be seated to the hilt.

However, before he finally gave them what they both wanted, they needed to get one thing straight.

His eyes locked with hers.

"I'll not release you," he growled. "Don't mention it again."

She moved her hips against his, seeking deeper contact, but didn't answer.

"Do you understand me?" he pushed.

She glared at him even as her hips pressed down.

His hands at her waist tightened. "Leah—" he grated warningly.

"I understand," she whispered.

He prepared to thrust, a thrill of desire tearing through his body, but before he could follow through, her frame went solid at the same instant he heard the distant dangerous noises.

Her wide eyes locked with his.

"Something's wrong," she breathed.

Her understanding of this when there was no way she could hear the approaching car or the conversation of the people in it, shocked him.

He couldn't think of that now.

Yes, sweetling, he spoke to her mind.

Her limbs tensed around him in a way he thought, after what just occurred, was strangely protective.

You don't want them to hear us talking? she asked.

With great regret and a tight control on his anger at The Council's very bad timing, he withdrew but stayed on top of her, pressing her to the bed.

No. You'll need to put on your pajamas. With what happens next, I want you to take your cues from me. They come in, don't speak unless they speak to you. Be very careful of your answers if they ask you questions and tell them as little as you can. He studied her a moment and then finished, *If you sense something's wrong, go with your instinct.*

Her body trembled beneath him. Her heart was still racing but now for a different reason.

Who are they?

You'll be safe.

Who are they?

No time for questions, sweetheart, you must trust me.

Lucien...

His hands went from her hips to frame her face and he looked into her eyes.

Trust me, Leah.

She stared. She swallowed. He watched as her face worked then her eyes flashed.

He knew, with grave disappointment, what her answer would be before she spoke it to his brain.

However, he was wrong.

Achingly sweetly, she whispered hesitantly, *Okay.*

15
The Menace

Before I could blink, Lucien and I were in the dressing room
He'd tagged my underwear during his dash, and when he set me
on my feet, he handed them to me.

The doorbell rang.

Without a word I began dressing swiftly.

There were a number of things to think about.

One being the fact that I punched him.

I'd never hit anyone in my life and I wasn't proud of it, not even
a little bit. I had a bad temper but I'd never been moved to violence.
Even if he was a big, bad, strong vampire who surely could take it and
arguably deserved it, there was no excuse.

Of course, he had declared he'd never let me go, which was a
total, complete, utter and very, very, *very* vicious lie.

But still.

Another was the fact that he'd spanked me.

Spanked me.

Like I was a naughty child.

Well, not exactly like that, but still!

And he did this *while* doing his mind control business.

It was so mortifying it was a wonder I could move at all and wasn't literally petrified. Especially coupled with the fact that he'd gone straight from the spanking right to playing my body against me yet a-freaking-gain.

And I couldn't fight it. I wanted to. My brain screamed at me to, especially after the spanking, which, during it, even though his strikes caused little pain to anything but my pride, I'd felt something break in me. Something integral to all that was *me*, Leah Buchanan, one in the centuries-old line of strong independent concubines (if Lucien's word was anything to go by). And there was something in the way that it broke that I knew it could never be mended.

The weird thing was, I didn't mind. Not in the slightest. It was as if it was meant to be.

It was as if it had been built solely for the purpose of it existing for when Lucien would break it.

Now how blinkety-blank freaky was that?

But I couldn't think of any of that now.

Not now when danger was at the door.

Bad danger. The worst.

So much the worst it wasn't danger, it was *menace*.

I felt it crawling—disquieting, threatening, evil—through the very air. To say it made me uneasy was a humongous understatement.

I didn't know how I understood this. I didn't even know *what* I understood. I just knew I understood it.

And what I understood was that, if this didn't go well, my life would be over.

And I also understood that the only thing standing between me and that menace was Lucien.

He'd keep me safe. Regardless of and contradictory to the scene I'd just endured at his hands, I knew to the depth of my soul that he'd do everything in his substantial power to stand between me and whatever was at the door.

Or he would die trying.

This shook me worst of all.

But I didn't hesitate. I put on pajamas and for good measure my robe, yanking the belt tightly. Then I turned to him, seeing he was waiting for me with his pajama bottoms on.

The doorbell rang again.

My heart raced.

Settle, sweetling. His voice sounded in my head as he lifted his hand toward me.

Without hesitation, I walked to him, sliding my hand in his, his eyes keeping mine captive while I did this.

The moment his long fingers closed around my hand, dwarfing it, I felt my heart settle and I saw his face gentle.

That's it. His voice, edged with pride, sounded encouragingly in my mind.

We walked together slowly, hand in hand to the front door. The bell sounded again as we walked.

He positioned me, his eyes caught mine in the dark and he placed his hand on my cheek, not letting go of my other one.

Your cues come from me, yes? he asked.

I nodded, and he gave me a reassuring smile coupled with a squeeze of my hand.

Then he let me go and moved away to switch on the light. He opened the door and stood strong in its frame, barring the way to whoever was out there.

I was behind the door. I couldn't see who was there and they couldn't see me. Lucien spoke and he did it in a way that provided me with the information I needed without letting on to our visitors he was doing so.

"Rudolf, Cristiano, Marcello," he drawled, his voice sounding amused. "They sent three of you?"

"My profound apologies, Lucien," a heavily-accented, definitely uncomfortable voice replied. "I know it's very late but unfortunately we're here to ask you to come with us."

What?

Why?

I held my breath.

"This can't wait until morning?" Lucien returned.

"No." Another accented voice, not uncomfortable but hostile, now sounded. "The Council waited for you to come to them. Now, matters have arisen and they will wait no longer."

Lucien was silent, considering this.

"Please, Lucien, don't make this difficult. It shouldn't take long," the first voice urged.

All amusement was gone when Lucien spoke again. "This does not make me happy, Rudolf."

"Don't tell us. Tell The Council," the hostile voice retorted.

Lucien's body changed like it did when Katrina came to visit. The muscles stood out, defined, deadly. I didn't take this as a good sign.

"Marcello," a third voice, also accented, said the name as a warning.

There seemed to be some kind of standoff happening. I could only see Lucien's half of it, but I *felt* it, and it scared the freaking heck out of me.

Finally, Lucien's body relaxed, he stepped back, opening the door wider, his voice now courteous. "Wait inside. I'll be a moment."

His eyes cut to me. I read his intent and moved to him. His arm curled around my waist, shifting us back so the three large vampires could fill the foyer. Two were dark, both looking Latin or Italian or something. One was fair. All were gorgeous.

My heart skipped a beat.

The fair one closed the door then turned, which meant all of them were staring at me. I pressed into Lucien's side.

"Leah, this is Rudolf, Marcello and Cristiano," Lucien introduced, indicating each with his hand. Rudolf was the fair one.

I nodded and gave a lame wave.

Cristiano and Rudolf smiled. Marcello scowled.

"It's a long-awaited pleasure, Leah," Rudolf murmured, his eyes calm and gentle on me. I suspected his words held greater meaning because Marcello's scowl deepened. At the same time Cristiano's smile widened.

"Thank you." My voice was soft and breathy and something changed in the room when I spoke. It was powerful, electric, weirdly both dangerous and seductive and it was emanating from all three.

"We won't be a moment." Lucien's voice cut through the thickened air and he started to move us away.

"Leah's to wait here," Marcello announced.

Lucien stopped and his eyes sliced to the vampire.

"Leah will come with me," he replied.

Marcello's gaze moved to me, raking me from top to toe, and something about the way he did this freaked me out. I didn't know how but I sensed Rudolf and Cristiano tense and I *felt* Lucien's body change to that freakishly scary alertness of moments before.

"Leah will stay," Marcello declared.

Lucien didn't reply; he moved us toward the stairs.

Before we even got close, suddenly Lucien was gone from my side.

I knew why. I'd only caught a flash of it but I saw Marcello dart forward, his arm extended toward me. Then there was a blur of bodies and Marcello was against the wall in a poof of broken plaster (boy, Edwina was going to be ticked, she'd just had the damage from the last vampire fight in the foyer repaired).

Lucien held him like he did Katrina, at the throat, but his body was close, pressing Marcello against the wall, his face not an inch from the other vampire's. I could only see their profiles but the expression on Lucien's was ferocious.

Cristiano got close to their sides as Rudolf circled.

"You'd touch what's *mine*?" Lucien ground out in a voice so sinister, a chill raced up my spine.

"Marcello," Cristiano murmured in soft reprimand and I found his accented voice beautiful even in this tense situation. "You know better, my friend."

"He made no contact with Leah," Rudolf pointed out quietly. "Let him go, Lucien." It was a request, not a demand.

Lucien and Marcello glared at each other. Finally Lucien released his hold and stepped back.

He walked to me and again took my hand.

"If The Council wants this to go smoothly, control him," Lucien warned Rudolf with a jerk of his head toward Marcello and Rudolf nodded.

Then Lucien turned us and guided me up the stairs.

As he did, he issued orders.

The minute I leave, call Stephanie, he told me.

Okay, I agreed promptly.

She'll come immediately. You can trust her.

Okay, I repeated.

Don't answer the phone. If it rings, Stephanie deals with it, he went on.

Okay, I repeated again

I don't want you to be frightened, sweetheart. I'll handle this.

I wanted to laugh. Not that it was funny, just that I was scared out of my ever-loving mind and no order, even from the Mighty Lucien, was going to stop that.

What's this about? I asked when we made it to the dressing room. *Why are they here? Why are they taking you away?*

I've broken the law, Lucien replied calmly, as if this wasn't a scary-as-shit announcement. He took off his pajama bottoms and started to dress in one of his suits like he was doing nothing more important than preparing to go to work.

While he did this, I stared at him frozen in shock.

Then, my mind breathed to his, *You've broken the law?*

Yes.

What law?

I'll explain later.

I didn't want him to explain later.

What did it mean, he'd broken the law? Did that mean they were going to throw him in vampire jail? Did that mean he was going to have to hire a vampire attorney and stand vampire trial? He'd just admitted to doing it! Was he going to plead guilty?

I needed *way* more information.

Okay, then at least tell me what kind of law? Was it like a jaywalking kind of law or a murder in the first degree kind of law?

Now dressed, he turned to me and lifted both hands to cup my face and bring me closer.

His eyes staring into mine, he repeated, *I'll explain later.*

I felt my patience, already strained to the breaking point, snap.

Un-unh, my mind retorted. *Give me something to go on here.*

He smiled like I was amusing.

Yes! *Smiled!*

I felt my eyes narrow.

He watched this, his eyes went that sexy-vampire-hooded I wished I didn't like so much, then he murmured, "Christ, you're adorable."

My temper flared and instead of shouting, out of necessity, I mumbled irately, "Boy, I wish I could kick your ass."

His hands left my face, his arms blurring around me with vampire speed, caging me tight against his chest. He threw his head back and roared with laughter.

Usually, I liked his laughter. Okay, being honest with myself, usually, I loved it. And I hadn't heard it in weeks. And, worse, even though I didn't want to lament that loss, I did. Every day. For *three stinking weeks.*

However at that particular moment, *I did not.*

"This isn't funny," I muttered angrily to his chest.

I felt him kiss the top of my head.

It's something between jaywalking and murder in the first degree, he told me.

That doesn't tell me much.

It's all you're going to get, sweetling.

I had no chance to reply. He took my hand and walked us back downstairs.

The three vamps were waiting for us. I knew Cristiano and Rudolf heard the very little we spoke out loud. It would be hard to miss Lucien's shout of laughter, even if you didn't have vampire hearing. Both of them looked highly amused.

Our whispered conversation made Marcello move from surly to openly hostile.

Casual as can be, Cristiano moved to and opened the door, walking through it. Rudolf and Marcello followed. All three stopped outside and waited.

Lucien walked me to the opened door.

Lock the door behind me. Stephanie has a key, he said.

Instead of nodding, I replied, *Okay.*

Then he demanded, *Kiss me.*

Did he just say what I thought he just said?

My eyes widened and I whispered, *What?*

Do it, now.

He told me to take my cues from him. That wasn't exactly what one would call a cue, more like a command.

Still, in this troubling situation, I felt it sensible to do as he ordered.

I leaned in, hands to his abs, getting up on tiptoe and tilting my head back. His own dipped down. I pressed my lips against his and his opened. Another cue I was forced to follow, my tongue slid into his mouth. The instant it touched his, his arms came around me like vises, pinning my hands between us, hauling me into his big hard body.

It had been three weeks since he'd kissed me like this. For three weeks, even during feeding, he'd been the perfect gentleman. Often during those weeks, he'd brush his lips against mine before going to sleep. Or he'd stop, bend and touch his mouth to the top of my head when he'd walk past me while I was reading. But he hadn't really kissed me.

Clearly my body missed it, so much I forgot our audience. My head tilted to the side, my hands forced themselves from between us, one wrapping around his waist, the other one going into his hair to hold him to me. Our tongues dueled, taking, giving, making my body burn and my heart race.

Like his laughter, it gave me sustenance. I demanded it and took it and more of it and even more because it had been so long, I was starving.

He broke the kiss, and when he did, I sensed he didn't like the fact that he had to.

"I'll be back soon," he murmured against my mouth and stepped away, but only after I took a deep calming breath and nodded.

He moved out the door and I finally felt the air. It was again thick with that seductive danger, so thick, the minute I sensed it, it nearly choked me.

All three vampires were watching me, now with no hostility and no humor. It didn't take a mind reader to know they were hungry. For what, I wasn't sure, but my guess was it was me. It wasn't my blood they were after but something far more profound.

Definitely a menace.

Lucien turned to me. *Lock the door.*

Then, *whoosh*, they were gone and all I saw or heard was the doors slamming on the car.

I closed and locked the door. Then as fast as my feet would carry me, I ran to the phone and called Stephanie.

Terror seared through me, all I could think was escape.

I collided with something strong, powerful iron bands went around me, holding me imprisoned.

"Leah, honey, what on earth?"

Loss. Pain. Anguish. Fear. Too much. I couldn't cope.

Burning, burning, the heat was too immense. Overwhelming. Scalding my eyes. Singeing my throat.

Falling, sharp, uncontrolled, something tightened around my neck. I couldn't breathe.

I struggled against my gentle prison.

"Jesus, Leah, calm down. What's the matter?"

Clawing at my bounds, I could hear my choking breaths hitching through my wracking sobs. Fingers forced open my mouth, pressed against my tongue, searching for the source of my suffocation.

Need. Need. Desperate need. Touch. Skin. Warmth. Strength. Power.

Him.

Needed him.

Needed his hands, his breath, his presence, *him*.

Soothing, soothing, soothing.

I had to have him. If I didn't get him, the noose would tighten, and I'd die.

"Please." It was my voice but I didn't recognize the rasping, raw, agonized noise.

"Oh my God."

Somewhere far away, the phone rang. My prison moved and I struggled to no avail.

"Lucien, thank God. Something's wrong with Leah. She can't breathe and I can't find out why. She's fighting me, and if I let her go, I fear she'll do herself more harm. You need to call an ambulance."

I gasped for breath. My lungs were burning. The blackness was encroaching.

"*What?* Are you *mad*? She's choking, goddamn it, call an ambulance!"

The noose tightened sharply. I feared it'd snap my neck and I sensed the sickening strangled noise I heard came from me.

"Listen, Leah, honey, please, listen to the phone..." the female voice implored urgently.

"Sweetling..." His voice sounded in my ear.

Breath filled my lungs.

I took it in in gulps.

"Hold on, I'm coming."

My mind cocooned, nothing came in, nothing went out, nothing went on.

Catatonia.

Then he was there, his arms sliding around me, lifting me. I was cradled in his lap, his heat enveloping me, his hold fierce and protective.

The aftereffects of the hideous living nightmare still held me in their thrall, and although my senses were returning, I was utterly powerless. A blind, mute ragdoll in Lucien's arms.

"How long has she been like this?" I heard him ask tersely.

"Since you talked with her on the phone, but trust me, this is better. Before that, I swear, Lucien, it looked and sounded like she was dying," Stephanie replied.

"*Christ!*" Lucien's word was a subdued explosion. His arms got tight, painfully so. It hurt and at the same time it felt beautiful.

"Has this happened before?" Stephanie asked.

"She has bad dreams," Lucien answered, his hand beginning to stroke my back.

"Bad dreams? Luce, that wasn't a bad dream. That was completely *fucked up*. I'm seven hundred and fifty years old and I've seen some serious shit in my life, but that was *fucked up!*"

Stephanie was in a state.

"Tell me exactly what happened," Lucien demanded.

Stephanie didn't hesitate.

"I heard her scream. It was intense. I came running just in time to catch her leaping out of bed. She was choking, crying. I thought she was just upset about what happened earlier," Stephanie explained. "Then I realized it was something more. The crying stopped, the choking continued. She fought me like no mortal has fought me before. I almost couldn't hold her. It was like she was being strangled by something invisible. She was fighting it and she was losing. Then you called and talked to her, the strangling stopped, but she went limp and unresponsive. Honest to God, for a minute, I thought she was dead, but I heard her heart beating and her breathing. I put her in bed and she just curled up, eyes open and staring at nothing. I think it's safe to say she *freaked me out!*"

Lucien said nothing but he stopped stroking my back, his hand went under my hair and curled warmly around my neck.

"She's still messed up. We need to call a doctor," Stephanie announced.

"I'm fine," I whispered and wished I didn't.

My voice scared me. It scared me because it sounded like I'd just survived being *strangled.*

At the sound of my voice, Lucien's body went solid.

"See!" Stephanie cried.

"Leah, sweetheart, can you look at me?" Lucien's tone was gentle, his hand moving from my neck to grip my hair and carefully pull my head back.

I nodded, the effort at that simple movement felt like running a race, but my eyes caught his.

"Do you remember anything?" he asked and I nodded again.

"All of it." My voice still sounded painfully abrasive because it *was* painful *and* abrasive.

Lucien flinched when I spoke.

"Ow," I whispered.

His face went hard before he commanded, "No more talking."

I nodded again. I was happy with that. Way happy.

He let go of my hair, but his fingers cupped the back of my head and pressed my face to his throat.

"We need to call a doctor," Stephanie repeated.

"She's fine now," Lucien replied.

"I...do...not...*think*...so. She sounds like she's been strangled!"

"Teffie, I'm here. She's fine."

The air in the room got thick. I tensed before Stephanie spoke angrily.

"I know pretty much everyone thinks you're all that, including me most of the time. But as far as I know, you don't have magical healing powers."

"Teffie, leave us. Get some sleep," Lucien ordered.

"You heard her voice!" Stephanie yelled and my body twitched at her anger.

I felt Lucien's frame turn to stone.

His voice was ominous when he demanded, "Get the fuck out of here, *now.* You're upsetting Leah."

"I—"

"*Now!*" he barked, and I jumped.

She must have left because the next second I was on the bed alone, bereft of Lucien. The second after that I felt his warm, naked body the length of mine, his arms tight around me, his heavy legs tangled with mine.

I felt the numbness go, my strength and wits returning, but the exhaustion stayed heavy upon me.

I melted into his heat and he gathered me closer.

Sleep was coming and I hoped it was the good kind because I needed it. I was battling real and invisible demons and I'd need all the rest I could get to endure.

I was nearly to dreamland when I heard his soft voice make a vow.

"That won't ever fucking happen again, Leah. You have my promise."

Tears slid up my throat, but silently I swallowed them down and burrowed closer.

He couldn't promise that. Even though I had no freaking clue what happened, there was one thing I knew through an intuition the source of which escaped me. Coming straight from the core of me, I knew the only way he could make good that promise was never to leave me.

Never.

And that was not going to happen.

I had more than one menace (the gentle one, Lucien) and more than two menaces (the frightening one, personified by Marcello, but also Rudolf and Cristiano), now I had three (my own mind, which freaked me out most of all).

I was dead woman walking one way or another.

And I was terrified out of my skull.

"I don't want Leah to overhear." Lucien's voice was low but angry. I shifted out of sleep and my eyes opened, seeing nothing but Lucien's vacant pillow.

"I'm thinking Leah should be in on this conversation," Stephanie snapped back.

"Teffie." Another voice, male, vaguely familiar. Cosmo.

"I don't understand." That was Edwina.

"Can we move to the kitchen?" Lucien asked a question which wasn't a question as much as a politely-formed demand.

Silence.

"I just went in there. She's sleeping. She sleeps very soundly," Edwina offered in a voice that said she was playing peacemaker.

I guessed Stephanie was digging in and Edwina was hoping she wouldn't have to repair plaster in the upstairs hallway.

Lucien must have thought that slamming Stephanie into the wall would likely wake me anyway and probably upset me, so he spoke.

And what he said freaked me out.

"She has a dream. It's recurring and it's connected to me. I know this because I hear her words in my head while she's dreaming." Lucien's voice was low, curt and impatient. "I spoke to her mother and these intense dreams have been happening her whole life."

I was totally freaked about me talking in Lucien's head when I was dreaming, about what I might have said and about the dream being about him *at all* considering what that dream did to me, both before my near death experience and during it.

But what he said after that took precedence.

He spoke to my mother?

Now that made me angry.

For the last three weeks I'd been calling all my family, even Aunt Kate (but not Myrna as I had enough of channeling Myrna in daily life, I didn't want to have to actually speak to her).

Desperate for advice, guidance and the lessons Lucien stopped giving me until last night, I was willing to talk to anyone. I'd even called Aunt Fiona twice.

Problem was, when they answered the phone, and I was suspecting they were avoiding that chore when they saw my name come up on their displays, they were busy.

Busy, busy, busy.

Even Lana, who could talk to a corpse until it reanimated, sat up and told her to shut the hell up.

This hurt.

I mean, I'd never moved away from home and I missed them a lot.

But it seemed like they were getting on with life without me just fine.

When Lana had been selected, she'd been lucky enough to move not that far away, a three hour drive. She was home all the time. My move was a two hour *plane ride.*

I thought they'd feel my absence, but the whirlwind of "I have a lunch date..." "We're about to catch a movie..." "I have a facial in twenty minutes..." "If I don't get to that sale, that pair of shoes is going to be gone and I'll just *die* if I don't own them..." (that was Aunt Nadia, she liked shoes nearly as much as me) was all I heard.

Not a single, "So, Leah, how are you getting on with the Mighty Vampire Lucien who you so desperately did not want to be separated from your adored family and pack of friends to go and service? Are you okay? Do you need, per chance, to talk to a beloved trusted family member?"

Silly, mean, awful Buchanan bitches.

Now I find my mother, *my mother,* was chatting with *Lucien.*

I was going to disown her. As soon as she talked to me long enough for me to share that morsel that was.

Stephanie's amazed words brought me back to my chore of just-woken-up eavesdropping.

"Like last night?"

"No, I talked to Lydia this morning and she said that never happened to Leah," Cosmo put in. "She said often her dreams would be frightening and she'd be nearly inconsolable afterwards but she only cried or screamed, sometimes fought. Nothing like what you described last night."

So, Mom was also not too busy to have a natter with Cosmo either.

Totally disowned.

"She's very concerned," Cosmo continued.

Yeah right, I seethed.

"She should be concerned," Stephanie clipped. "It was fucking scary."

"I'm concerned," Edwina said quietly, and I knew she meant it.

I liked Edwina and at that moment I liked her even more. Maybe I'd ask her to be my new mom.

"She has abilities," Lucien shared and you could tell he didn't much like it.

My body tensed and my ears perked up.

"Abilities?" Cosmo prompted.

I imagined Lucien nodding before he spoke. "She can fight mesmerization. Not long, seconds, but longer than anyone else. She can talk back when you're communicating with her, hold entire conversations, like you." I didn't know who he meant but I guessed it was either Stephanie or Cosmo. "She can also get into my head, speak to me without me calling to her. She can do it on her own, again, like you."

I couldn't believe what I was hearing. Not everyone could do that?

Lucien continued, "Her senses are advanced, particularly her sense of danger. Either that or she has the reciprocal ability to mark *me*, making me attune to her in a way that I don't feel it and she doesn't know she's doing it. Either way, when there's danger or a situation is uncertain, she senses it."

"Fucking hell," Cosmo muttered.

"You're joking," Stephanie whispered.

"I knew she was special," Edwina stated.

Edwina was *so...totally...my new mom.*

"I think it's marking," Lucien decreed and my heart started tripping. "I've never been marked. I do the marking, but twice I've felt her trying to attune herself to me, sense my thoughts, my mood. It took effort to hold her back."

Oh my God.

That whole pulsating thing. I remembered wanting to know his mood. I thought he was trying to probe mine, but I was probing his!

And he was blocking me out which must have been why I was pulsating.

"How bizarre," Stephanie mumbled.

She could say that again!

"I have a theory," Lucien declared, and I stopped breathing like this would help me hear better. "Her bloodline has been absorbing vampire essence for a long time. Each respective generation taking in more than any other concubine line. I think it's affected her line and mutated, giving her powers other mortals don't have."

I started breathing again.

Wow.

I was maybe mutated. Vampire powers spliced in my genes.

That was *huge*! And cool!

I know you're awake, my pet.

My body jerked.

Holy heck!

Lucien was so freaking *annoying*. I couldn't even eavesdrop without him cottoning on.

"I wouldn't share that with The Council," Cosmo warned, tearing me away from my thoughts.

"I've no intention to," Lucien replied, his voice closer, coming my way, and I assessed my options.

I didn't know if he was angry, but eavesdropping was never nice. Of course, in my defense, they *were* standing outside the door and the door *was* open.

I considered throwing myself out the window but I didn't think my mutant vampire abilities translated to not breaking my leg upon such a feat. And I hadn't been servicing Lucien long enough to get my super-healing vampire mojo going yet so I figured I should just face the consequences.

"Lucien, we're not done talking," Stephanie called.

"Leah's awake," Lucien informed her, sounding like he was right at the door.

Silence then, "Shit, she is. I wasn't paying attention."

Boy, vampires hearing heartbeats and breathing really sucked sometimes.

Lucien appeared. He closed the door and walked slowly to me.

"Hey," I said hesitantly, testing his mood.

My voice was rough as sandpaper.

This was a good move on my part. His expression had been thoughtful as if trying to decide which irritating dominating vampire punishment to mete out. Upon hearing my voice, his eyes flashed then gentled as did his face.

He threw back the covers and got in bed with me, even though he was fully-clothed, wearing jeans and a tight-fitting black T-shirt.

He pulled me in his arms.

"When did you know I was awake?" I rasped.

"The minute you woke," he informed the top of my head scarily. "Now, stop speaking."

"I'm fine," I argued even though I didn't sound fine, I really was. I didn't feel any different than normal except my throat was kind of sore.

"I'm not arguing about this."

"But—"

Quiet, Leah. He mind-controlled me.

Big, bad, vampire *jerk*!

I hate it when you do that, I snapped.

Why would you use your voice when we can converse perfectly well like this?

He had a point. Still, for good measure, I pouted. Seeing as my face was in his neck and he couldn't see me pouting, this was a moot pout but at least it made me feel better.

Talk to me about last night, he ordered.

What do you want to know? I asked.

Everything, he answered.

I sighed then gave in. No sense fighting it, he was even more stubborn than me.

I had the dream again, I told him and stopped sharing.

When I said no more, he prompted, *I guessed that.*

I kept going. *I don't know what happened. I still don't remember what I dream, but it's like the dream kept going even after I woke up.*

How?

I shook my head but answered, *It felt, I know this is going to sound totally unhinged, but it felt like I was being hanged.*

His body went completely taut. I'd felt this before, of course, many times, but there was something different about this time. Very different and very wrong.

Lucien?

Tell me more, he commanded, even his voice in my head sounded tight.

This alarmed me, so I continued, *I could feel Stephanie, sense the real world around me. I even heard the phone ring when you called. But I was still in the dream and it was more powerful. It felt like the floor went out from under me and the noose was strangling me.*

Did you see anything?

Like what?

Like me.

This time, my body grew tight.

I know you're dreaming of me, Leah. Now his voice was soft and coaxing.

I don't know that.

You are, sweetheart.

What do you hear me say?

Let's focus on you.

I'd rather focus on what you hear.

Later.

Now.

His arms grew tight and the breath went out of me.

"Do you see me in your dream? Did you see me last night?" he demanded to know.

I shook my head.

"Did you feel heat?"

That confused me.

Heat? I asked.

"Like a fire."

My head jerked back and I looked up at him with wide eyes.

Yes, I breathed.

I watched as his eyes closed slowly and his jaw got tight, not like he was angry, like he was in pain.

I felt his pain. It hurt.

His look was also familiar. I didn't know why, but it was very familiar, like I'd seen it before and it scared me.

Lucien! I cried.

His eyes opened.

What? I asked.

His hand at the back of my head tucked my face in his throat again as he answered, "Nothing, sweetling."

That wasn't nothing!

"Just relax," he ordered.

Yeah, right, you *relax. I'm freaking out!*

"Everything will be fine."

Sure. Everything will be fine. You're a vampire renegade, breaking laws and getting carted in to talk to The Council in the middle of the night. Your estranged mate wants me dead. Creepy Marcello-with-a-death-wish nearly touches me and you morph into Super Lucien, the Mighty Concubine Protector. And even my dreams want me dead! Yep, all's normal! Nothing to worry about here!

After my mental tirade delivered directly to his brain, which was totally bizarre *in itself* (the most bizarre of all was that I was communicating with him like this and it didn't feel bizarre in the slightest), I felt his body shaking.

He was laughing.

It started silently then it became chuckles. He pulled me up, lifted his head and buried his face in my neck.

This isn't fucking funny, I declared, and it sure as hell wasn't.

He kept laughing.

What happened last night? I demanded to know.

"I'll tell you later." His voice was still filled with mirth as he spoke against my neck.

Now.

"Later," he murmured.

Now, Lucien! I insisted. *You can't just leave me after that drama, all worried about you, and then not...*

I stopped nagging his brain and went still.

I did this for two reasons. One, because he went still too. Completely. Nearly as solid as when we were talking about my dream. Two, because one part of my idiot brain caught up with what the other, more idiot part of my idiot brain was actually saying.

His head came up. I twisted my neck to look up at him and wished my possible vampire abilities extended to turning back time so I could take back words.

"You were worried about me?" he asked.

I tried to cover. *Well, you know, anyone would get worried when someone was carted off in the middle of the night.*

"They wouldn't be worried if they hated the person who was being carted off," he pointed out logically, but his voice was pure velvet and it seemed to glide across every inch of my skin.

Why oh why was I such a freaking loser!

Don't read anything into that, Lucien, I warned.

He grinned and it was his arrogant grin. "Hard not to, pet."

Well, try, I pushed.

His face got closer and his voice was still velvet. "I rather like what I'm reading."

May I remind you that you spanked me last night? Spanked me! I snapped.

"Oh, I remember." Still velvet, still gliding across my skin, now I was getting goose bumps. Then his eyelids slowly lowered to half-mast and he muttered, "I'm thinking I should have done that at your initial bloodletting. Saved time."

My body went tight then it jerked against his hold. I knew this would have no effect but I felt better doing it.

It was high time to change the subject.

I need food, I declared.

"Me too," he whispered.

Damn it all to hell, that got a response. I felt my nipples get hard and I went instantly wet.

He knew it. I knew he knew it because I saw the flash of a satisfied, smug smile before his face disappeared in my neck. His lips traveled down my chest, and with one arm locked around my waist, the other hand came up to my camisole and tugged it down sharply to expose one of my breasts.

I gasped.

Then I felt his tongue at the side of my breast, fire shot between my legs, and I squirmed.

Let me speak, I whispered and the instant I did, his mind released mine, and I felt the blood flow. "Oh my God," I breathed.

Powerless to stop them, my hands went to his head, fisting in his hair, holding him to me as the sweet, familiar thrill from his feeding shot through me.

His hand came up, fingers wrapping around my wrist, he pulled it away and down. Taking my hand in his own, he guided it into my pajamas, my undies, straight to the heat of me. His fingers manipulating mine against my most sensitive part, he coaxed a deeper response. I took over and his hand moved, a finger sliding inside, then two, then he stroked, the rhythm sure and strong, practiced and powerful, building in intensity and quickness.

With the feeding, my own fingers and his thrusts, it took only moments for me to come.

"Lucien," I whispered in my raspy voice and when I did, my fisted hand in his hair tightened at the same time holding him to me.

It was consuming. It was beautiful. I hadn't had that in three weeks. It nourished me too.

He imprisoned my hand cupped under his between my legs, lashed the wound at my breast with his tongue, pulled up and rolled into me.

With his weight pressed against my side, his face in my hair, he spoke.

"You've broken," he declared, victory warm in his tone.

I suspected he wasn't wrong.

I didn't tell him that.

"Now, you're mine," he went on, the warmth of victory turning heated, brutal, savage and fierce.

I suspected he wasn't wrong about that either.

Boy, was I *so* fucked.

His head came up, his hand pulling mine from between my legs, it lifted it, curling my arm around his waist. He tugged my camisole back over my breast, rolled deeper into me so he was almost on top of me and then he rested his hand against my neck, thumb stroking, head up, eyes locked to mine.

"Tonight, we join," he decreed, his voice still fierce as were his eyes.

I felt something unsettling.

His eyes were blazing, the triumph blatant, searing into me, so hot, so fierce, I felt branded.

But it wasn't the first time I felt that. I'd felt it before. Even though I knew I hadn't. Just like earlier, when he'd closed his eyes in pain.

"Leah? Did you hear me?"

My mind was elsewhere but I still answered, "I heard you."

"Leah," he called.

I shook off my troubling thoughts and focused on him.

"What we'll have will be beautiful," he told me, voice back to velvet.

I suspected he wasn't wrong about that either.

The problem with that was, even though it would undoubtedly be beautiful, whatever it was, it would be temporary.

Tarnished beauty. Could I live with that?

"Sweetling," velvet still but there was an odd throb to it like an ache, "whatever that is working in the backs of your eyes, let it go. You give this to me; I'll take care of it." His voice dipped lower before he finished, "That's a vow."

Of course, seeing as I was expelled from Vampire Studies, I had no idea how binding a vampire's vow was. I had no idea they'd kill to protect it and die before they'd break it. I had no idea they'd quest to the ends of the earth for centuries to fulfill it or that they'd endure torture to keep it safe.

So, even though I believed that *he* believed he wasn't feeding me a line, I knew different.

Still, with that thing in me broken, unable to keep him out any longer, I had no choice.

So I looked him in the eyes and whispered, "Okay."

My submission was immediately rewarded.

He pulled me tight into his arms and gave me one of his demanding, bruising, possessive, branding and undeniably savage kisses that left me breathless.

Then he carried me all the way to the kitchen, deposited me on a stool, ordered a concerned, fawning Edwina and an equally concerned but not fawning Stephanie and Cosmo out of the kitchen and he made breakfast.

Amongst many other things, that morning I found out Lucien could cook.

16

The Aunties

I lay curled in the big beanbag in the comfy seating area off the kitchen while Edwina made dinner and Avery sat on the couch, chatting to her.

Avery was who I guessed was my protector for the evening.

Even though it was Sunday and Edwina was supposed to be off, she didn't leave.

And even though it was Sunday and ever since our first Sunday together Lucien had made a habit of being with me in some way all day (even these last three weeks when he'd not been pushy domineering Lucien), Lucien *did* leave. He took off with Cosmo after breakfast and another demanding, bruising, possessive, branding and undeniably savage kiss—right in front of *everyone*—going to places unknown and unshared with, oh, say, *me*.

Stephanie hung out until Avery arrived that afternoon then she immediately took off.

This was how I knew Avery was my protector.

The only thing I knew they were protecting me from was what Lucien commanded Edwina and Stephanie to look out for before he left. In fact, he had a load of commands.

"She rests and she doesn't speak. Got me?" was his first.

His second, "No phone calls. No visitors. She doesn't go near any door and she doesn't go outside."

His third, "She doesn't sleep, not even a nap, not without me in the house. Not just today, *every day*. Am I understood?"

He could, of course, have told me these things. However, it was very likely I'd give him lip, which was probably what he was trying to avoid.

Instead, I spoke directly to his mind.

Seriously bossy vampire! I snapped.

His head jerked toward me. I figured I was in trouble, but his lips twitched, he walked right into my space, and that's when I got The Kiss.

I had the sneaking suspicion Lucien was providing protection for me not because my own flipping dream nearly killed me and he needed someone around to keep me awake. But because there were other, more dangerous menaces from which he needed to keep me safe.

I didn't want to go there but I couldn't anyway. Lucien was gone before I could form a word in his mind.

It would have to wait for that night and the good thing was, it would delay "the joining" something which, I had to admit, I was looking forward to rabidly. In fact, if I let myself think about it for more than two seconds, I'd start panting and my legs would get restless.

It also scared the hell out of me mainly because if just thinking about it made me pant, what would happen when *it* happened? Would I spontaneously combust?

I had a pad of paper in my hands on which I was meant to write whatever I wanted to communicate. I was doing this even though I tested out my voice in the bathroom, and seeing as my throat felt better (because Edwina kept giving me throat lozenges), my voice sounded almost normal. Edwina gave the pad to me, and if I even opened my mouth, her hand would shoot up, palm facing me, and then she'd point at the pad.

At that moment, instead of using it to communicate, I was doodling on it.

I felt Avery's eyes on me, so mine slid to him.

He smiled.

Really, even though he was somewhat weird-looking, he was also very attractive.

I ripped the doodling sheet off the top, wrote him a note and passed it to him.

He read it and shook his head, handing the pad back to me, "I'm not a vampire, Leah."

I wrote another note and passed it to him.

He did the reading thing and gave it back to me. "Yes, I'm immortal."

Wow!

I was guessing!

My brows shot up.

"Maybe you should—" Edwina started, all of a sudden there, standing behind the couch looking a little worried.

Avery lifted a long, knobby-knuckled, quieting hand and Edwina was silenced.

"What?" I asked and Edwina gave me a look.

I wrote *sorry* in big block letters on the pad and showed it to her.

Her head tilted to the side. She winked at me and fluttered back to the kitchen.

Avery spoke. "She's concerned. As you're in the life, you're entitled to know about vampire culture. But other cultures are kept from you. They're secret as the vampire culture is secret from all mortals outside of it. In other words, I can't tell you what I am."

My eyes went wide then I wrote on my pad and turned it to show him.

"Yes, Leah, there are other cultures, other kinds of immortals," he paused then continued, "and other creatures."

This was news. Seriously nutty outrageous news.

I wrote on my pad again and showed him. He read it and smiled.

"I trust you to keep my secret, little one."

Only Avery, who was seven foot tall and mammoth, would be able to get away with calling *me* "little one."

He went on, "Though, if anyone ever knew I told you, I'd be sentenced to death."

I felt my eyes bug out in horror, he laughed and continued, "We take our secrets very seriously."

I wrote *no kidding* on my pad. He read it and chuckled again.

Then I wrote *why?*

"Do the words 'angry villagers' mean anything to you?" he asked, trying to make it a joke, but I didn't take it as such.

I felt my heart hurt like it did last night when Lucien explained the world he was forced to live in. Not only hiding his magnificence, but also being roundly and kind of sickeningly used and misunderstood.

I wrote angrily on my pad again and showed it to Avery. When he read it, his face grew soft, his big hand came out, and he tugged a lock of my hair.

Then his gentle eyes looked deep into mine and he whispered, "Not all mortals suck, Leah."

His words washed over me and I smiled at him. It was shaky, my heart still hurt, but I was glad he didn't blame me for whatever tortures his people endured from my people, either advertently or inadvertently.

The phone rang. Edwina answered it then brought it to me.

"Lucien," she said and my heart skipped an irritating beat. I took it and put it to my ear.

Then I didn't know what to do, his command was no talking.

Could I do long distance, mutant vampire abilities, telepathic communication?

"Leah?" he called.

I was silent.

"You can talk, sweetling," he said softly.

I was relieved. Then I was cross.

"You know, it totally sucks that I have to wait for you to let me speak," I informed him waspishly.

He chuckled. Damn the vampire!

I ignored the chuckle.

"Did you manage not to get arrested today?" I asked.

More chuckling, but, I noted, no answer.

"For my peace of mind, I'll take that as a yes. So, did you break any laws?"

"Leah—"

I cut him off with, "Speeding ticket?"

He burst out laughing.

I fumed.

"You're sounding better," he commented after his hilarity died down.

"Like I said this morning, I'm fine."

"You're fine because you've rested your throat all day," he returned.

He was probably right. That and Edwina's obsessive administration of throat lozenges. I didn't share either of these tidbits of knowledge with him.

"I'm on my way home," he informed me.

"Goodie," I said with saccharine sweetness, but I felt my pulse race.

I ignored my pulse. Lucien ignored my grumpiness.

"Have you eaten?"

"Edwina's making dinner now."

"Good. I'll be home in five minutes."

"You know," I said chattily, "you don't have to call when you're five minutes from home. We could have had this extremely pressing conversation five minutes from now, when you *are* home."

"Yes, my pet, but I worried about you all day and found I couldn't wait five minutes more to assure myself you were all right."

That took the bitchiness out of me. Mainly because his words made me feel really, *really* good.

And that scared me silly, or in this case, it scared me right back to bitchy.

"Stop being so nice," I snapped.

"Why?" His voice held a burgeoning chuckle.

"Because I don't know what to do with it," I replied.

His tone turned velvet. "Tonight, I'll teach you what to do with it."

My womb (and parts south) rippled and it felt *great*.

Moving on!

"See you soon," I told him.

"Soon, pet," he replied and then disconnected.

I hit the button to turn off the phone, ignored my still rippling female parts and announced to the room, "Lucien says I can talk and he'll be home in five minutes."

Edwina flitted forward, wielding a throat lozenge. "One more, dear, just to be on the safe side."

I caught Avery's amused grin as I took it and popped it in my mouth, even though I didn't need it and I didn't want it. She was concerned. It made her feel better. I wanted her to feel better, and furthermore, I wanted her to be my new mom so I didn't want to scare her off with Leah Attitude before she took on the role.

The attitude would come later, the first time she told me to behave myself, which would happen, no doubt about it.

Lucien had been wrong. He wasn't home in five minutes. He was home in four. It was embarrassing to admit, but I watched the freaking clock.

To hide the fact that I'd had such a girlie, obsessed-with-a-hottie-vampire-who-was-going-to-*join*-with-me-that-very-night thing, I didn't bother to rise from the beanbag when he came in.

I should have known better.

He hooked the keys on the holder, nodded to Edwina's greeting, shook hands with Avery, and then came direct to my beanbag.

"Yo," I said, looking up at him.

Mistress Cool.

His mouth twitched. My female parts rippled.

Before I knew it, I was plucked out of the beanbag and found myself in Lucien's arms. *Not* like a normal, give your concubine a hug upon arriving home.

No.

He had my legs wrapped around his waist, my arms automatically went around his shoulders to hold on and his hands were at my ass.

His head tilted back to look at me and he murmured, "How was your day, sweetling?"

"I wrote everything I wanted to say on a pad of paper all day," I answered. "Do you know how annoying that is?"

"Was it that difficult?" he asked, his black eyes dancing with suppressed humor.

It wasn't.

"Yes," I answered huffily.

I got another lip twitch, one of his hands left my ass, slid up my back and tangled in my hair.

"Your torture's over," he muttered before pressing down on my head so he could kiss me.

Not a normal, because you have company, give your concubine a seemly peck on the lips upon arriving home.

No.

A full-on, mouths open, tongues dueling, ravenous, feasting *snog*.

I was panting when it was done and I'd totally forgotten Avery and Edwina *existed* much less they were in the room.

I'd like to take you upstairs right now, his mind told mine and his voice sounded deliciously hungry in my head.

One could say, at that precise moment, I'd like that too.

I decided not to speak.

Then he asked, his voice in my head sounding both sweetly intimate and even more sweetly teasing, *Throat lozenges?*

I couldn't help it and I didn't know why I couldn't, but I giggled.

Edwina, I answered. *All day. I've had six hundred of them at least.*

His eyes were on my mouth, his mouth was grinning.

Ah, he murmured in understanding.

Avery cleared his throat. "I think we're missing something."

I looked at Avery then at Lucien before I pushed against his shoulders and placed the blame squarely and publically on him.

"You're being rude."

His brows went up but he dropped me to my feet and curled me into his side with an arm around my shoulders.

"You're staying for dinner?" Lucien asked Avery, and I marveled that even a courteous invitation from Lucien sounded like a command.

"Leave now and miss Edwina's cooking? I'd rather..." Avery started, I tensed, and Lucien's and Avery's heads snapped toward the front door.

"Company," Avery muttered.

Reflexively, my hand lifted, fingers fisting in Lucien's shirt at his stomach as I looked up at him.

This was wussy behavior, I knew, but we hadn't had a lot of luck with the front door. Usually, someone at my front door meant a call to the handyman.

Lucien's head was cocked and I knew he was listening.

Then he mumbled, "Fucking hell."

"What?" I asked.

His eyes caught mine. Then he said, "Buchanans."

He said this right before there was an imperative and constant knocking at the door, confirming Lucien's words.

Only Aunt Kate could knock on a door like that. It was her signature. Even when she was coming over for a cup of coffee and a gab, she eschewed doorbells and knocked on the door like she was Queen of the World and how dare the lowly commoner inside not anticipate her arrival, sweep open the door and throw rose petals at her feet.

"Aunt Kate," I whispered.

"Kate," Lucien agreed.

"Oh dear, oh dear," Edwina fretted as she fluttered toward the hall. "How many are there? I don't know if we have enough food."

Avery followed Edwina, but Lucien curled me into his front.

I looked up at him when he asked, "If it seems your family will interrupt our plans for this evening, if I'm forced to eject them bodily, how would you react?"

He was teasing again. It was frustrated teasing but he still did it really, really well. I was seeing the benefits of having a kind of like boyfriend who was centuries old. He had a lot of good stuff down *pat.*

"I've decided I'm mad at them. They've been ignoring me," I admitted. "But not sure about bodily ejection. Could you, you know, Mighty Vampire Lucien Command them to leave?" I said the words "mighty vampire Lucien" in a fake pompous voice which was why I think Lucien yanked me in his arms and gave me a tight hug as he threw his head back and shouted with laughter.

This was what my family saw when they filed into the room looking uppity and in dire need of a martini.

I decided to glare.

I mean, in my hour of need, they'd ignored me, and here they were when my hour of need was beyond me (not exactly, but in a way) and the good parts (one particular one I had in mind) were happening *that very night.*

"I need a drink," Aunt Kate announced grandly.

"Leah, honey, are you okay?" Mom asked worriedly.

"Is that roast chicken I smell?" Aunt Millicent inquired, sniffing.

"*Ohmigod*, I love your blouse!" Aunt Nadia screeched excitedly.

"Well, hello to you too," I replied to them all. "So, you remembered I exist?"

Aunt Kate's eyes narrowed.

Mom looked guilty.

Aunt Millicent glanced away.

Aunt Nadia bit her lip.

Lucien gave me a shoulder squeeze and murmured, "Leah."

"Sorry, but I *was* expelled from Vampire Studies and I *did* happen to find myself living with a vampire and my family *does* happen to be the premier family of vampire concubines, so forgive me for expecting a little guidance and support!" I fired off.

The collective of Buchanan women's eyes moved to Lucien. Once they did, so did my own. Lucien let me go and shrugged off his suit jacket.

He dropped it on the arm of the couch and suggested, "Perhaps we should all have a drink."

I didn't think this was good.

Aunt Kate disagreed.

"Capital idea!" she announced.

"Lucien?" I called.

Drink, he said in my head. *I'll explain in a minute.*

He'll explain? What did this have to do with Lucien?

Then it hit me. The aunties visit a month ago when I didn't get the chance to talk to them.

I was right, this wasn't good.

I crossed my arms, jutted my hip, threw out a leg and tapped my toe. If *any* of my past boyfriends saw me in this stance, they would ask no questions. They wouldn't utter a *noise.* They would cut and run straight for the hills.

Lucien glanced at me as he headed for the drinks cabinet. When his eyes hit me, they traveled from chest to toe then straight to my face. Then I saw him bite back a smile.

Big, fat, vampire *jerk*!

I immediately changed my mind regarding our later activities. If he thought we were "joining" tonight, he had another think coming.

"I'll make more stuffing and potatoes and warm up more rolls." Edwina was fussing in the kitchen. "Maybe whip up a pie."

I was about to offer my help when I was interrupted.

"You were expelled from Vampire Studies?" Avery asked, his amused stare locked on me.

"I was caught texting, passing notes, throwing spitballs and writing my Last Will and Testament," I declared.

Avery burst out laughing.

"Spitballs?" Lucien voice came at me from behind.

I turned and saw he had a bottle of vodka in his hand, his brows were up, and he didn't look amused.

"Spitballs," I snapped rebelliously.

"Oh, can we *please* not talk about that? It took some palm greasing to get that instructor to keep his mouth shut," Aunt Kate lamented and sent me her look that, since I was four and even now that I was forty, never failed to pin me to the spot. "Anyone *else* learns of this and it's sure to taint the Buchanan name."

"I still think it's kind of funny, Katie," Aunt Nadia whispered, giving me a wink.

"Um, excuse me, but does anyone want to talk about my daughter nearly dying from a bad dream last night? Anyone? Anyone? Or is it *just me*?" Mom demanded tetchily.

I stared at Lucien's back and stated, "I'd prefer to know why my family has been avoiding me for a month."

Don't try me, Lucien warned in my head.

Kiss my concubine ass, I returned to his.

He didn't turn but I saw him shake his head in that way men do when they think women are entirely too ridiculous for words. But, seeing as this was Lucien, he did it far better than any man of my acquaintance, and there were *lots* of men of my acquaintance who would shake their heads like I was too ridiculous for words.

It was then that I saw the drawbacks of having a kind of like boyfriend who was centuries old.

He had a lot of bad stuff down pat, too.

"Leah, I asked you a question when I came into this room." Mom commanded my attention. "Are you all right?"

I turned to my mother and told her, "I'm fine."

"What happened?" she asked.

"Oh, not much, except I woke up but my dream wasn't quite done with me yet. I had the highly disturbing experience of being hanged, literally, but without actually being hanged."

Every single one of my aunties gasped and even Avery winced.

Lucien's sharp voice cut cleanly through the horror filling the room.

"Leah, a word."

Then he handed the martini shaker to Avery and walked out.

After the last incident that happened when I defied him in front of my aunties, I felt it prudent to follow him. He turned into the study and I followed him there too. He shut the door behind me, grabbed my upper arm and pushed me against it.

I looked up to see he was angry.

He didn't delay. "You're mother's concerned. So concerned she flew across four states to check on you. You just told her something grisly, terrifying and *life threatening* happened to the daughter she loves like you'd relay the time of day."

"Please, do *not* think to tell me how to handle my own mother." I tried to make it as nice as I could. He might be the Mighty Vampire Lucien everywhere else, but he was treading on thin ice if he thought he could get between me and my family.

He crowded me, dropping my arm and putting his hand on the door by my head.

"I see you need to learn respect for more than just me, pet," he said in a low, dangerous voice, clearly thinking he could get between me and my family.

"You have brothers? Sisters? Cousins?" I shot back and his eyes narrowed.

"What the fuck does that—?"

I cut him off before he could finish, "No? Well then, you don't understand what it means to be the black sheep in very close-knit family. They love me and I love them, like, a lot, but mostly, except Aunt Nadia, Lana, my cousin Natalie and sometimes my mom, they put up with me. I didn't want to come here. They *made* me. Then they left me to deal with it all by myself with only Edwina, Stephanie and *you* to help me out. I didn't know any of you and *you* I didn't even *like*."

His face lost some of its anger, not all, but there was a hint of concern (and, dare I believe it?) even regret in his eyes.

"I curtailed their communication with you, Leah."

"I figured that out in there, Lucien," I informed him with a toss of my head toward the other room. "But do you think, for even a minute, *I* would listen even to *you* if my sister Lana needed me? Or Natalie? Or Mom? Or even Aunt Kate? Hunh? Do you?"

His hand left the door and came to my neck. Then his forehead came to rest on mine.

Then he muttered, "Not even a minute."

"No, not even a minute. I was drowning, Lucien. I called out to them and they gave me no lifeline, just floated on their merry way."

His other arm slid around me and he pulled me from the door into his warm, big, solid body.

"Sweetheart," he whispered.

Yep, definitely regret.

It was time to let him off the hook. What he did was uncool, but it was very Lucien. What they did was just plain *wrong*.

I looked up at him and put my hands on his chest. "So, seeing as you're new to the Buchanan family dynamic, let me clue you in. I'm going to go out there and be sarcastic, bitchy and obnoxious. Aunt Kate's going to be overbearing because she's never wrong. Mom's going to be guilty, as she should be. Aunt Millicent is going to be mostly worried about when dinner will be served. And Aunt Nadia and I'll probably talk a lot about the clothes you bought me and whatever new man is in her life. Then all will be forgiven. We'll eat. We'll probably get drunk. And, except for Aunt Kate, who will find the best guest room and lay claim to it before any of the rest of them even think about getting their suitcases from the car, we might end up dancing to eighties pop music and doing the robot. Just hope Aunt Nadia doesn't try to breakdance. The last time she did that, she threw her back out and was down for a week."

The regret was gone, his hand was moving up my back and his eyes were smiling even though his mouth wasn't.

"Two problems with the evening's festivities, pet."

"And those would be?"

"I don't want you drunk and I don't want a house full of Buchanans when I finally have you."

Oh.

I'd semi-forgotten about that.

"*Definitely* no breakdancing," he went on, and because he was funny, I laughed out loud.

When I did, his gaze dropped to my mouth, the smile left his eyes, and they went intense. His hand sifted into the hair at the back of my head and he kissed the laughter right off my lips.

It was a good kiss. One of the best in a lineup of seriously top-notch kisses.

My arms were wrapped around his neck and my body was plastered against his when he lifted his head.

When my thoughts unjumbled, I whispered, "We have a wee problem then."

"No, we don't."

I tilted my head to the side. "We don't?"

"Leave it to me."

For some reason, I got worried and my arms tightened.

"Lucien, I'm not sure you understand. The Buchanan women can be kind of..." I couldn't believe I was saying this to *him* of all people, but I had to warn him as I would have to warn *anyone* who went head to head with the aunties, "*daunting* when they're riled. Whatever they did made my dad leave and never come back and—"

Lucien interrupted me, "First, they're concubines. I'm a vampire. Your father wasn't. They won't say a single word to me."

Oh yes. That was true.

He went on, "Second, your father left because of your aunts, but he never came back because of Cosmo."

My arms tightened again, this time spasmodically because at the same time I felt like I'd been kicked in the gut.

"What?" I whispered.

"If concubines find a man after their Arrangement and wish to stop their care, they can ask their vampire to stop it. Most of them do. Your mother did too. But your father couldn't give her the life Cosmo gave her or the ones her sisters had. This made him mean. Mean turned to nasty. Drink made him dangerous. Your aunts got rid of him, Kate told Cosmo about his behavior, and Cosmo reinstated your mother's care and made certain he stayed gone."

I stared at him, uncertain what to do with this knowledge.

"Did Cosmo...did he...*kill* my father?"

Lucien's brows knitted. "Of course not."

"What'd he do?"

"He gave him a very large sum of money."

My mouth dropped open.

My father vanished from my life because Cosmo gave him money?

"He, Cosmo, Dad..." I stuttered, composed myself and then went on, "Cosmo made it so my father didn't even send me a birthday card, a graduation gift, a—?"

"Cosmo made no stipulations about you girls. Only Lydia. Your father chose to disappear from *your* life."

This rocked me and my eyes moved to stare unseeing over his shoulder.

What a *schmuck*!

Of course, I already knew this but to have it confirmed totally stunk!

Lucien's arms gave me a gentle squeeze.

"Leah?"

"What a schmuck," I whispered.

"Leah."

My gaze returned to him and I declared, "Men suck."

His lips turned up at the ends. "Not all men."

I wrinkled my nose and then stated, "No, you're right. Avery seems relatively nice."

His arms gave me an affectionate squeeze this time but I didn't feel in the mood for affection.

"Do you know everything about me?" I asked snottily.

"Not everything, no. But most things, yes."

"That's not fair," I declared.

His small grin got bigger. "Why's that, pet?"

"I don't know hardly anything about you."

His hand twisted in my hair then started playing like we had all night and my aunties and Avery weren't in the other room and Edwina wasn't blustering around in the kitchen in a dither at how to feed twice as many people as expected.

"What would you like to know?" Lucien asked.

I looked over my shoulder at the door mumbling, "The aunties—"

Another arm squeeze and I looked back at him.

"What would you like to know?"

I had a million questions. No, a billion. Enough where the aunties would have to find ways to amuse themselves and breakdancing would no doubt commence.

"Lucien, we have company."

"Two questions," he returned.

"Sorry?" I asked.

"Later, you can ask me whatever you want. Now, you'll ask two questions."

I stared at him and curiosity, as it had a way of doing, got the best of me.

I started with, "How old are you?"

"Eight hundred and twenty-two."

I felt my lips part and my eyes grow wide. The instant he caught my look, his eyes went hooded.

"Wow," I breathed. "You're old."

His eyes stayed hooded and he smiled, making it the sexiest smile I'd ever seen in my life, except the first one I witnessed from him at my Selection the minute I clapped eyes on him when he heard me verbally drooling over how handsome he was.

This one, however, was up close, so it was even better.

"Second question," he prompted, taking me out of my sexy smile reverie.

I tried to decide. There were too many.

Then it came to me. "How do you stop from hurting me?"

His head cocked sharply to the side and he asked, "Pardon?"

"You can throw a car, Lucien," I said softly. "How do you hug me and not crush my bones?"

His hand slid through my hair then twisted back in it and he explained, "It's like speaking two languages from birth. It's second nature. You can think, speak, read and write in them both. You just learn from the minute you're born how to be a vampire and how to live in the mortal's world. It's rare I'll lose control or any vampire will and it only happens when emotions are high," he paused, "or when it's deliberate."

"It's like you speak two body languages?" I asked. "Fluently?"

"Exactly like that, yes."

I thought that was kind of cool. Then something occurred to me that was seriously not cool and my heart skipped a beat.

He heard it and called, "Leah?"

Before I could lose my courage, I blurted, "Emotions are high when you have sex."

His hand fisted in my hair, his other arm growing tighter.

"Yes," he agreed.

My breath caught, my body tensed, then automatically I tried to draw away.

His arm got even tighter and his face dipped closer. "I'll not hurt you."

"Have you ever hurt anyone else?"

"Never."

"You said that about the feeding," I whispered.

"Leah—"

"Maybe we should—"

His face got even closer. "No you don't," he warned. "I was a week without food when I lost control at your first feeding and you were far more excited than I could imagine. Not than I could desire, but definitely than I could imagine, especially at that point in our relationship."

This was highly embarrassing and even more highly annoying, so I tried to cut him off.

"Lucien—"

I failed at cutting him off.

"I wasn't prepared. It won't happen tonight."

I stared at him.

For three weeks I knew he didn't go to Feasts. If he did, he was a glutton. He fed morning and night and even would come home some afternoons. And, on top of that, the last time I thought he had sex with someone else, he said he couldn't, even though she tempted him.

As far as I knew, he'd been without for three weeks or longer.

I'd had Lucien-induced orgasms. He'd had nothing.

If that wasn't a recipe for disaster, nothing was!

"What's working behind your eyes now, pet?" he demanded, watching me closely, too closely.

I looked over his shoulder.

"Nothing," I lied.

He gave me a shake.

I looked back at him. "Seriously! Nothing!"

His hand in my hair pulled my head back and his face got close.

"Waking up every day after sleeping next to you, smelling you, feeling you, I take care of myself in the shower. In the beginning, during your punishment, I'd have to do it two or three times a day." I stared up at him in shock and wonder and maybe a little turned on at his frank honesty, but he saved the best for last. "It's been a long time, too long. It'll be good to come inside you, sweetling."

Oh my *God*.

Yes, *totally* turned on.

Before my brain kicked in, I whispered, "Can we kick the aunties out right now?"

I saw the flash of his smug smile before he buried his face in my neck and muttered, "You're adorable."

I wasn't trying to be adorable. I was trying to get laid.

"No, seriously."

His head came up and he touched his lips to mine.

Then he promised, "Soon, Leah." His eyes went all vampire sexy and he whispered, "Very soon."

My female parts rippled. He smiled like he knew it.

And he probably did.

I rolled my eyes. He burst out laughing.

Then he walked me out so I could be sarcastic, bitchy and obnoxious to my family.

I was padding on bare feet down the hall when I heard them.

Lucien's "very soon" didn't come about because Stephanie showed up during dessert. Then Lucien, Avery and Stephanie went behind closed doors in his study.

While they were plotting whatever it was they were plotting, I sat and talked with Mom and the aunties for a while.

Since Lucien was hogging the study and the desktop computer was in the study, I had to go to the laptop upstairs to search online for someplace for my family to stay. Lucien might not have been right about the "very soon," but he *was* right about my mom and aunties not giving him any backtalk when he told them they had to stay somewhere else. Not a single word was spoken, except Aunt Millicent asking, "Could someone pass the potatoes?"

Luckily, Dragon Lake was a picturesque town so there were tons of posh bed and breakfasts. Unfortunately, most of them were booked up.

I lucked out on the seventh call when I found a place that not only was a B&B but also had a big guest house which had a cancellation.

I booked them in and was heading toward the comfy seating area in the kitchen where they were all gabbing (seriously, that huge house and we used, like, four rooms, it was such a freaking waste) when I heard them.

"*Lifemates?*" my mother cried in a weird strangled voice that sounded both thrilled beyond belief and scared stupid.

At her words, I stopped dead. I thought they were talking about Lucien and Katrina and I felt like a knife had been plunged in my gut.

I hadn't exactly forgotten about her but I had also not let myself think about her. Lucien had moved on from her, that much was clear. What wasn't clear was how I felt about how easily he could leave what amounted to his wife of fifty years and carry on with another woman, namely me.

"What else could it be?" Aunt Nadia replied to my mother.

"There's no such thing as lifemates. That's romance novel balderdash," Aunt Kate proclaimed.

"Sounds fishy to me too," Aunt Millicent agreed.

"Well, it doesn't sound fishy to me. She's marking him and only Lucien can do that. She can talk to him with her mind. That's *never* happened, not from a mortal. And she's dreaming about The Sentence," Aunt Nadia said.

The Sentence? What on earth was that?

I moved to the wall to better hide myself and decided to full-on eavesdrop since they weren't talking about Katrina, they were talking about me.

Me being lifemates with Lucien.

I read romance novels, loads of them, and lifemates were what some of those books called the unions between immortals or mortals and immortals.

The concept was, there was one being on all the earth through all of time that belonged to the immortal. She was destined for him (it was usually a him), even so far as created for him.

And of all the millions and billions of beings on the planet through time, he had to find her. Through all his centuries and sometimes millennia of living, he had to search out his one true love, the other half of him, and bind himself to her.

Of course, he found her. They usually had lots of hot sex. Though how they got to the sex when all the rest of the time they were bickering, or there was some huge misunderstanding, or they had to fight against some grave evil, or he'd done her some wrong for which she hated him, I'd never know. Still, it worked.

Eventually she soothed his savage soul, he'd find some way to make her immortal if she already wasn't, and they lived happily ever after for eternity.

Aunt Kate was right.

Balderdash.

"What do you think, Avery?" my mother asked and my eyes went to the study door, which, I noticed belatedly, was open and no one was inside.

Where was Lucien?

"I think I'll respectfully decline participation in this conversation," Avery murmured.

"Oh come *on*, Avery. You have to speak up," Aunt Nadia urged. "Mortals don't have those powers. Leah didn't even have those powers until she met Lucien."

"She'd had the dreams," Aunt Millicent pointed out.

"Okay, she had the dreams," Aunt Nadia allowed. "But the rest? It's crazy! Sounds total lifemate to me."

"Can you imagine? My Leah, lifemate to the Great Lucien. She's already famous, but she'll be a *legend*." Mom sounded ecstatic.

I was famous?

I didn't have time to ponder my celebrity, Aunt Kate spoke.

"I hope you jest, Lydia. I hope to *God* you jest," Aunt Kate whispered, but her whisper was strange.

It was angry and it was afraid.

"Katie—" Aunt Nadia started.

"You'd wish that on *your daughter*, to build *a legend*?" Aunt Kate hissed.

There was silence.

Then Mom replied, "Kate, I just want to see Leah happy."

"Happy for what? A few years? Until they cotton on, they hunt them down, they torture them, and they hand down The Sentence?"

"Kate—" Avery said gently.

"No, Avery, no," Aunt Kate cut him off. "If such a fool thing as lifemates exists, and if Leah is Lucien's lifemate, I hope she doesn't figure it out. And I *especially* hope he doesn't. There is no way the Great Lucien will denounce her. Not *ever*. And Leah's so stubborn, she wouldn't denounce him either. He'd burn, and while he did he and the rest of us would watch her *swing*."

My breath stuck in my throat, stars exploded in my eyes, and I thought I might faint.

My dream, the heat I felt, the noose around my neck, Lucien telling me he was in it. Was that what it was? A premonition of this sentence thing?

Lucien *burning*. Me *swinging*!

Oh my God!

"For a month, Lydia," Aunt Kate went on, "you and Nadia, Lana, Natalie, Kendra, Melissa, you've all been after me to let you speak to Leah, to let you disobey the wishes of a vampire to make sure she's all right. And now you want her life to be at risk?"

They wanted to speak to me? Even Kendra?

My cousin Kendra and I fought before I left because she couldn't find that kickass belt I loved so much that I wanted to bring with me but I'd lent to her. She was always losing my stuff (like my kickass belt). Why I let her borrow it, I'd never know.

"Do you think Lucien would let anything happen to Leah?" Mom asked, sounding uppity and taking me out of my thoughts about my belt. "You saw them when we walked in. Have you ever, once, seen Lucien *laugh*?"

More silence.

I guess they hadn't.

Wow.

Mom went on, "We agreed to this because this is bigger than all of us. This is *huge*."

"Yes, and this is about Leah," Aunt Kate returned. "The reason I didn't allow you to go against Lucien was because I had every faith Leah would have the *exact* effect on Lucien that we witnessed when we walked in. She's the best of the lot of us. She's a true Buchanan. She's a Buchanan of old."

At those words—uttered by Aunt Kate no less (I always thought she thought I was a big crazy loon)—I felt my chest get tight and I had to put my hand to the wall to hold myself standing.

It was Aunt Millicent who spoke next and she did so softly.

"Let her work her magic, Lydia. She's got the strength to see this through at Lucien's side to however it ends. No other concubine I know, living or dead, has that same strength. But lifemates, which is a ridiculous notion, Nadia, even for you, don't even consider it. And *definitely* don't put that idea in Leah's head. She'd run and Lucien would have no choice, now he's come this far, to hunt her."

More silence. More swirling in my head.

Finally Aunt Nadia muttered, "I still want them to be lifemates."

"Oh, for heaven's sake, *why*?" Aunt Millicent snapped.

"Because, you and Katie are right, this is *Leah*," Aunt Nadia snapped back. "And she's *special*. We've *always* known that. And I'd rather her have however long Lucien can give her of something beautiful before The Dominion puts a stop to it, if they can defeat Lucien at all, then for her to be set aside like the rest of us."

At that I backed away slowly, carefully, not making a noise.

My heart was racing, my eyes were stinging, my stomach hurt and my head was filled with loads of junk, none of which I could sort. I really, really, *really* needed to talk to Stephanie.

Or maybe Edwina, because I had the sneaking suspicion she knew more about everything than she let on.

Or even, possibly, Avery.

I turned and walked up five steps, shutting out their murmurs while deep breathing.

When I had myself under control, I bounded down, shouting, "Found you guys a guest house!"

Their murmurs stopped. I sauntered in like I'd heard nothing.

"That's great, honey," Mom, sitting on the couch, said, and since I was close to her, she grabbed my hand.

She gave my hand a squeeze. I gave her a squeeze back.

"Are you still disowning me?" she asked, giving me a cheeky grin because she knew my answer.

I had, of course, in my efforts at being sarcastic, bitchy and obnoxious, told my mother I disowned her.

"I haven't decided," I replied but she knew I wasn't serious.

She gave me another hand squeeze.

I saw movement outside and looked out the windows. One wall of the kitchen was made of floor to ceiling windows making the indoors seem kind of outdoors, which was really cool. And I saw Lucien and Stephanie stroll out of the woods.

So Stephanie and Lucien had gone for a stroll, which was why he couldn't hear my family's mind-boggling, earth-shattering,

Leah's-place-in-the-family-and-all-her-foundations-and-everything-she-ever-thought-about-life-herself-and-the-world-as-she-knew-it rocking conversation.

They were walking slowly even for mortals and I watched Lucien's body move.

It was a sight to behold.

Even walking slowly across a yard, he looked imposing. Not like he was walking across a yard, but as if he was strolling broodingly across a battlefield, pre-battle. A battle he'd eventually win, of course, soundly.

As I had this thought, his head came up and he looked right at me.

I hoped he didn't hear my thoughts.

Then his lips tipped up in that sexy way of his. Not smug or arrogant, just smiling at me.

He didn't hear me.

I smiled back.

Then I felt something strange. I looked toward its source and saw Avery was watching me musingly. And somehow I knew that he knew I'd heard every word of the earlier conversation.

But it was something else. And that something else was somewhere I did *not* want to go.

I wrinkled my nose at him and he grinned.

Lucien and Stephanie walked in.

I went to sit down on the arm of the couch next to Aunt Kate, which, incidentally, had the added benefit of being closer to Lucien. Then, I couldn't help myself, I bent and kissed the top of Aunt Kate's head.

"What on earth!" She batted around her head, her hands getting nowhere near me. Aunt Kate, by the way, *hated* public displays of affection, or affection at all for that matter. "What's the matter with you, Leah Buchanan?" she snapped.

"I'm trying to find new and interesting ways to annoy you," I informed her.

"Well, you found one," she retorted.

"Good," I returned. "Next I'm going to force you to cuddle with me and a tub of ice cream and tell me about all your secret crushes as a teenager," I hesitated and finished, "in minute detail."

Aunt Nadia, Aunt Millicent and Mom giggled, Stephanie out and out laughed, and I heard Avery's chuckle.

Aunt Kate stood and announced, "We've a guest house to check into. Ladies, we're going."

The rest of my family and also Avery and Stephanie made their moves to leave.

Nicely done, pet, Lucien said to my brain.

I looked at him. He looked amused and hungry and very, very sexy.

My heart skipped a beat.

I hadn't actually kissed Aunt Kate to piss her off enough to leave and drag everyone with her.

But at that moment, I also wasn't upset to see them go.

17

The Joining

Three weeks ago, Lucien came home and gave me a black-colored credit card, a checkbook and a bank card.

The credit card, he told me, was for my use whenever I wanted, whatever I wanted. The bills would go to him.

The checking account, he told me, had its first deposit. The same amount would be deposited every month and that was for my use whenever I wanted, whatever I wanted when cash was required.

When he left me, I looked and the amount of the deposit was a quarter of my yearly salary.

It was the kind of thing dreams were made of, if you didn't hate the person who made that dream come true, as, at the time, I'd hated Lucien.

Two weeks ago, Stephanie came over one morning and told me we were having a girlie day. Then she whisked me off to a spa, we had facials and massages, and then sat in a sauna where, incidentally, her super-vampire senses came in handy because all that steam made me blind. I tripped over the wooden mat by the door and she caught me before I took a header. Then we had a gourmet lunch followed by manicures, pedicures, makeup and hair.

After that, we went shopping and she took me to the place where she bought the outfit I admired so much.

And she also took me to a place that sold lingerie that cost more than most people's monthly mortgage payments.

It was there that she made me (and she *did* make me, I didn't want to do it) buy the getup that I was wearing at that very moment. She heard my heart start racing when I eyed it in the shop, she forced me to try it on, and then she vampire-talked me, as in no protesting allowed, into buying it.

Now I was standing in front of the three-way mirror in the dressing room and examining myself.

I had to admit, I loved it. It was kind of naughty, but it was also cute.

The problem was I didn't know if Lucien would like it.

It was a camisole and panties in sheer baby pink. The camisole was bloused from under the breasts and the cups had rows of tiny black lace frills that ran at diagonals. The thin straps were made of baby pink satin and there was a little black frill around the hem. The panties were also sheer baby pink but they were covered in rows of tiny black lace frills, like little girl panties.

Very sexy. Very sweet. Very cute.

But definitely kind of naughty.

I fancied I heard a noise, jumped like the scaredy-cat I was and ran to the black silk man's tailored robe that came down to my knees that I also bought at that store. Both purchases cost more than my food budget for six months when I was at home. Lucien was going to have a conniption when he got the credit card bill.

I covered up, tugged the belt tight on the robe, and wondered if I should put on lip gloss. Then I decided that was a supremely stupid idea since I was, essentially, going to bed.

I took a deep ragged breath, walked out of the dressing room through the bathroom and into the bedroom.

Lucien was laying in bed, back to the headboard, covers up to his waist, gorgeous chest bared. He was reading a book.

I stopped and stared. His eyes came to me. I fought back the need to start panting. To hide my distress, I latched on to something else.

That something else was the fact that he was lying in bed reading and he was blinkety-blank eight hundred and twenty-two years old.

"After eight hundred years plus, haven't you already read every book ever published?" I asked.

His thumb holding his place, he dropped the book to his side.

Then he answered, "No."

Hmm.

Next question.

"Do vampires ever get so old they have to wear glasses?"

"No," he repeated.

"Hearing aids?"

"No."

"Dentures?" I went on stupidly and maybe semi-hysterically.

His lips turned up at the ends. "No, Leah."

"Do they ever have to walk with canes?"

The lip-turn morphed into a sexy smile.

"Come here, sweetheart," he ordered gently.

Seeing as, if I decided to make a run for it he could be on me faster than I could blink, I thought it best to do as he ordered.

As I walked toward him, he put his book on the nightstand.

I stopped at the side of the bed.

With vamp speed he twisted, grabbed me by the waist, slid down the bed, and I was on top of him over the covers. I arched my back and rested a forearm on his chest, catching my breath at his sudden movements. He gathered all my hair in both of his hands at the back of my neck and his eyes caught mine.

"Nervous?" he murmured.

Nervous? No.

About to have a cardiac arrest? *Yes!*

"No," I lied to save face.

He grinned and told me, "I can hear your heart, pet."

Why was I always forgetting that?

I wrinkled my nose and informed him, "You're very annoying."

He put pressure on my neck, enough for my arm to buckle and get trapped between us as he lifted his head and buried it in my neck.

"You're very adorable," he replied against my skin.

I was pretty certain my heart was accelerating past the point of cardiac arrest straight to cardiac *explosion.*

Regardless of this fact, since I was me, I retorted, "That's part of you being annoying."

His lips slid up the side of my neck and I did a full body tremble.

"What is?" he asked the underside of my jaw.

"You calling me adorable," I answered, tilting my head back to give him better access.

I felt his smile. Then I felt the tip of his tongue move along my jaw and down my throat. I held my breath while he did this and my female parts rippled.

"Are you going to feed?" I whispered.

"No," he answered.

This surprised me. He hadn't fed that night except on roast chicken, stuffing, potatoes, rolls and Edwina's whipped up at the last minute strawberry pie.

"You're not?"

One of his hands slid up to cup the back of my head, the other one glided down my back. He guided my mouth to his and touched his lips to mine.

Eyes holding mine captive, he replied, "If I feed, the numbing agent will release. I don't want any part of you numbed with what I do with my mouth tonight."

Oh my *God.*

Another full body tremble, female parts ripple, and goose bumps formed on my flesh. He felt it, he knew it, he grinned his smug grin, and then he kissed me.

It wasn't a claiming onslaught. It wasn't a wild ravenous duel. It was sweet and soft, coaxing and discovering, a *new* kind of kiss that was quite like our first one but *a whole lot better.*

My body melted into his and I kissed him back.

His hand at my back slid over my bottom, down my thigh and then started to bunch the robe in his fist. From somewhere far away, my naughty-girl undies popped right into my head and I jerked straight up to straddling him.

He allowed this, why, I didn't know. He just laid there looking up at me, his eyes alert but not angry, his hand now caught in the crease of my leg, his other hand coming to rest on my other thigh.

I stared down at him thinking one thing.

I needed to change clothes. Like, *now*.

"There's something I forgot," I muttered.

"Leah—"

I prepared to move and while I took the nanosecond to do this both his hands settled firmly on my hips.

"Leah, you aren't going anywhere."

I was mentally inventorying my lingerie drawer (he'd filled it full himself, he had to like *those* things, he bought them!) when I replied, "This won't take a second."

His hands tensed, his face gentled, his eyes grew warm just as his voice dipped low—a killer combination. "Sweetling, there's nothing on this planet you have to worry about right now."

"Lucien—"

His hands slid up my sides at the same time putting on pressure to pull me toward him.

"Just relax," he muttered.

My mind searched wildly for ways to delay.

"Can I...?" I muttered, coming up with nothing as his face got closer. "Can I...?" I repeated stupidly. Then it came to me. "Will you let me...explore?" I whispered.

The pressure stopped.

Thank *God*.

His hands drifted down my sides, my waist, my hips, to come to rest on the tops of my thighs.

"By all means," he murmured, my heart skipped, his eyes had gone hooded, and now I was really in trouble.

Since I'd been really in trouble before like, lots, as usual, I just winged it.

And, anyway, his chest was right there. And I'd never really touched him before. He touched me, but I'd never got the chance to have a go at him.

I took my chance.

I lifted up to straddling again, and using my fingertips, I explored. Drifting softly as my eyes followed my movements, I touched all the planes and angles of his chest, his abdomen, brushing my fingers across the top of the bedclothes under his navel.

I discovered he felt good. His skin was soft, his muscles hard. The angles fascinated me. The planes fascinated me more. I lost myself so much, it came as a surprise when he took in a sharp breath and his fingers tensed on my thighs as I ran the pad of my thumb across his nipple.

My eyes flew to his and his were intense. So intense they were blazing.

For the first time since I met him, I felt power.

And I liked it.

I liked it so much, I couldn't stop my smile.

Totally forgetting my lingerie, I bent at the waist. I followed the trail my fingertips had made, this time with my mouth, often my tongue, tasting him.

His skin tasted just as delicious as his kisses.

My lips slid across his nipple then my tongue did the same then I swept the front edge of my teeth against it.

Suddenly, he knifed to sitting, his hands no longer at my thighs, they were yanking at the belt of my robe.

"I'm not done exploring," I protested.

Looking in my eyes, he tugged the robe off my shoulders and tossed it aside. Then his hand fisted in my hair and he steered my mouth to his.

"You can explore all you want when we're both naked." His voice was a low sexy rumble.

I had no chance to speak further. He kissed me, hungry, even needy, and demanding. So demanding it rocked me, my arms circled him, for I had no choice but to hold on.

I was dazed, trembling and feeling ripples *everywhere* when his mouth tore from mine, he leaned a bit back, his hands at my camisole, and he stilled.

Then, eyes on my middle, in what could only be described as a raw groan, he growled, "Jesus, Leah."

"What?" I breathed before I remembered and I stilled too.

Damn!

He didn't like my naughty-girl undies.

His hand went into my hair, twisting and fisting, and he used it to bring my face close to his.

His eyes were burning.

I quit breathing.

He ground out, "Leave it to you to wear something I want to fuck you in when I've been fantasizing for twenty years of fucking you wearing nothing at all."

Okay, maybe I was wrong. One could say he liked the lingerie.

Good to know.

"Is this our only shot?" I asked, still dazed and now slightly confused.

"Pardon?"

"Are we only having sex once?"

"Fuck no," he clipped.

"Then can't you do both...eventually?"

I'd barely uttered the "ly" in "eventually" when I was flying through the air, landing on my back.

Before his mouth took mine in another hungry demanding kiss, I guessed I had my answer.

I learned very quickly that Lucien hadn't only used his eight hundred plus years on this earth to become a master with his hands and mouth.

Lucien had used those years to become a master at *everything*.

He also used the lingerie to his advantage. His mouth did the same on me as mine did on him, but trailing the edge of the camisole at my breasts, pushing the blousing up and gliding his lips and tongue across my midriff and belly, tracing the edge of my panties then up. Over the frills, I felt his tongue dart aggressively against my rock-hard nipple, then again and again, before he sucked it into his mouth over the fabric.

When he did, it felt so freaking fantastic, I moaned for a very long time.

Not done, he tugged the fabric down so it dragged across my sensitive nipple in a sexy way that made me whimper before his mouth locked on my nipple and he drew it in sharply.

Vampires understood suction like no one else.

It was sheer ecstasy.

After a while, he did this to the other nipple too.

I was paying attention, of course, *lots* of attention.

But I was also busy moaning and writhing and gripping his hair to hold him to me. I was so turned on I thought I'd have an orgasm just by what he did to my nipples.

But I wanted more.

I pushed off on a foot, rolling him to his back.

He let me do this, his arms sliding around me, crushing me to him for another wet, hot, demanding kiss.

"My turn," I whispered against his lips when he ended the kiss.

Before he could say a word, my lips went down his throat, down his chest and down his stomach, pushing the bedclothes lower and exposing him.

He was thick, rock hard and looked utterly delectable.

I could not *wait* to explore.

I wrapped my hand around him, thrilling when I heard him suck in a sharp breath.

I no sooner twirled the tip of him with my tongue when he bent double. He wrapped an arm around my waist and yanked my body around so I was facing his lap but my knees were in the bed beside his shoulder as he lay back.

I looked at him in question and his eyes were on me.

"Enjoy, pet," he murmured his encouragement, his voice resonating deep, and I didn't know how long my shot would last so I didn't hesitate further.

I enjoyed.

A couple minutes into my enjoyment, his hand went between my legs, stroking my inner thighs, gliding along the edges of my naughty-girl panties between my legs and over the swells of my bottom, his touch whisper-soft.

This felt really, *really* nice. So nice, I slid my legs wider to give him better access.

And so nice I wanted to give Lucien something really nice too.

I stopped licking and stroking and slid the tip of him between my lips. When I did, his hand moved, delving into my panties, filling me with his finger just as his hips bucked, filling my mouth with him.

It was divine. He tasted good there too.

Luscious.

I groaned and immediately got greedy.

He pulled my undies down to my thighs and he played with me while his hips jerked into my mouth as deep as he could go.

It was unbelievably hot. Too hot.

I lost my concentration and drew back, wrapping a fist around him, thumb absently circling the tip. I arched my back, which pressed my chest into his stomach, and threw my head back, my hair flying over my shoulders and drifting across his abs.

All I could do was focus on what was happening between my legs.

And what was happening between my legs was the makings of an orgasm so cataclysmic, I wasn't certain I would survive it.

Whimpers of pleasure sounding from low in my throat, I spread my legs further, ground my hips into his hand, and regardless of my uncertain survival, I sought more.

His fingers stopped swirling and thrusting and disappeared. Before I could react to this sudden loss, he swept an arm behind my knees and I was on my back, my panties were gone, his hips were between my thighs and his weight was pinning me to the bed.

I felt the tip of him enter me.

"Yes," I breathed, wrapping my arms around him.

I closed my eyes, so freaking ready, I would have begged him without hesitation.

His hands coming down the backs of my thighs, he pulled them up at the knees and slid in a centimeter deeper.

I arched my neck.

"Look at me, sweetling." His voice was a deep aroused rumble that moved across my skin like a touch.

It took some effort but I looked at him.

I thought I knew what he wanted and immediately whispered, "Please, Lucien."

His eyes went dark, his face got close, and he framed mine with his big hands.

"That's beautiful, Leah, but I don't want you to beg."

My body moving on its own, desperate for release, desperate for *him*, I pressed my hips into his, but he withheld.

"Leah," he gritted between his teeth, clearly seeking control, "before the joining, you need to answer one question."

I nodded, too far gone to do much else.

His lips came to mine, his eyes still open, in his rumbly voice that now seemed even more intense, he asked, "Are you mine?"

My body stilled.

This was it. I had to make a choice and once I did there was no going back.

The answer came to me, the only one there was.

My arms held on tight just as my legs circled his hips and did the same.

"If you give me you, Lucien, then I promise, I'll give you me."

I watched close up as his eyes flashed.

Then he drove in deep.

I arched my neck in pleasure and cried out as it mingled with a hint of pain.

Seated to the hilt, he filled me completely. He was so big, I had no idea how I accommodated him. It didn't matter. It was so beautiful to be joined to him, connected to him, filled by him, I welcomed the pain.

"You have me, Leah," he murmured in my ear and he was *not* wrong. I had him, *all* of him, or likely all that I ever was really going to get.

I knew this and at that moment I couldn't bring myself to care.

Because all of Lucien, what filled me, what pinned me to the bed, and everything else that he'd gifted me with this past month was far, far more than I'd ever had from anyone else.

I twisted my head to look at him, my arms and legs tightened, and I whispered, "Then I'm yours, Lucien."

At my words, his mouth took mine in a hungry dueling kiss and he started moving.

It was gorgeous.

While driving deep, his thrusts opening me, widening me, filling me full again and again and again and again, the pressure built, excruciating and fantastic.

Cataclysmic *was* the word for it. I was rocking underneath him, lifting my knees, giving him more, taking more from him, insatiable, the pressure building, becoming unbearable, ripping through me.

His lips released mine, his hand went into my hair, tugging my head back.

His mouth went to my neck and I felt his tongue. Then I felt him feeding. I felt my blood flow into his mouth, pouring out with each deep savage thrust. Once, twice, three times, four.

Suddenly I hit paradise and came.

And I came hard, wrapping him as tight as I could in my convulsing limbs and forgetting everything but Lucien, his heavy body, his scent, the feel of him, his mouth at my neck, my blood nourishing him while I felt him plunging deep inside.

There had never been better and there never would be. Maybe not only in my life but in the history of Buchanans.

I was sliding down the wave, my body still jolted by his thrusts, small contented whimpers escaping my lips when his tongue swept my neck, his mouth claimed mine and his tongue drove inside so I could taste myself on him. The taste of me on his tongue enhanced the intimacy in an unexplainably profound way that shattered my soul.

Finally, he slammed inside me until he was seated full to the root and I felt his body spasm powerfully, shaking me with him as his deep groan filled my mouth. His orgasm, and the depth of it, caused a sense of triumphant elation so powerful, it felt like it shredded me straight through to my core.

Shredded, shattered, sated and moved beyond anything I could imagine by the splendor of our joining, uncharacteristically of me I didn't fight the feeling.

I drew it in, pulled it close, held it safe and wrapped my limbs even tighter around my vampire.

My eyes opened when Lucien set me in bed.

I saw the sun peeking weakly through the curtains. It was nearly morning.

I'd been dozing, or more accurately, passed out.

He slid in behind me, his arm curling around my waist, pulling me to his heat, holding me close.

I settled against him.

After the first time, we'd done it four more times.

Four.

More.

Times.

That was five, in total.

The first was by far the best, but it was up for grabs which reigned supreme of the other four. I could likely argue in favor (for hours) for all of them.

The last time was on the couch in the comfy seating area off the kitchen. We'd gone down to raid the fridge. Or I had, I was starved. Lucien had been feeding a lot, he couldn't be hungry.

We got sidetracked.

It was the first time he let me be on top. After we were done, still joined, I rested my torso on his wide chest, burrowed my face into his neck and fell fast asleep.

I didn't know how long ago that was. It could have been minutes or it could have been hours. Now I was awake, and out of nowhere, it hit me.

It felt like I'd been struck by lightning.

Lucien's behavior was not about making me cow to him, to submit, to change, to be something he wanted to force me to be.

He'd said and demonstrated more than once that he always wanted me.

Just me.

It was about me submitting to what *he* was.

I had to accept *him*, in all his bossy domineering vampire-ness and the other sweet or gentle or generous parts besides.

He wasn't taming *me*.

He was taming that part in me that held me away from his differentness. He was showing me who he was, what he was, how he behaved, and I had to accept it, all of it, without *him* being anything but Lucien.

You live your day to day life hiding the essence of who you are; you don't want to let someone into that life who won't accept you for that same thing.

Even embrace it. Even rejoice in the beauty of it.

I felt tears fill my eyes.

I was *such* a moron!

"Sweetheart?"

Oh my God.

Could he *hear* tears? That would suck!

"What?" I asked and I was pleased my voice sounded normal.

"You aren't asleep."

"Um..." I couldn't answer. I was busy trying to control my tears, and I succeeded, but just barely.

"Is there something on your mind?" he queried gently.

Yes, many things were on my mind. Weighty things. Ayers-Rock-style weight, or at least it felt like it.

"Not really," I lied.

His arm grew tight. "You can sleep, Leah. What happened last night won't happen again."

He thought I was worried about my dream.

I wasn't worried about my dream.

Though, now that he brought it up.

"How do you know?" I asked.

"I'm here," he answered.

All right, so I pretty much believed that Lucien was big enough, bad enough, fast enough, and strong enough to kick anyone's ass, but a phantasmagorical dream that mysteriously hangs its victim? I was thinking even he couldn't beat that.

I made a decision. It was a scary decision but I made it, and seeing as I was so freaking stubborn, once made I'd see it through, no matter that it scared the heck out of me.

"Are you tired?" I asked.

"Yes, pet." I felt his face move into my hair before he muttered, all vampire sexy, "I'm very tired."

Oh. Well then.

Maybe I couldn't see it through.

Knowing I'd tired out the Mighty Vampire Lucien with all our sexual antics, and thinking that was pretty cool, thus being pretty pleased with myself, I decided I didn't care.

He went on, "But if you wish to talk..."

As was my way, instantly, I changed my mind (again) and took my shot.

I turned in his arms so I was facing him.

It was time to get some questions answered.

I started with one that might not freak me out (much).

"Am I famous?" I asked.

"Pardon?" he asked back, seeming surprised by my question.

I explained, "Everyone I meet when I'm with you seems to know me. Even at The Selection people were looking at me like they knew me, or at least were curious about me so they knew *of* me."

"Most members of a concubine family are known by vampires, Leah."

I studied him.

He was *so* holding back.

"Not like me," I whispered my challenge.

He blew out a sigh then curled me closer.

"No, my pet, not like you."

I knew it!

"Why not like me?"

"Because of me."

I held my breath. I didn't know why, I just did.

I heard his chuckle. "You can breathe, sweetheart."

I breathed and wrinkled my nose.

"I'm so glad I amuse you."

His mouth touched mine before he murmured, "Always."

I shivered in his arms. Those arms grew tighter. Even though this felt good, curiosity was killing me.

"Well, are you going to explain?"

He rolled to his back taking me with him so I was pressed mostly to his side but partially lying on top of him. He tucked my forehead in his neck and started to play with my hair before he began.

"During The Revolution, I was a general. A very..." he hesitated then went on, "*successful* general." I shivered at his words, but this time reading the meaning behind them it was in a different way. He stopped playing with my hair and wrapped his arm around me before continuing, "After The Revolution, I was a hunter." His voice dipped low. "And very successful at that as well."

I'd quit breathing again.

I did not like this.

At all.

He hunted mortal and immortal mates!

Oh. My. *God.*

His arm gave me a squeeze and he whispered, "Not that kind of hunter, Leah. Never that. I'd burn before doing that."

I started breathing again. In fact, my breath came out in an audible gush of relief.

"What kind of hunter were you?" I asked.

"I hunted the remainder of our enemy, my kind and those who allied with them. Once warriors, they'd become renegades. They had to be found and stopped before they planned another revolution. I was the one who stopped them."

I got up on an elbow and looked at his face in the weak light. I could tell something was not right.

"How many of you were there? Hunters, that is."

"Just me."

What? This didn't make sense.

"Really?"

"They only needed me. I was good at what I did."

Was he serious?

"How many renegades were there?" I asked.

"Thousands."

My mouth dropped open. He couldn't be for real.

If he was, this gave a whole new meaning to the words "Mighty Vampire Lucien!"

"Were there...were there..." I stammered, "any *other* kind of hunters as good as you?"

"You mean the hunters of mates?"

I nodded.

"No."

"None?"

"There were at least twenty hunters, only hundreds of mates to be hunted."

Wow.

"Why was it only you who hunted the renegades?"

"I wasn't the only one at the beginning. The Dominion recruited and dispatched other hunters. Most of the others didn't survive. As

I mentioned, I not only survived, I excelled. They pulled the others back and sent only me."

This was crazy. Lucien was Super-Vamp, singlehandedly crushing a possible rebellion!

This was remarkable, unbelievable and very, very cool. But that something that I sensed was wrong niggled at me, making me uncomfortable.

I watched him for a moment, thinking of his magnificence, Stephanie's, Cosmo's, Lucien's obvious pride in his people, and I said softly, "You hunted your own."

His hand came up, fingers curling around my neck, and he explained as if I'd made a gentle accusation, which I hadn't, "They were also hunting, Leah, and they were hunting mortals. Feeding and killing. Without thought or remorse. Making a point, living their lives in the old ways. They were not only murdering innocents, they were putting everything we vampires fought for at risk."

I stared at him.

Then I guessed, "You didn't like doing it."

He shook his head. "Regardless if I didn't believe in their way of life, enslaving your brethren and delivering them to their executions is not a fun job."

He could say *that* again.

I understood what that something wrong was and it made me incredibly sad.

For Lucien.

Something I never expected to be, but there it was.

I felt my body get soft and I pressed into him.

Lifting my hand to touch his face, I whispered, "Lucien."

When my palm rested against his cheek, I saw his eyes close slowly and the deep feeling so obvious in his handsome face made me catch my breath.

He was immensely good-looking, but looking at him in that moment, he'd never been more striking.

Not ever.

I felt my mouth part in awe and I desperately wanted to kiss him. And through my kiss I wanted to draw away his demons, absorb his emotion, take it away from him forever.

Before I got the chance to attempt this feat, his eyes opened and he murmured in a way that said he was trying to reassure *me* even though it was him I sensed reliving a nightmare, "It was a long time ago, sweetling."

"It bothers you still."

His hand went from my neck to my hand on his face. His long fingers curled around mine and he drew my knuckles to his lips, brushing them there.

His eyes locked on mine and he repeated, "It bothers me still."

I understood then why people acted the way they did around him and I shared, "You're a vampire hero. They admire you."

"They do," he agreed in a casual way that said it mattered very little to him and went on, "They also fear me."

I was thinking they probably should. He could hunt down thousands of vampires on his own, that was pretty freaking scary.

"What does this have to do with me?" I asked.

He rested his hand still holding mine on his chest. "Because of the status they've placed on me, people take an interest in what I take an interest in. That, plus other annoying things, goes with the territory. However with you, I marked you twenty years ago and waited. This isn't my usual behavior. *Your* behavior isn't the usual concubine behavior either. This intrigued my people and they started watching and waiting to see what would happen. Now, I fear, they're no less intrigued."

"So, in a way, we're like the mortal and vampire Elizabeth Taylor and Richard Burton, without the weddings and such, of course," I muttered.

I felt relief sweep through me when the air cleared, his face softened and his lips twitched.

"Something like that."

Well, that was one question answered, and as usual, it made sense.

Now for the one that might freak me out, not that the last one didn't.

"Why do you think you can make me safe from my dream?"

He rolled us to our sides, pulling me up so I was face to face with him and gathering me close.

"You remember the conversation you overheard this morning?" he asked and I nodded.

How could I forget?

He continued, "I think you're attuning yourself to me."

"Yes, I remember you saying that. What does that have to do with—?"

He interrupted me, saying, "You're dreaming of The Sentence."

I fell silent but my heart tripped.

His eyes grew contemplative. "Has your mother or one of your aunts explained The Sentence?"

They hadn't, as such.

I shook my head deciding not to lie out loud.

"Edwina? Stephanie?" he asked.

I shook my head again, this time not nonverbally lying.

When he spoke again, it sounded like he was speaking aloud to himself, not to me. "Then you must have somehow sensed it from me."

"Sensed what from you? What's the sentence?"

His eyes refocused and he murmured, "It's not pretty, sweetheart."

"I could guess that," I replied.

His lips turned up before he began to explain, "The Dominion created The Sentence for mortal and immortal mates who would not denounce each other. They did it in hopes that the others being tortured or yet to be caught would spare their partners from this by quickly denouncing them. What they understood, and I reminded them, as did Cosmo, Stephanie and other advisors at the time, was that a vampire's vow is his or her bond. He, or she, will never denounce any vow, no matter what might befall them." He took in a breath then continued, "In many cases, when vampires mate, their claimings are a promise, not a vow. There is a nuance of difference, but it's there and for a vampire that nuance is crucial. The understanding being that eternal life with another may not work out after centuries. To promise forever opens the relationship to Severance. To vow forever, never. However, in most cases when a vampire took a mortal as a mate, during the claiming they vowed to be with their mortal forever. This, a vampire would never denounce. The Dominion was, however, with some experience of the behavior of mortals, counting on the mortal being less devoted. Unfortunately, they were wrong and dozens of Sentences were carried out."

"Let me guess," I whispered, "the mortal was hanged, the vampire burned."

He gave me a squeeze and nodded, but said, "Worse."

What was worse than *that*?

He answered my unasked question, "It happened simultaneously. The fire was lit so the mortal could watch the burning commence. Then the hanging proceeded so the vampire could watch his beloved swing before he died."

I knew that too but I still gasped when Lucien confirmed it.

"The Dominion enjoyed one success from this," he informed me. "It proved a healthy deterrent from any such future matings."

I dropped my head, looked at his throat and muttered, "Not surprising."

He kissed my forehead and I tilted my head back to face him.

"I don't remember my dream but that's what it felt like," I told him.

"I've no doubt that's what it is," he replied.

"Why am I dreaming about that when I didn't even know it existed?"

"I've no idea."

"Can you explain what happened last night?"

He shook his head, but said, "I have a theory."

When he didn't continue, I prompted, "And that would be?"

He pulled me closer and whispered, "You're connected to me, my pet, in a way I've never experienced before."

He wasn't wrong about *that*. And it made me a tad bit uncomfortable at the same time I found it made me a lot more than a tad bit safe.

More contradictory emotions.

Great.

When I made no reply, he continued, "And you have a strength of will that's astonishing. This most likely means your subconscious strength of will is indestructible. When you dreamed the dream when I wasn't here to soothe you, hold you, me there living and breathing and not burning, something that would prove your dream false, your subconscious carried forward the dream."

"That sounds crazy," I told him, because it blinkety-blank did!

"Yes, you're correct. It does," Lucien agreed. "Even so you can't deny that the dream carried on, you felt it physically and it continued until you linked to me on the phone."

This was even crazier. But it was also true.

I stayed silent.

Lucien went on, "And your mind shut down, you descended into catatonia until you connected with my physically and only then did you reanimate." After saying this, his face got closer, only a breath from mine, and his voice went soft. "Sweetling, this tells me I'm the catalyst to stop your dream. It tells me that I can keep you safe."

His words and the way he said them, softly but with confidence and more than a hint of satisfaction, made me tremble.

Nevertheless, although his explanation was logical and plausible, as Lucien tended to be, I still didn't buy it. Something else was at work here.

There might be no paranormal, supernatural, black, or any other kind of magic happening in the world of vampires and other creatures, but what I was experiencing with my dreams was something different. I didn't know if it was magic but it was something—something *otherworldly*—I just knew it.

And it frightened me to bits.

"Leah?" Lucien called.

"Mm?" I replied, deep in thought.

"Listen to me," he ordered, and when I focused on him, he continued, "I want you to listen closely, pet." He was being serious, deadly serious, and I nodded. "I don't want you sleeping when I'm not close. Until these dreams subside, you sleep only when I'm in the house preferably when you're in bed with me."

I nodded my head again, not because I was submitting to his order, but because I guessed he was right. He was the catalyst that stopped the dream, and seeing as I didn't want to be hanged by an invisible rope while sensing Lucien burned at the stake, I was willing to give in this time.

"Okay."

I felt his big body relax against mine and I hadn't noticed he'd grown so tense. I tucked my face in his throat and slid my arm around him, burrowing even closer.

"Are we done talking?" he asked the top of my head.

"I have a million more questions," I answered his throat.

"Will they wait until tomorrow?"

Considering it already *was* tomorrow, and for other reasons besides, the answer was...not really. Now that I was on a roll, no matter that it freaked me out, I still wanted to know as much as I could so I could know what I was up against.

However, much of what I wanted to know I needed to ask Stephanie.

"Yes," I told him.

He kissed the top of my head and tangled his legs with mine. In his Lucien way, something which I realized was now endearingly familiar, he was settling in for sleep.

I settled with him.

And I allowed myself to feel what I hadn't allowed myself to feel the many times he'd done this before.

Content.

My throat clogged as my mind protested, but my heart, for once, refused to be denied.

Aunt Nadia was right. Many people never had something beautiful, not even for a short while. Lucien was giving me something beautiful, and even though it was temporary, it was a gift my heart knew it was imperative to accept.

"Leah?" His voice was husky and sleepy when he called my name and my heart accepted that too.

"Hmm?"

"Thank you, my pet." His voice was still husky, but there was a depth of meaning to those four words that made my heart stutter.

I wasn't entirely certain what he was thanking me for, but I could guess.

He was thanking me for giving him *me*.

Another gift.

I closed my eyes and burrowed deeper while my heart accepted that too.

18

The Nightmare

Stephanie, Cosmo, Avery, Rafe, Fiona, Edwina, his children, his mother and Leah's entire family attended the Ancient Claiming Ceremony. A ceremony that was performed for all vampire unions. A ceremony that hadn't been conducted between a mortal and immortal in over five hundred years.

Eschewing the traditional blood red, she wore a sophisticated ivory satin gown, a nod to her culture.

He'd given her diamonds for her ears and wrists and dozens nestled in her upswept hair.

A black diamond already adorned her left ring finger, its matching bands, another nod to her culture, would be placed at its base.

But her exquisite throat was bare.

He took of her blood. She took of his.

When she did this, her nose wrinkled before her lips locked to the wound he tore into his own flesh at his wrist. However, when she suckled, her eyes lifted to his and grew wide with wonder.

Lucien laughed.

He swept his tongue against his wound and drew her close in the circle of his arms.

His voice resonating through the small assemblage, he declared the words of claiming, words he'd said twice before, to Maggie, then, five hundred years later, to Katrina.

Regardless of what happened with both of his earlier unions, the words were not bitter.

They were only sweet.

And this time, he did not speak them as promise.

He spoke them as vow.

"Until the sun falls from the sky."

Tears filled her eyes and she pressed deep into his body.

Unlike his commanding declaration, when she spoke she spoke only to him.

In a soft voice, Leah repeated, "Until the sun falls from the sky."

Cheers went up all around them along with happy sobs, but Lucien processed none of it.

The only thing in his universe was the woman in his arms.

Lucien was running, Leah's hand in his. He could hear her panting even though she had uncommon speed for a mortal, something else she'd picked up from him.

Even so, she was nowhere near as swift as him and he could hear them getting closer.

He wasted precious time, stopped, and flung her over his shoulder.

Then he *ran*.

Their hunting meant that Stephanie had failed. As had Cosmo, Avery, Rafe, Hamish, Jordan, Duncan, Hermes, Orlando and scores of others. His army. His and Leah's personal guard.

He would never have guessed their defeat. Their loss, which surely meant their deaths, caused a searing pain to slice through his gut, but his legs didn't falter.

"Lucien." Leah's voice was harsh, his name broken with his strides.

He didn't reply. His focus was distance, escape.

"Lucien, let me down."

"Quiet," he grunted, his own breath coming fast and short, not from the effort, but from his dread.

"Let them get me."

Silence, he commanded.

Let them have me, darling. You go.

Of course, being Leah, she wouldn't leave it be.

We're not discussing this.

He sensed their pursuers losing ground, but he didn't slow.

Let me go. You need to live to fight so other vampires can be free, she urged, her voice thick with emotion. *So my people can stay free.*

Not without you, never without you.

They're counting on you.

I don't give a fuck. They want it, they can fight for it on their own.

Silence.

Then, *So stubborn!* she snapped to his brain.

He kept running.

The drug coursing through his system making him weak, he watched Leah walk up the scaffold.

Lydia cried out, the sound the definition of agony.

Lucien's eyes never left his mate.

Denounce me, Lucien ordered.

Never, Leah shot back, a tremble betraying the strength behind her tone.

He thrilled at her word even as it tore at his heart.

This time, when he spoke, it was a plea, *Denounce me, my pet.*

I'd rather die with you than live without you.

He nearly smiled.

Drama, he muttered into her mind.

This isn't funny.

She was absolutely correct.

Using what strength he had, his next words were a command he knew she couldn't defy.

Denounce me.

Her body jerked, her pale worn face going all the more ashen. But her eyes were defiant.

Never.

He was stunned and horrified and now unbelievably frightened.

He'd not had to control her mind for years and in those years she'd obviously built up an immunity.

They stopped her under the noose and put it around her neck.

She stood, arms tied behind her back, wearing her ivory claiming gown.

Another defiance, not of him, of The Dominion.

Even facing certain death, she was magnificent.

That vile feeling he'd felt so long ago when he thought he'd broken her, a feeling he hadn't had in years, ripped through him.

Without delay, they touched the torch to the kindling around his feet.

Another scream of agony, this piercing the air and coming from Katrina.

Lucien's eyes never left Leah.

I love you, she whispered to his mind.

He closed his eyes.

He sensed the heat but nothing could slice through the altogether different, far more powerful pain.

I love you too, sweetling.

He opened his eyes to see her smile, radiant and beautiful.

Then the trapdoor opened and she fell.

With a jerk, Lucien came awake.

The sun was blazing around the curtains but the room was still dark.

He felt a tightness in his gut, his skin dampened with sweat, Leah curled into the curve of his body, her heartbeat and breathing steady.

Asleep.

"Holy Christ," he whispered.

He remembered every vivid, horrifying second of his dream.

Every excruciating second.

He could actually feel the smooth satin of her claiming gown under his hands, the weight of her body over his shoulder as he ran, the touch of the flame.

"Holy Christ," he repeated.

Was this what she was dreaming? Was this what sent her fleeing the bed, terrified and sobbing?

It had to be.

"Holy *Christ*," he gritted between his teeth.

She stirred.

He moved, turning her still sleeping body into his arms, he put his mouth to her, tasting her, his hands stroking at the same time. Down his mouth went to her breast, he rolled his tongue around a nipple.

"Lucien?" Her sleepy voice sounded, her hands came to his shoulders.

He moved south.

"Lucien," she breathed, the fingers of one hand sliding into his hair.

He spread her legs, shifted her calves over his shoulders and put his mouth to her. Relentlessly, he feasted on her as she gasped and panted, her fingers clenched in his hair, her hips bucking.

Voracious, always voracious, his Leah, this time, demanding more of his mouth. Her muscles tensed, heels digging into his back, and she cried out his name when she came.

He surged over her, controlling his heart, calling out to hers, making them beat as one while slamming into her lush wetness savagely in one, long, smooth, brutal thrust as she panted out his name again, still in the throes of her climax. He nearly forgot to sweep his tongue along her neck before he extended his razor-sharp fangs and tore through her flesh.

Then he was thrusting, her body jerking, her blood pumping into his mouth with each deep violent plunge, every beat of their hearts throbbing in tandem.

He'd been correct.

Fucking *rapture*.

She wrapped herself tightly around him and came again, harder, nails digging into his skin, breath catching and halting, heart tripping. He felt the pressure building in his own body, sharp and fierce, his cock aching to release.

He closed her wound with his tongue and used her hair to force her to face him.

Her eyes half-closed, somnolent, sated, he shook her head with his fist in her hair, trying to be gentle and fearing he'd failed when her eyes snapped open.

"You're mine," he growled, surging into her.

"Yes," she panted without delay.

"Say it," he demanded.

She acquiesced, again immediately, "I'm yours."

"Always."

As he thrust into her, faster, harder, the pressure building, her body jolting under him, he felt her limbs tense and watched as her face paled.

She didn't speak.

"Say it, Leah. *Always*," he ground out.

"Lucien..."

He thrust into her, deeper, harder, and she whimpered in pleasure.

"Say it!" he commanded.

Her eyes locked with his.

"I'm yours, Lucien," she whispered. "Always."

It was at that moment he came, long and hard, an orgasm unparalleled in eight hundred years. It was even better than the one she'd given him last night during their first joining, which he would have thought impossible.

After, he allowed his weight to collapse on her for long moments before he heard her breath turn heavy from taking his burden.

Then he rolled them, careful to keep them joined, so he was on his back, she was straddling him, her torso to his, her face in his neck, breath still coming fast and brushing lightly against his skin.

Moments passed, Lucien matching his heart to the pulsing rhythm of Leah's as he tried to shut down his mind. To shut out the images burned there from his dream. The traces of satin on his hands. The dread tearing through his soul as he sought to escape the hunt. None of this reconciled with Leah in his arms, her sweet wetness still tight around his cock, her breasts crushed against his chest, her heartbeat thumping rapidly.

Belatedly, he smelled her fear.

"Leah?"

Her heart skipped and his skipped with it.

Then she whispered, "What was *that*?"

"Leah—"

She started to lift up but he held her captive with his arms.

"Don't move," he ordered, "we'll disconnect."

She stilled.

Then she asked, "Lucien, what just happened?"

He had no earthly idea. He'd never behaved with such a driven, even desperate need before.

This wasn't true. When he discovered the enemy had tortured and murdered his mate, he'd behaved with a driven desperate need for fifty years. First fighting then hunting anyone who had anything to do with those who brought about Maggie's death.

Why he felt that need now, outside a reaction to the nightmare, he didn't know.

What he did know was that he wasn't going to tell Leah that he'd shared her dream. This would likely alarm her, and until he understood what was happening, he intended to shelter her from that.

So in an effort to shield her, Lucien lied.

He moved his hips and her muscles contracted deliciously around his still-hard cock.

"I think the answer to that is fairly obvious, pet."

"I...you...we," she stammered. "It's never been like that."

His fingers sifted in her hair and he murmured, "We've only been lovers one night, Leah."

Her body jerked and he caught her again before her movements could break their joining, something which he was compelled to prolong, again for reasons unknown.

"I don't mean it's never been like that between you and me. I mean it's never been like that for me *ever*. Maybe for any woman *in the history of time*."

Drama, he thought in a moment of amusement before his gut clenched in memory.

I'm not being dramatic! she retorted and his body jolted in shock.

He hadn't been speaking to her. Or, more accurately, he hadn't meant for her to hear.

"Did you hear me?" he asked.

"Yes, you *were* talking to me. Or, I should say, making fun of me." She tried to move again but he kept her pinned to him. "Let me up," she demanded.

His arms grew tight before he responded, "I want to feel you around me for a little while longer."

She pressed against him. "Let...me...*up!*"

He let her up but only her torso. He kept her hips fixed to his with an arm about her waist.

She glared down at him, her hair falling about her face in waves. Looking at her, finally he felt the clutch of the nightmare release.

This was Leah, his Leah, now fully his, all of her.

Not running, not hiding, not climbing a scaffold, she was alive and, apparently, angry.

This made him smile which made her glare turn to a scowl which, in turn, made his smile deepen.

"You seem in an immensely foul mood for someone who just came twice," he remarked.

Her eyes widened, her anger accelerated, he knew because her heart did as well, taking his with it. She opened her mouth to speak and then suddenly shook her head and looked to the side.

"Why couldn't I be some *other* immortal's concubine?" she muttered. "A werewolf. Or Frankenstein. I could escape Frankenstein. He doesn't move very fast. A wraith would be good, they're ethereal. I could probably slip..."

She hadn't noticed his body freeze but she stopped talking when he whipped her to her back. Disconnecting their joining, he settled on top of her, pinning her to the bed.

She stared up at him in surprise.

"What do you know of other immortals?" he demanded, savage fury tingeing his voice, primarily because he was *savagely furious*.

She reacted to the fury. He smelled it and he heard it and he didn't give a fuck.

"Wh-what?"

"What do you know of other immortals? Werewolves? Wraiths?"

"Oh my God," she whispered.

Lucien shook her and he didn't do it gently. "Tell me, damn it!"

"I don't know!" she gasped. "I mean, Avery..."

She stopped speaking, her eyes dropping to his jaw as it went rigid.

Between clenched teeth, he gritted, "I'm going to fucking *kill* him."

"Lucien?" Her tone was uncertain and very frightened.

His gaze bore into hers. "Don't tell anyone you know of the existence of other immortals, Leah. Not a single soul. Not your family, not Stephanie, not Edwina—"

"Edwina knows," she admitted softly. "She was there when Avery—"

He closed his eyes and ground out, "Fucking hell."

"He didn't say anything, Lucien. Not anything," Leah defended hurriedly and he opened his eyes to glare at her. "He just said he was immortal but he wasn't a vampire. He didn't tell me what he was. He didn't tell me what other immortals there were. He said if he said anything it would mean his death. Earlier, I was just guessing."

"I'll wager, my pet, he didn't tell you that if anyone found out *you* knew then *you'd* face certain death."

She pulled in a sharp breath.

"Yes," Lucien clipped. "So no one is in on this secret. No one. I'll have a word with Edwina and I'll have several with Avery."

Her hand came to his neck, fingers curling there, and he could feel the slight tremor.

"Please don't be angry with him. He was trying to be kind," Leah whispered.

"Putting your life in danger is far from kind," Lucien returned, his anger not abating, the nightmare too fresh as was this new danger.

Pain slashed through her face before she went on, her voice gentle, "Maybe he's tired of hiding, Lucien. Maybe he felt he was among friends. Maybe he knew I'd accept him. Maybe he trusted me. That isn't something to be angry about. That's an honor he bestowed on me."

"Letting me break you one day doesn't make you friend and protector of all immortals the next, Leah." His tone was sharp and derisive because her words had no effect.

He was still angry.

And troubled.

The Council was considering his request. They owed him and he had friends on The Council, friends who he had no doubt would become allies if things didn't go his way. Therefore friends who would do all in their considerable power to make things go his way. No one wanted war.

Those who were not friends, those who wished to defy change because they feared it or because they hated him were using Rafe's behavior as grounds to deny Lucien's request.

Rafe had not yet taken Lana as a lover but he'd told Lucien he wanted to and he was now spending the night with her, this being the reason why The Council finally called him in. Rafe had not joined with her because he feared for her safety.

Lucien approved of Rafe's intentions and when speaking to him encouraged them.

As he would encourage any vampire who wished to bloody well behave like a fucking vampire.

If this was known, this would not sway The Council in his favor, even his friends might demur. Allowing Lucien a boon was one thing, allowing rampant and widespread change to centuries of tradition was another.

However, if it was known that Leah held the knowledge that other cultures existed, he'd not get his request granted for she'd be executed.

No, she'd be *hunted* then she'd be executed.

They had enough to worry about, most of it she didn't even know, they didn't fucking need *this*.

He caught her flinch at his mocking words. It wounded him, but he ignored it. He'd make it up to her and she'd forgive him. At that moment he had to make her understand.

"That wasn't nice," she whispered.

"No, it wasn't. I wasn't trying to be nice, pet. I was trying to get it through that thick stubborn head of yours that this is serious."

Her eyes flashed. "I may be stubborn, Lucien..." she hesitated, looking strangely but also hilariously confused for a second then repeated, "Lucien Whatever-your-last-name-is, but I'm *not* stupid. I think I get it. Certain death is a pretty big motivator to keep a secret."

When she stopped speaking, she glared at him. He returned her glare. He felt her discomfort well before he was ready to back down.

Finally and waspishly she demanded to know, "What *is* your last name anyway?"

Lucien relaxed, partially because he believed she understood his concern, mostly because she was amusing.

"Vampires don't have last names."

Her anger dissipated, her eyes grew wide, and she replied, "So, you're like Cher? Madonna? You're just Lucien?"

"Cher and Madonna were born with surnames, they simply don't use them. But I am 'just Lucien.'"

Her eyes slid to his shoulder and she mumbled, "How weird."

Gently, Lucien reminded her, "It's far from weird."

Her gaze shot back to his, it went soft and her body became pliant underneath him.

"I didn't mean that in a bad way," she whispered, each word clearly heartfelt.

Christ, she was sweet.

Twenty years of watching her and hearing of her, he'd had a good idea of what he'd get when he finally had her.

At that moment, he realized he'd had *no* idea.

And this added blessing settled warmly in his gut.

His weight eased into her soft body and she automatically accommodated it.

He touched his lips to hers and rested their foreheads together. "I know you didn't, sweetling."

Her hand slid up to rest on his chest before she asked softly, "Are you going to stop being Scary Lucien now?"

"I'm never Scary Lucien," he replied, and she gave him a look so disbelieving it was comical.

Therefore he shoved his face in her neck and burst out laughing.

He rolled them yet again, positioning her against his side partially on top and she raised her head to look at him as his laughter died down to a chuckle. He lifted his hand to touch her eyebrow with a finger and he smoothed it across the arched line. With his movement, as he'd intended, her face gentled and his finger drifted down her cheek where he touched her lips with his middle three fingertips.

"You never have to be scared of me, sweetheart," he told her quietly but firmly as his hand dropped away.

She surprised him by asking, "What about when your anger fills the room like a physical thing?"

He wound his arms around her and gathered her closer. "If that happens, Leah, then it happens. There are times when I'll get angry, but no matter how angry I get, you never have anything to fear."

Regardless of his words and the feeling behind them, she persevered. "What about when your body goes all funny?"

He blinked slowly before repeating, "My body goes all funny?"

"Yeah, it gets stiff, the muscles all tense, stand out. I can't explain it, but—"

Lucien was appalled. "I've done that to you?"

She studied him, her look wary, and she nodded before saying, "Just now and when, um...that time Katrina came over."

"Christ," he muttered, stunned and disgusted with himself. He hadn't even felt it.

"I'd said some awful things..." she defended him and his arms gave her a gentle shake to stop her exoneration.

"That won't happen again," he declared.

Leah watched him, her eyes wide, lips parted, and this time he didn't revel in a look that made her adorable.

"What is it?" she whispered.

His reply was swift and terse. "Preparing for battle."

"Wow," she breathed.

"Against an immortal, Leah," he went on, tone still curt. "My strength is twenty times yours. When I'm in a fight or flight situation, my adrenaline releases, just as yours does, but it makes me twice as strong as I was before, twice as fast. If I were to—"

"You didn't," she cut him off.

"And I *wouldn't*," he stated. "I'll repeat, my pet, when you're with me, you never have anything to fear."

At that, she replied, "That part I know."

After she spoke, he watched as her face stilled before horror filled it and she grew pale.

Her heart started racing. In his anger, he'd ceased attuning his to hers and his remained steady.

But she'd given something away and it wasn't that she trusted he'd never harm her.

"Leah?"

She looked toward the door and quickly changed the subject, "Maybe we should call my family to come and have breakfast."

"Leah—"

"I'll make breakfast today. Crêpes Suzette."

The idea of Leah attempting Crêpes Suzette, which she'd fail to do (not to mention it was dessert), was infinitely amusing, especially considering flambéing was key to the dish's success.

He mentally located the fire extinguisher, just in case.

But at the thought of witnessing this endeavor and her reaction at her inevitable failure, Lucien was tempted to let her off the hook.

However, he didn't.

"Look at me, sweetheart."

Her gaze flitted to his eyebrow.

His arms tightened and his tone was a warning. "Leah."

She sighed and her eyes caught his.

"What did you mean?" Lucien asked.

"What did I mean what?" Leah asked back.

His eyes narrowed. She wrinkled her nose.

"Tell me, Leah," he ordered.

"Oh, all *right*," she snapped and frowned at him before admitting something astonishing and tremendously gratifying, but doing so with extreme ill-humor. "You make me feel safe."

Again, Lucien was stunned. This time in a much better way.

"I make you feel safe," he repeated.

"Yes. You," she poked him in the chest, "make me," she pointed to herself then her hand fluttered in the air, "feel safe." She dropped her hand and stared at him. "You're big and fast and you can throw a blinkety-blank car, for heaven's sake. You make me feel tiny and sheltered and...well, safe!"

That warmth in his gut started spreading.

"Leah—" he began, his hand inching up her back, sifting into her hair.

But she wasn't quite through.

Glowering at him, she admitted irritably, "My father left me, which was enough to twist me in a way that I'd never feel safe. We were *girls* on our *own*. Mom's strong but, you know, sometimes..."

She trailed off, losing track of her theme. She found it and kept going, "Then every guy I've ever been with has hit the top bell on the jerk-o-meter. You can be a jerk but, get this!" she fairly shouted. "One of my boyfriends sat in the car while *I* changed the tire. Another one didn't do a freaking thing when some guy was pawing me at a bar. After I got away, I asked him why he sat there and watched and did *not...one...thing* and he said he didn't want to get 'into it' with some 'moron' and it was obvious I could 'sort myself out.'" She lifted her hands and used two fingers to put quotation emphasis on her words before dropping them again and finishing, "Can you believe?"

He couldn't. In fact the very idea infuriated him.

He didn't get a chance to share this, she kept talking.

"*You* wouldn't make me change the tire and *you* wouldn't let some guy paw me and *you* haven't told me I have a fat ass and perhaps I should lay off the fried chicken. You're big and heavy and strong and cart me around like I weigh as much as a kitten. And you're tall and I have to look up at you, *even* when I'm wearing *heels*," she uttered this last like it was a total impossibility for her to look up at anyone and to look up at him was akin to a miracle. However, she wasn't quite finished. "And *you* could probably change a tire just by glaring at it."

Lucien bit back laughter as he rolled her to her back and decided they weren't having Crêpes Suzette. And *definitely* her family wasn't coming over.

His mouth went to her throat and he muttered, "I'm sorry to say I can't change a tire by glaring at it."

Her voice was no longer loud but breathy when she replied, "You know what I mean."

His mouth moved up and over her jaw to meet hers.

Looking into her eyes, he murmured his understatement, "I'm glad you feel safe with me, sweetling."

She tried to make light of it by announcing, "Anyone would feel safe with you. I'll repeat, you can throw *a car*."

"Maybe," he allowed, "but I'm thrilled that *you* do."

Before she could speak again, he rewarded her admission with a kiss.

Without hesitating, her arms stole around him and she kissed him back, her mouth sweet, her tongue sweeter.

His hand moved to her breast and cupped it, his thumb stroking its peak, feeling it harden instantly.

His cock responded in kind.

She gasped into his mouth.

He lifted his head to watch her face as his thumb stroked back, and as he did, he liked what he saw.

Her cheeks warmed and she bit her lip.

Then she said, "I'm hungry."

"I'll feed you," he assured her, executing another nipple swipe before he finished, "Later."

Her eyelids fluttered lower, desire evident in her face. He felt a further tightening in his groin, but even so, she whispered, "My family—"

He added a finger to his thumb and rolled. He was rewarded at once. Her breath caught, her heart started hammering, and he smelled the rush of heat between her restless legs.

Magnificent.

"Later," he repeated, his head descending and his mouth was on hers when he heard it.

Her body froze beneath his as his head jerked up. His two fingers stopped rolling but all of them curled possessively around the swell of her breast.

He listened and he couldn't believe what he heard.

"What is it?" Leah asked, a tremor of fear in her voice.

His eyes caught hers.

The doorbell rang.

Her body went solid and her fear permeated the air.

Lucien's temper spiked.

"What is it?" she asked again, the fear stronger.

"It's *my* fucking family," he growled.

He watched as her eyes grew wide, her lips parted, and yet again he found no pleasure in her endearing expression.

This was mainly because, instead of being able to do something about it, something they'd both like very much, he had to go answer the fucking door.

19
The Family

Lucien walked the small pier to the end where he stopped and examined the lake.

His children followed.

He didn't speak for long moments and Julian and Isobel astutely left him to his silent contemplation of the serene water.

Finally, quietly and menacingly, Lucien spoke to the water. "Explain."

"He came to see me, Father," Isobel replied swiftly.

"And?" Lucien prompted.

"I thought—" Isobel started but stopped when Lucien's head turned and his eyes sliced to his daughter.

"No," he said softly, "you didn't."

Her eyes slid to her brother. Julian's gaze locked with hers a moment before he looked to his boots.

Julian had his father's build, his father's hair, but he had his mother's startling blue eyes. They were clear sky blue. In all his years, Lucien had never seen eyes that color except in the face of his ex-partner and his son.

Isobel had her mother's curves and delicate bone structure, but she had her father's dark hair and eyes. She was petite for a vampire, an inch shorter than Leah, her mother's height.

Lucien was close with his children. He visited them when time allowed. They visited him the same. And he spoke to them regularly.

At that moment, however, he'd gladly throttle the both of them. Starting with Isobel.

This was because she brought Lucien's father, Etienne.

It was safe to say Lucien was *not* close to his father.

This was because Etienne was not a vampire you could get close to. He was cold, unfeeling and superior.

This was also because Etienne was not a vampire you'd *want* to get close to because he was cold, unfeeling and superior, but also because he was avaricious, sly, duplicitous and cruel.

And lastly this was because of Maggie.

Etienne had little to do with mortals except partaking of them as food, and at The Feasts he liked to attend, partaking of them in other ways. Some of them, in the cold, unfeeling, superior and savage ways he did it, not entirely welcomed by the mortals who attended The Feasts and usually those mortals were up for everything. He'd been called on this by The Dominion on more than one occasion and therefore had learned to hide these proclivities, but Lucien, as did many, knew he had not ceased this behavior.

Etienne held no regard for mortals, never had. Therefore he had hated Lucien's union with Maggie. And lastly, he had not kept this feeling a secret from Lucien *or* from Maggie.

This was not something Lucien had forgiven nor would he ever forgive.

Further, Lucien was not brimming with excitement to have his ex-partner, Julian's mother, Cressida, in the home he shared with Leah.

This was not because he didn't enjoy an amicable relationship with Cressida. He enjoyed a lot of things about and *with* Cressida, things he no longer intended to enjoy.

This was because Cressida was like a cat and cats liked to play with their prey and she would see Leah as prey, no doubt about it. Although Leah would need to show respect to Cressida as vampire, Cressida would not offer that same respect to Leah as concubine regardless if this was Leah's due and Lucien's demand. It would amuse Cressida to play with Leah and to defy Lucien's demands.

She had, since he'd known her, liked her challenges. She did it often with him and others. With Lucien, even after they'd ended their relationship, these challenges always ended physical, first as vampire combat then as something altogether more pleasant. This had carried on for centuries until Lucien had tied himself to Katrina. And this would be what she would take delight in throwing in Leah's face.

Luckily, they'd also brought Lucien's mother, Magdalene.

Now Lucien *was* close with his mother. It was a mystery Lucien had never solved how Magdalene and Etienne had coupled. Magdalene was the opposite of Lucien's father. After years of contemplating this enigma, the only answers Lucien could come up with were that they were both very young vampires when they started their union and it lasted less than twenty years, which was clearly all Magdalene could take. Unlike Lucien and Cressida, their relationship was *not* amicable.

Therefore, upon sensing who his company was, he'd ordered Leah to shower and get ready and fortunately she'd obeyed. He'd gone down to greet his family and then he'd called Leah's family and taken her himself to their guest house where he'd left her. Leah had not even glimpsed his family on her way out of the house nor, unusually quiet and docile, had she questioned his actions. On his way home, he'd called Avery to ask him to go to the guest house to guard her. He'd come home and left his father, mother and ex in the house in order to speak to his children privately.

Which brought him to now.

Lucien looked to his son. "And you?"

Julian's head came up as did his brows. "Me?"

"Cressida," Lucien answered, striving for patience for Julian was being purposefully obtuse, something he did more than occasionally.

"Cressida was curious," Julian answered, and Lucien decided this was likely the truth. He also knew his son shared a close bond with his mother. It was a rare occurrence when Julian didn't give in to her every whim. It was a rare occurrence when *anyone* didn't give in to her every whim. The only person who didn't was Lucien.

Lucien's voice was low with meaning when he reminded them, "I think I spoke to you both about this."

"You did, Father, but—" Isobel started.

"But nothing," Lucien cut her off. "Not only was your judgment poor, your decisions were dangerous."

Julian spoke quickly. "Cressida would never—"

Lucien interrupted, "Etienne would."

Julian sighed and nodded his agreement for, indeed, Etienne would.

"People are talking," Isobel put in, "quite a bit."

"I'm aware of that," Lucien informed her.

"You had to know the talk would reach Etienne's ears," she went on.

"Yes, I knew that as well," Lucien replied.

"Therefore," she continued, "when he approached me, I thought about it and decided that it would be better for him to think he was in the family fold rather than for him to maneuver outside of it."

"Keep your enemies close," Julian muttered, his eyes on his father.

This was, Lucien had to admit, sound logic.

Regardless, it didn't explain why they'd perpetrated a surprise visit.

"And he'll maneuver, we all know that," Isobel carried on. "He doesn't agree with what you're doing even though he's told me he does and he only wants to offer you his support and allegiance."

"He might even be a mole," Julian added.

"Absolutely," Lucien agreed, turning to face his children. "Which is why I understand your logic, but your judgment is still in question as to why you'd bring him *here*."

"We thought—" Julian began but Lucien again interrupted.

"We've established that you *didn't*." On his last word, he leaned slightly toward his son and saw a muscle in Julian's cheek twitch. "That vampire should be nowhere near Leah."

"Father," Isobel whispered. "It was my idea. Etienne wanted to take you off guard. He said it was because he knew you would not wish his visit so he didn't want to forewarn you of it, but I know it was so he could take you and your concubine by surprise. I decided if I didn't agree to come with him, he'd do it himself. So I talked Jule and Magdalene into coming with us and Cressida is, well...Cressida so she's here too. Now your mortal is protected. Even Cressida wouldn't allow Etienne to harm your concubine if he should do the impossible and get past you."

"There are a number of ways to harm Leah," Lucien replied. "Many of which you can't know. However, if you'd phoned and warned me of this visit, I could have explained them to you."

Julian was openly curious. Isobel's face went blank, which meant she was equally curious.

Julian had the brute strength of his father and thus didn't play his cards close to his vest. He could best practically anyone (save Lucien), and if challenged, didn't hesitate to do so. Lucien's son was hot-headed and acted on his emotions, therefore he was lucky he was a strong, capable, intuitive fighter.

Isobel, being petite, had to rely more on her cunning, for most vampires were stronger than her and almost all were bigger. Her focus, craftiness, and endurance were the most dangerous weapons in her arsenal and she used them well. Also like her father.

"You've already tamed her," Julian guessed.

"Indeed," Lucien replied.

"Oh my God," Isobel breathed. "You've taken her as lover? Before The Council agreed?"

Lucien's response was to lift his chin in the affirmative.

"Brilliant," Julian muttered, failing at fighting his grin.

Isobel's body jerked to face her brother. "Jule! Are you nuts?"

"No," he was still grinning, but now it was directed at his sister. "There are a couple tasty mortal morsels I wouldn't mind having. It'll be nice to have that door opened."

Isobel's body jerked back to face her father. "Father!" she snapped. "Listen to him! This could mean—"

"I know what it means," Lucien cut her off. "And I don't give a fuck."

"Can't wait to meet this Leah," Julian murmured, still grinning.

Isobel ignored her brother and spoke to her father. "I understand what you're doing, why, and you know you have my loyalty, no matter what," she paused then repeated in a voice that vibrated, "No matter what, Father. But this is too fast. Vampires everywhere are having the same thoughts as you and Jule and we're not prepared."

"It took me ten minutes to talk The Council into considering my request, Bel," Lucien replied quietly. "I'm sensing they understand that they may need to reconsider things, not just for me and Leah, but for all vampires."

"Yes, perhaps," Isobel allowed. "But this is going beyond you and your mortal and Rafe and her sister and even Julian wanting to get himself some. Orlando was seen at a Feast with his concubine and they were embracing. And Hermes selected his new concubine only a week ago, and just like you, he moved in with her the night of her Bloodletting."

Lucien knew this as Avery had told him just that morning. He couldn't say it was unwelcome news. Orlando was vicious in battle and Hermes equally coldblooded. Both, like Lucien, Cosmo and Stephanie, were roundly feared. It was surprising news that they'd acted so swiftly, but it wasn't disadvantageous. If it came to it, his army was clearly amassing and their ranks were such others would avoid challenging.

Isobel kept speaking. "So now it seems The Council's hand is being forced. They don't like that. They *so much* don't like that, even if they were to find in your and your concubine's favor, they'd find against it just to retain a vestige of control."

Lucien's jaw got hard before he said, "Leah."

Isobel's head twitched to the side before she asked, "What?"

"You call her my concubine, my mortal, but her name, Bel, is Leah," Lucien returned, and Julian looked to his boots again but Lucien kept his eyes locked on his daughter.

Her face went hard before she replied, "I'm not like Etienne."

"No, I know. I know your words are said out of concern for me. But that doesn't change the fact that she is not my concubine, my mortal. She's *Leah*," Lucien replied.

He watched his daughter's face pale. "But she is, Father. Regardless of the taming, of what you're doing, she's still your concubine." She hesitated before asking, "Isn't she?"

"She is. She's also Leah," Lucien stated.

"I don't get it," Julian put in.

Lucien crossed his arms on his chest and he looked between his son and daughter before saying, "Then I'll give it to you. As you know, I've been waiting to have her for twenty years and I can tell you now that wait could have been a hundred years and I would not have been disappointed."

Isobel pulled in a sharp breath. Julian's gaze grew intense.

Lucien continued, "There is more to her, much more than I expected. Just Leah being Leah and more." He studied his children and shared, "She can mark me, with practice she may even be able to track me, tune *me* to *her*. I sense when she's trying and it takes some effort to stop her from doing it."

"Oh my God," Isobel breathed.

"You're kidding," Julian whispered.

Lucien didn't answer his son, he went on, "She senses danger either on her own or through me. She can speak to me with her mind, not only when I'm reading hers, but when she wishes to do so."

Neither of his children responded, they both simply stared at him in shock.

Lucien continued, "And she and I are sharing dreams of The Sentence."

"Christ," Julian muttered on a wince, but Isobel's face went even paler.

Lucien carried on, "Leah's dreams are vastly more powerful to the point where, if I'm not with her, even awake the dream doesn't leave her. Indeed, the other night she nearly died by hanging, such is the power of her mind."

"Oh, Father," Isobel whispered.

"She's special," Lucien stated. "It will be intriguing to watch and see if these abilities form more fully and how. But I need to guard her, protect her in ways I didn't fathom when I began this. I need to protect her from those who would harm her because of what she means to their way of life, concubines who wish to halt a change or vampires who wish the same. I need to keep her abilities a secret. And I also need to protect her from these dreams. I shared her dream just last night. It's hideous. Simply her having them is bad enough. Her physically experiencing them, I will not abide. Her dying from one, I will not tolerate."

"Of course not," Isobel said softly. "That's terrible."

"It is," Lucien agreed. "Now, we need to be certain Etienne doesn't discover these things. We also need to be certain that Cressida nor even Magdalene learn about what Leah can do. And we need to be certain that Leah does not learn from any of them about Maggie or the fact that the additional component to the physical nature of our relationship is not commonplace with concubines."

Isobel lost her ability to hide her reactions and her mouth dropped open.

"What?" Julian asked. "She doesn't know?"

"No, she doesn't know," Lucien answered. His children glanced at each other but wisely did not question this and Lucien went on, "Also, Julian, you need to keep a tight rein on your mother. Leah is not like other concubines. She's not even like other mortals. She's spirited and unused to obedience. If Cressida presses for a reaction,

Leah will likely give it to her, and if that should happen, I will side with Leah."

"You'll side with Leah?" Julian asked. "Against a vampire?"

"Absolutely," Lucien answered.

Suddenly, Isobel's eyes narrowed and she queried, "Why are you both dreaming of The Sentence?"

"I've no idea," Lucien replied.

Isobel instantly shot her next question at him. "Do you intend to take her as your mate?"

Lucien felt his body go solid as he heard Julian take in a sharp breath and he spoke low and slow when he answered, "No, Isobel, I do not."

"Then why would you both be dreaming of The Sentence?" she pushed.

"I've answered that question, Bel," Lucien returned.

Isobel kept pushing. "You obviously hold her in deep regard. You marked her twenty years ago. You've stated you'd back her even if she disrespected one of your own kind. And you're putting yourself, your family, your friends and our way of life in danger, and you're saying all of that is just so you can fuck her?"

"Bel," Julian hissed.

"No!" Isobel snapped back, her eyes cutting to her brother. "I want to know. I want to know what he'd risk burning for. I heard she's not hard on the eyes and she smells divine, but no mortal blood and definitely no mortal pussy is worth *burning*."

"Okay, but you don't have to be a bitch about it," Julian bit out.

But Lucien had had enough.

Silence! Lucien commanded. Both his children's mouths clamped shut, and when they turned to face him, he continued, *Be still*, and their bodies locked.

"Do not," he spoke aloud, his gaze on his daughter, "*ever* speak that way in regards to Leah. What I have with her and why I'd risk what I'd risk for her, if you don't understand it when you see it, is none of your fucking business. If you know nothing, you know *me* better than to think I'd take this risk if it didn't mean something to me and that should be enough for the both of you. Am I understood?"

He freed their minds and Isobel clenched her teeth but nodded. Julian tipped up his chin.

"There will be no more talk of mates," Lucien declared.

Julian tipped up his chin again but Isobel pulled in a deep breath.

Then her face changed. It melted and it so reminded him of her mother, who was the most gentle vampire he'd ever known, much like Maggie was the most gentle mortal he'd known, that some of Lucien's temper fled.

"You're loved," she said quietly.

The rest of Lucien's temper fled and he replied, "I know that, darling."

She shook her head and looked to the water before she went on, "I'm just worried about you. I wasn't around when vampires could take mortal mates but," her eyes came back to him, "I heard that was what it was like. That they didn't respect vampires. That they were treated as equals. That—"

"You're wrong and you're right," Lucien interrupted her. "You've never experienced a taming. It's about respect *and* equality. But, Bel, when you see Leah with me, you'll understand." He closed the distance between them, lifted his hand and put it to his daughter's neck, his thumb moving to stroke her delicate jaw, also just like her mother's, before he murmured, "I promise, my darling, you'll understand."

Her black eyes hit his and it took a moment before her eyes grew warm and she nodded.

Lucien smiled at her and he received a hesitant smile in return. Then he felt Julian get close to them and both he and Isobel looked to their sides to see Julian grinning.

"Seriously," he said through his grin, "I can't wait to meet Leah."

Lucien strode into the guest house on the annoying errand of claiming his concubine to take her back to meet his family. The annoying part of this errand was the last part.

The minute he entered, he saw her through the windows at the back of the house, sitting out on the deck in the sun, drinking coffee with her mother, aunts and Avery. Seeing her sitting there, smiling, the sun kissing her skin, glinting in her long thick hair, he wondered if he would ever grow accustomed to her beauty.

Drinking it in, he decided he would not.

He stopped only steps into the unit's living room because he caught a familiar scent and heard a heart beating.

He turned his head to the side and waited. It took only a moment for Kate to walk into the living room from the small kitchen.

She'd been waiting for him. He knew this by the way she held her body and the expectant look on her face.

"Kate," he greeted and he heard her heartbeat escalate as he smelled her fear.

She had something to say. Something she didn't want to say. Something that was important enough for her to power through her fears to say it. And lastly, something that would take time.

This was a nuisance. All of it. Leah's family being there, his as well. He'd been waiting for Leah for twenty years. And he'd had one day, the length of which he was away, and one night of her being tamed. Being his. And it was far better than he'd expected it would be. He wanted their families gone and his attention focused on nothing but Leah, with hers on nothing but him. And he didn't want this for the day. He didn't even want it for the next week.

He wanted it for as long as he could keep hold of it.

"Lucien, if you wouldn't mind, I'd like a word," Kate spoke quietly.

He minded. But seeing as this was Kate Buchanan, the matriarch of the Buchanan concubines, and Leah's aunt, Lucien did what he did not wish to do. He lifted his chin to indicate assent.

Then he watched the indomitable Kate Buchanan press her lips together.

Fucking hell, she was nervous.

He didn't have time for this.

"Kate, please begin," he ordered.

"Leah is in fine spirits this morning," Kate noted, and Lucien's head turned to the windows.

Through them he saw Leah smiling at Nadia, her manner relaxed, her beautiful face aglow, warmth emanating from her. Even if their family dynamic was strange, it was clear she adored them and he liked that. But more, the taming was complete. She was not holding back, not hiding, not on guard.

She was just Leah.

His Leah.

Finally.

"She's told us your family is at her house," Kate went on and Lucien's eyes went to her.

"They are indeed," he confirmed and her head tilted to the side.

"Etienne?" she asked quietly.

Lucien sighed with irritation.

"You have nothing to fear, Kate. She's safe under my protection," he assured her of something which she should not need assurances. Even if Leah was not who she was to him, she was his concubine and he was Lucien. He'd never allow anything to harm her.

"She feels that way," Kate bizarrely replied.

"Pardon?" Lucien asked.

"She feels that way. Safe. Your family is at her home, there's a possibility she'll be meeting them, and she's not anxious in the slightest," Kate explained. "In fact, she's quite content and even..." she paused, "cheery."

Lucien thought that was excellent. Mainly he thought this because he knew it was he who made her that way. But Leah in a relaxed cheerful mood, feeling safe under his care would aid greatly in her impending meeting with his family.

Kate kept talking. "She has no idea she should be nervous with Etienne there. Even so, they *are* your family and you two have a..." she hesitated before finishing, "special relationship. In normal circumstances, that is to say, amongst mortals who are starting a relationship, meeting each other's families is a significant thing."

Lucien turned fully to her and crossed his arms on his chest. "Please," he invited, "stop beating around the bush and explain what's on your mind."

"My grandmother knew Sasha," Kate said softly and swiftly.

Lucien tensed.

Kate continued, "This is, as you undoubtedly know, a story passed through the concubines now for decades. Only cautionary, of course, but nevertheless it is well known. But we Buchanans, as my grandmother was confidante to Sasha, know even more. Except Leah who, for obvious reasons, we kept this from. And Leah feels safe with you, as she would." She hurried to say the last. "But Etienne, he's...she's... well, we both know Leah and—"

He knew what she was saying.

Sasha, his father's concubine some decades ago, was a legend and not in a good way. She was one of the rare concubines who had demanded to be released from her contract. And she was one of the very few who did so on the grounds of extreme cruelty. It was investigated and The Dominion found that Etienne regularly and often fed from his concubine without anesthetizing her, getting off on the agonizing pain he inflicted.

Obviously, she was released. She was also endowed with a fortune, this commanded by The Dominion to be provided upon her by Etienne. He was infuriated, but he did it. He also never again treated a concubine in this manner. However, he often engaged in this pastime elsewhere.

It was the first such occurrence for over two hundred years and the last of its kind since then.

It was not a secret the vampire Etienne held no regard for mortals and this was only one incidence of proof of that fact.

It was also not lost on Kate that Leah was spirited and rarely showed him the respect he was due. If pushed, she could earn Etienne's ire and his attention, neither of which would be advantageous. Especially not now.

However, with his children and mother in attendance and Leah tamed, he had matters in hand.

Therefore, Lucien interrupted her. "Do not concern yourself with this."

She leaned into him and whispered, "Lucien, you know I say this respectfully, but there is no way I can *not* concern myself with this. What you're doing with Leah...what you've already *done*. Etienne—"

"Kate," Lucien cut her off, "I'll repeat this only once. This is not your concern. It's mine. I am aware of it and I'll keep Leah safe."

"She's dreaming of The Sentence," Kate reminded him.

"I'm more aware of the meaning of that than you," Lucien clipped, losing patience.

"Okay then, why? And how?" Kate pressed, her heartbeat escalating further, her breath coming faster. She was pushing him, she knew it. But she loved her niece and was concerned.

For that reason, Lucien sought patience.

"This I don't know," Lucien admitted through his teeth.

"Then Etienne being involved at this juncture, with so many unknowns, so many dangers—"

"I will keep her safe," Lucien repeated impatiently.

"She's falling in love with you," Kate blurted and Lucien's entire body went tense. Kate saw it and leaned back, then took a small step away from him. Still, even as she moved away, her eyes studied him closely. Quietly and with some surprise, she whispered, "That eventuality had not occurred to you."

She was wrong. Stephanie had warned him of this possibility. Cosmo had concerns of it. His children.

But it could not happen.

"She is concubine. I'm vampire. She's mortal. I'm immortal. She's dreaming of The Sentence, and after I explained it to her, she knows what it means. It would be beyond foolhardy for her to fall in love with me. Even before she knew of The Sentence, she knew vampires did not mate with mortals. She knew this," Lucien replied, feeling something in his gut. Something new. Something he hadn't felt in centuries. Something he only felt once in his very long life.

Something he felt with Maggie.

I love you.

Christ, he'd heard it through her dreams. He'd even heard it in his.

Christ! Could these dreams be premonitory?

No. It simply could not happen.

"You've spent much time watching Leah, hearing of her, and now, being with her. But you still have much to learn about her," Kate said softly, taking his attention back to her.

Lucien held Kate's eyes before he sighed.

It was time to do something about this, for their families, those who cared about them and especially for Leah.

Therefore he announced, "I'll speak to her."

Kate's brows shot up. "You mean, to tell her not to fall in love with you?" she asked incredulously.

"No, to remind her of things she should keep in the forefront of her mind through our time together. Once I remind her of these things, she'll stop herself from being controlled by these types of emotions."

Kate shook her head. "Lucien, this is Leah we're talking about."

"Yes, and she is far from stupid. I can see, as our relationship has progressed, the intensity of feelings we've shared, matters could cloud better judgment. I'll simply call her attention to what she should bear in mind."

"You can do that, of course, and Leah *is* clever. But Lucien, I warn you, if you haven't already noted this, my niece follows her heart. She's ruled by emotion. She can understand something logically in her head, but her feelings guide her, especially if they're intense. Her head has absolutely no sway over her emotions."

"Then I'll explain things fully," Lucien returned and Kate fell silent. When this lasted several moments, Lucien inquired, "Are we finished?"

"One more thing," she answered quietly.

"One more, Kate," Lucien allowed. "But make it fast."

"If you intend to have this talk with Leah, please, I implore you, do it quickly."

"Unfortunately, at this time there are a variety of other matters—" Lucien started and was surprised when Kate cut him off.

She did this to whisper, "Make this a priority, please, for my niece."

"Kate—"

"She's falling in love with you."

"And I will speak with her."

"Yes, but you must do it soon..." she hesitated and concern washed through her features as she finished, "Before she lands."

Lucien drew in breath and acquiesced, "I'll make it a priority."

"Thank you," she whispered.

Lucien was done. He communicated this by tipping up his chin and moving toward the back door of the house.

As he moved, he noted Avery sense his approach and Lucien watched through the windows as Avery rose and moved to the door.

His eyes went to Leah to see she'd noticed Avery's departure. Her gaze then came to the window, caught his, and she smiled and waved.

Hello, my pet, he called to her.

Hello, darling, she replied.

She meant it, calling him *darling*.

He smiled back.

Avery came through the door.

"A moment, Lucien."

Lucien stopped, his eyes going to Avery, his control on his patience slipping.

"I'll just head outside," Kate murmured, slid past Avery and Lucien and out the door, closing it behind her.

Lucien leveled his gaze on Avery, warning, "I have very little time and less patience."

"Only a moment," Avery replied quickly.

"Then take your moment," Lucien allowed.

"Gregor requests a meeting."

Lucien held his eyes but didn't expose his reaction.

Gregor was a member of The Council. Lucien had known him for years, but even so, he didn't know him at all. He could be ally, he could be enemy.

Centuries ago, Gregor had shocked all vampires by denouncing his mortal mate during The Hunt. He was the only vampire to do this. Many didn't understand Gregor's actions, however Lucien did. If Maggie had lived, for her, he would have considered it. It was fortunately unfortunate that this decision never needed to be made.

Lucien, having had a mortal mate himself, could believe Gregor denounced his mate to give her a longer mortal life, even if they had to live the sudden brevity without each other.

This could mean that all these years, Gregor was holding resentment about the loss of his mate. This meaning he desired vampires to have their freedoms restored, to have what he lost, if only the taming.

It could also mean that, having lost his, that resentment could have turned bitter and he wished no other vampire to mate with mortals, not even for a taming.

The only thing Lucien had to go on with Gregor was that he'd taken a young mortal into his care after her parents were assassinated. Lucien had never met the girl, who now was a woman. However he had heard talk that Gregor was devoted to her in his way. The vampire was cold, but Lucien sensed he wasn't unfeeling. Further, Gregor's son, Yuri was attached to his father's ward, perhaps unhealthily. Or at least The Dominion would feel that way.

This could work in his favor if Gregor wished his son to be free to claim the mortal child he raised, not only to keep her in the family, but also to keep her alive for eternity.

"Arrange it," he ordered Avery.

"With Stephanie and Cosmo," Avery added and Lucien's gaze sharpened on his face.

"Why would he wish Teffie and Cosmo to be there?"

"I've no idea. He just does."

Lucien was silent a moment.

He didn't like that Gregor wished to speak with him and his two closest friends who would be his two chief lieutenants should hostilities escalate. Further, having all of them there would mean he would be forced to leave Leah unprotected as, at that juncture, he did not feel he could trust another vampire enough to add to her security detail.

This could be a plot. It could also bode bad tidings. Or it could mean further inroads into The Council.

He wouldn't know unless he took the chance and took the meeting.

His protection of Leah primarily involved his control of information shared with her, her interaction with vampires who might wish to frighten her into distrusting their culture, including Lucien, thus driving her emotionally away from him, and, most importantly, her sleep.

Edwina and Leah herself would see to it that she did not slumber while he was absent.

Leah was not immune to fear but she'd demonstrated more than once that she trusted him and she further admitted, gratifyingly, that she felt safe with him. If vampires were to approach with the intent to scare her, she might get frightened, but she'd await him to explain and make her feel safe.

Lucien did not fear for her experiencing bodily harm. Being Lucien, no vampire alive would be foolish enough to harm her physically. Except Katrina, and his ex-mate only had the courage to act when pushed by emotion she was too weak in the heat of the moment to control. Further, Katrina had made it clear through copious communications with anyone who would listen that her emotion had shifted from anger irrationally directed at Leah to anger at Lucien. She was no longer a threat.

But it would be Lucien who told her, eventually, of the differences of their Arrangement. It would be he, perhaps, who would share with her about Maggie. And it was unlikely she would be approached by another vampire who wished to drive a wedge between them in the time it would take to have this meeting.

Making his decision, he repeated, "Arrange it."

Avery nodded.

Lucien dismissed him by moving his gaze to Leah.

He wanted no further delays. The sooner the meeting with his family was conducted, the sooner he could get them on their way.

Therefore, he called, *Tell your family good-bye, sweetling, and come to me.*

It was an order, but not mind control. And he was pleased to see Leah turn her head to look at him, tip it to the side, then give him a small smile. Then he watched as she did as she was told.

Lucien returned Avery's farewell and Leah passed Avery on her way in, stopping to get up on her toes to brush her lips to his cheek. She came through the door, the small smile still on her face.

"Is everything okay?" she asked as she arrived at him.

Not even close, he thought, studying her.

She was beautiful. Even more beautiful than Maggie. And like Maggie, Leah's beauty had depth. It was in the inquisitiveness of her eyes that didn't hide the warmth—a warmth she felt upon see-ing him. It was in the hint of concern she also didn't hide. Concern because she knew he was not pleased his family had arrived unan-nounced, but further, he'd also taken her away without explanation before she could encounter a single one of them. It was in her bear-ing. The way she wore her clothes. The way she felt about her fam-ily. It was his knowledge that she could and would say or do practi-cally anything and most of it he would find interesting or amusing but none of it he would ever find boring.

Until the sun falls from the sky.

The words of the Ancient Claiming Ceremony hit his brain.

Any immortal would seek these things in his mate. Beauty, depth, warmth, concern, but more. Eternity was just that and that was a very long time. Any man would wish his mate to surprise him, amuse him, interest him and never, ever bore him.

If they had five years or five hundred, Leah would never bore him.

He knew this in that instant right to the depths of his soul.

Until the sun falls from the sky.

"Lucien?" she called softly, her voice warm too, inquisitive, concerned. She moved in to him and laid a hand light on his chest. "Is everything okay?"

Until the sun falls from the sky.

Yes. Kate was correct. He needed to discuss things with Leah as a priority.

Finally, he answered, "They will be, pet. We're going home now to have lunch with my family. However, I need to speak with you before we return."

"Okay." She was still talking softly and getting closer. When she did, he slid his arms around her.

She relaxed into him.

Yes. He had her. All of her. His.

Finally.

Until the sun falls from the sky.

"So, uh..." she broke into his thoughts when he didn't begin. "Are we actually going to *speak*? Or are we going to stand here staring at each other?"

Lucien relaxed, grinned and told her, "I could stand here and stare at you for some time, sweetling, but I suppose we should speak."

At his grin, she relaxed deeper into him. At his words, even deeper and her face went soft.

He liked that. All of it.

And all of it was his. Only his.

Until the sun falls from the sky.

He drew in breath and addressed the matter at hand.

"At home are my children, Julian and Isobel. My mother, Magdalene. My father, Etienne. And Julian's mother, Cressida."

She looked into his eyes with interest until the last. When he mentioned Cressida, he saw something cut through her features before she wiped her face blank. And what he saw cutting through features he did not like. He did not like that she felt it and he did not like that her feeling it meant he felt it as well.

"Leah, sweetheart, what we had was a very long time ago," he assured her and this was true, for mortals. For vampires, seeing as he ended the physical side of his relationship with Cressida only fifty years ago, it was not.

"Okay," she said quietly.

"There is nothing there," he told her.

"Then why is she at our house?"

Our house.

Until the sun falls from the sky.

"I mean, um..." Leah went on, "I don't know how vampires roll, but the ex isn't normally in on surprise family visits, unless that family is a little bit weird."

Lucien again grinned. "Vampires are the same way."

"Well then?" she prompted.

"Cressida is..." he searched for a word, "unusual."

Her eyes slid away and she muttered, "Great."

He gave her a squeeze and regained her gaze.

"It is your home, Leah." He dipped his face closer to hers and stated, "*Our* home. She will respect me in it and I will make certain she respects you."

He watched her brows draw together. "She wouldn't?"

"Cressida is unpredictable."

"Great part two," she again muttered.

"I'll need you to have patience with her, my pet. And I'll need you be cautious around her. She will attempt to goad you. Take the high road."

Leah stared up at him and whispered, "Uh...something to know about me. I'm not very familiar with the high road."

This time Lucien smiled. "I am aware of that, but today, you'll need to embark on an adventure and discover it."

She smiled back, humor lighting her eyes, making them luminescent, as she whispered, "Embark on an adventure."

Lucien very much wanted to savor the amusement he gave to Leah but he didn't have the time.

So he continued, "Cressida will be irritating. She will say things, perhaps even do things that might be maddening or even hurtful. Do your best to ignore her. I'll deal with her and I promise to talk through with you anything you may have questions about after she leaves." He waited for her nod, received it and went on, "My father is another matter."

Her head tipped to the side. "Your father?"

"We do not share a close relationship," he disclosed.

"Oh," she whispered.

"Not even slightly," he went on.

"Oh," she repeated on a whisper.

"I do not like him. I do not respect him. And I do not trust him. He has reached out to Isobel and therefore she brought him to our home. I've had words with Bel. But I cannot know his intentions. He may be charming. He may be condescending. Either way, you must treat him with respect no matter what."

"Okay." She was still whispering.

Lucien gave her another squeeze. "No matter what, Leah. I'll do my best to control him, but like Cressida, he's uncontrollable and unpredictable. The only thing I can ask is that *you* control your reactions."

"I'll control my reactions, Lucien."

After her immediate response, he studied her again. The inquisitiveness was gone. The warmth muted. The concern evident.

He did not like this but he nodded.

"I also ask you not to share anything about you and me," he went on.

Leah blinked before she asked, "What?"

"Nothing about us, Leah. They know I live with you. They know you are my concubine. They know I hold deep regard for you. Any personal information is not theirs to have. Not your nightmares. None of your abilities. Not what you are to me."

He felt her body stiffen and she asked quietly, "What I am to you?"

"That we're lovers."

Understandable confusion suffused her face and she started, "But—"

"It is none of their concern."

"Of course not," she replied. "But won't they know that already?"

"They would make that assumption," he lied. "I simply wish you to avoid any discussion about it. Any at all."

Her head tipped to the side again and the confusion in her features increased. "Why would they discuss it?"

"Again, Cressida and my father are uncontrollable and unpredictable. They may bring it up to provoke you. Don't be drawn in, and if I ask you to leave the room, you do it. Immediately."

She stared at him a moment before she admitted, "This is kind of freaking me out, Lucien."

He gave her another squeeze and his neck bent so he could touch his mouth too briefly to hers. When he lifted his head, he held her eyes.

"You feel safe with me," he reminded her, her lids lowered slowly for a languid blink he liked very much and she nodded. "Then you must trust me because I promise you, my pet, I will keep you safe."

"Okay," she whispered.

Lucien sighed.

Then he stated, "Let's go home."

"Okay," she repeated.

He touched his mouth to hers again and let her go only to take her hand and draw her to the front door. He knew she turned back to the windows to wave to her family and Avery.

He did not.

He took her out to his Porsche and took her home.

20
The Lunch

"**M**other," Lucien's son hissed. "Stop it."

She wouldn't. I knew this. I'd been in Cressida's presence for an hour and I knew this.

Lucien's ex was a total bitch. I hated her. I tried not to be a hater but she was the kind of woman that even Mother Theresa would consider bitch-slapping.

But Cressida wasn't my concern. I was a woman. I'd encountered bitches.

It was Lucien's father Etienne who gave me the creeps. And he did this because he enjoyed Cressida playing with me. Every catty comment out of her mouth, his eyes flashed with a sick happy light and they moved to me to assess my response. I didn't know how I knew it, but I knew he was waiting for me to break no matter what way that was. To be hurt. To get angry. Just as long as it was negative or damaging.

Vampires were human-*ish*. This meant that Lucien shared this man's DNA, which I found impossible to believe.

Lucien could be a jerk, but he was a hot jerk who could be funny, sweet and gentle.

Etienne was none of these (except, damnably I had to admit, the hot part) and proud of it.

If Magdalene wasn't sweet and openly loving, I would think she stepped out on Etienne.

There was nothing in Lucien that was like his father. They didn't even look alike, Etienne being blond and blue-eyed, tall, but lean for a vampire. Lucien looked like his mother. In fact, he was the uber-masculine image of her classically beautiful femininity.

Cressida turned her (damnably I had to admit, gorgeous) sky-blue eyes to her son and asked with fake innocence, "Stop what?"

Julian glared at her and ordered, "We need to talk in the study."

She threw out an elegant hand to the dining table at which Edwina was currently serving us dessert. "But, we haven't finished lunch."

Julian pushed his chair back, declaring, "*You* have."

"Julian, don't be rude," Cressida returned.

I looked to my lap and smiled because that was hilarious coming from her. She'd been rude from the get-go when she took my hand, squeezed it and murmured, "Mm...tasty."

"Study, Mother, now," Julian growled, and I looked to Lucien's son.

It was bizarre how Lucien, who I knew was over eight hundred years old, but this didn't penetrate considering his looks and vitality, had two grown children. It was also bizarre that his parents looked like his contemporaries. And it was equally bizarre how both his children clearly got the best selections in the gene pool they were offered.

Julian was gorgeous in his father's raw manly way.

Isobel was beautiful in what had to have been her mother's delicate way, but Lucien was still stamped all over her.

I liked them both. They were obviously close and affectionate with each other, their father, and their grandmother, and until now, patient with Cressida. They also were cautious and watchful with their grandfather, which meant they were far from stupid. And they were kind and welcoming to me, which was nice.

On this thought, I heard Lucien command, "Go with Julian."

My head came up and I looked down the table to the head where Lucien was sitting. I was at the foot. Lucien seated me where I was and I didn't think anything was amiss with this, considering it was my house. But when he did this, the rest exchanged looks and I jotted this down on my mental list of what to talk to Lucien about later.

He was also glaring at Cressida and it was clear he did not find anything amusing.

Cressida looked to Lucien and grinned cattily, "I don't want to miss Edwina's dessert." Her head then turned to me and she finished. "I've known Edwina for *years*. She's the best cook. Don't you agree?"

Her meaning was clear.

See?

Total bitch.

"You can go or I can carry you," Lucien bit out, Cressida looked to him, and I pressed my lips together.

"Oh," she purred, her eyes flaring with a sultry light, her face softening seductively. Neither of which I liked. Neither of which I could do a thing about. "I'll take the second option."

Bitch.

Lucien opened his mouth to speak but I took my chances and got there before him.

"Lucien, really, Cressida's right. No one should miss Edwina's dessert." Lucien's eyes cut to me, but I looked to Cressida. "As you can see," I pointed to the bowl Edwina had set in front of me, "it looks delicious. Of course, if you wish to chat with Julian and not tax yourself after that rich lunch, Lucien can carry you to the study." I shrugged and smiled at her. "Anything goes in Casa Leah. So, whatever you wish."

Cressida's eyes narrowed on me.

My smile got bigger.

I heard Isobel chuckle.

Cressida's eyes narrowed further.

I forced myself to quit smiling.

"The Buchanan smell."

This came from Etienne and I looked to him to see he was studying me in a way that made my flesh crawl.

"I have, of course, smelled it at Selections over the years, but haven't partaken. You, my dear, have changed that. I believe you have cousins who'll be attending their Selections soon?" he asked, but didn't wait for me to answer. "I'll be certain to arrange it so I'm free of concubine and I'll act quickly at their Selections to declare my intentions."

Oh yes, my flesh was crawling and I tasted bile considering it suddenly crept up my throat.

I didn't want my cousins to service this man and my eyes flew to Lucien to communicate this fact. The instant they caught his, his locked on mine and they were intense. I knew what that meant and I swallowed the bile, deciding I disliked Etienne even more, considering he put me off Edwina's dessert. I didn't know what it was, but by the looks of it she'd used a heavy hand with whipped cream, so I also didn't care.

Now I knew I'd have to force it down.

I pulled in a breath, looked back at Etienne and lied quietly, "I'm sure they'd be honored."

Actually, what I was sure of was that I'd warn my aunties about this and prepare my cousins for this eventuality. They could refuse him and would have to wait for another Selection, but it would be worth it.

"And how do you find serving your master?" Etienne asked what I considered a rude question. I hadn't sat down to lunch with vampires, except, of course, Lucien and Stephanie, but what I did for and *with* Lucien was personal, not a topic for luncheon conversation.

And I didn't like the way he put it. Lucien had called himself my master in the beginning, so I guessed this was accepted language in their culture. But I still didn't think the way Etienne phrased this was nice.

My gaze again went to Lucien to see his jaw was hard and his eyes were still intent.

I was right, it might be accepted language, but Etienne wasn't being nice.

I forced myself to smile a small smile at Lucien, take in the elegant dining room where we were seated, and I looked back at Etienne.

"I believe I've done well," I replied. "At least for my part. You'd have to ask Lucien if he agrees."

"Oh, Lucien always enjoys his meals to their fullest," Cressida put in. I fought against my back going straight even as I felt the air in the room get thick, but she wasn't done. "Of course, considering all that is you, he's enjoying it even more."

"That's enough."

This was said quietly and surprisingly by Magdalene and all eyes went to her to see she was looking at Cressida.

"You are at Leah's table in Leah's home eating Leah's food. She is concubine. She is Buchanan. And you have repeatedly disrespected her," Magdalene went on, again quietly, her voice soft, and if it wasn't for the sharp look in her eyes, you wouldn't know she was angry.

But that sharp look was in her eyes, so sharp it was piercing, so you couldn't mistake it.

Magdalene wasn't done.

"I know for a fact that if Lucien referred to your Teo as your 'meal,' you'd challenge him without hesitation. And yet here you sit, at his concubine's table in her presence and his, and treat them both to your insolence. I've shown you patience, Cressida, until now. One more demonstration of your lack of regard for this family, it will be *me* who challenges you."

Cressida's brows went up. "This *family*?"

Magdalene sat back. "Are you not seated at a table with your son, his sister, their grandparents?"

"Are you not inferring that Leah is family?" Cressida shot back.

"If that is what you wish to read into my statement, be my guest. I, for one," her eyes intriguingly slid to Etienne before going back to Cressida, "hold my concubines in deep regard, so I have no issue with that."

Cressida had no retort and it was clear she didn't like this because her face went hard and her nose scrunched.

Magdalene dismissed her and looked at me.

"My apologies, Leah. I'm deeply sorry we've intruded on you and my son only for you to be treated to this behavior."

"Good Christ," Etienne muttered in clear contempt. "Apologies to a concubine?"

I *so* did not like Lucien's father.

But with effort I ignored him, held Magdalene's eyes and said quietly, "Thank you."

She nodded to me and her face went soft.

I so *did* like Lucien's mother.

I smiled at her, picked up my spoon and forced myself to take a bite of dessert. I was right. Lots of whipped cream with a hint of strawberries and chunks of moist rich yellow cake. I was also wrong. Even the antics of Lucien's crazy family didn't make me not enjoy Edwina's scrumptious dessert.

Edwina was a genius.

I was scooping up more dessert when I heard in my head, *I'm proud of you, pet.*

I kept my attention on my bowl when I replied, *Thank you, darling.*

Only when I swallowed my next bite did I look to Lucien.

His eyes were on me.

I grinned.

He grinned back.

I liked that. Therefore my grin got bigger and I gave him a smile I had no idea was dazzling. Not even when Lucien's eyes warmed and his face got soft upon witnessing it.

I turned my attention back to my bowl and thus missed his family again exchanging glances.

Some were relieved. Some were hard.

All were knowing.

It was after dessert and coffee. Lucien had come down to my end of the table to pull out my chair, help me up and guide me out of the room with his hand at the small of my back.

We were walking through the double doors when I saw Magdalene and Isobel were hovering. As was Cressida, if farther away. Julian and Etienne were moving to the formal living room, which I found a relief.

No lounging in the comfy seating area off the kitchen for Etienne. No way.

I was wondering if I could tell them I needed to powder my nose and Lucien had to help me, whereupon I would barricade us in our bathroom until they all went away, when Magdalene came forward and wrapped her fingers around my elbow.

"Girl talk," she said on a smile tipped up to her son.

I felt Lucien's body get tight even as mine did the same.

"Oh goodie!" Cressida exclaimed.

My body got tighter and Lucien's hand pressed into the small of my back

"Magdalene said 'girl talk,' Cressida, not cat talk," Isobel stated instantly.

Cressida sliced her a look, but Lucien relaxed and I did too.

"I'll behave," Cressida declared, I knew lying through her teeth.

"No you won't," Isobel returned, knowing better than me that Cressida was full of it.

"Reap what you sow," Magdalene stated in her quiet voice. "You came here full of curiosity, like a cat, and recklessly indulged yourself in that curiosity, like a cat. Now you bear the consequences."

Not giving Cressida the opportunity to reply—but I got a funny feeling I didn't like all that much when her angry eyes cut through me—Magdalene drew me away. I saw Lucien give his daughter a look and felt his hand slide around my waist to curl at its side.

I stopped and looked up at him just in time for his mouth to touch mine.

When his head lifted slightly, he said gently, but I still knew it was an order, "Don't be long."

I nodded. I could do not long. I could definitely do not long.

I had to say, it freaked me out he was so cautious about me being with his family. Sure, they were strange and he'd forewarned me about Cressida and Etienne, but I sensed there was more.

I needed to ask him, Edwina, or Stephanie about this. I didn't know if I missed this when I missed my studies. Perhaps concubines didn't socialize with a vampire's family and his was just weird or weirdly nosy. I did know, whatever was happening, Lucien didn't like it.

He let me go and Magdalene again commenced in moving me away. I followed, as did Isobel. Neither woman talked even after we moved outside. And they continued their silence as they moved me to the trail that led to the pier.

I knew what this meant. They didn't want their family's vampire hearing to catch our conversation.

I wasn't certain this was good.

I was so uncertain, we walked in silence to the pier, and when we arrived I was a bundle of nerves.

"You can relax, Leah, we're all friends here," Magdalene assured me softly as we moved on to the wooden slats, the serenity of the lake all around us. A serenity that did nothing to calm me. She could hear my heart, I knew, and read me.

"We just wanted to apologize personally for showing up out of the blue and bringing Etienne and Cressida," Isobel added when we stopped. "I hope you see they both need to be handled with care."

Oh, I saw that all right.

"Of course," I murmured.

"When we return to the house, we'll do our best to conclude the visit swiftly," Magdalene told me.

"No, that's unnecessary," I semi-lied, seeing as I liked them. I just didn't like Etienne and Cressida. "Stay as long as you like. Lucien is enjoying his time with you." That last was also a semi-lie.

They'd both known Lucien for a long time (and that long for them was *long*), therefore they both burst into laughter.

Slightly sobering, Magdalene's hand came up and squeezed my biceps before she dropped it and said, "I appreciate the sacrifice you'd make for my son, but as gracious as that is, we'll do our best to conclude the visit."

"Okay," I whispered then rallied, "But, just so *you* know," I emphasized the "you" so they'd understand exactly which "yous" I was talking about. "You're welcome anytime. Edwina likes company, so do I, and Lucien has shared with me his fondness for the both of you."

"That's very kind, Leah," Isobel replied softly.

"And to return the kindness," Magdalene pulled a business-card-shaped piece of paper out of the pocket of her awesome, tailored, loose-legged slacks and offered it to me, "this is our contact information. Bel's and mine. If you should need anything," her eyes held mine, hers communicating something I didn't get but something I wasn't sure I liked, "*anything,* Leah, call on us."

What was *this* all about?

Taking the card from her, cautiously I asked, "Are you talking about the trouble Lucien is in?"

Magdalene's head tilted slightly to the side but her face gave away nothing. "Trouble?"

Uh-oh. Maybe she didn't know Lucien was hauled away in the middle of the night by The Council. She might look like his sister but she was his mom and that wouldn't be stellar news.

"Uh..." I mumbled to cover.

It was lame but I didn't know where else to go.

"Do you know of Father's troubles with The Council?" Isobel asked, clearly knowing herself and not afraid to mention it in front of Magdalene, which meant she knew too, so I relaxed.

"Not, um...exactly. I know he had an, uh...visit from them, but he hasn't shared more," I answered.

"Actually," Magdalene cut in, "that card is for you to use whenever you feel you need it, my dear. Whatever concerns you have. Whatever you wish to discuss. My son endures an interest amongst our people that can be trying. Not only for him, but for those with whom he shares his time. We just wished you to know, regardless of how Cressida and Etienne behaved at lunch, that you have his family's support, a listening ear, whatever you need."

Wow. That was super nice.

"Thank you," I replied quietly.

"Whatever you need," Magdalene repeated, getting slightly closer to me in a way I found contradictorily both reassuring and a little scary.

Great, now Lucien's mother was causing me to have bizarre, conflicting emotions.

"Okay." I was still talking quietly. "Thank you."

Her hand came up and she again gave my arm another squeeze.

I smiled then looked to the path and back to the women.

"I really should get back to Lucien," I told them. "As you know, he's not a big fan of his father, Cressida worked his nerves at lunch, and he can sometimes have a temper. I don't know you all very well, but I'm thinking Julian working on his own can't keep the beast at bay. And anyway, Lucien would much rather spend time with you, so maybe we should return."

"I see you have grown to know my son well," Magdalene noted in her soft voice.

"He's an immensely knowable guy," I replied and heard Isobel chuckle. "I mean, he's a guy you'd want to know, uh...immensely," I clarified stupidly.

"A guy," Isobel murmured, amusement vibrating in her voice.

"It's refreshing, my dear," Magdalene started and my attention went to her, "to see my son with someone, anyone, who enjoys his company, *his* company, without veneration."

Well, I worshipped her son, but not in a way I'd share with her.

"I'm pleased you find that refreshing," I told her, and she moved into me again, this time to slide an arm around my waist and turn me back to the path.

"Let's get to know each other better, you and I," she stated as she started us on our way, Isobel following. "Use that card to call on me just to chat."

"Me too," Isobel called from behind us.

Wow, totally nice. They completely made up for Cressida being a bitch and Etienne being super creepy.

"Okay," I agreed.

"And perhaps we'll return. Take you to lunch, just girls. Maybe shopping," Magdalene went on.

I would love that.

I didn't share that.

I just said, "That'd be great. Maybe we can invite Stephanie."

"Excellent idea," Magdalene stated on a waist squeeze.

We were on the path, woods surrounding us, when it hit me and I found my feet suddenly stopping. Thus I stopped Magdalene with me and Isobel was forced to halt behind us.

I turned to them, moving out of the curve of Magdalene's arm, and that was when I found my mouth moving.

"I...Lucien...he's shared with me a variety of things and I... well, being me, being mortal, I mean, it's very hard to wrap my mind around them. But at lunch, I was worried...um, I mean to say..."

Damn! I was screwing this up!

I took in a deep breath and forged on, "What I mean is, he's very strong, but still, I sense he's suffered. That will happen to everyone at times in their lives, I know. It would just suck if it happened to you and you didn't have good people, family, friends, at your back. At lunch I worried that he didn't." My eyes took them both in and I finished quietly, "I'm glad to know that he does."

Magdalene's normally soft friendly face got softer and friendlier. Isobel, who played her cards closer to her vest, smiled a genuine heartfelt smile.

I kept talking.

"Lucien would never thank you and it isn't my place to do it, but I'm going to do it anyway. So, uh...thank you."

Magdalene looked at Isobel, Isobel looked at Magdalene, then Magdalene again moved in to me and wrapped her hand around my elbow.

She turned us and started us forward again, but she did this walking close and saying softly, "And thank you, my dear. It's lovely to know my son spends his time with a woman who cares."

"I do," I said softly back, and actually (shocker), I did.

Her fingers gave my elbow a squeeze.

"Good," she murmured and I looked to the side to see her facing forward, her expression thoughtful but content.

I threw a look behind me and caught Lucien's beautiful daughter's smile.

Totally weird. Either one of them could be his sister.

Still, I smiled back.

Then I concentrated on walking close to Lucien's mother as we made our way back to her son.

Wearing a raspberry satin nightie with a deep edge of black lace at the bottom, I wandered out of the dressing room, through the bathroom and into the bedroom.

Although Magdalene and Isobel had been true to their promise to conclude the visit from Lucien's family shortly after we returned, five minutes after they left, my family descended.

This did not make Lucien happy and his frustration was apparent. He only put a clamp on it when Aunt Kate explained their plane left early the next morning and that evening was the last opportunity they had to visit with me. Therefore, they stayed for dinner and beyond, leaving only fifteen minutes ago.

However, during their visit they were all watchful of Lucien and me. I didn't get the opportunity to ask them to explain, though it felt weirdly like they were taking our pulse after the visit from Lucien's family.

The second we walked back from me giving them hugs and kisses at their rental car and Lucien closed the front door of the house, he turned, looked down at me and growled, "Bed."

I felt his growl in secret happy places and this feeling was so strong, I totally forgot I wanted to ask him about his family and my family seemingly worried about my visit with them. So I called my goodnight to Edwina and skedaddled up the stairs to peruse my lingerie drawer for Lucien's next treat.

As I changed, I heard him in the bathroom brushing his teeth. Then I heard him leave the bathroom.

Now I was walking through the bedroom to see he was as he was last night. Reclined against the headboard, chest bared, book in hand, but eyes on me.

He immediately flipped his book shut and set it on his nightstand.

I immediately walked to him, put a knee in the bed, threw my other leg around and settled astride his hips.

"You don't use a bookmark," I noted, moving my hands to rest them lightly on his upper abs.

"No," he answered shortly as I felt his stomach muscles tighten even with my light touch.

Power.

My power over the Mighty Vampire Lucien.

I liked that.

"What?" I tipped my head to the side. "Do you memorize the page number or something?"

"Do you really care?" he shot back.

I smiled at him. "No."

His hands came to my hips. I felt the pads of his fingers press in and just with that my body heated.

"I like your kids," I whispered, sliding my hands up slightly, my torso moving down a smidgeon as I did.

"Good," he muttered, sliding his hands up too, pulling me down a smidgeon more.

"And your mom is lovely," I told him, my hands sliding up more as I bent just a touch closer.

"She is," he agreed, his hands doing the same, pulling me even closer.

That was when I moved down. Folding one of my arms between us, the other hand slid up to curve around his strong jaw as my thumb slid out to glide along his beautiful lips.

"I like that for you," I whispered, and he blinked.

"Pardon?"

"You're Mighty Vampire Lucien," I told him and felt his lips twitch. "But even superheroes need good folks at their backs. Batman has Robin and that butler guy. Iron Man has that dude in the military and Pepper Potts. Spiderman has Aunt May. The Fantastic Four are, well...*four*. And—"

"You don't have to recite your knowledge of all things superhero, sweetling," Lucien said against my thumb, his voice vibrating with humor. "I think I've got it."

My thumb swept his cheekbone and I repeated softly, "I like that for you."

"There's a problem with this scenario," Lucien noted and my head tilted.

"What problem?"

Suddenly I found myself on my back with Lucien's weight on top of me and his lips brushing mine.

"Superheroes don't often get the girl," he murmured against my lips and that made my body heat more.

"Okay, then you're a new, better, *real* kind of superhero who gets laid regularly," I murmured back, my hands traveling light on his skin.

"Better?" he whispered, his hands traveling light on the satin of my nightie.

"Oh yeah," I whispered back.

His mouth grinned against mine and I watched up close as his eyes got smug.

That used to annoy me.

Now I thought it was hot.

I wrapped my legs around his hips as his lips trailed down my cheek to my ear. One of his hands pushed between me and the bed so his arm could wrap around me tight.

His tongue touched the skin under my ear then his lips moved against it. "I'm going to feed from you, my pet."

My whole body trembled.

Lucien wasn't done.

"And I'm going to do it everywhere."

Oh yes. That sounded nice.

He kept going.

"There will be places you'll be numb."

Hmm. That didn't sound nice.

He went on.

"But there'll be other *better* places where you absolutely will not."

Goodie!

"Are you ready?" he asked.

Was he crazy?

"Yes," I breathed.

He lifted his head so his burning eyes caught mine and my entire body felt the burn.

Then in a blur of motion he was between my legs. I felt his tongue run along the inside of my thigh as his finger ran feather-light along the outside edge of my panties between my legs.

Another full-body shiver.

Yes. I was right. This was nice.

He repeated, his tongue running up my thigh, his finger running over my panties between my legs.

My womb spasmed and I whimpered.

Then I felt him feed from my thigh as his finger pressed in at the perfect spot over my panties and my hips surged up as my neck arched and my eyes closed.

Definitely right.

Nice.

God, God.

I thought I had the best the night before, the excruciatingly beautiful intensity of that morning.

But now, Lucien crouched back on his calves, me straddling him, his hips powering up, his cock ramming into me, his mouth at my neck feeding from me, his big hand curled at my cheek, his thumb in my mouth and I was sucking, I knew *this* was the best.

My hips jerked, it was almost on me and he sensed it.

His thumb slid out of my mouth but only to glide along my lips before it happened. Then his thumb slid back in sideways and my teeth automatically clamped down on it as my hips bucked. A moan stuck in my throat, my arms clenched him tight and my back arched, pressing my torso into his hard body.

Through my overpowering orgasm I vaguely felt his tongue lash the wound at my neck. His thumb moved from between my teeth so his fist could clench in my hair to position my head where he wanted it.

Then his mouth was on mine as his cock kept driving up inside me, filling me so full it felt like he was an essential part of me.

"When you come, the world stops," he growled against my lips as I kept trembling through my orgasm. "The whole world becomes nothing but you, your pussy, your pussy taking my cock and me."

Oh God, just his words and tone were going to make me come again.

"Darling," I whispered, holding tighter as my body jolted with his thrusts.

"Eight hundred, twenty-two years, I've never felt anything this beautiful," he whispered, still driving and my eyes, half-closed, shot open.

Oh God.

I loved that he thought that.

He wasn't done.

His gaze held mine. "Eight hundred, twenty-two years, I've never seen anything this beautiful."

Oh God.

God!

"I could fuck you for eternity," he whispered.

My hands slid up and fisted in his hair as my hips bucked again.

"Lucien."

"Eternity," he murmured against my lips then his head slanted, his mouth claimed mine, our tongues dueled and his thrusts became savage. Suddenly I was on my back in the bed taking the force of him between my legs and it was pure brutal beauty.

His mouth broke from mine, he buried his face in my neck as he buried his cock in me, and I listened to the power of his groan.

I gave him that. Me. Just who I was. All that I was. I gave him that. I made him feel that beauty. My beauty was what he saw.

I *loved* that.

He barely finished before he rolled to his back, taking me with him, keeping himself a part of me. When he settled, one strong arm held me tight around my back and his other hand in my hair pressed my face in my throat.

"Christ, I'm sorry, Leah."

I blinked at his throat.

These were words I didn't expect to hear.

I lifted my head to look down at him.

Wow. He even looked sorry.

"You're sorry?" I asked.

"Yes, sweetling," he replied gently, his black eyes filled with remorse, his hand sliding out of my hair to cup my cheek.

"For what?"

"For taking you that hard."

Was he serious?"

"Uh, darling, it seems you might have missed this, but I liked it," I informed him.

His thumb slid along my cheek as his gaze moved over my face.

His eyes came back to mine and he murmured, "You aren't lying."

"Why would I lie about that?"

"Because that would be what I wanted to hear."

It was my turn for my eyes to move over his face.

Cautiously, I asked, "Do people tell you what you want to hear often?"

"Except for Cosmo, Teffie, and occasionally others, always."

I felt my lips part and my eyes grow wide.

Whoa.

I didn't know what to do with that.

"Seriously?" I asked in amazement, the shadow moved out of his handsome face, and he grinned.

"Seriously," he answered.

"I don't know if that's cool or if that would suck," I shared.

"The latter," Lucien clarified.

I tipped my head to the side even as I dipped it closer to his and I grinned before saying, "I don't know. I think it would be cool to have everyone tell me what I want to hear. Like, 'Leah, your butt absolutely does not look big in that.' And, 'Oh no, this hollandaise sauce isn't runny and disgusting. It tastes great.' Stuff like that."

Lucien's hand left my face so that arm could also wrap tight around me and his hips adjusted slightly so he slid out of me as he grinned and stated, "For the record, your ass never looks big in anything."

"Good to know," I said through my smile.

"But please, don't attempt hollandaise sauce."

I burst out laughing, and as I was doing it, Lucien rolled me to my back. We ended with his torso on mine but most of his weight on a forearm in the bed beside me. I was still giggling, and although Lucien was smiling a beautiful smile, he wasn't laughing. He was watching and he was doing it like he liked what he saw.

And I liked that.

"All right, darling," I replied. "I won't attempt hollandaise sauce. But I'll inform you that this is mostly because I already have about seven thousand times. I've always ruined it, so I know that's a road I shouldn't go down."

"This is good," he muttered, his eyes holding humor.

"But I make no such assurances about béarnaise sauce. I think I could kick some béarnaise ass."

Lucien kept muttering as his eyes kept dancing when he said, "Heaven help me."

"Just saying," I muttered back.

He held my eyes, his still lit with amusement, then I watched the amusement die and he said quietly, "We must talk."

I sighed, replied, "I know," and finished, "Cressida."

His head jerked slightly and he asked, "Cressida?"

"Darling, I have to say, and please, no offense, but I'm concerned you're into me considering the two other women that have been in your life that I've met. Am I like them?"

"Not in any way," he stated firmly.

Interesting.

"Then why did you pick them?" I asked.

"I'm not certain you want to know."

I totally did.

"Call me crazy, but I do."

"Then I'll amend my response," Lucien returned. "I'm not certain I want to tell you because, having you, I'm no longer certain why I chose them."

Oh my God.

That was sweet.

"Lucien," I whispered.

Lucien changed the subject. "But that isn't what we need to talk about."

I nodded and said, "The table thing."

Lucien's brows drew together. "Pardon?"

I fluttered my hand in the air and explained, "The table thing. I saw it. When you seated me at the foot, everyone went kind of weird. What *was* that?"

"Tradition," Lucien answered. "You're a mortal and you were amongst vampires. My mother would normally take the foot."

I didn't think that was good.

"Then why'd you seat me there?"

"Because it's your house, your place, and my seating you there was my way of telling them they should respect you in it. Unfortunately, even this did not deter Cressida and my father from behaving badly."

He was right about that.

Still.

"I hope your mother wasn't offended," I whispered.

"She understood why I did it and therefore she wasn't."

Well, that was good.

Lucien went on, "That also isn't what we need to talk about."

Again I nodded and stated, "The Council."

"Leah—" he started, but I interrupted him.

"You still haven't told me about what happened and I'd like to know."

His eyes moved over my face again and he noted, "You're worried."

"I told you I was, but that was then, only the morning after. Now I've had two days of inexplicably being under guard at your demand, something else you haven't explained. And, I should tell you, I kind of figured it out that I don't have a guard to stop me from sleeping without you close. Then *both* our families descended unexpectedly. Not to mention lots of hot sex. But bottom line, time has passed. So before I was worried. Now I'm *worried*."

His eyes warmed and his head dropped so he could rest his forehead to mine.

What he didn't do was answer.

Therefore, I prompted, "So can you either tell me everything is all right or tell me what's wrong so I can pinpoint my freakout rather than making shit up in my head?"

Lucien lifted his forehead from mine and caught my eyes but I kept talking.

"Because you should know, I have this thing I do. So I can prepare for the worst, I worry about the worst. Then I find out what's happening or what's going to happen happens and it's never the worst and I'm relieved. And, seriously darling, the shit I make up is really not good, so give me something to go on here."

When I shut up, instantly he stated, "I broke a rule. Not an insignificant one. However, it is one that was created a long time ago for reasons that might have been sound then, although that's debatable. What isn't debatable is that they no longer are. It's antiquated and confining. I've explained my reasoning to The Council and they're considering it. They'll find in my favor and all will be well."

I studied his face and asked, "You're sure?"

He held my eyes and I had no idea that he lied when he replied softly, "I'm sure."

"And, say, just for the sake of discussion, they *don't* find in your favor. What happens to you?"

"They'll find in my favor."

"What if they don't?"

"Leah, they'll find in my favor."

"Okay, Lucien, but what if they don't?"

"They will."

I pressed both hands to his chest, not to push him away, but to communicate my need to know, and repeated, "What if they don't? Will they punish you? Vampire torture? Vampire prison? What are we talking about here?"

Lucien grinned. "There is no vampire torture or vampire prison."

"So what if someone does something wrong?"

"If their transgressions are discovered, they're told to stop doing it and pay compensation, if The Council deems it necessary."

My eyes got wide. "That's it?"

"Often the compensation is significant."

I couldn't believe this.

"So all forms of vampire punishment are paid through fines?"

"No. If a vampire breaks a *very* significant rule or continues to break a rule they've been penalized for before, they'd pay with their life."

I sucked in breath and my body went solid.

Lucien's big hand framed my face. "The rule I broke wasn't that significant."

"Holy heck," I breathed.

His hand pressed gently into my head, even as he gave me some of the weight of his torso. "Leah, listen to me. The rule I broke was not that significant."

"There aren't any crazy redneck vampires on The Council who pass down insanely ridiculous sentences for minor infractions are there?" I asked.

Lucien stared at me a second then threw his head back and burst out laughing.

I slapped his chest and snapped, "I'm not being funny."

He visibly struggled to quell his laughter and looked back at me. "Sweetheart, there are no crazy redneck vampires *at all*. So no, there definitely aren't any on The Council."

That was a relief.

"So, they rule against you, they'll make you pay a fine?"

The laughter moved out of his face but he held my eyes and I didn't know he lied again when he stated, "Yes."

"And you're a gazillionaire," I remarked.

Humor hit his features again when he murmured, "I might fall short of that."

"A billionaire then," I stated, and Lucien didn't answer, which meant yes. I powered through understanding this insane, totally unbelievable but still true tidbit of Lucien's life and carried on, "So, essentially, it's water off your back."

Something drifted through his eyes, it wasn't fast and it didn't seem pleasant, but I still couldn't read it.

It was gone like it had never been there when he replied, "Essentially, yes."

"Okay then," I mumbled.

"Feel better now?" Lucien asked gently.

"Yes, but you're a billionaire so we can probably access arms dealers. Therefore we're buying a flamethrower and I'm manning it should someone on The Council get a wild hair, do something stupid and they come after you."

At that, a statement I made in jest (partially), Lucien's entire face changed and I felt his body get tight. I also couldn't read this change, but I knew to my bones it was significant.

"Lucien?" I called when he didn't speak.

He blinked, his body relaxed and his hand slid into my hair on the pillow where he started to twirl a lock around his finger.

"A flamethrower is unnecessary," he whispered, his eyes warm, his face soft and even the air around us in our bed felt snug and safe.

"Of course," I whispered back, sliding into his mood, the look on his face, in his eyes. "You could probably take on the lot."

"Without a doubt."

"So I have nothing to worry about."

That thing drifted through his eyes again even as he murmured, "No, my pet, you have nothing to worry about."

I didn't like whatever was drifting through his features, but even so, I decided to trust him.

"Good," I whispered.

His gaze moved over my face then his head dipped, and even as his fingers kept twisting my hair, his lips moved on my neck. Lazy. Sweet. Nice.

My arms circled him. "Are we done talking?"

"Absolutely."

"Are we going to sleep?"

"Absolutely not."

I grinned. Then I twisted my neck, his head came up and our mouths met.

And we absolutely didn't sleep.

Not for a long time.

And when we did, we did it close. Our bodies snug.

And, for my part, I did it feeling safe.

21
The Attack

I turned the faucet off, wrung out the washcloth, smoothed it over the edge of the basin and looked into the mirror as I grabbed a towel to dry my hands.

Lucien and I had just made love and he'd fed. It was beautiful. As good as always. Ecstasy.

I'd cleaned up and was wearing nothing but a short ivory silk nightie. In the mirror, I could see the angry pink wound at my neck morphing, fading, healing. It didn't take long now, less than half an hour, then it would be gone.

I watched the wound grow fainter for long moments thinking that was wild and totally freaking cool.

I folded and returned the towel to its loop and looked back at my reflection the mirror.

It had been a week and a half since we had the visits from our families.

I was surprised but definitely not displeased that Lucien spent that entire time with me. We made love. He fed. We cooked together. We ate together. We walked to the lake and swam together. Ditto in the pool. We lay in bed or on the couch in the comfy seating area off the kitchen and whispered together or napped, doing both holding each other close. Lucien took me out to dinner twice. He took me shopping once. I made him watch a movie with me snuggled on the couch. I learned about his life, his family and vampires. I also learned he knew most everything about me, but still, he liked hearing me tell my stories anyway.

The outside world intruded, of course.

Edwina was there, quietly taking care of the house, stocking the fridge, sometimes clucking around us like a mother hen, but usually making herself scarce because she felt the mood.

My mother called, Aunt Nadia too, Stephanie, my sister and a couple of my cousins. They were worried about the nightmares I assured them (truthfully) I was no longer having. But I made short work of allaying their fears so I could get back to Lucien.

He also received calls, mostly business, which he would take with me close. Sometimes they were about other things. Those he would take elsewhere.

I was curious and wanted to ask because I sensed they were about me. But I didn't because if it was bad, I didn't want to know. Not then. Not in that golden time I fell in love with a vampire.

I stared at myself in the mirror, smiling.

There it was. Proof.

I was demented. Totally.

I was in love with Lucien.

I couldn't have him, not like I could one of my own, to take vows with, make children with and grow old with. I also couldn't have him like in the time before The Revolution, to take vows with, not make children with, but to spend eternity together.

And I didn't care.

I had him now. I loved him now.

And I knew it was in a way that I would love him for my forever.

To put it simply, there were not many girls who got the chance to fall in love with a vampire. To have his attention, his protection, his body, his humor, his generosity, his gentleness. He could be bossy and annoying, but that was just him and he was hot doing it, so although we exchanged words because he was who he was and I was too, it never amounted to much.

I had been right, as crazy as it sounded. He had all the good stuff down pat and was the best boyfriend *ever*.

I didn't know how long it would last, what we had. And I no longer cared.

Because I had it now and I would have it for a while, and even when it was gone, I'd always have the memories we were making. And the moments we shared were so much better than anything I'd ever experienced, anything *any* woman would ever experience, were enough for me.

I knew it down to my bones.

The Mighty Vampire Lucien was mine...for now. So I was going to do whatever I had to do to make really fucking great memories.

But even more important, I was his. And, just as he promised, me giving him me meant something to him.

Not something small.

Something huge. Something meaningful. Something sweet.

I knew that down to my bones too.

He loved me. He couldn't be the way he was with me and not feel what I was feeling. It was impossible.

The strictures of his culture meant we couldn't have forever. But he was just as intent as me to take what he could from the now and make it sweet.

I knew it. I *knew* it.

Right to the heart of me.

And he had been right. What he could give me when I gave him myself was beautiful.

I looked away from the mirror still smiling and wandered into the bedroom. Today was the end of our long romantic interlude. He had an important meeting to attend that morning. To spend time with me, he'd postponed it twice, which, he told me, was two times too many. However, he assured me, once it was done, he'd be back.

Therefore, I was a little surprised when I hit the bedroom that he was still in bed, since I knew he needed to leave soon. But there he was. The covers down to his waist, chest exposed, arms lifted, his head resting on his hands, and he was staring at the ceiling.

The urge came over me and I didn't even try to suppress it.

I had memories to make.

So I took off running across the large room. I saw his head come up and I launched myself on the bed, my body landing full-length on his large one.

He grunted, cocking at the hips, but his arms locked around me as we bounced.

"Jesus, Leah," he muttered when we settled, his lips twitching.

I planted my hands on his shoulders and smiled into his beautiful face.

"Right, so, something to take with you to your meeting that we'll celebrate when you get back with fillet mignon smothered in homemade béarnaise sauce," I started. His lip twitch became a grin and my smile got bigger before I did what I needed to do to make one, huge, beautiful fucking memory, and without further ado announced, "I'm in love with you, Mighty Vampire Lucien."

His grin died instantly even as his arms spasmed around me.

I felt my stomach clench.

Oh God.

"Leah," he whispered, his deep voice sounding funny, rough, tortured. Exactly like it did the morning after the first time he fed when he'd nearly killed me.

Oh God!

I thought he felt the same, or if not the same, then *something*. He had to. With how hard he worked to get it, everything we shared, he had to.

But looking at his face I knew he didn't.

Oh *God!*

He didn't.

I didn't expect this. I never dreamed he didn't feel the same as me. I could rejoice in the time we had, albeit short, if he returned my feelings.

I couldn't bear it if he did not.

I didn't know what to do.

But my body knew what to do and it prepared for escape.

Lucien felt it and in a nanosecond I was on my back with Lucien on top of me.

I knew I had no shot at getting away from him so I did the only thing I could do. I turned my head away and closed my eyes tight.

God. *God.*

My vampire didn't love me.

"Sweetling, look at me," Lucien urged softly.

"Please, get off me," I whispered and my voice sounded funny too.

Rough.

Tortured.

His big hand slid between my cheek and the pillow and he whispered, "Leah, sweetheart, please, look at me."

I didn't look at him but I said quietly, "I shouldn't have said it. Forget I said it."

"Look at me."

"It didn't happen. Just wipe it from your mind. Go to your meeting. We'll both forget it and everything will be okay," I whispered desperately.

"Leah, *please look at me.*"

It was then it occurred to me that his hand was cupping my face but he wasn't forcing me to do what he wished. And it was then I opened my eyes, turned my head and looked at him.

I shouldn't have done it. His handsome face was gentle and God, *God,* more beautiful than ever. His eyes were warm and openly troubled and that looked good on him too.

"I must attend this meeting," he said gently. "It's important or I wouldn't leave you. Not now. Not when it's essential we talk about a variety of things."

I didn't want to talk about a variety of things. I wanted to curl up in a ball somewhere and remind myself to stop being my...*fucking*...self. Doing stupid shit. Getting myself in trouble. Breaking my own fucking heart.

"Leah, did you hear me?" he asked.

"Yes," I whispered.

"I'll make this meeting short. I'll get home as soon as I can and we'll talk."

"Okay," I agreed, knowing I'd take the time he was gone trying to figure out how I could get out of that talk even knowing I'd never get out of that talk.

"We should have talked before," he told me, his thumb sweeping the apple of my cheek. "I knew that. We didn't because I was enjoying you and I didn't want that to interfere."

He was *enjoying* me.

God, how could I forget?

I was his meal. His fuck buddy. His pet.

God! How could I forget?

I should have remembered. I should never have fucking forgot.

It took everything I had, *everything*, but I fought back the sting of tears in my eyes and the ball of fire burning in my throat.

When I accomplished this herculean task, I whispered, "Go to your meeting. We'll talk when you get back."

"Back home," he returned immediately, and I blinked.

"What?"

"When I get back home."

I knew what he was saying and it felt like he'd plunged a knife in my gut.

Why did he persist in this? Expecting me to give everything while holding himself away.

"Yes, when you get back home," I forced out.

His face dipped closer and I braced, every part of me. I knew he felt it. I knew he heard my heart stuttering, my breath coming uneven. I knew he felt my body tightening. I knew it because I knew he had those abilities. And I knew it when I saw his face get even gentler, his eyes warmer and more troubled.

God, why wouldn't he just go away?

"I told you what we had would be beautiful," he reminded me, twisting that knife he left in my gut, making me bleed. "And I knew even before you said what you said earlier that you finally understood what I was giving to you. Now, you must understand our future."

He was wrong.

I already understood it. I'd *always* understood it.

I just chose to ignore it.

Stupidly, as usual. Stupid, stupid, *stupidly*.

"Okay," I agreed quietly.

His eyes roamed my face as his thumb moved over my cheek then he captured my gaze and whispered, "It will still be beautiful."

Wrong again.

"I promise, Leah," he continued softly.

Fucking *liar*.

"Okay," I repeated.

His eyes again roamed my face before coming back to mine.

Then, in perfect Lucien style, he demanded, "Kiss your vampire before I go."

His words sliced that knife up from my gut right through me, carving me open, laying me bare.

But I did what I was told. Wrapping my arms around his shoulders, I lifted my head the inch it needed to press my lips against his. His opened as did mine.

That was when I kissed him hard, wet, long, giving him everything I had, showing him exactly how I felt, offering him everything that was me. And I did it because that was how I'd been kissing him since this began, at first against my will, then gleefully.

But that was the last.

He'd never get that from me again.

Never.

When he tore his mouth from mine, he immediately shoved his face in my neck.

His arms again locked around me, his weight heavy on me, he growled, "Fuck, Leah," against my skin.

He felt it, I knew it. Whether he understood that was the last he'd ever get from me, I didn't know. I also didn't care. I didn't care about anything. Not anymore.

My life yawned before me. Years of being forced to live with a man I loved but didn't love me back and I could never really have. Then years of bitter memories taunting me.

I knew this. From the beginning I knew this.

But did that stop me?

No!

Stupid, stupid Leah.

I forced my arms to squeeze him and my lips to whisper, "You need to go."

He lifted his head and looked down at me. Then he dipped it, touched his mouth to mine, pulled back slightly and murmured, "I need to go."

I drew in breath.

All of a sudden I was no longer in his arms. With vamp speed, he left the bed.

Numb, I lay still and listened to him brush his teeth, his short shower. Before I knew it, he was wearing one of his fantastic suits, looking gorgeous standing by the bed. Then I was mostly out of bed, my legs dangling, my feet brushing the covers, my torso held close to his with his arms tight around me.

I looked up at him and blinked away the disorientation his speed created.

"I'll be home soon," he whispered.

"Okay," I replied, my hands drifting to rest on his broad shoulders.

He closed his eyes and dropped his forehead to mine.

I used everything in my reserves to stop myself from sobbing.

He lifted his head and opened his eyes.

"Thank you, sweetling, for giving that to me." He was still whispering, his voice deeper, again rough, but now with a different kind of feeling. In any other circumstance, I would think it was beyond beautiful.

Right then, obviously, I didn't. Because he was expressing gratitude for me giving my love, and outside of a great house, fabulous clothes, beautiful shoes and unbelievable orgasms, that gratitude was the only thing he would ever give to me.

"You're welcome," I replied, my voice strange, void, dead.

He didn't miss it.

"Sweetling—" he whispered.

"You need to go," I reminded him.

His arms gave me a squeeze before he ordered, "Busy yourself. Don't think of this while I'm gone. When we talk, Leah, I promise, you won't feel the way you feel right now."

He was full of it. He'd promised me a lot. And all of it was bullshit.

"Lucien, you have to go," I told him.

"Busy yourself and don't think of this," he repeated.

"Okay, I'll busy myself and not think of this," I lied.

He held my eyes and whispered, "You're lying."

Whatever!

Jeez!

Why wouldn't he just *go*?

I held his eyes right back.

Lucien sighed and reiterated, "I'll be home soon."

"And I'll be here."

His arms spasmed around me again as his gaze continued to hold mine captive.

Then, if you can freaking *believe*, the big, fat, vampire *jerk's* lips tipped up.

His lips tipped up!

"Yes, pet, you will," he whispered and touched his mouth to mine.

Then he was gone.

It happened after I made my plans and executed them.

I couldn't get out of the talk, this I knew.

So I would be prepared for it.

I did not cry. I did not curl up and give my mind over to contemplating my bleak future. I didn't open up the forgotten Why I Hate Lucien Vault, catalog its multitudes and nurse my fury. I didn't immediately hit the kitchen and consume everything edible within reach.

I took a shower. I took forever doing my hair. I spent a great deal of time on my makeup. I studied my vast wardrobe selection and picked the perfect outfit. And I strapped on a pair of fabulous shoes.

I did this with only the aid of coffee supplied by Edwina, who took one look at me and knew things were not right. And fortunately she also knew that I was in no mood to discuss them. So she brought me coffee but otherwise let me be.

I was coiffed. I was made up. I was wearing a freaking great pair of dark bootcut jeans that I paired with a fabulous dusky-blue, somewhat see-through top that clung to my midriff and hips but had a deep scoop at the back. I had a white racerback tank under it. And my feet were in high-heeled, beige suede, wedge sandals that had a wide strap across the toe and a wide, sexy ankle strap. In this getup, mentally prepared for what lay ahead, I walked downstairs.

My stomach felt hollow but I wasn't hungry. This was unusual. Usually, when I stupidly broke my own heart by picking the *way wrong guy* to give it to, I could and did eat everything in sight, but only if it wasn't good for me.

Now it felt like I'd never feel hungry again.

And the alarming thing was, now it felt like I'd never feel *any-thing* again.

That was how deeply Lucien wounded me.

No. That wasn't correct.

That was how deeply I allowed Lucien to wound me.

He fought to get in and I let him get in. But he knew he'd never give himself to me. And I knew he never could.

I just chose to ignore it.

My foot hit the floor of the foyer, my mind shoving away these thoughts, forcing itself toward eating something.

I needed to keep my strength up. Lucien had been gone for nearly an hour. His office was half an hour away if you didn't drive a Porsche. He drove a Porsche and did it fast, considering he couldn't die unless his crash was fiery. So he could drive it in twenty minutes and he did. Regularly. He said he'd make the meeting short, but I didn't know what that meant. I just knew there was a probability he could be home any minute.

When my foot hit the floor of the foyer was when it happened.

The front door flew straight off its hinges. It blew right by me through the foyer at least ten feet to crash to the floor and skid down the hall.

Every molecule in my body froze for an instant before I turned to flee up the stairs. My cell was on my dressing table in the closet.

I needed to call Lucien.

I got one step up and heard Edwina scream. Sheer dread coursed through my body, but I had no chance to react. No chance to do anything.

There was movement everywhere but nothing I could see. Solid things dashing through the house causing blurs. One of them cut me off on the stairs. I ran into it, and before I could see what it was, I fell back the step I took, landing painfully on my ass in the foyer.

Then I was up, my body like a rag doll, bent double at the waist, held tight to someone's side, my hair blowing in the breeze created by our movement down the hall. As suddenly as we were moving, we stopped, my frame swaying with the rapidity of us halting. I was swung up and around, my body jerking unnaturally with the speed, and it was sheer luck my neck or spine didn't snap.

I was held, my back to the front of someone, iron arms clamped around me, holding me captive, my arms held tight to my sides, rendered useless.

But I didn't try to move. This was because, in the comfy seating area, I saw Nestor, the vampire that had words with Stephanie at my Selection. And he was holding Edwina like whoever was holding me except he had one big hand over her mouth.

Her eyes were wide and filled with fear.

"Tape her to a chair in the dining room." I heard from behind me and I knew that voice.

Lucien's father.

Etienne.

Oh my God!

What was happening?

Nestor and Edwina were there one second and I felt the gust of wind they created when they sped by Etienne and me. Then they were gone.

I heard movement in the dining room but my attention was caught on something else.

My head jerking around, I saw Katrina, Lucien's ex, or soon-to-be-ex mate and Marcello from the night The Council sent vampires to collect Lucien. Katrina was standing in my kitchen staring daggers at me. Marcello was moving with a mortal's speed toward Etienne and me. My tight body got tighter but he stopped five feet away.

Then my tight body got so tight I thought it would snap when, his eyes burning into me with a light I did *not* like, he muttered heatedly, "God, I want to drain her while I fuck that fear."

"She is still my son's concubine," Etienne stated, and Marcello's eyes jerked over my shoulder.

"He's taken her as lover. All bets are off," he growled.

"We court his wrath already and you know it," Etienne shot back. "Don't be foolish."

"Agreed, so it should be worth my while," Marcello returned.

"My brother," Etienne said quietly, "in the coming war, we will need your strength. I ask you to restrain your instincts. Soon, all mortals will again be prey and you can take what you wish. My son falls or fails to protect his meal, you will have what you desire."

His son *falls*?

Oh my God!

What was happening?

I breathed hard as Marcello held Etienne's eyes. I felt no relief and kept breathing hard when he took a step back.

"Now, Leah," Etienne whispered, his mouth at my ear, "I'm going to let you go and we're going to talk. If you do anything unwise, I will let Marcello have you. Are you going to do anything unwise?"

Fuck no. These were vampires. No way I was going to do anything unwise.

I shook my head.

"Excellent," he murmured then let me go.

I took two quick steps away then turned my back toward the hall and moved back two steps more. But it was there I stopped because I had three vampires' eyes on me and I felt Nestor come out of the dining room behind me.

I looked amongst them, feeling my chest rise and fall, my fingers tingling, my legs quaking, but I kept my shoulders straight and stood tall.

I moved my eyes to Etienne.

"What's going on?" I asked and was pleased beyond reason my voice didn't shake.

"We've decided it's time you knew a few things," Etienne answered.

I didn't want to know a few things, of this I was certain. I also was certain I had no choice.

"What things?" I asked.

"Things about our culture. Things about your culture. Things about my son. And things about this world and your place in it," Etienne replied.

That was a lot. Some of which I knew or thought I did.

Though, not their versions of it.

"Okay," I whispered.

"Now be a good girl, Leah, and let your superior speak. I'll tell you when and if you're allowed to ask questions," Etienne stated, and I swallowed.

God, seriously. He was *such* a dick.

Still, with no other choice, I nodded.

"Very good," he leaned in, his eyes lighting, creepy, amused and terrifying, before he finished, "*Pet*."

Oh God.

"Did you know," he started, "that for five hundred years, it has been strictly forbidden for a vampire to take concubine as lover?"

I couldn't help it. I wanted to but I couldn't. My midsection swayed back like he'd struck me.

Etienne grinned.

I opened my mouth to say no, but remembered his order and instead shook my head.

"I didn't think so," he muttered then spoke louder when he informed me, "But it's true. No vampire has taken anything but blood from their concubine for centuries. *Centuries*. But my son had your contract altered. He did this without the knowledge or the assent of The Dominion. They've since found out and they are not happy."

The rule he broke.

The not insignificant rule he broke.

And he broke it to have me.

Please tell me this wasn't happening.

I stayed silent.

Etienne kept speaking.

"Vampires do not live with their concubines. They don't kiss them at Feasts. And seeing as he's obviously fucking you, he's done whatever the fuck he wished to do prior to receiving permission from The Council. They will not take to this kindly."

I pressed my lips together and nodded so he knew I heard him.

He went on.

"Whether willfully or coincidentally, this has made other vampires question this law. We," he flung his arm out to indicate Marcello, Katrina and Nestor, "welcome this. Because this means war. And we are ready."

Okay. Right.

This wasn't just not good.

This was *not good*!

"It has been a long time coming," Etienne whispered. "Vampires *hunt*. Vampires *feed*. Immortals should rule this planet, not be ruled by *rules*."

I fought it but I couldn't stop myself from trembling.

Etienne was far from done.

"We do not wish to take your kind as *mates*." He spat out the last word, and if I didn't already have a fair inkling about how he felt about "my kind," I would know by the way he spat that word. "We simply wish to take your kind whatever way we like, whenever we like. And this is how it will be."

Yes.

Not good.

I pressed my lips together.

Etienne kept going.

"Lucien, either wittingly or unwittingly, began that process. Everyone within our culture is positioning. Vampires who do not wish change and are willing to fight for status quo. Concubines who desire to keep their place as the parasites of our culture. Vampires who wish to be free to find their mates whatever form they take. And my brethren," again with the sweep of his arm, "wishing simply to be free to be vampires."

Well, one thing I could say about that: that was pure Lucien, doing what he wanted to do and damn the consequences.

When Etienne stopped and didn't start again, even though I didn't want him to continue, I nodded anyway.

So he continued.

"Do not fool yourself into thinking my son cares about you. He wants you to believe this, of course, it is the way with a taming. But it is not real."

Another body sway when the impact of his words slammed into me and he smiled. He was loving every second of this.

The bastard.

He went on but this time he did it quietly, slowly, savoring the pain he knew he was going to cause.

"He had his mortal mate. The delectable Maggie."

God. God! *God!*

"Maggie was captured, tortured and killed during The Revolution."

Oh no.

Oh God.

God. God! *God!*

"Maggie was my son's one and only true love. As sickening as that may be, it is the truth. Maggie's death was the reason Lucien was unstoppable during that conflict. Maggie's death was the reason he was unstoppable in hunting his own who would plot to resurrect the conflict. Maggie was everything to him. Maggie was his reason for being. Without Maggie, he exists. He does it well, he enjoys his life and the fruits of his endeavors, but it is simply existence. Nothing more. You, delicious Leah, he is using. Our lives are long, we must have our challenges, and even if you're simply breathing, you must find diversions to break up the monotony. That is what you are, Leah. A diversion. An enjoyable one, a succulent one, but simply a diversion."

Love is a blanket that keeps you warm.

Lucien knew that to be true because of Maggie.

We'd talked a lot. He'd spent time educating me. He'd told me stories of his family.

But he'd never mentioned Maggie.

I fought the tears that filled my eyes.

I didn't succeed.

And I hated it when Etienne grinned a triumphant creepy grin when he saw them slide down my cheeks.

"I will educate you about our taming," he said with false gentleness. "We have been forbidden to do this as well, but we all yearn for it. We all enjoy it. But once a taming is complete, we will take pleasure in the spoils of our victory and then we will retreat. Move on to the next taming, the next meal, the next diversion that makes a vampire's life sweet."

Every word, every single word he said was killing me.

Lucien had lied. He'd not only broken promises, he'd flat out *lied*.

From the beginning. The very beginning.

He'd played with me like a toy.

Like his *pet*.

He'd played with me.

The tears kept coming.

"You are nothing, Leah," Etienne whispered, his eyes boring into me. "A plaything now and always a parasite. But in the end, in the course of a vampire's life, a few years spent enjoying a morsel, we release you and in no time at all, we don't remember how you taste, what you look like, even your name."

More tears. That was all I had to give to what he was saying to me so that was all he got.

But he loved each salty drop.

"And now you understand your place, do you have any questions?" he asked.

"Is Edwina all right?" I asked in return and his eyes shifted behind me. Nestor must have made some nonverbal reply because they shifted back and he nodded.

I nodded back.

"That's all you wish to know?" he prompted when I said no more.

"I think you've been thorough," I whispered and heard Nestor's chuckle from behind my back, but I didn't turn.

I kept my eyes on Etienne.

"I'm pleased you think so," Etienne muttered, grinning his sadistic grin at me. "Now, we will be leaving."

I blinked.

Was he high?

Break into the Mighty Lucien's house and then just leave?

One could say I was thrilled beyond belief they were going, but Lucien was going to lose his mind!

He must have read my face for he carried on.

"You can tell him what you wish. We're prepared for his response."

Oh shit. That didn't sound good either.

"Yes, Leah, we are prepared. You can tell my son that too," Etienne whispered menacingly.

I swallowed again.

He kept going.

"And tell your aunts, your cousins, your friends to enjoy their lives as they are to their fullest. The days when a concubine could provide us nourishment for a spell then suck from *us* for the rest of their days are numbered. Do you understand me?"

Oh yes. I understood him.

Totally.

He didn't like mortals. But he *really* didn't like concubines.

Boy, I understood him all right.

I nodded.

"Good girl," he murmured patronizingly and bile slid up my throat.

He studied me. I stood still and let him, just happy that I'd quit crying.

"You know," he whispered thoughtfully. "It's almost sad, you mortals handing your hearts to vampires. It's been a long time since I've seen that look on a mortal's face after she learned of a vampire's true nature." He cocked his head to the side, his lips twitched, and he finished, "Thank you, delicious Leah, for giving that back to me."

I knew it then. He'd played with many women, scores of them, maybe hundreds of them. All of them just like his son had played me.

God, I hated him.

Hated him.

More than I hated his son and that was saying something.

He jerked up his chin, my body swayed and my hair flew back when they all sped by me.

I stood solid and staring at nothing.

Then it hit me.

Edwina.

I turned on my foot and ran to the dining room. I halted on a skid in the door when I saw her duct taped to a chair, more tape on her mouth, tears sliding down her cheeks, terror stamped on her features.

I shook myself out of my horror and dashed to her.

"I'm sorry, I'm sorry, I'm sorry, Edwina," I whispered. "In the movies they do this fast. I'm going to do it fast. Get it over with. Please, forgive me."

With that I tore the tape off her mouth. She cried out in pain and the sound cut through me.

"I'll get these off," I muttered, shaking the piece of tape away from my fingers and going to work on the tape at her wrists. "Are you okay?"

"I'm...no," she answered shakily.

No. Of course not. She wouldn't be.

"I'll just...I'll..." I stopped talking and my hands stopped moving.

You are nothing, Leah...a plaything...we don't remember how you taste, what you look like, even your name.

My eyes moved to Edwina's wet ones.

She read mine immediately.

"Leah, I heard him. Every word," she whispered.

Do not fool yourself into thinking my son cares about you. He wants you to believe this, of course, it is the way with a taming. But it is not real.

"Leah, listen to me. Don't believe what he says," Edwina urged, her voice insistent.

That is what you are, Leah. A diversion. An enjoyable one, a succulent one, but simply a diversion.

"Those vampires with him, they are few," Edwina kept whispering urgently. "Everyone knows of Etienne, no one respects him. Katrina was only here because she's angry. A week, a month, she'll rethink and she'll retreat. Nestor, Marcello, they have been enemies to Lucien for years. Jealous of his fame, his abilities, his fortune. They have allied with Etienne for no other reasons then to make Lucien suffer. Don't believe what he says, Leah. Not a word of it."

I didn't hear anything she said.

I heard Lucien telling me, *It will still be beautiful.*

I told him he had my love and he didn't return it. Still, he thought he could talk me into continuing to service him by convincing me the emptiness he could give me was fucking *beautiful.*

He'd had the love of his life. It sucked she was tortured and killed, but at least he'd had her.

I didn't have anything.

Nothing.

Everything had been taken from me.

Everything I had, everything I owned, everything I was.

Taken by Lucien.

I focused on Edwina's face.

"Please, someday, understand what I'm going to do now and forgive me," I whispered.

I straightened away from her and ran out of the dining room on my high-heeled, kickass wedges.

"*No!*" she cried. "Leah! No! Don't listen to him. Unbind me! *We must call Lucien immediately!*"

I ran to the phones first. Each one I grabbed and ripped free from the wall. Each one I ran to the pool and threw it in. Then I ran to the key hooks by the back door, grabbed Edwina's keys, went to her purse, snatched out her cell, and I took those to the pool too and threw them in.

I didn't have much time.

I had to hurry.

I ran upstairs and found the two suitcases I brought with me stored in the hall closet. I dragged them to the wardrobe. Quickly but carefully, I packed. Not the things Lucien bought for me (except my undies and nighties since I'd thrown all my old ones away seeing as the ones Lucien gave me were much nicer). Makeup. Shampoo. Lotion. Jewelry. Everything that was mine that I could see.

I shoved my phone in my bag, ran to the desk in the bedroom and grabbed my passport.

I dragged the bags down the stairs and didn't look into the dining room as I rolled them right past.

"Leah! Don't! Please call Lucien! Don't leave! If nothing else, it isn't safe!" Edwina called after me.

I felt like a bitch. Worse than a bitch, leaving her tied there. That was mean. It was selfish. It was ugly.

But I had no choice.

I had to get away.

I had to escape.

And Lucien could be home any minute.

Edwina was a nice lady so I hoped to God one day she'd forgive me.

I went out to the Cayenne and loaded up my bags. I got in and hit the garage door opener. I buckled my seatbelt and noticed belatedly my hands were trembling.

This wasn't the only thing trembling. My whole body was.

As were the tears in my eyes.

I forced my thoughts on what was next. Bank, drain the accounts where Lucien deposited my concubine plaything money. Find an ATM and take a maximum withdrawal from my account at home. Get out of Dragon Lake. Stop at the nearest used car dealership, ditch the Cayenne and get another car.

I made my plans then I executed them. Bank. Thank God, no line. ATM at the same place. Easy.

And as I drove out of Dragon Lake, I grabbed my cell and dialed 911.

"Nine-one-one, what's your emergency?" they answered.

"There's been a break in..." I told them the address where to find Edwina and finished with a whispered, "Hurry."

I disconnected the call, hit the button to roll down my window and threw my cell phone out.

I didn't know how it worked, but on TV they could track you with phones.

Not mine.

Not anymore.

Lucien would hunt me and he was within his rights to kill me.

I knew I'd see him again. I knew when I did he'd be infuriated. I knew it would be done, one way or another.

Done.

Over.

And I would be free.

22
The Secret

Lucien drove into the car park under his office building. He was furious.

The drive to his office took well over an hour. A four car pileup caused a massive backup with subsequent delays. More times than he could count, he stopped himself from turning around and going back.

Back home.

Back to Leah.

Back to explain things to her, smooth that hideous look out of her features, the pain out of her eyes, inject the life back into her voice.

But he couldn't. This was Gregor. Gregor was a member of The Council and with Gregor's alliance he could assist with making Leah safe. Twice, he'd postponed a set meeting and he'd done it to spend time with Leah. He couldn't delay again. Gregor was impatient, the meeting important, even imperative, he'd told Lucien through Avery.

He had to take the fucking meeting.

He guided the Porsche to its spot thinking she loved him. His Leah loved him.

He knew it. He knew it was happening. Not only because Stephanie warned him, Kate told him, but because he felt it.

And that was why he'd done what he'd done. Selfish in the extreme, but it was too beautiful, Leah's love. Better than her beauty. Better than her smell. Even better than her blood. It was like a drug. The feeling of ecstasy. Constant, from waking until sleep and even in his dreams, having her close.

Fuck.

Fuck!

He should have talked to her as Kate asked. As a priority.

He should have talked to her.

He parked, shut the Porsche down and exited the car without delay.

He needed to get this meeting done. He needed to get back home. Back to Leah.

I'm in love with you, Mighty Vampire Lucien.

The words pierced his brain as he closed the door to the car and he lost control. The door slammed to and the entire car shuddered and shifted four feet into the next, luckily vacant, spot.

He stared at his vehicle as it continued to rock then as it stopped. He closed his eyes, leaned into his forearms on the roof of the car and dropped his head.

Sweetling, look at me.

Please, get off me. Husky. Agonized.

Leah, sweetheart, please, look at me.

I shouldn't have said it. Forget I said it.

Look at me.

It didn't happen. Just wipe it from your mind. Go to your meeting. We'll both forget it and everything will be okay. Whispered. Desperate.

Agonized.

Desperate.

He'd done that. He'd made her feel those things. Being selfish. Taking and forgetting he couldn't give. Taking and forgetting his duty was to keep her safe. Taking what he couldn't stop himself from taking and forgetting to protect her, causing her agony, just like at her Bloodletting.

He'd never forget she'd said it. He'd never be able to wipe it from his mind. It was burned there, literally for eternity.

"Fuck," he whispered.

His eyes opened, he lifted his head and looked blindly through the car park.

He thought of Gregor. Not the impending meeting. Gregor's decision five hundred years ago.

Lucien had three choices. Keep taking from Leah. Make her his mate and put her in even more danger, conceivably making their nightmares come real.

Or, for her sake, release her.

No. He had only one choice.

The last.

Fuck.

He sucked in breath, straightened from the car and eschewed the elevator in order to race up the forty flights of stairs with vampire speed. If a mortal saw him and it came to the attention of The Council, fuck it. Let them fine him. In mere hours he was losing everything.

Everything.

He slowed when he hit the hall and stayed slowed as he opened the door and moved through his busy offices. He took out his cell and turned it off in preparation for the meeting while employees nodded to him, lifted their chins, Lucien returning the gestures.

He saw Sally behind her desk through the glass wall that exposed her office. She'd been in his employ for ten years. In that time she'd met and married her husband, had two children and lost her mother. In that time, he hadn't aged a day.

It was time to move on. Create new companies, sell his vast holdings to himself, distribute severance packages, references, let his workforce go and move. This time, he'd need to disappear, hire someone young and competent to act in his stead for twenty, thirty years. Then he'd need to go through the motions again, managing his holdings as a ghost. In sixty, seventy years, he'd resurface, or perhaps continue as a phantom looking after his fortune.

He'd been considering it awhile. He'd even planned to discuss the destination for their future home with Leah.

Now he decided Singapore. Magdalene had moved there three years ago. She loved it. And he'd never lived there. It was as good a place as any.

In order to protect the knowledge he was vampire, he'd done this times too numerous to count. It was a chore that was never less than trying. And every time he wished he could simply be who he fucking was and not be forced to engage in this aggravation.

He pushed through the glass doors to Sally's outer office. Sally looked up and smiled. Then she read his face and the smile died.

Therefore, instantly, she reported, "I've given them coffee and bagels, told them you called and explained your delay."

"Thank you, Sally," he muttered, moving to the glossy wood panel double doors that led to his office.

"Would you like fresh coffee?" she called to his back.

He'd had nothing but Leah's blood and he'd had her blood not knowing it was the last taste of her he'd ever have. He always savored her. If he'd known, he would have taken the time to savor more. Not just her blood, all that was her when she gave it to him.

"No coffee and no interruptions," Lucien answered, turning the knob and pushing open the door.

He took in the room before he closed the door behind him.

Cosmo leaning against the side of his desk, arms crossed, ankles crossed. Stephanie lounging in an armchair in the seating area at the side of the room, legs crossed, coffee cup in hand. Avery and Gregor both seated on the couch, Avery's posture relaxed but alert. Gregor, however, was lounged back like Stephanie, legs crossed, looking bored.

Lucien walked to the seating area as Cosmo pushed away from his desk and approached from the other side.

"I apologize for the delay. Traffic," Lucien muttered, stopping at the back of the vacant armchair across from Stephanie.

"These things happen," Gregor murmured, studying Lucien.

Lucien crossed his arms on his chest and leveled his eyes on Gregor, ignoring the others.

Rude, he knew, but he didn't give a fuck. He needed to get this done and he needed to go home and release Leah so she could begin healing from the wounds he'd willfully inflicted, enjoying every fucking second of it.

"Unfortunately I must apologize again. I know my postponements have been frustrating and today's delay the same, but the reasons for this meeting are now moot. This afternoon, I'll be releasing Leah from her contract."

He heard the swift hiss of Stephanie's indrawn breath at the same time he heard Cosmo's whispered, "What the fuck?" Both of these came with Avery growing more alert and Gregor's gaze turning sharp.

"I'm sorry?" Gregor asked softly.

"I'm releasing Leah," Lucien answered.

"Fucking hell, Lucien!" Stephanie snapped as she shot out of her chair. "What's going on?"

Lucien looked to Stephanie. "It's none of your concern."

Her eyes got big. "None of my concern? Are you *mad*?"

Lucien took in a long, slow breath and held her eyes, but he did not speak.

Stephanie didn't like that, leaned forward and demanded, "Answer me! Are you mad?"

"I'll repeat, Teffie, it's none of your concern."

"You *are* mad," she whispered, her eyes narrowing.

"Lucien even *you* cannot expect to tip our culture on its head after five hundred years of convention then, weeks later, change your mind on a whim," Cosmo put in, his voice low with anger.

Lucien's eyes moved to Cosmo as he spoke, and when he was done, he stated, "It's not a whim."

"What is it then?" Cosmo retorted.

"What it is, is none of your *fucking* concern," Lucien shot back.

"This is unbelievable," Stephanie hissed, and Lucien looked to her.

"Teffie, calm," Avery murmured.

Stephanie's head was a blur when she turned to Avery and shouted, "I will not be calm! We're on the cusp of *war*!"

"You're in love with her."

The room went still when Gregor spoke these words and Lucien's eyes moved to him.

"Yes," he confirmed without hesitation.

"Oh my God," Stephanie whispered.

"Jesus fucking Christ," Cosmo said softly.

"You know my choices, Gregor," Lucien stated calmly. "You're the only one in this room who does. I can keep her safe but for how long? The feeding I've done from her, it won't have had the chance to have much effect, give her a longer life. She has forty, fifty years left of mortal life. That's better than living whatever length of time I can keep her alive, doing it on the run and her life ending on a scaffold while she watches me burn. You know that better than anyone in this room. Therefore, this afternoon, I'm releasing her."

"How long have you known?" Stephanie asked quietly and Lucien's gaze went to her.

"The minute I saw her twenty years ago," Lucien answered.

"Why didn't you say anything?" Her voice was rising.

"Because I only admitted it to myself two minutes ago," Lucien replied.

Stephanie closed her eyes and dropped her head.

"Why?" Cosmo asked, and Lucien looked to him.

"Why?" he repeated.

"Yes, Lucien, *why*? If you love her, why are you releasing her?"

"You've never mated. Seven hundred and fifty-three years, Cosmo, you've been on this earth and not one woman, mortal or immortal, have you stood beside and exchanged blood and vows. When you do, you'll know why," Lucien returned.

"None of this was about the taming," Cosmo accused. "It's bullshit that you only knew two minutes ago you loved her. You've known it all along."

Lucien inclined his head. "On some level, yes. But I was denying it for Leah's safety. And bullshit it might have been, Cosmo, but you knew too. So did Stephanie. And Isobel. And anyone who really knows me. If you're honest, all of you knew I was doing this for more reasons than to tame and fuck a concubine."

"So on some level you knew you couldn't have her and she couldn't have you and you did it anyway," Cosmo reminded him.

"What I knew from what I had with Maggie was that having Leah for even a little while was better than not having her at all. Not only for me, but for her. And our time together proved me right. And I knew, this time, our time together would be short. So I knew I couldn't waste any. What I did not factor was that Leah would return my feelings so swiftly."

At this, understanding dawned. Lucien knew it when Cosmo flinched and turned his head away.

Lucien looked to Gregor.

"She shared she was in love with me today. As The Council is considering my request, I've reflected on this. My first instinct was to talk logic to her in an effort to prolong our Arrangement. But this is Leah. I know her better than that. She consumes life, she's ruled by emotion. She won't enjoy what we have for a short time. And she cannot know I reciprocate her feelings. If she does, she'll never let me go. And I'll not want her to. Thinking I don't share her love, she's already shut down on me. She's retreating in an effort to control the pain I've caused. I must release her for her sake. Therefore, I do not need The Council's permission. That said, if other vampires wish to indulge in a taming, you should know I will champion them."

"Please sit, Lucien," Gregor requested quietly.

Lucien shook his head. "I must get back to Leah."

"Please, Lucien. Sit," Gregor said more firmly.

"This is done. I must get back home."

Home.

Home.

Not anymore.

Fuck.

Fuck!

Gregor held his eyes.

Then he stated, "What I'm about to say is known by very few. A very *select* few. If anyone outside of that sacred circle and the occupants of this room ever speak of what I'm going to tell you, it won't matter which one of you shared the secret. All of you will be hunted. All of you will be captured. All of you will be tortured until you beg to be burned. Every member of your family will have the same fate. And everyone you love, immortal or," his eyes sharpened on Lucien's face, "mortal will share that fate too."

"Holy shit," Stephanie breathed, sitting back down.

"*Speak*," Lucien barked and Gregor lifted his chin.

His gaze swept the room as he announced, "Immortal history is a lie."

Lucien felt his eyes narrow.

"I beg your pardon?" Cosmo asked.

"Immortal history is a lie," Gregor repeated. "Millennia ago, a decision was made. There was much fighting. Bloody battle after bloody battle was waged. Immortals tortured, beheaded, burned. It was gruesome, it was destructive, and in the end it simply decimated the number of our species. Tragically. There were very few of us left. *Any* of us." He lifted a hand to gesture to Avery. "Vampires. Werewolves. Wraiths. Phantoms. Golem. The Wee. So the remainder of the species came to an agreement and made their decision. Many of our people need humans to survive. A way needed to be found that we could live amongst them peacefully. The battles were mostly fought over conflicts about domination. Being vastly stronger and extremely difficult to kill, there were immortals who felt our kind should rule mortals, and when I say that I mean enslave them. The others were bent on a more democratic co-existence, even if they knew it would mean hiding who we are."

"This is not news, Gregor. These ancient battles are known amongst all immortals. To this day it is a very ill-kept secret that there are those who still harbor these different political opinions," Lucien informed him.

"Yes, you do know of that, of course," Gregor stated, looking up at Lucien. "What you don't know is that the different species are not mutated from homo sapiens, a transmutation of wolf and human, an evolutionary process based on geography, or a metamorphosis of natural forces into human forms. Nor did we evolve to what we are today from primordial slime. We were made from magic."

"Holy shit," Stephanie breathed.

"That's ridiculous," Cosmo bit out.

Gregor looked to Cosmo. "It may seem so, but it's absolutely true. We are otherworldly. We are supernatural. There is no explanation for us. We are magic."

"Explain," Lucien growled and Gregor's eyes came to him.

"I cannot, Lucien. As I said, there is no explanation for us. There has been much research on the topic, but whenever and however we came into existence, in those ancient times there were no records kept. And there were so many of our species killed in these battles and the secret has been kept for so long, even the ancients who made the pact have since expired. If they knew the secret of our origin, they took it to their deaths."

"This can't be possible," Stephanie whispered.

"It isn't," Gregor informed her. "That's what makes it magic."

"If that's the case, explain how we share the same exact body structure as humans. We mate the same. Reproduce the same. Breathe, sleep and, for the most part, eat the same," Lucien demanded.

"I do not know the answer to that either. But think about it, Lucien," Gregor encouraged softly. "Each species does, indeed, share the same exact body structure as humans and yet, unless we are beheaded or burned, *we do not die*. On this earth, nearly everything dies eventually. Even the ancients who made that pact didn't die naturally. Some were killed and others killed themselves."

"We consume mortal blood to nourish us, keep us alive," Stephanie put in. "We'd die without it."

"You'd be weakened significantly. But you would not die. This is not a fact understood by our kind because none of us have tested this theory by abstaining. But it is nevertheless true," Gregor stated.

Stephanie's eyes got wide and Gregor carried on.

"But wraiths and phantoms consume mortal energy. How is that possible? It seems natural to us since we've known it for what seems like eternity, but, Stephanie, it...is...*not*. If you think about it logically, you know it too. Not to mention, werewolves are immortal and they don't consume anything mortal or anything different than mortals do. Except to say they consume a lot of it and metabolize it much faster."

"Why would immortals be told we're humans?" Stephanie asked. "Lying to us about who we are doesn't make sense."

"We already are different from humans and unfortunately that species is prone to fearing the unknown and we all know that fear often manifests unpleasantly. To convince immortals that they share integral parts with humans gave immortals a sense of humanity. A oneness with the other beings inhabiting this earth. Doing it built in immortals an affinity between the species. If you feel you've evolved from a species that is inferior to you, but you have the capacity to feel compassion, it would assist in eradicating urges to subjugate your inferiors because they are an extension of yourselves. And, for millennia, you must admit, this has worked very well."

"This is bloody insane," Cosmo muttered.

"Indeed but it's also absolutely true," Gregor returned.

"And this great secret," Lucien stated and Gregor's attention returned to him, "you're sharing this with us now because...?"

"Because of The Prophesies," Gregor answered.

"Oh shit. Here we go," Stephanie murmured and Gregor turned to her, his eyebrows snapping together.

"You know of The Prophesies?"

"No," she retorted. "But two minutes ago I learned I'm supernatural. It would stand to reason right on the heels of that you'd spout nonsense about prophesies. Fuck, Gregor, I'm hundreds of years old. I've read my fair share of books. With supernatural shit, there's always fucking *prophesies*."

Stephanie was pissed but she was also amusing.

Even so, Lucien did not laugh.

Gregor responded, "Well the ones you'll learn of today all have to do with The Three. The Three being The Sacred Triumvirate which includes a vampire whose strength and cunning know no equal, but who also has added abilities beyond any shared by his species. He will find his lifemate, a mortal woman of great spirit, who also has her own abilities. Those she was born with, one of which is the ability to absorb her mate's powers through his feeding."

The air in the room went thick and Lucien's gut wrenched as his chest squeezed.

Gregor wasn't finished.

"The second is the King of Werewolves who will find his lifemate and she too will have otherworldly powers. And the last is a werewolf, vampire hybrid whose mortal lifemate will also be exceptional."

"Werewolves and vampires cannot produce children," Cosmo declared.

"Yes, and neither can vampires and mortals, but if The Prophesies come true, Lucien will sire four children on Leah in the next ten years," Gregor returned.

Lucien couldn't have held back his reaction if he tried. But he didn't try. His hand shot out, his fingers curling tightly around the top of the chair in front of him.

"My God," Stephanie whispered.

Gregor looked to Lucien.

"Times are changing," he stated softly. "War is nearly upon us. And this is not a war amongst vampires who wish to be freed from the constrictions of the Immortal and Mortal Agreement against those who do not. It will be war amongst *all* immortals allied with mortals who will fight against the immortals who wish to rid the planet of their brethren who think differently than they do. Brethren who want to live amongst what their enemies consider their inferiors.

And our enemy wishes to enslave their inferiors to serve them in all ways. And, I'm sorry to say, Lucien, as you have endured much in your years, you and your Leah are part of The Three. A trio of lifemates who will be instrumental in stopping this or the six of you will perish trying."

Fuck.

Fuck!

"What does this mean?" Cosmo asked.

It was Avery who answered.

"This means it is time for immortals to make inroads *as immortals* into the mortal world. And to do this, this means The Council have already amended the Immortal and Mortal Agreement. It means that not only will vampires be free to tame their concubines, they will be free to tame any mortal they desire. And lastly," his eyes moved to Lucien, "they will again be free to mate with mortals officially. The Sentence has been done away with. They'll be making an official statement on Monday."

Lucien's hand released the chair, he turned and moved swiftly to the door.

"Lucien," Gregor called, Lucien stopped and turned back.

But not because of Gregor's call.

"Are these Prophesies written?" he demanded.

"They are," Gregor replied. "But—"

Lucien interrupted him, "I must get to Leah. Later, you'll arrange for me to read them."

"That's impossible," Gregor returned.

"Make it possible," Lucien clipped.

"You don't understand," Gregor said carefully.

"And you can explain it to me after I speak with Leah," Lucien retorted.

"I might be able to arrange for you to see some of them, but it is highly likely you'll only be allowed to see those Prophesies that do not concern you, but instead the other two sets of lifemates in The Triumvirate," Gregor explained.

"Pull strings, grease palms, exchange favors, but find a way for me to read those Prophesies," Lucien gritted.

"Luce, do you believe this nonsense?" Stephanie asked in disbelief and Lucien's eyes cut to her.

"That Leah's my lifemate?" he asked, Stephanie nodded, and Lucien finished, "Absolutely."

Stephanie's head jerked right before her eyes narrowed and that was right before she grinned.

"Okay, then do you believe about The Prophesies?" she queried.

"If anything is written about Leah and me, I want to read it whether it was written yesterday or three thousand years ago and whether I believe it or not," Lucien replied.

"Understandable," she muttered, still grinning.

"There is much still to talk about," Gregor cut in and Lucien's attention went to him.

"We'll arrange another meeting. Two weeks," he stated.

Gregor's eyebrows shot up. "Two weeks?"

"Gregor, I'm about to walk out of this office, go home and ask the woman I love to spend eternity with me. Yes, fucking two weeks, and consider yourself lucky I'm not going to arrange a fucking meeting until after two months."

Gregor's eyes dipped to his knees but not before Lucien saw them light.

Jesus, the vampire wasn't entirely cold and unfeeling.

This was good to know.

On that thought, the door opened and Lucien turned to it to see Sally's head stuck in.

His body went solid when he registered her pallor, her wide eyes and smelled her fear.

"I'm so sorry, Lucien. I know you said no interruptions, but Edwina's on the phone and she said it's a dire emergency."

Fuck, he'd turned off his cell for this meeting. And with Cosmo, Stephanie and Avery at the meeting, he'd necessarily but unwillingly left Leah unprotected.

Fuck!

He strode swiftly to his desk, forcing himself to do it at a mortal's pace, demanding to know, "What line?"

"One," Sally replied.

He yanked the phone out of its cradle and put it to his ear, hitting line one at the same time.

"Edwina."

"Lucien," she breathed, her voice hitching. "Oh, Lucien."

"Talk to me," he ordered.

"Your...your father, Ka-Katrina, Marcello and, um...I don't know his name, but there were four vampires here. They busted through the door. They—"

Fuck. No.

Oh fuck, no.

"Leah?" he barked.

"She's gone," Edwina whispered and Lucien's gut twisted as his free hand curled into a fist and his chest started to burn.

"Gone?" he whispered back, stunned at their audacity as well as livid. "They took her?"

"No, no...she left. They, your father that is, he said the most awful things to her, Lucien. You wouldn't...I couldn't even believe it. He told her such awful things. And he told her about some woman named Maggie."

Lucien closed his eyes as his fist tightened. He put it to his desk and leaned into it.

Edwina kept talking.

"He...he...oh Lucien, I'm sorry to tell you this about your own father, but...he *touched* her."

Lucien opened his eyes but he saw nothing but red.

"He *touched* Leah?"

"Oh fuck." He heard Stephanie whisper but Edwina was again talking.

"He touched her and he spoke to her, such vile things. She was... she was crying, Lucien. It was...oh goodness, the look on her face. I'll never forget it. I tried to explain, but she...I'm sorry, she packed her things and left. She was so desperate to get away, she left me tied up, but called the police to come get me. They're here now. They got here just minutes ago. I called you as soon as I—"

"Do not leave. Do not make a complaint to the police, but keep them there until I'm home. I'll bring others with me so you'll be safe."

"All right, Lucien," she whispered. "I, uh...you should know, your father said they would be prepared for your response."

Fuck.

"Did they harm you?" he asked belatedly.

"They scared me and taped me to a chair. It hurt when they ripped the tape off, but I'm fine."

They would burn for the hurt Edwina endured when the tape was ripped off.

They would scream before they burned for attacking Leah.

And his father would beg for his life to end.

And he'd do this for a long fucking time.

"I'll be home in twenty minutes," Lucien told her.

"All right."

He put the phone down and turned to see Avery and the three vampires all on their feet.

"What do you need from us?" Cosmo asked immediately.

"You hunt Katrina," Lucien ordered.

Cosmo's face went hard but he nodded.

Lucien looked to Stephanie. "You bring me Marcello."

Stephanie smiled a humorless smile before she nodded.

Lucien looked to Gregor. "There was another vampire there. I want to know who he was."

Gregor simply nodded.

Lucien looked to Avery. "Gregor finds out, he tells you. You send Rafe."

Avery tipped up his chin.

"They're expecting you," Lucien warned all of them.

"We heard," Cosmo replied.

Lucien nodded and looked at Avery. "I'll need you to follow me. Guard Edwina."

Avery lifted his chin.

Lucien moved to the door.

"Are you hunting your father?" Stephanie asked his back.

"No, he can wait," he turned, hand on the doorknob and looked at Stephanie, "I'm hunting Leah."

He heard her indrawn breath but he walked out the door.

23
The Vow

My eyes on the television set, I pulled the two scrunched pillows I was holding deeper into my body. I was curled tight around them, my neck bent, my cheek resting on the rough material.

The TV wasn't set too loud. This was because I wanted to hear what was happening outside. Not that I could get away if Lucien caught up with me. I just wanted the half a second I'd have to prepare myself to die.

But my mind wasn't on the TV.

My mind, as it had been for days, was on everything.

Would I be able to sleep that night, alone in a bed in a hotel room after spending weeks sleeping every night curled into a vampire?

Where would I go tomorrow? North, south, east, west? Canada? Mexico?

Should I take the chance to phone my family? I'd left nine days ago and it was likely they'd been informed I'd escaped and they were probably worried about me. Not to mention, it would be my last chance to speak to them if Lucien was enraged when he caught up with me, went the way of the vampire and took my life. I clearly didn't know him (at all), but what I now knew of him, I convinced myself he would go the way of the vamp.

And lastly, wondering how much time I had and if I should just stop moving, let him catch me and be done with it.

I was ready to die and this was messing with my head too. It was sick and crazy, but I was tired, hungry, heartbroken, on the run, and I knew to my soul my future was fucked. I'd fallen hard for a vampire who'd spent months playing me against me. And I was just *so* done with it.

But weirdly, considering what Lucien had done to me, I had to admit that a lot of my headspace was taken up with worry about things his father had said. Things that meant Lucien was in danger in a variety of ways.

I shouldn't care, I knew it.

But I did.

I was totally messed up.

And then there was the incessant beating myself up. Asking myself why I was so stupid. Asking myself when would I learn.

I tried to cut myself some slack. He *was* Lucien and there weren't a lot of men like him (in fact, none). He'd worked hard at it, vowed to break me. And a vampire vow was a bond. So, obviously, he pulled out all the stops to succeed.

But I couldn't cut myself any slack. My decisions were my own. My capitulation was on me. My flight and the consequences of it were mine to bear. I knew it would hurt my family, which made it harder for me not to call them. But I told myself, if what Etienne said was true, it might be time for the Buchanan women to get out of the concubine business.

I stared unseeing at the TV. This was the ninth hotel room I'd been in. I'd splurged this time. I'd stayed in crappy places off the beaten track the last eight nights. But I was tired. I'd had little sleep. This place wasn't great and it certainly wasn't the luxury I'd grown accustomed to. It was old, but at least it was clean. I needed clean. I needed sleep.

Hunger pains gnawed at my gut, but I knew I couldn't eat. I'd tried. The thought of it made me nauseous and the one time I tried to eat something it made me flat out sick. So I stopped trying.

I just drove wherever my hands on the steering wheel took me. I drank loads of coffee to stay awake. Then I found a place to settle in and pray for sleep.

But sleep eluded me.

I was so damned tired. I'd never been that tired. That hungry.

I'd never been that heartbroken.

I missed him. I missed my vampire who would never be mine. I missed him every second of every day I was away from him.

And I hated myself for it.

I felt the tears gather in my eyes and I blinked them away, trying to concentrate on the TV screen.

This didn't work. I knew it but I didn't give up. Every night, the tears came, and no matter how I'd struggle to beat them, they'd always silently fall.

If this was a romance novel and he wasn't Lucien, I could believe we were lifemates. My tears and heartbreak weren't about knowing I was on the run from the man I loved who would find me and kill me. They were about losing the man I loved (see? Messed up!). I'd never felt this way when a relationship ended with one of my other boy-friends. I didn't even know you could feel this badly. I didn't know this kind of pain existed.

I wished I still didn't know.

I was cold. I was wearing a pale pink cotton nightgown that fell to my knees and had a wide v-neck and short sleeves. I'd stopped and bought a few and some underwear so I could throw away the stuff Lucien gave me. To try to warm up, I curled my knees tighter to my chest. I was too exhausted even to move to get under the covers.

The tears slid out the sides of my eyes making the TV screen blurry and I sighed.

I wondered, if I actually managed to get to sleep, if I'd have the nightmare. I hadn't thought of that when I took off and each night this thought also served to keep me awake. But in the snatches of broken sleep I was able to get, it didn't come.

I knew what this meant. We'd been connected, even if it was in a fucked-up way.

Now we were not.

Who would have thought I'd ever want that dream back?

It stunk but I did. I wanted any connection to him. Even a connection that might bizarrely kill me.

Jeez, I was messed up. Totally.

I sighed again, the tears slowed and my eyelids started to feel heavy.

Yes. Sleep, please. I needed sleep.

The tears stopped and my eyelids drooped.

Yes, sleep.

I blinked slowly and closed my eyes.

Then, thankfully, nothing.

I woke and instantly knew he was there because I could feel his fingers wrapped around my ankle.

Knowing I wouldn't succeed but doing it anyway, I tensed for flight.

I felt my ankle jerked. Suddenly, my body was on its back and the weight of Lucien was on top of me. He had his long fingers around my jaw, his palm warm against my throat.

I'd fallen asleep with the lights on. I could see him right there, his face an inch away, his eyes filled with heat.

Hungry.

I felt my heart hammering in my chest, fear burning through me, my fingers and legs tingling.

"Leah," he whispered, my name coarse on his lips.

I didn't speak. I waited for whatever would befall me. It sucked but I was ready.

Nine days. It took him nine days to find me. I was surprised and impressed. Not impressed in a good way, but still, that was pretty unbelievable.

"I haven't fed in nine days, sweetling," he murmured.

Sweetling.

Still persisting in this charade when we both knew it was *way* over.

God, I hated him.

But this surprised me. I vaguely wondered why he hadn't fed. Then again, if he was going to drain me dry, he'd need to be super hungry.

"Sweetheart, I need to feed," he whispered.

I swallowed, my throat moving against his palm, my mind hazy with exhaustion, wondering why it seemed he was asking for permission to kill me.

Maybe it was some crazy vampire tradition.

I did the only thing I could do. And anyway, I might as well get it over with.

I turned my head to the side, exposing my neck, his hand moving with me.

I just hoped he anesthetized me. I didn't want to die but I *really* didn't want to experience that agonizing pain before doing it.

I sensed his head dip but I definitely felt his tongue move up my neck.

I licked my lips. That felt good and I was pleased he didn't intend to hurt me unduly before he killed me. But as good as it felt (and it felt *great,* as always, which also sucked) I wouldn't allow myself to react.

His tongue moved down.

I felt the numbness then I felt him feeding.

My eyes closed slowly and I finally found it fortunate I was so tired. I didn't have the energy or strength to react no matter how good it felt.

His hand moved. His thumb tenderly gliding over my lips, his fingers drifting over my cheek, down my jaw, down to wrap around the side of my neck and pull me up as he deepened the suction.

God, I used to love it when he did that. And even right then, as exhausted as I was, I felt a faint tingle in my nipples and between my legs.

His thumb moved, stroking my throat and that, I thought, was so Lucien. Even while killing me, he was playing the game, pretending gentleness, giving me something beautiful.

My eyes opened slowly and just as slowly closed again. I was so exhausted. I wasn't going to fight no matter how futile it would be. I had nothing left in me. I wasn't even going to stay awake through my death.

This, I decided, was probably good.

Lucien's weight, his heat, his feeding, his big warm hand at my neck, his thumb stroking soothingly, his other arm wrapped around me tight, my eyelids fluttered one last time.

So he'd give me a beautiful death.

That was Lucien too.

I let go, allowed the glory of his feeding to overwhelm me and drifted into oblivion.

"It may take a few days. I need to see to Leah."

As I swam toward consciousness, I heard Lucien's deep voice saying these words quietly.

Then I heard, "I don't know. What I do know is she hasn't been seeing to herself. Nine days and she's lost an alarming amount of weight. Her color is not good, there are shadows under her eyes, and she fell asleep during a feeding." There was a pause and then, "Yes, Teffie, *during.*"

I struggled against the weight of the fatigue that still held me in its grip. This was aided by the fact I was held snug and tight to Lucien's side, part of my body on top of his, my cheek resting on his chest.

Lucien kept talking.

"I'll be moving her to a decent hotel, feeding her, getting her rest. Then we'll be talking. I don't want to start the journey home until I'm satisfied she's fit for it. So hold them. I'll deal with them when I return." Another pause then, "If you wish. Play with them all you like."

What was he talking about?

And more importantly, why was I alive and being held snug and tight to Lucien?

My eyes opened and I blinked.

Lucien's arm around my back shifted, his hand drifting up my spine, his fingers tangling in my hair.

"She's awake, Teffie. I'll phone you later when I know more."

His fingers moved, twisting a lock, and my heart skipped a beat.

"Right. We'll speak soon."

I heard a beep and I knew he was done.

I had a second to process this before Lucien shifted. He ended settled on his side, his other arm going around me, pulling me up so my head was not on his chest but on the pillow and I was eye to eye with him.

God, his eyes were beautiful. Nine days and I thought I remembered everything, but I forgot just how beautiful his eyes were.

"You slept deep, sweetling. How do you feel?" he asked gently, his fingers still playing in my hair, his other arm holding me close to his heat.

"Uh...what's going on?" I whispered cautiously.

"You're about to tell me how you feel," he replied.

"Well...uh..." I trailed off.

He hadn't killed me. In fact, looking at him, he didn't look angry at all. He looked like Lucien except better. *Way* better. His eyes filled with concern and a warmth so deep I'd never seen anything like it. His face was soft. His voice was gentle and quiet.

Was this part of the taming? Your prey figured it out, took off, and you got to go after her and do it all over again?

Oh God, I hoped that wasn't it. Like, I really, *really* hoped that wasn't it. Seriously, I preferred it if he'd kill me.

"When's the last time you ate?" Lucien asked when I trailed off and didn't start again.

"You mean, ate and kept something down?" I asked back and watched his eyes flash and his mouth go hard.

Oh boy.

"Yes, the last time you ate and kept it down," he replied, his voice now tight but somehow not menacing.

"Well, the night before..." Oh shit. I didn't want to go where I had to go. Well, I had to say it because I knew he wouldn't let it go. "The night before I took off."

"Ten days," he murmured, surprising me when he looked thoughtful, not angry at my mention of my escape, his arms going tight, his eyes moving over my face, then they locked on mine. "That was foolish, my pet."

Okay. Now. Seriously.

What was happening?

"We need to get you food," he declared. "Do you have the strength to go with me to a restaurant or do you wish for me to go and bring something back? If the latter, tell me what you'd like. And I'll warn you, you've slept twelve straight hours, not counting however long you were asleep before I found you. It's not morning. It's one in the afternoon."

Learning this, I felt my eyes go wide as my lips parted. Then I felt my stomach flutter when he took in this look, his face again went soft and his fingers stopped playing in my hair and fisted gently in it.

Still, he'd just asked me what I wished and inferred he'd go off and do as I asked.

Was this a new tactic?

"Uh..." I mumbled, not alert enough to process this, defend myself, figure out what was happening. Not alert enough for anything.

He rolled me so I was on my back, he was looming over me, but his torso was deep in mine and his face was super close.

"Leah, my love, we cannot delay in getting you fed and rested. We need to get back home. There is much we need to discuss, but more, there is much that needs to be done. Teffie and Cosmo have captured Katrina and Marcello. The Council has sanctioned their torture and burning and I need to get back and see to that. So now I need to find you food, feed you, get you in a decent bed with sheets that don't feel like cardboard, you need to rest, we need to talk then we need to go home."

Okay, there was a lot there.

First, he'd called me his "love." He'd never done that. Never, ever, ever.

Second, The Council sanctioned torture and burning?

Third, Lucien was going to "see to that?"

"What's going on?" I repeated.

"Leah—"

"Lucien," I cut him off. "What is *going on?*"

"We'll talk about it later, after you've eaten, you have some of your strength back, and we've moved to a different hotel."

"We'll talk about it now."

"Later, Leah."

"Now, Lucien!" I snapped, still fatigued, definitely, but not so fatigued I was going to fall for his games. Not again. And he needed to know that. "I want to know what's going on, now, not later. I don't want to die 'at home' as you put it. I don't understand why you're delaying it. I don't get why you're still playing me. Just do it. Drain me and get on with your life."

His brows shot up. "Drain you?"

"Yes," I hissed. "I knew when I left that you'd hunt me and I knew leaving you gave you the right to feed until I was dead. So what are you waiting for?"

His brows knitted, his eyes narrowed, but contradictory to the ominous look stamped on his features, his hand left my hair to frame the side of my face.

And furthering his contradictions, his voice was soft and sweet when he replied, "I'm annoyed with you for making the very unwise decision to attempt to escape me considering the danger you knew was inherent being away from me when you might dream. Not to mention, you and Edwina had been attacked by vampires who stated vile intentions, so you also knew the dangers were not singular, but many. Nevertheless, it would be reckless of me to punish you for carrying through this rash decision by killing you, my pet, considering that would significantly fuck with my plans for spending eternity with you."

I stopped breathing.

Yes, stopped breathing.

Entirely.

So it came out in a gust of air when I forced a, "What?"

Lucien smiled and he used his whole face to do it. I'd never seen him smile that openly and the effect was staggering.

Still smiling, he dipped his face closer to mine and whispered, "I plan to spend eternity with you."

I stared and whispered back, "You do?"

He nodded. "I do."

"I...I..."

Oh my God!

Was he serious? Or was this another game?

"How? Why? When did you...? But you can't," I stammered.

"I can," he replied.

"But, it's against the rules," I reminded him.

"The rules have changed," he informed me.

Oh boy. Here we go again. Lucien doing whatever he wanted to do and fuck the consequences.

"Lucien—"

Suddenly he wasn't lying on top of me and I wasn't on my back.

He was on his ass in the bed and I was straddling him. One of his arms was tight around my back holding my body close to his. His other hand had sifted in my hair, cupping the back of my head and holding my face super close to his.

The instant he got us in this position, before I processed I was in it and therefore was by no means ready for what he was going to say next (not that I ever would be), he stated, "I'm in love with you, sweetheart."

Oh my God!

Was he...?

No.

No!

"Don't," I whispered, pain piercing through me, and I watched Lucien blink.

"Don't?" he whispered back.

"Don't do it again. Don't play me," I explained quietly and I watched the gentleness fade from his features as fury infused them.

I braced.

"I'm in love with you," he repeated.

"Don't," I whispered, that word breaking in the middle, and his hold on me tightened mightily.

"Leah...I'm...in...*love with you*," he growled. I opened my mouth but his arms squeezed so hard all breath left me. "He lied to you. My father *lied*. I told you I did not respect him and you knew he was not a man to be respected. Eating lunch with him, you figured it out. And at lunch, he was on his best behavior. During the attack, he treated you to exactly the vampire he really is. He lied, Leah. Edwina told me what he said and what he said to you about what's between you and me, every bit of it, was a fucking *lie*."

I wanted to believe that.

I really did.

But...

Before I could even think through my "but," Lucien sensed there was one and kept talking.

"There are things I'll explain more fully when I've seen to the woman I love, but for now, The Council has amended the Immortal and Mortal Agreement. Vampires are again free to take mortal mates. And I'm taking my mortal as mate. You love me. I love you. We're connected. What we have is beautiful and that's all it'll ever be. For eternity. Until the end of days. Until the sun falls from the sky, all you and I will share is beauty."

I felt my heart leap, tears fill my eyes and hope suffuse my system.

But what came from my mouth was simply a whispered, breathy, "Please."

I didn't even know why I said it, but Lucien did.

So he replied in a voice filled with tenderness, "Yes, my love. I'm not lying. I am not playing you. Swear to God, this is all truth." He pulled me even closer. "I love you, Leah. I've loved you for twenty years and I'll love you for eternity. My beautiful Leah, listen closely. What I say is pure truth. And on this truth, you have my vow."

The tears slid out of my eyes, coursing down my cheeks. I knew Lucien saw them but his eyes never left mine.

And mine didn't leave his.

I looked deep. I felt his arms around me, his big strong body, and I paid close attention to the wonder of his vow sinking deep.

He loved me.

The Mighty Vampire Lucien *loved me.*

Oh God.

That felt *great.*

I pushed my hands that were trapped between us up until my fingers could curl around his neck and I whispered, "You can be bossy and annoying. I can just be annoying. We're going to fight. So my guess is, we'll clash, like *a lot.* Therefore it will be awesome, but it won't be an eternity of *just* beauty."

I barely got the last syllable out before his hand at my head crushed my mouth down to his. Our lips opened, our tongues dueled, and then I was on my back giving everything to my vampire and experiencing the beauty of finally, *finally* getting everything from my vampire in return.

And, let me tell you, it was *amazing.*

After a long time, he lifted his head and I dazedly opened my eyes to see his heated but gentle, searing into me.

"Right. That's done," he declared. "Now tell me, what do you fucking want to eat?"

I stared up at my vampire.

Then I burst out laughing.

I blinked the sleep away hearing from a distance Lucien talking and I knew he was again on the phone.

I stared across the sheets that did not, by a long shot, feel like cardboard.

Lucien had fed me. After our kiss, suddenly ravenous in a way that didn't mingle with nausea, I'd asked for burritos. Lucien told me burritos were out of the question considering I should have something bland and filled with vitamins and energy in my stomach after not eating for ten days. I told him I had a craving for burritos. He told me there was no way in hell I was getting burritos. I asked him why he asked me what I wanted when he was going to get me what he thought I should have anyway. He kissed me until I was dazed, left me in bed and came back fifteen minutes later with a bunch of bananas and a jar of chunky peanut butter.

I sat cross-legged in bed, using a plastic knife to gouge out peanut butter and glop it on my two bananas, eating them all the while glaring at Lucien, who was seeing to the not taxing chore of packing up my things.

I didn't admit to him I loved bananas and peanut butter and it tasted awesome. I also didn't admit it filled me up and made me feel human for the first time in days.

I dressed. Lucien dragged my stuff to his Porsche. We got in and he drove us forty-five minutes to the nearest city. Upon entering the city, like it had a homing beacon and Lucien was the receptor, he guided us straight to what had to be the most exclusive hotel in the city. He valet parked, grabbed one of my bags and his only bag and walked us in. He then proceeded to check us into the presidential suite which had its own butler (no joke!).

We took the elevator up and Lucien let us in.

It was phenomenal. I lived in a mansion and the man who loved me was a billionaire, and still, I'd never seen anything so opulent.

Lucien ordered me to take a shower and get in bed. I told Lucien I wanted to explore our sumptuous suite. He repeated he wanted me in the shower then in bed. I told him it would take ten whole minutes for me to look around so he should just keep his pants on.

Approximately three second later, both Lucien and I were naked, in the shower and he was turning on the water.

At least I got to see the bathroom before he led me to the bedroom and gave me one of his long-sleeved tees. He then made a point by digging through my bags and depositing my new nighties right in the trash. His point being discount department store nighties were not good enough for his Leah. I rolled my eyes but I didn't protest. They were cute and comfy. What they were not was the finest silk and lace. He then ordered me to bed.

Unfortunately, after a long hot shower with Lucien, I had nothing in reserve.

I pulled on his tee, crawled in bed, and slept.

This brought me to now. It was dark in the room but there was light coming around the not entirely closed door to the sitting room.

I felt rested but again starved. Tossing back the covers, I listened to his murmurings as I hit the bathroom. It was bigger than the living room in my old condo.

Wow. Really, this suite was *it*. I wanted to live there.

I did my thing, wandered out through the bedroom and to the door.

Before I got the door open, I knew Lucien's eyes were on it. I knew this because when the door was open they were on me. He was sitting in the chair at the desk. His cell held to his ear, he lifted up his chin to me then gestured with his hand to his lap.

I wandered his way, pushing up the sleeves of his tee.

When I got within reaching distance, Lucien reached, my ass was in his lap and his arm was wrapped around me.

"No, I'll do it," he said into the phone as I settled in, cheek to his shoulder, my forehead pressed to his neck. His arm got tighter. "I understand," he went on. "But it will be me who hunts him."

I sighed.

Lucien's arm got tighter.

His voice was quiet when he continued, "Julian, I know this attack was perpetrated on the family. And yes, normally you would be correct that every member of the family is within their rights to exact vengeance. And you know I appreciate your and Bel's show of loyalty. You both can be there when I deal with him. But it will be me and only me who hunts Etienne."

Well, the good part of that was that Julian and Isobel had their father and my backs and clearly thought of me as family.

The bad part was that Lucien was intending to hunt down his father.

I wasn't entirely surprised by this. He loved me and I loved that he loved me. I was certain it was partly about that. But his father had touched me, scared me and was just plain old mean to me. I knew Lucien enough that I knew he wouldn't let that be.

I didn't like Etienne. He scared the beejeezus out of me. Still, hunting him down, torturing and burning him was pretty extreme.

"Right," Lucien continued. "Leah is up, she needs to eat then I need to feed. I'm turning my cell off now. I want no further interruptions tonight. I'll phone you tomorrow."

He needed to feed and he wanted no further interruptions.

I liked this idea.

"Goodnight, Julian. My love to Bel," he muttered.

I heard a beep then I saw his phone clatter on the desk.

I lifted my head to look at him.

"Is it time to talk?" I asked.

"No," he answered, reached out to the hotel phone on the desk, grabbed the receiver and put it to his ear. Then he stated, "We're ready to order dinner."

Without another word, he put it down.

"That was kind of abrupt," I told him.

"I don't have the time or inclination to befriend a man I'll see occasionally the length of our stay here and never see again. You're rested. Your color is back. You're sitting in my lap with no underwear on. We were separated for nine days and reunited for one, the vast majority of which you've been sleeping. I want you fed and you'll eat sitting next to me not wearing any underwear. Then I want to feed and do it while I'm inside you. You need your strength. That, at the moment, is all I have time for."

I was blinking at him, half turned on (okay, fully turned on) when out of nowhere a man wearing a spiffy hotel uniform walked into the room.

Lucien wrapped me tight in both arms and looked up at him.

"Dinner, sir?" he prompted.

"Thank you," Lucien replied then launched into it. "A French baton. Pâté fois gras with truffles. Two fillet mignons rare with béarnaise sauce. Sautéed potatoes. Fine greens. Rolls. A bottle of red, a Bordeaux. This followed with two chocolate crème brûlées and a bottle of Moët."

It seemed while I was sleeping that Lucien had familiarized himself with the menu and it was clear he was in the mood for French food. This was good since all that sounded *great*.

"Yes sir," the hotel butler murmured.

"Bring the crème brûlées and Moët half an hour after you serve the main and then don't disturb us for the rest of the night."

He nodded, muttering, "As you wish," and moved out of the room.

Okay, that was still abrupt, but one could not say this presidential suite business wasn't totally cool.

On that thought we were up, me held in Lucien's arms and he was striding across the room. I barely got my arms around his shoulders when we were down again. Me on my back in the couch, Lucien partially on me, partially with his side in the seat. His head was up, his eyes on me, and he lifted a hand, trailed a finger down the side of my face then curled all of them around my neck.

"You remembered the béarnaise sauce," I whispered.

"Of course," he whispered back. "We've something to celebrate, if belatedly."

I felt my nose begin to sting as I whispered, "They'll probably make it better than me."

"Undoubtedly."

I grinned but it faded and I ordered, "Tell me you love me."

His hand slid up my neck, my jaw, to cup my cheek as his head dipped closer.

"I love you, sweetling."

Dinner sounded great.

But those words sounded better than anything.

I sighed, my arm moving around him, and I turned to my side. Lucien shifted with me so we were face to face and in each other's arms.

"Why didn't you say it before?" I asked.

"Because I couldn't," he answered immediately. "Because I hadn't admitted it to myself. Not when you gave that to me. Not before. Not for twenty years. If I admitted it to myself twenty years ago, I wouldn't allow myself to have you because I knew if I did, I wouldn't let you go. When I had you, I wouldn't admit it again because I wouldn't let you go. I was already flying in the face of the rules of The Dominion with what I would allow us to have. They were going to accept that, I knew. They owe me. But they'd never allow me to take you as mate. We could do it, but they would hunt us, eventually find us, and we'd be given The Sentence. I had to protect you from that." His eyes went strange and I knew why when he finished, "But it seems I failed at protecting you from everything."

"It worked out in the end," I whispered reassuringly on an arm squeeze.

"Yes," Lucien replied, not looking or sounding very reassured.

I decided to change the subject to a far happier one. "Why did they change their minds so suddenly about immortals mating mortals?"

"They had their reasons," he answered vaguely.

It had to be said, I wasn't in the mood for vague. I'd had a lot of vague, not to mention seriously vague (in other words, stuff kept from me). Therefore I was *so* over vague.

"Seems strange," I probed, "all the trouble they took, all the heartbreak they caused, five hundred years and then, *poof,*" I fluttered a hand in the air, "whatever. Mate with mortals. We don't care."

Lucien grinned then clarified, "All right, my love, how about they had very good reasons."

"War?" I whispered.

"Yes, amongst other things."

"Etienne told me about their plans and—"

"Don't worry about it."

Don't worry about it? Was he crazy?

"Lucien, what he told me was pretty scary. And they didn't say it straight out, but it seemed you're a specific target. How am I not supposed to worry about that?"

His arms gave me a squeeze and his voice was low and firm when he repeated, "Leah, my love, don't worry about it. You know I can take care of myself. What I must do is be certain I take better care of *you*."

That was nice, very nice.

Still, I studied him and I did it closely.

Then I noted, "You're not going to share, are you?"

"Not now, no. I need to have a meeting with a member of The Council, discuss things, and if it's safe for you to know, I'll tell you."

I had a feeling I had no choice but to leave it at that. So I left it at that and changed the subject again.

"You didn't feed," I whispered and his arms gave me another squeeze.

"You don't like me taking from anyone but you. I don't like to feed from anyone but you. So I didn't feed until I found you."

God, that was *so* sweet.

"Thank you," I said softly and Lucien leaned into me to touch his mouth to mine.

When he pulled away again, I held his eyes.

I didn't want to go where we had to go but we had to go there. We were starting an eternity together. There were a few things to get straight.

"You kept a lot from me," I said quietly, trying not to make an accusation sound like one.

"I did, pet, and I'm sorry," he replied.

"Why?" I asked.

Lucien sighed then pulled me closer. "First, I didn't tell you about the restrictions against physical intimacy and living together because I knew you well already. And knowing you, I knew I had my hands full. I didn't need you having more ammunition to use to keep yourself from me."

This, I had to admit, was true.

"Second, I didn't tell you about Maggie because it served no purpose."

"It's a part of you, a part of your history," I reminded him. "And I was falling in love with you. But even if I wasn't, we were sharing our lives together and would be doing so for a while. You already knew everything about me and you had to know I wanted to know everything about you.

"I did, sweetheart, but I'll remind you we've known each other a very short time and only a small portion of that has been time you've let me in. I cannot say, had my father not intervened, if I would have told you. But it's likely. You're right, I intended for you to be a part of my life for years to come, which would mean you being around my friends and family. There was a high probability someone might let something slip. Secrets have a way of revealing themselves, and I tell you true, when you learned about Maggie, I would have wanted it to come from me."

"I believe you," I said softly and that got me Lucien's smile.

He went on gently, "Edwina told me what my father said. And part of it is true. I loved her. I thought I'd spend the rest of eternity with her and I was happy with that. We were together for seventy-five years. I was a young vampire when I met her but I knew my heart and her place in it."

Okay, suddenly, I didn't want to know so much about Maggie.

Lucien read my face and gathered me even closer as he leaned into me, pressing me partially on back and he kept going.

"But she died, Leah. Her death incensed me and I avenged it. It took decades, blood was spilled, lives were lost, but I avenged Maggie's. And baring this to you, you also need to know that until very recently, I had not recovered from her loss. That was how much I loved her. She was a good woman and she made me happy."

My face must have given something away because Lucien got closer and his arms got tighter.

"She was a good woman, my love, and she made me happy. I missed her. I hate having the knowledge in my brain that she endured what she endured prior to her death at the hands of my people simply because she fell in love with a vampire. And that love will always be true. But I have not lied to you the times I told you I'd never had more beautiful than what I have with you. You are what I've been looking for for five hundred years. You and me, we were meant to be. Maggie was my mate, but she is gone. *You* are my lifemate."

I sucked in breath as my heart flipped over and whispered, "You believe in lifemates?"

"I didn't until the day you told me you loved me and I could no longer deny I felt the same for you. Then I did. Absolutely."

His tone was firm, his eyes held mine, his gaze was unwavering and intense.

He meant it.

Absolutely.

"Even running from you, believing your father, still, the pain I felt losing you, I often thought if we were in a romance novel, we'd be lifemates," I admitted.

Lucien's eyes grew warm and his arms relaxed.

"I'm sorry you lost her and the way you lost her, Lucien," I whispered.

"I am too," Lucien whispered back.

I kept going. "And I'm sorry I believed Etienne, took off and didn't talk to you."

His lips twitched and he repeated, "I am too."

"Still," I started to defend myself, "you kept things from me and—"

His hand came up to curve around my jaw and his thumb slid to press against my lips.

"My father attacking you was his decision, he carried it through, and he'll bear the consequences." His thumb slid from my lip and along my cheek. "But you are correct. It was me who kept things from you, even after the taming was complete, which left it open for my father to plant those seeds. That was my error in judgment. And I left you unprotected. I didn't think I would be gone that long. I had no idea they were lying in wait to instigate their plan. And even if they did, I must admit I'm shocked that any of them touched you, even my father. Scared you. Warned you. Threatened you. Shared things with you I was keeping from you. Yes. Touched you. No. Not any of them and especially not my father."

"Maybe we should talk more about this," I suggested. "What are you planning?"

"Marcello and Katrina have been caught, as you know. They're holding them awaiting me. Cosmo and Rafe are hunting Nestor. They will hold him too. I will deal with them then I'll hunt my father and deal with him."

"Deal with them how, uh...*exactly*?"

His mouth went hard, his eyes started burning in a scary way that (yes, I'm deranged) was totally fabulous, and he answered immediately, "I will torture them until they scream their pleas for me to burn them. Then I will burn them."

I wasn't certain how I felt about that.

So I turned, pressing myself to him, and whispered, "Darling, isn't that a bit—?"

He interrupted me. "It is my culture, Leah. It's how we deal with these things. It isn't only accepted, it's expected. And it will be done."

"But you were married to Katrina," I reminded him.

"And she attempted to attack you twice prior to the events of ten days ago. That was enough for me to seek permission from The Council to hunt her and end her life. And they would have granted it, Leah. Without demur. But this was worse. Far worse. Not only did they penetrate a concubine's home, manhandle her, frighten her and lie to her, they tied up her servant, who also has my protection. Further, what Edwina told me they told you, they are planning revolution. So not only are their deaths expected, they are necessary for the safety of your people, and, in a way, mine."

I couldn't deny that.

His hand left my jaw so his arm could wrap around me while he reminded me, "This is your world now, pet. You must learn to accept these things."

I nodded because he was right. It was wild, it was scary, but then again, I had a long time to get used to it.

"Do you have any more questions?" he asked.

I shook my head.

"Then we must talk about The Claiming," he stated.

I blinked.

"The what?" I asked.

"If you wish a mortal's wedding, I'll give you one. But we'll also have a Claiming Ceremony."

Oh my.

I felt my belly turn squishy.

"What's a Claiming Ceremony?" I whispered and his face got soft at my tone and probably the look on my face and also probably the fact he heard my heart skip a beat.

"It's our ceremony, pet. Words are spoken, I take of your blood, you take of mine, then we share the words of claiming. Much like the mortal's 'I do.'"

"And what are the words of claiming?" I was still whispering.

"Until the sun falls from the sky," he whispered back.

That was nice. He'd said that earlier to me. I loved it then and now I loved it more knowing its meaning.

"I like that," I told him softly and he grinned.

"For us, it will be real and right now, I need to know you understand that."

"Understand?"

"That it's real."

"That what's real?"

"That we will be together until the sun falls from the sky."

Oh yes.

That was nice and I loved it.

"I told you I liked it."

"You told me, Leah, but you're forty years old. I'm eight hundred and twenty-two. I have a fair understanding of what immortality means. You have no idea. Although it was understandable, it was a loss to all of us when Isobel's mother took her life. Living forever may seem alluring, but life is the same whether you're mortal or immortal. There are highs and lows, good times and bad. And, bottom line, there's a lot of time. A lot of time to travel, read, make love, eat, and a lot of time to disagree, fight, get frustrated with each other. And there will be a lot of time to get bored."

"I never get bored," I informed him.

"Everyone gets bored," Lucien informed me.

"Well, I don't, unless I have absolutely nothing to do like when you left me in the house with no wheels and no books and that was an extreme circumstance. Still, I found something to do. And, if you're with me," I grinned at him, "*you* won't get bored either."

Lucien returned my grin then leaned in and touched his mouth to mine. But when he pulled back, his face was serious.

"You'll well outlive your entire family, sweetling," he warned gently.

My mood subdued at a thought I hadn't yet had. A thought that really stunk.

But I nodded and whispered, "Yes, but I'll also get the chance to know their children. And their children's children. So I'll always, in some way, have family."

"That's a nice way to look at it," he muttered and I felt my lips tip up.

I pressed even closer and told him, "I know what you're trying to make me understand, darling. And I can't tell the future. But I'm looking forward to it, as long as it seems, as far as it goes, as long as you're in it."

He pulled me tight to him, his mouth descending to mine, his tongue sliding inside as he rolled to his back, shifting under me. My hands went into his hair on either side of his head to hold him to me, even though he wasn't going anywhere. His hands went up my shirt to my bare ass, his fingers curving in to hold me to him, and I was definitely going nowhere.

I broke my mouth from his, slid it down to his ear, and whispered, "I could study to be a doctor." Then I slid my lips to the hinge of his jaw and kept whispering. "And when I get bored of that, I could study to be a sculptor." My lips moved to his neck. "Then I could become a lawyer." My lips moved to his throat. "And I'd have centuries to perfect my béarnaise sauce."

I felt his body shaking under mine, his fingers pressed into the cheeks of my ass and my head went up so I could smile down at him.

The smile slid away from my face and I whispered, "I'll never get bored, darling."

His heated eyes turned soft and suddenly I was on my back with Lucien covering me.

I caught my breath at this maneuver but understood it five seconds later when I heard the clinking and jingling of a cart being rolled into the room.

"Dinner," the hotel butler called. "I'll set it at the table in the sitting room. Is that okay with you?"

"Perfect," Lucien answered, his eyes on me.

I giggled.

The butler laid out our food.

Lucien's gaze roamed over my face.

"Perfect," he repeated on a whisper and my stomach dropped

Then his head descended and he resumed kissing me.

Epilogue
The Future

Her fists in his hair became insistent.

He felt it, stopped feeding, lashed his tongue along the wound and gave his bride what she wanted.

He tipped his head back and looked at her.

She slid down, filling herself full of him, her eyelids heavy, Christ, so beautiful.

But her focus was all on him.

"This is our eternity," she whispered and his arms, already wrapped around her, went so tight he felt it as the gentle wind of her breath stroked his face.

All he could see was her beautiful features. All he could feel was her body in his arms, her sex wrapped around his cock, her thighs pressed tight to his hips, her breasts to his chest, her arms curved around his shoulders holding him close. All he could smell was the overpowering scent of her excitement. All he could taste on his tongue was her blood mingled with her skin and her pussy. All he could hear was her heart beating, her excited breaths.

"This is our eternity," he agreed quietly.

Her lids grew heavier even as she smiled an alluring smile.

"Give me beauty, my vampire," she demanded.

Instantly, he flipped her to her back and gave in to her demand.

Lucien's eyes opened, the dream still on him. So real it was like it happened.

The moment his eyes opened, he felt Leah shift against him. His arm around her grew tighter. His other arm moved to circle her. She slid up his body and looked into his eyes.

Hers were wondrous, her lips parted.

Fucking hell, he loved that look.

But he knew.

He knew even before she whispered, "Darling, I just had *the best* dream."

"This is our eternity," he stated, his voice rough with sleep and her eyes got wider.

"You dreamed it too?" she asked.

Lucien nodded.

"Wow. Awesome," she whispered.

He grinned, thinking, sharing dreams like that with Leah, eternity, already sweet, just became sweeter.

Then his arms grew taut around her, he rolled her and continued living the dream.

Her scream still ringing around the room, Lucien stepped away while watching Katrina's head drop.

"Now, you burn," he said softly.

He watched her breathe, the effort visibly taxing, and he did this for some time.

"You tried to teach me," she whispered, hanging from her wrists pinned to the wall, her body limp, lifeless, nearly bloodless.

"It's too late to tell me you've learned, Rina." Lucien continued to speak soft.

To his shock, her sagging body slumped deeper.

He gave her time, and as he expected, she again spoke.

"I'm okay with this," she went on in a whisper. "I couldn't live without you."

"I know," he replied and watched her put extreme effort into lifting her eyes to him.

"Not at all," she admitted. "Not even for a second."

"I know," he repeated.

"You love her?" she asked, the stamp of agony in her face twisting with new pain.

"Yes," he answered shortly.

She'd endured enough. Now it was time for her pain to end. But just like Rina, she begged for more.

"I wanted you to love me like that," she told him something he already knew.

Lucien made no reply.

"Why couldn't you love me like that?" she asked.

"Rina, let Julian take you to the stake," Lucien replied gently.

"Give me that before I die. Tell me why. Why couldn't you love me like that?"

Lucien sighed then reminded her, "I've told you why."

She smiled a humorless smile before she whispered, "I'll listen now."

He held her eyes as he answered, "Because you wanted it so badly."

"That's not good?" she asked, genuinely perplexed.

Lucien shook his head. "The moment I understood Leah's love for me caused her pain, I knew I had to let her go. Even knowing losing her I would lose everything. I was willing to sacrifice everything to ease her pain. And when I understood I loved her, but if we stayed together our time would be short and end in tragedy, I understood this more completely. I was determined to let her go to prolong her life in hopes, during it, she might find happiness. What you failed to learn is that true love is not selfish, Rina. It's selfless."

She gazed at him, even in her state the unhealthy, fevered, obsessive love she had for him burned in her eyes.

Quietly, he finished, "You never understood that."

"No," she whispered. "And I still don't. Today, I die for my love for you, Lucien."

"If it makes you feel better to believe that, Rina, then I'm pleased you do," Lucien returned on a whisper.

She continued to gaze at him he knew in order to steal more of his time and attention.

But he was done.

He stepped away and jerked his chin at his son.

Julian moved forward.

Lucien didn't watch as his son carried his ex-mate over his shoulder out of the room. Instead, he pulled out his phone and made three calls. Two were business. One was to Leah to tell her he'd be home soon.

She told him she was making her fried chicken.

This was something over the past week since they returned that he was growing accustomed to. A new nuance of his soon-to-be bride. She didn't ask about the unpleasant business, simply waited for him to tell her if he so desired.

But she was attuned to him. Now that he'd opened it to her, both of them could sense each other's moods with an acuity that had nothing to do with body language, facial expressions, or tone of voice. They tracked each other easily. So she knew when he had them and she made certain she did something, sometimes large, sometimes small, to make his unpleasant days end well.

He finished his call with Leah and moved outside. Bel was there. Stephanie. Rafe. Duncan. And Cristiano was there to represent The Council.

When Lucien arrived, Julian handed him the torch. Without delay, he threw it at the wood and kindling at Katrina's feet.

He gave her one last thing. Lucien held her eyes as she burned.

When she was no longer of this world, he left, leaving Cristiano to gather the ashes and scatter them to the winds.

Lucien sat back and yanked off the white gloves they'd asked him to wear before he handled the ancient parchments.

It was over a month after he'd found Leah. He was in the ancient city of Speranza in a windowless, air-controlled, intensely secured room in the basement of The Dominion's international headquarters.

He lifted his head and looked across the table at Avery, Gregor and Rudolf.

"This does not make me happy," he muttered his understatement.

He'd just seen The Prophesies, or what they would allow him to see. He had no idea what else there was. However, they had shown him some of what referred to Leah and himself.

"That's understandable," Rudolf replied.

"Do you now understand why we've asked you to refrain from hunting your father?" Avery asked carefully.

"I understand it, but I don't like it," Lucien answered tightly.

"As you can see from those documents, he is surely the general of the insurrectionists noted in them. If his death is precipitous, it could tip war and we're not ready," Rudolf explained.

"I did read that in the parchments, Rudolf," Lucien muttered with irritation.

"You will have your time," Avery assured him quietly.

He fucking well would.

Lucien nodded.

"She's already exhibiting the abilities," Gregor stated, looking at him closely.

Lucien briefly weighed the wisdom of answering, glanced at Avery, who already knew, and decided.

"She has exceptional powers of the mind. She can mark me. Track me. Sense my mood, and therefore, when she's with me, sense danger when I do. She can speak to me with her mind, and as the days go by, this power increases significantly. Indeed, if I wished, I could call to her where she's sitting at a café across the street and she'd hear me. She could do the same. We also have begun to share dreams, having them separately and, on occasion, simultaneously." He gestured to the papers on the table before him. "However, she does not demonstrate uncommon speed or strength."

"You are vampire, she is mortal, Lucien, would you know if she had uncommon speed or strength for a mortal?" Rudolf asked an excellent question.

Before he could answer, Gregor spoke.

"We would like to ask you to speak to her about submitting herself for testing."

Lucien's felt his body prepare for battle, his adrenaline releasing, his muscles expanding, and he immediately replied, "Absolutely not."

"Lucien—" Gregor began but Lucien leaned forward.

"You get near her without my permission, I'll tear you apart, and then you'll burn," Lucien vowed, his voice low and unmistakable.

Gregor gestured to the table. "You can see from what you've read that it's important we understand we're in the position to combat this threat."

"My bride is not a mutant warrior in this war to be prodded and researched," Lucien clipped. "There are yet two other lifemates to unite. We will allow matters to play out, and as they do, she and I will decide how we will proceed."

"We don't have a great deal of time. Callum will mate with Sonia before Christmas this very year," Gregor told him and Lucien held his eyes.

Callum was King of the Werewolves. Lucien knew him. Lucien respected him.

Sonia, he knew, was the name of Gregor's mortal charge.

"Sonia?" Lucien asked.

"Yes, Sonia," Gregor answered then clarified, talking quietly, "*My* Sonia."

"So this is why you took her into your care," Lucien surmised.

"That and I held deep regard for her parents prior to their deaths and affection for her prior to her losing them," Gregor replied.

Lucien nodded but he did not share further words on the topic. The Prophesies were vague as Prophesies tended to be, but it was not vague what would befall Sonia, the woman who would soon be the mortal Queen of the Werewolves. Gregor knew of this. And Gregor was hiding his despair at the knowledge.

Instead, he asked, "Does she know? Callum?"

Gregor shook his head. "No. And they won't. As this was kept from you and Leah, it will also be kept from the other mates. As you read, it is essential that every immortal demonstrates his ability to make a crucial selfless sacrifice for his mortal lifemate. And it is essential that every mortal demonstrate her generosity to or protection of immortals. To establish an eternity of peace between the species, The Three must personify that we can live together through diversity *and* in harmony."

He'd read this in The Prophesies. It was annoying, but it was understandable.

"And the third lifemates?" Lucien asked.

"They have not been located," Rudolf answered. "We believe the male is living amongst mortals. Their story is vaguer in The Prophesies, but we believe from studying the parchments that he knows who he is, what he's capable of. He feeds from mortals, he morphs to wolf. But he does not know of the existence of others of his kind. He thinks he's an anomaly, hides his abilities and lives underground. Therefore, it is difficult to find him."

"Perhaps he has not yet come into existence," Lucien suggested.

"No," Avery whispered, "Sonia's destiny will play out shortly. The Noble War is nearly upon us. He's out there, as is she, whoever she may be."

Lucien tipped up his chin then remarked, "If he thinks he's an anomaly, he's correct. Unless I'm mistaken, he would be the only vampire, werewolf hybrid in history."

"In the years to come, many things will change, Lucien," Avery replied. "*Many*. What was impossible will be exceptional, but possible. Then it will become commonplace."

As it always had been. As, he hoped to Christ, it always would be for a very long time.

Lucien moved on.

"I'll be telling Leah of The Prophesies," he announced and the three other men in the room tensed.

"This is unwise," Gregor muttered.

"Why?" Lucien shot back and Gregor's eyes slid to Avery. "It isn't unwise," Lucien stated and Gregor's gaze came back. "You're intent to keep your secrets from being revealed. But I can assure you she won't speak of them."

"Can you be certain?" Rudolf asked.

"She is mortal but there are many mortals who are far from stupid, Rudolf," Lucien returned. "I'll explain to her the importance of keeping the secret and she'll understand it. I'll also explain the consequences of not keeping it and she'll definitely understand that."

"Of course, but she is also in the life. Her family is in the life. What is to come, her part in it, she may be moved to warn them," Rudolf replied.

"She won't speak of The Prophesies," Lucien repeated.

"It's essential she doesn't," Gregor pressed,

Lucien looked to Avery then back to Gregor and impatiently reiterated, "She will not speak of them."

Gregor took in a breath. Then he nodded.

Lucien wanted to get back to Leah so he demanded in the form of a request, "I wish to speak to Avery alone."

Glances were exchanged but Rudolf and Gregor assented, said their farewells and moved to leave the room.

Gregor, however, stopped at the door.

"The Council wishes you to know that the access provided you to these documents means our debt is paid."

"Servicing The Dominion by hunting my own and taking them to their deaths for fifty years is hardly paid by providing me access to documents that describe, however vaguely, that myself and my bride face mortal perils in a Noble War," Lucien returned. "That is surely my due and I regard it as such. Tell The Council I consider that I still hold the marker and I will call it when I need to use it."

Gregor held his eyes before he sighed, tipped up his chin and left the room.

Lucien didn't speak until he sensed they were well out of hearing distance. Then his eyes moved through the room. Not finding what he was looking for, he turned his gaze to Avery.

"Is this room monitored?" he asked.

"No," Avery answered.

"What I wish to discuss, it would be foolish to lie," Lucien stated quietly.

"As has been explained, very few know of The Prophesies, Lucien. This is a humidity, air and temperature controlled room that holds nothing but The Prophesies. Access to it is strictly limited. Security is state of the art. However, it does not include cameras or microphones. It wouldn't do for security guards to be able to catch a glimpse of the parchments or hear those allowed in this room discussing them."

Lucien nodded once.

Then he crossed his arms on his chest and stated quietly, "You're an Ancient."

Avery slowly closed his eyes.

He was.

Fucking hell.

"Do you know our origin?" Lucien asked and Avery opened his eyes.

"I vow to you, Lucien, that this is also a mystery to me," Avery answered.

"Are there others older than you?" Lucien queried.

"I cannot say," Avery demurred.

"But there are other Ancients," Lucien went on.

"I cannot say," Avery repeated.

"How many people know that Ancients still exist?" Lucien pushed.

"One," Avery answered. "You."

That was what he was looking for. An indication of trust. And he had it. This secret was more crucial to guard than The Prophesies.

Lucien took a moment before he reminded Avery quietly, "My future bride and I risk much for this world."

Avery studied him a moment, then whispered, "You do. And therefore I will give you another vow. There will be those who will do everything in their considerable power to keep The Sacred Triumvirate safe. But right now, this is all I can give you."

"I have children and The Prophesies state that I will have four more. For reasons that, if The Prophesies are true, are no longer accurate, Leah and I do not use protection. If this Noble War means my bride and I will perish and our children will live without parents or worse, die themselves, I need to know what you know and take precautions."

"You must find out along with me," Avery replied.

"You know no more?" Lucien pressed.

Avery extended a hand to the papers on the table. "I wrote those parchments. I wrote everything I knew, Lucien, everything that came to me. If I knew more, I would gladly tell you. I don't. Therefore, you must find out along with me."

Lucien held his gaze and read nothing. And he knew from this that when Avery gave away the knowledge he was indeed an Ancient, this was his intention.

He tried once more by reminding him, "I lived eight hundred and twenty-two years waiting for the woman who was destined for me."

"And we're counting, very much, on your desire to keep hold of that destiny," Avery returned.

"If that's true, Avery, then you are very lucky," Lucien whispered.

At that, Avery smiled.

Lucien didn't smile back. He lifted his hand in a brief gesture of farewell and left the room to make his way to his mate.

"Okay, seriously, this is *awesome!*" Leah exclaimed.

She was sitting astride him. Lucien was on his back in their bed in their hotel room in Speranza, Leah straddling his hips. She was wearing a black silk nightie adorned with thick edges of cream lace. They'd just made love and her hair was a wild tumble around her shoulders.

Prior to their making love, he'd given her an emerald cut black diamond engagement ring. After, he told her of The Prophesies.

As was her way, her reaction surprised him.

"My pet, we're talking about war," he reminded her quietly.

She leaned in to him, putting her hands to his chest, her face getting close to his. Hers was still excited.

"Yes, and you, me and the other four are going to *kick ass,*" she declared, lurched back to sitting and cried, "I can't wait to get superhuman abilities!"

Lucien shook his head, finding he couldn't stop himself from grinning.

Then he sat up, his grin died, and he wrapped his arms around her loosely.

"My love," he started to caution, "anything can happen in war."

She wrapped her arms loosely around his shoulders and tipped her head to the side.

"Darling, are you the Mighty Vampire Lucien?"

His lips twitched but he didn't answer.

"You are," she whispered, her arms getting tighter. "You're unstoppable. And you're giving me your abilities. So *we'll* be unstoppable." Her expression grew serious as she pressed closer. "Before you get all mature vampire and impart wisdom on me, I'll tell you, I get it. I've never been in a war, but everyone knows wars are to be avoided. And I hate to remind you of something that upsets you, but Edwina and I were attacked by four vampires. I had no power in that situation and I was terrified out of my mind. So it may be that my powers won't be akin to a vampire's. But at least I'll have a fighting chance."

She was right. She'd reminded him of something that upset him. Greatly.

Lucien didn't share this and Leah wasn't done.

"But I also get something else. And I've thought this for a long time even when you told me before that you were mostly like me. There is magic at work. And that magic, I know in my heart, led me to you. And if that's the kind of magic we're dealing with then it's the good kind. And we have that on our side. And we have love on our side. And the other four will have love on their side too. And when you have our kind of love, you can't be beat because you won't *allow* yourself to be beat."

"I can't argue with that," he muttered and was rewarded with her smile.

Her arms left his shoulders so her fingers could wrap around the sides of his neck and she tilted her face close.

"Nothing will take you away from me, darling," her fingers squeezed, "*nothing.*"

Lucien stared into her beautiful eyes.

Then his arms tightened around her and he twisted her to her back as his mouth took hers in a searing kiss.

When he lifted his head, she took in an unsteady breath.

She finished their conversation with a whispered, "I get all this," her limbs gave him a squeeze and her lips gave him a smile, "*and* kickass superhuman abilities. I...can't...*wait.*"

Lucien grinned down at her, dropped his head and kissed the smile away from her face.

After that, he took his time doing a great many other things.

Things he couldn't wait to do.

It was after the Ancient Claiming Ceremony. After the celebration following. After Nadia threw her back out breakdancing at the celebration. But before they would board a plane in the morning to travel to Italy for their honeymoon.

Her fists in his hair became insistent.

He felt it, stopped feeding, lashed his tongue along the wound and gave his brand-new bride what she wanted.

He tipped his head back and looked at her.

She slid down on his cock, filling herself full of him, her eyelids heavy.

Christ, she was beautiful.

So fucking beautiful.

Her lids were heavy but her focus was all on him.

"This is our eternity," she whispered. His arms, already wrapped around her, went so tight he felt it as the gentle wind of her breath stroked his face.

All he could see was her beautiful features. All he could feel was her body in his arms, her sex wrapped around his cock, her thighs pressed tight to his hips, her breasts to his chest, her arms curved around his shoulders holding him close. All he could smell was the overpowering scent of her excitement. All he could taste on his tongue was her blood mingled with her skin and her pussy. All he could hear was her heart beating, her excited breaths.

"This is our eternity," he agreed quietly.

Her lids grew heavier even as she smiled an alluring smile. A smile for his words. A smile because she, like he, knew they were living a dream.

"Give me beauty, my vampire," she demanded.

Instantly, he flipped her to her back and gave in to her demand.

Fuck, but he loved it when their dreams came true.

Literally.

The Three Series will continue with **With Everything I Am**, *the story of Callum and Sonia.*

Printed in Great Britain
by Amazon

84454396R10294